MARGARET ELPHINSTONE is currently a
lecturer in English Studies at the University of
Strathclyde. She lives in Edinburgh, and has two
daughters.

D1439745

By *the same author*

FICTION

The Incomer (Women's Press)
1987

A Sparrow's Flight (Polygon)
1989

An Apple from a Tree (Women's Press)
1991

POETRY

Outside Eden (Sundial Press)
1990

A Treasury of Garden Verse (editor) (Canongate)
1990

NON-FICTION

The Organic Gardener's Handbook (Collins) 1994

Organic Gardening (Greenprint)
1990

ISLANDERS

Margaret Elphinstone

Polygon
EDINBURGH

© Margaret Elphinstone 1994

First published by
Polygon
22 George Square
Edinburgh

Set in Goudy by ROM-Data Corporation Ltd, Falmouth, Cornwall
Printed and bound in Great Britain by Hartnolls Ltd, Bodmin, Cornwall

A CIP record for this book is available.
ISBN 0 7486 6178 6

The Publisher acknowledges subsidy from

THE SCOTTISH ARTS COUNCIL

towards the publication of this volume.

For Vicki

map: Sean R. Milligan

PEOPLE ON FRIDAREY

The people at Byrstada

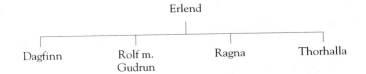

Erlend

Dagfinn   Rolf m. Gudrun   Ragna   Thorhalla

The people at Shirva

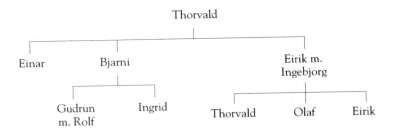

Thorvald

Einar   Bjarni   Eirik m. Ingebjorg

Gudrun m. Rolf   Ingrid   Thorvald   Olaf   Eirik

The people at the Smithy

Snorri m. Gunnhild

Acknowledgments

I would like to acknowledge the assistance of the Scottish Arts Council and Hawthornden International Writers' Retreat during the writing of this novel.

I am also indebted to the following friends for their generous help and advice: Anne Sinclair of Busta, Fair Isle; Sean Milligan, of the Dept. of Seamanship and Navigation, Stromness Academy; Barbara Crawford, of the Dept. of Medieval History, St Andrews University; Eileen Cadman, Vicki Coleman, members of Pomegranate Women's Writing Group; and various others.

Part One

Astrid

Chapter 1

The sea appalled her. It was huge beyond anything she had imagined, heaving and falling under her like molten slate. Her hands and face were stiff with salt that burned her lips. Holding her stomach rigid to stop herself shaking, she clung to the gunwale aft. She saw the helmsman above her, a wild sky surrounding him, then falling, falling with water banked behind him. The sail, half-reefed, blocked out the sea ahead as the ship rose, riding the invisible wave which lifted the quarter. For a moment they were poised again, dark clouds scudding round them, then the dip began, with a lurch in the pit of her stomach. The depths loomed and vanished in a flurry of white water that clattered like stones on the canvas above.

Her father was still beside her. He hadn't looked up now for hours. Since they left the Sudreyjar he had clung there most of the time, not like the man she knew at all. He had been sick again and again, and on his own ship too. She had not been sick, and didn't like watching when other people were. But she wasn't thinking of that now, only of the heave and fall, the impossible swell, and the vigilant helmsman. When the water cleared each time, she saw his eyes still fixed on the luff of the sail and the receding wave.

Bracing her legs so she didn't slide, she let her mind drift; it was too much to take in. Too much, and so quick. A life gone, and she still only thirteen years old.

Astrid Kol's daughter, she said aloud.

The name was swallowed in a roar. Giving her name, she became aware of sheer noise, the rigging stretched to it, the boat taut against it; noise in the wood to which she clung.

When they had embarked the ship had not seemed small, lying between stone jetties in the still harbour water. It was a strong trading ship, as Kol's daughter should know very well, and this was not the first time it had made the long voyage from Monige to Noreg, though never before so late in the season. Standing on the aft deck in harbour, with the sun beating down on hot planks, Astrid had looked down to the dirt of the harbour floor, to muck and fish guts, and shoals of fish like gleaming shadows. The water stank in the heat. There had been fear in the air, as if the smell of burning were still with them.

Burning. She shuddered and clung to the gunwale. A wave broke out of rhythm, taking the ship broadside on. The hull jarred, the sail flapped, and water drenched them. There were two helms-men now, bent and straining at the steerboard. Water rose like a grey hill to her left. She felt the ship being sucked under.

With death so close, suddenly it was her mother she prayed to. Not God, not the saints, but one who knew her, waiting for her just beyond the wall of wave. In death, Astrid might reach out and touch her. She closed her eyes.

At the last moment they began to slide upward. The grey hill subsided. Astrid's breath came back in a whimper, drowned by the sea. The deck righted, and someone clutched her shoulder. Her father's arm came round her, real, solid, not like this nightmare sea.

'Astrid?' He was shouting. She held his arm hard, as the ship dipped and swung down.

There was movement at the helm. The captain was speaking to the helmsmen. The wind tore at their cloaks and hair, and the words were whipped away so she heard nothing. Kol edged along the gunwale and shouted something to the captain. There was a nod to the man at the helm, who pushed the steerboard hard over until the ship turned and the swell was behind them. Huge seas still followed them, sweeping them on in the ceaseless heave and fall, but the ship was no longer fighting, and Astrid felt the easing.

Death receded, and so did the image of the mother that waited. Mary Mother of God, deliver us from evil. Pray for us now and at the hour of our death. Sweet Jesus Christ, make these waters calm. Saint Olaf and Patrick, who also sailed these seas, have mercy on us. Mary Mother of God, pray for us now, and do not let us be drowned.

Kol scrambled down beside her again. 'All right?'

'All right.' She shifted her hand on the gunwale and faced him, so she could see what he said. 'What's happening?'

His mouth was close to her ear. '. . . Turning easterly . . . too strong . . . well clear now. Best to run before it. No chance of Hjaltland now . . . Into the Norweg sea. There before we know it.'

He was still white and gaunt from seasickness, and she could feel him shivering. She turned back to the sea, as if the sight of his weakness were something forbidden. This fleeing had forced them so close. At home they had been more distant, although friendly and companionable.

For a long time there had only been the two of them. Home was a city street. Their house was a fine one at the top of the hill, where the air was fresher. They had moved there when she was three, when the money began to come. It was a good house, with a big square room, leading through to a small private yard. A rowan tree grew in the yard next to the wattle boundary fence. Uprooted by some fool who knew no better, and found by her mother among the rubbish put for burning, it had been replanted in July. Astrid had not turned four, but she remembered. She saw her mother's hands, dirty and firm, pressing the soil down hard, drawing symbols in the new-turned earth. Protect this house. If you plant a rowan in July, the leaves drop off and wither, but the bark keeps its grey sheen, and the next year there will be buds, then white flowers, and in the autumn, berries like blood. Her mother never saw the berries. They had buried her in summer, on the hill outside the city where the dead lay. The sky had been empty blue, gulls from the river circling and crying, the land green and sunlit beyond the walls. A hole in the earth, impossibly deep, a cold smell, the sound of earth spattered on wood, like spray on canvas.

The light was growing thicker. It would soon be quite dark. She was so cold it exhausted her, and there was an ache behind her eyes, with staring at the sea. It was becoming harder to remember to hold on. Her hands were numb. She never noticed her grip slacken, but Kol's arm round her grew tighter.

The day her mother had died, there had been strawberries in a wooden bowl. Astrid had sat eating, until her fingers were stained red, and her stomach felt gorged. There was no one there to stop her. Ten years ago, nearly. At some point since then she had realised that the dead do not come back.

Mary Mother of God, pray for the souls who depart in faith. Mary and my mother, watch over us. St Patrick watch over us. St Olaf watch over us, take us safe to Noreg where you too belong.

She must not sleep. If the sea were not watched it could grow dangerous, and its rhythm might break if she did not count. Memories slid away until she could no longer grasp them, the old life dissolving in a storm of wind and water. If there were a future, with warmth and dryness in it, it was beyond imagining. Sense vanished into nightmare, a ruined yard, a broken tree, rubble heaped over her mother's herbs. The chickens slaughtered, a shower of russet feathers over devastation.

She cried out, and woke. Pitch black, the world heaving and falling. Her father was still there. She clutched at his cloak. Her hand closed on wrought silver, and the smoothness of aquamarine. The brooch-pin stabbed her. She let go and sucked her numb hand.

Nothing had ever been so cold. In Monige they had said it was the shock when she couldn't stop trembling. In the house there, they had wrapped her in a quilt, on the sleeping platform nearest the hearth, and put a hot stone at her feet. 'I'm all right,' she kept saying to them. 'I'm only cold. It's only that I'm cold.' The humiliation of it. Always so tough, Astrid, tough as a boy. She should have been a boy, then she would have been apprenticed to succeed her father. He was still holding her to him; his arm now felt tight and firm. They had survived. It was just that she kept on shaking. And it was so cold.

They had put her mother in a hole in the earth, and said she was going on a journey. Astrid used to lie in her bed at home, while shadows from the fire danced on the wooden ceiling, imagining a coffin with a sail. Her mother on a wild sea, sailing, and never coming back. Or herself, being put to sea in a coffin, or in her bed perhaps, when she was asleep. As a child, she used to wake up screaming. Her father would come over to the corner where she lay, carry her back to the hearth, and sit her on his knee, so she could lie back and watch the firelight in the middle of the room, where it was safe.

Her teeth chattered, and her stomach hurt from shuddering. Huddled against Kol she fancied he still smelt of home, even through the wet, the odour of woodsmoke caught up in rough woven fabric. In the dark it helped her to remember. It was a blue tunic he wore, a brave summer blue, tied by a belt with a gold clasp that gleamed in fire or sunlight. Kol liked fine things, and could afford them.

She thought of him as he had been only that morning, standing beside the helmsman, confident aboard his own ship, in spite of the seasickness which had dogged him ever since they left Monige. He had pointed out the north-west tip of the Orkneyjar to her, and she had seen a faint blue line on the horizon. Vestrey. All was set fair then, a light south-westerly, and nothing to worry about. They had been heading up for Hjaltland; there was a man her father knew, and it seemed likely now they would be able to make a landfall. During the day the wind had veered westerly. As dusk began to fall it freshened, and the sea started getting up. But she had never imagined it could be like this.

If she slept again, it could only have been for a moment. The waves grew wilder. They could have been alone in the chaos that surrounds the world. The men struggled through the long night, keeping the stern into the sea. If the ship were not a masterpiece, it would never have lasted. Kol must have thought of these things, as he clung to his ship and to his daughter, waiting for dawn.

A city in flames behind them: filthy smell of burning, crash of roofs, thunder of invasion. Fire taller than houses, heat over water. Heave and fall. Fleeing for their lives, hooves on cobbles. Heave and fall. Flames following, faster than footsteps.

Astrid woke again, gasping and wet. She could see men at the ropes, then suddenly the sail came down. The yard fell to the deck. Canvas flapped and billowed, swamping the deck space. The men fought to control it, holding it down with their bodies, struggling to lash it down. The ship tossed, while the seas rolled past her. Everything slowed down, the men fighting the sail, the tearing wind, the waves, all like a dream. She didn't know what was happening, only that the sea felt wrong.

Men struggled with the oars, while the deck bucked and heaved. The helmsman kept glancing back to the seas that came on from behind.

The next wave lifted them.

There was a line of broken white ahead, and something grey which was neither sky nor sea. Astrid screamed, or thought she did. There was too much noise to know. She clung to the gunwale, and stared.

The helmsman must have seen it too. His eyes were fixed ahead. Why didn't the ship turn? Astrid fought down another scream. They had the oars out on the starboard side, two men to each oar, but the sea leapt under them so the oars did not grip. As the ship rose with the wave Astrid saw the line of white again. Nearer. One hand was over her mouth, with the other she kept her hold.

From the peril of the storm, Good Lord deliver us.

Kol was beside her again, holding her to him. She wriggled out of his grip so she could see. She couldn't take her eyes off that line of white. She tugged at his cloak, pointing. 'Don't they see?' It came out as a thin scream.

His mouth was at her ear. 'Trying to turn. . . . the groundswell . . . shoals. . . .'

The line of white drew nearer, and the noise of the sea changed. The next wave flung them closer. She held her breath.

They were turning at last. The starboard oars gripped the sea, and the helmsmen thrust the helm over. The next sea caught them broadside on. The ship rolled to starboard. On the port side next to Astrid a wall of water rose, and she shut her eyes.

The sea never broke. They were being carried sideways with a speed that made her stomach lurch. The ship righted itself, and began to slide down the back of the wave. It finished turning as it went, and they took the next wave bows on.

The crew had the port oars out. The men rowed desperately, but they were losing ground. The line of grey loomed larger. Neither sky nor sea. Solid. All they could do was keep her prow into the waves.

A heavy sea broke over them. When Astrid could see again there was chaos. No mast. Figures clinging. A rock like a needle, a handsbreadth away.

Rocks scraped alongside, then astern. A sound like falling roofs; a sudden jarring. The ship flung shorewards, stern first. Astrid let go. A moment later the sternpost was wedged against the rock wall, with a foul grating noise.

'Up!' Kol was shouting at her, pushing her. For a second she fought him. He was trying to thrust her overboard, into that sea. She hit out, then understood. 'Up! Up!'

She let him push her then, and was half flung over the side. She had her feet on the gunwale, then she was on her hands and knees among rock and weed and water. She scrabbled for a hold. A sea caught her, but she clung like a limpet while the water swirled back. Wedged in a crack in the rock, she looked round for Kol to follow.

No ship. Only broken sea, hungry waves. Wood. An oar. She dragged herself into a crevice slippery with weed. The world spun, the darkness at the edge of the world.

Chapter 2

There was a man named Einar Thorvaldsson who farmed the lands at Shirva with his brother. On the day of the shipwreck he woke before dawn, listened to the wind, and knew that the gale which had blown up from the west yesterday was now dying with the beginning of the day. There was a big sea running on to the cliffs a few hundred yards from where he lay. The tide would be almost halfway out by now; he could hear the waves, and that told him where they were breaking.

The house itself was wrapped in quiet. The dogs lay in curled humps, as close as they could get to the long hearth, where the peat fire was smoored under fresh turfs. The people made bigger humps than the dogs, huddled in their blankets on the sleeping platforms that lined either side of the hearth. The women slept at the far end from the door, next to the gable wall. The only other sleeper in the hall was his brother Bjarni, who occupied the bench opposite Einar's own. Einar himself slept in the place next to the high seat.

Einar laid his hand flat against the stone wall beside him. Last night he had felt the vibration of every gust of wind through two feet of stone. It was still now. A thin light filtered in round the board over the chimney hole. No rain. Clouds still scudded across the small patch of sky that was visible. Einar pushed away his blanket, sat up, and swung his legs out of bed. Cold air eddied around his feet, although the room was stuffy after the night. The old dog stirred, whining in its dreams. The young bitch cocked her ears and looked at him, waiting for the word that would let her jump up. Einar ignored them both, scratched himself under his woollen shirt, and rubbed the sleep out of his eyes. Then he shook out his tunic, which he used as a pillow, and put it on over his shirt.

He stood up and stepped round the hearth. Some of the banked up peats had broken apart in the night, and a red glow showed in the heart of the fireplace. Einar ignored it; keeping the fire in was nothing to do with him. He found his boots drying at the hearth, and pulled the straw out of them. The damp straw, dropped on the fire, made a halfhearted flame, green against gold. He spoke to the young dog, who leapt up at once and came eagerly to heel. Then he put his boots on and opened the door. The day was grey and drear, the autumn grasses flattened to the wind. In front of the house the brigstones gleamed wet. Einar huddled his sheepskin cloak around him, and stepped into the wind.

Shirva stood on a small hill. Only to the east was it overshadowed, by a knoll so round and symmetrical it hardly seemed natural. The crops in the west rigs were often drenched by sea and burned by salt, in spite of the sheltering cliffs. This year they'd only saved the kale by drenching it with buckets of fresh water after the gales. Last night Einar had heard the waves echoing under the two arches at Raiva, beneath which lay long tunnels and hidden beaches. The hall itself had shuddered with the impact of water on rock far underground. The edge of the island, silhouetted against the western sky, was fierce and jagged, and Einar had seen big lumps crumble away under the constant barrage from the sea.

Southward was the Sudvik where Einar kept his boat, safely drawn up now and tied down in its noost. There was no sheltered harbour at all on the island. It was part of Einar's morning ritual to watch the waves breaking on the two skerries at the entrance to the wick, and so to assess the day's sea. Today, they were still half lost in spray.

Lastly, Einar looked north. Across his mown hayfields a sheer grey cliff, the southern face of the Seydurholm, shone in the rising sun. The day would be fairer than the night.

Because the gale had been westerly, Einar went straight to the cliffs at Raiva. He had his sheep round to do, but first he wanted to see if the sea had brought anything in the night. These shores were so familiar after over forty years of observation, that he would notice at once the faintest mark of any change.

Einar scanned the rocks. The sea was foaming round the feet of the cliff. There were few crevices there to hold driftwood, and while the sea was still running like this the shore was inaccessible. He glanced down at Hjukni geo, and stopped.

There was something there. Something extraordinarily, unexpectedly, blue. The sea was far from blue today, but something was spread across the stack at the end of Hjukni beach, like a patch of summer sky. It was high and dry. Einar stared, and examined the surrounding water.

Wood. There were spars, jostling together in the swirl of breaking waves. Further out, a barrel, and pieces of something larger.

If a ship had come ashore there, in that gale, one could expect nothing more. Einar narrowed his eyes, gazing at the scrap of blue marooned above the dropping tide. Then he began to edge his way down. He had once been fast and sure-footed, but age had made him cautious, and the loose gravel on the cliff path was slippery.

Einar's leather boots slid on wet boulders. The stack was almost out of the sea's reach. There were spars caught in the surf, dragged back with each undertow. He might have salvaged them at the price of a soaking. Safer with two. He was still only a short distance from home, and Bjarni would be awake by now. Einar hesitated, but then there was that patch of blue spread on the rock. It was less than five yards away on the seaward side of the stack.

Einar moved along the shore to where he could get a better view. There it was, not just a patch now, but a little lump. A body, probably, huddled among brown seaweed. A body in a cloak dyed blue might be adorned with other luxuries.

Einar pulled his boots off, and scrambled down into weed-sodden rock in his socked feet, the wool giving him some slight purchase. On the shore side the stack was almost sheer, but there were cracks in it. He had climbed it before, and knew exactly where to feel for them, toehold by toehold. As he edged seaward, water brushed his knees.

He edged round the corner of the rock, clung to bunches of seaweed and hauled himself up.

It was a body, very small. It must have edged itself into the crevice which had protected it from the sea, and then collapsed. Spray still spattered it.

He rolled the body over. There was soaked hair across the face. He pushed it back, and saw the white pinched features of a child. He noticed freckles, pale against white skin. The eyes were shut. Maybe it had not been dead when it came ashore. The spray reached up desultorily, wetting them both.

The blue was a cloak. He tugged it back. Bare white child's legs, a sodden skirt pushed up over the knees. In an automatic gesture he pulled her skirt down. Her flesh was cold. He thrust his hand under her dress and felt a small breast under his fingers. He tried to find her heart, feeling for a pulse of life. He watched her face at the same time, caring without knowing why. All at once he was convinced she had not died. Another spray broke over them.

He couldn't climb back the same way with a burden in his arms so, recklessly, holding her tightly to him, he slid down into four feet of sea. A wave met him, chest high. Einar staggered, handless because of his burden, and caught his balance against the rock as the undertow surged past. Then he was stumbling through rock and water, and was up on the stones, over the tideline to the grass above the beach, the child from the sea clutched to his chest, as cold as water.

He turned her face down and began to work on her, as urgent suddenly as if she were his own, raising her arms, pressing her back, pushing down, raising up, pumping with all the strength he had.

There was no water in her. He rolled her over. There was grit on her face. Her eyes stayed shut. But he was sure she was not dead.

He lay down beside her, his warmth against her body, and put his mouth over hers, his hand on her chest. He began to breathe hard into her lungs, as if her body were his own.

Chapter 3

The stone just above her head was pinkish, with lines scored by a long gone sea. The next stone was grey, with a straight edge that still had the marks of a chisel on it. Above the grey slab white roots hung down from the turf roof, searching for nourishment. Where the pink stone ended she could see a thread of light under the roof.

The roof went up to the main beam, which was huge, blackened with soot, and sea-smoothed at the corners. Her eye was drawn to the light coming in at the chimney hole. There was blue sky up there. The chimney shutter was pulled wide open, and a thin coil of smoke wreathed out. She watched it for a long time.

The storm was gone, as if it had never happened. This was another world, inhabited by strangers, but she was too tired to take it in. As long as she stayed numb, suspended between what had gone before and the inescapable fact that she was still alive, nothing needed to matter. The pain stayed safe so long as it was merely physical. Her chest ached, as if a rock had been dropped on it. Her body imprisoned her, and she was grateful, because she didn't want to face anything outside it.

The fair girl's name was Ingrid. She didn't remember being told that, but by the time her thoughts became coherent again she already knew it. She hadn't been told the name of the other woman, who had hurt her, prodding her and turning her over, and had then left strange leaves burning, so the place smelt like an altar to the old gods. Nor could she name the one who smelt of old age, and talked incomprehensibly. Only Ingrid made sense. Her accent was strange, but she had taken the trouble to speak clearly. Later she had heard men's voices, speaking low in the dark. It was quiet now. A cloud crossed the sky from one side of the chimney hole to the other. Astrid watched it pass, and decided that she could not lie on her back for ever. Once, then twice, she thought to move, and found herself still lying. The third time she struggled to sit up.

It was a free man's hall. She knew that at once, because in the centre of the room, she could see the carved pillars of the high seat dividing the sleeping platforms. A shield hung on the wall beside the high seat. It was hardly the seat of a great warrior, but she was relieved to know that she was in the house of a free man, with the right to carry his own weapons. If she had fallen among serfs, it would have been hard to find people of her own kind.

The hearth before the high seat was large and lined with blue clay. The peat fire was banked down on the cracked hearthstones. An iron pot hung on a chain over the fire. A wooden table was set flush to the hearthstones, and sleeping platforms lined the wall all along her side of the room. They were covered with sheepskins and blankets, like the one with which they had covered her. The floor was swept, and the broom marks had left tidy circular patterns on the hard earth. The implements hanging on the stone walls sug-gested fishing and farming rather than battle, but the metal blades gleamed, catching the glow of the peats. Hangings were tied back at the far end of the hall, and a couple of chickens wandered to and fro, finding some peckings in the half light. Stores hung from the rafters: herbs and dried meat, and a cheese in a cloth set over the hearth to smoke.

A long finger of sunlight groped into the dark. Painfully, Astrid swung her legs down. She was wearing a woollen dress that was much too big for her. She stretched out her bare foot until it touched the sun. Her feet looked unnaturally clean with all the dirt of summer scoured out of them by salt water.

She thought about standing, and pressed her hands against the edge of the platform to push herself up. Her right hand was sore,

and she winced. There was a deep red scratch across the palm.
Silver and aquamarine. A faceted stone as pale and blue as water.
My father. The scratch stretched from just under her third finger
to the base of her thumb where it had gouged a deeper cut in the
soft flesh. Don't think of that. Stand up.

She rested for a moment, then struggled to her feet. Heave and
fall. The stone walls sloped and righted themselves, then began to
tilt the other way. Astrid sat down again abruptly. The room went
on moving to the ghost of a swell.

What had happened was no dream. There was no waking to
morning, no point of return to life as it had always been. No Kol.
She could not take that thought in. Her legs shook, and she felt
cold. Shock, like in Monige. For a moment she seemed to be outside
herself, looking down on the small trembling figure on the sleeping
platform.

Presently she stood up again. The room bucketed to and fro. The
floor tilted perilously. She walked unsteadily to the door.

The doorway from the hall led into the byre through a hanging
of sewn sheepskins. Astrid clung to the door jamb. The byre, being
smaller, swayed even more than the hall.

'You're up. Are you all right?'

It was Ingrid, coming in from the outer door, carrying two
wooden buckets of water on a yoke. 'You look much better,' she
said. 'Do you want to get dressed? There's porridge from the
morning meal if you want it.'

The clothes Ingrid brought were Astrid's own. That surprised
her; she had expected them to have vanished along with the rest
of her past. Sitting shivering on the edge of the sleeping platform,
she managed to pull the borrowed dress off, and then to struggle
into her own. She dragged her tunic over it and tied the belt.

'That's pretty,' said Ingrid. 'You can get that purple colour from
lichen, can't you? Gunnhild uses a dye like that. Are your feet cold?'

Astrid nodded, trying to quell the dizziness. Ingrid pulled down
a line that hung over the fire. There were some fish drying on it,
and several socks. She unpinned two socks and Astrid put them on
slowly.

'Here,' said Ingrid proudly, placing a pair of rough leather boots
sewn with big stitches on the floor in front of her. They were
patched, scuffed at the toes and somehow friendly. 'I got them from
Ingebjorg.' Ingrid made it sound like a triumph. 'I remembered she

told me about Olaf growing out of his boots, not that he ever wears them anyway, even in winter.'

'What happened to mine?'

There was a silence. 'You'd lost one,' said Ingrid. 'But don't try to remember. Not now.'

'I'm going to have to remember.'

Ingrid ladled boiling water from the cauldron on the fire into a smaller soapstone pot, and began to stir in a handful of oatmeal.

'Do you have a comb?' asked Astrid.

Ingrid searched in the basket that hung on the wall above her own sleeping platform, and handed Astrid a big horn comb. Astrid began to struggle with the knots in her hair, while Ingrid stirred the porridge. The only sounds in the room were the licking of flames, the hiss of steam under the lid of the cauldron, and the scratching of a solitary hen around the flour barrel. The sun shone in at the doorway where Ingrid had tied back the hangings, and an old dog was stretched out on the patch of warmth cast across the floor. Peace wrapped itself around Astrid, and suggested moments out of the past, other days in other sunlit houses. She began to relax. A strand of the harder knot inside her loosened itself as she combed out her hair. She sighed, leaned back against the wall, and began to plait her hair again. Ingrid gave her a bone clasp to fasten the end, much plainer than the one Astrid had lost.

'Would you like to sit outside?' Ingrid asked her. 'We should make the most of the sunshine while it's here. Take this to drink. I'll bring your porridge.'

The drink Ingrid gave her looked like whey, but it smelt sour, and bubbles floated to the top. Astrid sipped it cautiously, and made a face at the taste.

'Blaand,' said Ingrid. 'Don't you like it?'

Astrid tasted it again. Buttermilk she knew, and ale. This was something between the two, bitter but tangy. 'Yes, I think so.'

'Good, because that's what there is. We only brew ale for feasts, and malt for the Earl's tax.'

Outside the door, Astrid was met by daylight so bright it hurt her eyes. All she could see, in a glare of white, were sea and sky, and vague shapes against their brilliance. It took a moment to focus on her immediate surroundings. There was a bench against the house wall, facing out to sea. Poultry foraged in the cracks between the brigstones. 'Sit down.'

Looking into the distance, Astrid felt the swaying begin to subside at last. She ate her porridge slowly, and looked about her. She gazed for the first time on the Shirva rigs, and beyond to the headland where this year's lambs were still grazing, and to the two skerries at the mouth of the south harbour. Across an innocent looking sea, the sun made ripples of silver that stretched from the horizon to the shores below them. The past was over. Everything external seem unreal, belonging only to people like Ingrid, whose lives had not been torn apart. Raw loss made Astrid feel untouchable, as if it were her fault for being different from the day, and all the bright things that belonged to it.

'Where is this?'

'This is Shirva.'

'Is that a country?'

'What? No, no, Shirva is just this farm. Ours. See the ditch there where the rigs run at an angle. Beyond that ditch, that's Leogh.'

There was a pause. Astrid watched four ducks parade past the bench in a line, making towards the stubble fields. 'But what country are we in then?'

Ingrid gave her a puzzled look. 'You mean the island? Didn't you . . .? This is Fridarey.'

An island. Astrid couldn't take it in. 'Are we in Noreg?'

'Noreg? Of course not. Noreg is three days' sail in spring, with a fair wind.'

'Then where are we?'

'As I said, this is Fridarey.' Ingrid pointed across the fields. 'The Orkneyjar, a day's sail, maybe.' She pointed back through the house. 'Hjaltland, the same again. If it's weather, that is. You can see Hjaltland from the island on a clear day. It's harder to see the Orkneyjar because there are fewer hills there, though we see them sometimes.'

'Does anyone go there?'

'Oh yes. But not until spring.'

'Have you been?'

'Me?' Ingrid was staring at her again. 'Of course not. This is my island.' She looked at Astrid with concern. 'Where did you come from?' she asked eventually. 'From the west, it must have been.'

'Dyflin.'

'Dyflin?' Ingrid's eyes widened. 'My uncle will want to know about that. Are you free?'

Astrid was indignant. 'I'm not a thrall,' she answered. 'I am Astrid Kolsdottir, and he is – was – a master shipbuilder of Dyflin.'

'My uncle will be glad. He said you would be freeborn, and father said we had no proof of it. But Einar minded. Maybe it's because he saved your life. What's the matter?'

Astrid's fists were pressed to her eyes. She held herself rigid and when she spoke her voice was thin and strained. 'Did they find my father?'

'Your father?' Ingrid put her hand on Astrid's shoulder. 'Was he on that ship?'

Astrid nodded slowly, not looking up.

'No one was found but you,' said Ingrid deliberately. 'Einar said that was a miracle. You were right on the rock, at Hjukni geo. It was a chance in a thousand. There's been nothing else but timbers.'

Astrid never moved. She ought to cry, thought Ingrid. She's so numb, it's like talking all the time to someone who isn't there. 'He's drowned,' she said aloud. 'It's a wicked place, and they'd know by now if it were different.'

But Astrid would not cry. All the time she had lain in bed, grief had hovered just below her, sometimes coming so close she thought it would suck her down. But she would not allow herself to fall. Nothing had meaning any more. The saints had abandoned her. Mary and Jesus had left her prayers unanswered.

She took her hands from her eyes, and looked out over the fields again. They looked pale and barren under a meagre sky. That was from pressing her eyes too hard. She could see green spots dancing. 'It's a poor land,' she remarked at last.

'It is not!'

Surprised, Astrid saw Ingrid was flushed and indignant. 'Shirva is the best farmed land on the island. We bring loads of seaweed up every winter. We'll be spreading it right across the rigs now the oats are gone, as soon as the cattle are in. You'll see. My father is the best farmer here. My uncle is the earl's own man. He's the lawman for this island. How could he be poor?'

'I'm sorry.' Astrid had not looked properly at Ingrid before, and realised now that she was beautiful. Ingrid had a very thick plait of fair hair which reached almost to her waist. She had a wide forehead, tanned golden rather than brown, and her skin looked silken, with no freckles or pock marks, just one small scar across her brow. Her eyes were a clear pale blue, and now that she was angry they were bright and hard like aquamarine. People would turn to look at her in Christchurch Square in Dyflin. No one had ever turned to look at Astrid, which was a great advantage. Even at thirteen she was still small and skinny. She had dark hair which was not quite curly, indeterminate greenish eyes, and a great many freckles. Various well-disposed neighbours had tried to give her lotions and ointments to cure these, but Astrid had liked having them when she was younger. She thought they made her more like a boy. Her father had never remarked on her blemishes; she didn't know if he had ever thought about them.

'I'm sorry,' said Astrid again. 'It's just that it's different here. I'm used to there being trees.'

She hadn't even realised what was wrong until she heard herself say it. No wonder the place looked so flat and bare.

Ingrid seemed to accept her apology, and the colour died out of her cheeks as fast as it had risen. 'Oh yes,' she said vaguely. 'I've heard about those.' She paused. 'Einar wants to talk to you.'

'Who is Einar?'

'I told you. My uncle. Einar Thorvaldsson. Einar and Bjarni are the farmers of Shirva. Eirik went to sea, but he is drowned. My cousins live at Setr, which is also part of Shirva. We don't see them much now.'

'Did you say that Einar saved my life?'

Ingrid looked at her cautiously. 'Do you want to talk about that? I mean . . . I could tell you what happened. You might not want to think about it though.'

Astrid felt sick of herself, of feeling like an invalid, to be treated so delicately. The blackness felt like a gulf beneath her. She banished it, and turned practical. 'I think you'd better tell me everything you know.'

Ingrid hesitated, then began. 'Einar found you. He was coming down from Raiva, and he saw you on the rocks. It had been a wild night; that was why he was out early. There wasn't anything left to see, he said, no hope. The ship hadn't a chance on a lee shore like that. If they'd become lost to direction, they'd still be thinking they had sea room. Einar can't imagine how you got high and dry. You hadn't been in the water at all, he said. Do you remember how it happened?'

'I don't want to remember,' said Astrid stonily.

'Of course not. I shouldn't be asking,' said Ingrid with a sympathy that Astrid found infuriating.

'My father got me ashore,' she said.

'Einar couldn't believe it. He said it must be fate, to be cast ashore so miraculously. He tried to pump the water out of you, but there was none.'

'I know.'

'You know? You remember?'

Astrid shook her head. There was hardly a memory, just bruises on her back, and the feeling of someone pounding her, crushing her back as if he meant to kill her. She hadn't been sure if the thing had happened at all.

Ingrid waited a moment. 'It seems so important to him. He keeps saying it's a fate. A child thrown up out of an impossible sea, and him chancing to be there. No one else came. He wouldn't have it you were dead. He found that you were breathing, then he wrapped you in his own cloak and carried you back here. We couldn't believe what he'd got. A child out of nowhere. It didn't seem canny. Some think it isn't right yet. But then timber came ashore, and they had to believe you were human. Einar won't let them make signs against you, I promise you.'

'I'm not a child.'

'I know that. Gerda and I undressed you. But Einar thought you were. You're not very big. We haven't told him different. But he wants to see you. He kept coming in while you were sleeping. Gunnhild said he shouldn't try to rouse you.' She eyed Astrid cautiously. 'It's as well the island does think that. There's a kind of fate about a child. They might think differently if you were a woman.'

Astrid considered. If being a child would save her from what they did to women, a child she would remain.

The afternoon passed in a slow dream. Astrid sat by the fire while Ingrid ground barley in the handmill by the door, and made bannocks from the fresh meal. When she had set them to bake, they went into the byre through a low oval door shaped for the kye, and Astrid watched Ingrid tie angelica in bunches and hang them up for winter. Then she suggested to Astrid that she come with her while she did the milking.

'You might as well see how it's done.'

Astrid didn't bother to tell her that there were kye in Dyflin too, but followed her meekly up the knowe that rose to the east of Shirva. The milking cow was tethered halfway up. Ingrid set down her stool and bucket, and began to milk.

The autumn day was drawing to a close. The western sky was deep pink, and silhouetted against it Astrid could see the cliff edge, jagged black rock only yards from the Shirva hall. She'd never seen a shore like it. Green slopes where sheep grazed rose and ended in extraordinary pinnacles of rock that might have been carved by trolls, or devils. She could hear, although she tried hard to shut it out, the muffled pounding of waves on a hard shore. Astrid turned back to Ingrid, who was milking steadily, her face pressed against the cow's flank. Astrid breathed in the smell of cow, and laid her hand against the animal's shoulder. She felt warmth, rough black hair, a sharp backbone, and watched milk, so white it seemed to glow in the twilight, squirt into the pail. The contrast was too great. Where she stood, the land was homely, full of familiar sounds and smells, a human, inhabited place. But over there it vanished in a chaos of rock and water, where events had caught at her and thrown her out of one world and into another.

Astrid looked the other way, but there was no getting away from the sea. She could see it all spread out to the south. The water on the darkening skerries glowed white like the milk, as if it had a light of its own.

Ingrid stood up. 'That's the Sudvik. We have our noost down there, where we keep the boat. See that house on the hill to the east there –' she pointed – 'That's where my sister lives. I'll take you to see her. You can't see the smithy from here, but that's where it is, just above the Sudvik.'

'Whose land is this?'

'I told you. It's ours. My uncle is the udaller of Shirva.'

'But isn't there a lord? To whom does he owe allegiance?'

'To the Earl of Orkneyjar,' said Ingrid proudly. 'There's been no other lord here, since Earl Paul was defeated, because of the beacons.'

Astrid said nothing. The household at Shirva didn't seem grand enough to belong to an Earl's retainer.

Back in the byre, Ingrid poured out the milk, and hung up what was left of the old milk in a cloth to make cheese. 'There won't be much more this year,' she remarked. 'The milk's beginning to go

down now, but we have plenty of buttermilk and pressed cheeses
stored from the summer.'

Ingrid cleaned the buckets and washed down the stone shelf at
the end of the byre where the dairying was done. As she did so she
kept up her flow of conversation about the work and the farm, this
year's harvest and the state of the fishing. She didn't seem to expect
Astrid to answer, and Astrid began to feel almost normal, even
interested. But then the pain would well back again, cutting her
off from everything around her. So her attention came and went,
while the day wore itself away.

The old woman appeared, and spoke to Ingrid. 'They're back.
They want to speak to her.'

Ingrid led Astrid back through the byre, and pushed her gently
across the threshold into the hall. This time the place was not
empty. There was a man sitting in the high seat between the carved
pillars. Kol. Her heart jumped. But when she looked again the man
was not like Kol at all. This man had thick curly hair, light brown
turning to grey, and was more plainly dressed than ever Kol had
been, wearing an undyed woollen tunic and hardly any ornaments.
Instead of boots he wore leather clogs, and thick trousers fastened
with plain cross straps. Red veins stood out in his cheeks, quite
unlike Kol. He had a beaky nose, and pale blue eyes like Ingrid's.
Since he was sitting in the high seat, he must be Einar Thorvaldsson, while the other man, sitting on the bench near the high seat,
must be Bjarni, Ingrid's father. He had dark red hair, and a crooked
nose that seemed too large for his face. He didn't smile when she
glanced at him, but looked away from her into the fire, as if he were
embarrassed.

'Come here,' said the man in the high seat. She stood before
him, the fire just behind her, so she felt warmth on the back of her
legs through her dress.

'Astrid,' said Einar. He regarded her as if she held an unusual
interest for him. Astrid felt uncomfortable. Then she thought of
the pounding on her back, thinking the man was killing her. She
coloured, and determined to keep her dignity. 'Einar Thorvaldsson?' she asked in return, and waited.

The man on the bench looked up from the fire, and suddenly
chuckled. Einar smiled at her without irony. 'I'm glad to see you
better. You must be tougher than you look. Can you tell us who
you are?'

'I am Astrid, daughter of Kol, who was a master shipbuilder from Dyflin. We were travelling to Noreg, from Monige.'

'From Dyflin?' Einar leaned forward eagerly. The redhaired man looked up. 'Ah, then you'll have news.'

She didn't want to look at him; staring past him, she saw a harp hanging on the wall in the shadows.

'Give the child a chance.' Astrid was surprised that Bjarni should be the one to say that.

'We?' Einar asked her, ignoring his brother. 'Who were "we"?'

'My father was on the ship with me. We had to flee the city, and we were going to Noreg. He has a cousin there, a man who was once apprenticed to him, who owes him a favour.'

She heard herself say the words as if they were quite normal. There seemed to be two of her: one calm and aloof, functioning in this world in which she did not belong; the other huddled inside her, knotted under her ribs. Dead.

'Child,' said Einar, and from him she didn't resent it. 'What is the news of Dyflin?'

'I don't know what you know.'

That was right. She sounded so calm, her voice high and far away. She held her breath to stop herself from shuddering.

'Rumour,' said Bjarni from his bench. 'Nothing but rumour. Dagfinn's tales.'

His brother gestured to him to be silent. 'We knew that Dermot of Laighen went to the King of Englaland, and that Henry's troops were in the south of Irland. Dagfinn told us they were saying in the islands that Dyflin had fallen, last year, but I also heard that the King of Connacht had defeated the English before they came near the city and the Norse had stayed out of it. Then I spoke to a trader from Ljodhus, and he said the Irish and Norse had made a treaty, and the English had fallen back on Laighen.'

'All our news is old these days,' said Bjarni, 'and there are fewer ships in the islands every year. If Irland is lost then the islands are in trouble. Whatever Dagfinn says, the markets are vanishing, and we grow steadily poorer. The world grows worse, whatever.'

They spoke as if it were a tale from Island, or someone else's dream. Men always talked like this, sitting outside their houses in the evening discussing news from far away, as if it were only thoughts. If she could do the same, this world might not be so unlike the old one at all.

'None of that is true exactly,' said Astrid. Suddenly it was a relief to be asked questions, and to have to think of an answer. It saved feeling, anyway, and Kol had always liked this kind of discussion.
'Then what is?'
'The English troops came years ago. When I was ten, no, eleven. There were troubles in Laighen, long before that. They were always talking about a siege in Dyflin. But everyone stayed. Then Strongbow came this summer.' She paused and took a breath. It was such a relief to talk again. She wanted to tell everything, so they would know. 'It was August when they took Vadrefjord. The King of Laighen came up to Dyflin with Strongbow then, and that's when they closed the gates, in the middle of harvest. The King of Connacht was supposed to stop them getting through, but Strongbow went right past him.
'They came very suddenly. Then we had the siege.'
'Was there a battle?'
They were both listening to her intently. She wasn't used to having two grown men hang upon her words. Feeling powerful at last, she was suddenly angry.
'No there was not a battle.' She was vehement. 'There was a siege. It was terrible.' The word wasn't hard enough for what she wanted to tell them, but she couldn't find a better. 'It was hot. They closed the gates. We knew we wouldn't get out, not until they won or we did. And we only could if the King of Connacht came to relieve us. They said he had gone home. But then we heard he was waiting to attack. We didn't know. And the harvest wasn't in either, so we knew we had no time. They were worried about the wells. Too many people, and it was too hot. It was horrible, knowing that until something happened we couldn't get out. Can you imagine that?'
The question obviously took them by surprise. They glanced at one another. Bjarni answered her. 'Yes,' he said without emotion. 'I can imagine it.'
She was beginning to like him after all. He treated her like an adult. Her father had always done that. 'It was when the gates shut,' she told him, as if Einar were not there. 'That's when I understood.
'It wasn't real until then. I'd been hearing it all for so long. Always fighting in the provinces, but never the Norse cities. Even though it was near it seemed far away. For me, anyway. I'm sure my

father knew differently. But when the gates shut I was scared. There was nothing we could do.

'They were supposed to be having talks, the governors and the captains of the raiders. So we weren't expecting anything to happen. It was supposed to be a truce. They breached the walls.' She faltered. 'I can't describe that.'

'You saw it?'

'No. I heard. All the church bells began to ring. And then there was the fire. Burning the city. So we ran. We lived close to the river, near the shipyard. The smoke was yellow, because of the thatch, choking. We had to put our cloaks over our heads. It was very hot. We could hear the fire roaring.' She stopped, as if she had just thought of something. 'Like the sea.'

'Yes,' said Bjarni. 'I can imagine that.'

'So we got to the shipyard, by St. Olaf's church. The church was on fire but the bell went on ringing. Ringing and ringing, even though there were flames at the door. I don't know how long they went on ringing. Father had a ship ready. Not just for us. We had to wait for the others. They didn't all come. But other people did, as many as we could take. There were small boats everywhere. It was a muddle, just a muddle. But we got a boat to take us aboard. There wasn't much wind, just enough to get down the river. The city was burning behind us. It was smoky all the way down. They were afraid for the sail, because of sparks. But we got away.' She looked at them, suddenly feeling helpless. 'That was all. We went to Monige. Other ships did as well. It was full of refugees. Father said we should get out. To Noreg. Everyone said it was too late in the season. But he trusted his own ship. We'd have made it too, if it wasn't for the island. The storm didn't bother him. As long as we have sea room, that was what he said. She can do it, she can take it. He was thinking he might stop in Hjaltland, if it was weather.'

She remembered it so well. She could hear his voice in her mind, saying those very words. If only it could be the moment before, when things could still be different. He seemed so close, but he was gone, drowned; and she was without him now forever. They were to have stopped in Hjaltland, if it was weather. It could so easily have happened, only it had not.

The blackness flooded back. She seemed to hear the hollow echo of her voice, talking too fast, too high, letting all the words out that told them how it was. Gabbling in the dark. Dead. The word fell like a hammer, but made no sound. There was no meaning in it. Why had she talked to these men so urgently? It changed nothing. Kol would have known what to make of it. She pressed her hands to her face to shut these strangers out.

'That's enough,' said Einar. 'No, Bjarni, we've asked her quite enough. We've got all winter to talk. So what are we to do with you now, Astrid Kolsdottir?'

Astrid would never let them see her cry. He had spoken just in time. Perhaps he knew that. She lowered her hands, glanced at Einar cautiously, and caught a look of appreciation. Maybe he still thought she was sent to bring him luck. It was as well that he liked her. Better still that he considered her a child. She gave him a level look. 'I suppose that's up to you.'

Bjarni stood up and leaned over his brother, muttering something in his ear. 'I don't think so,' said Einar. He continued to regard Astrid steadily.

'It seems you are our guest at Shirva,' said Einar at last. He spoke as if he were giving a judgement, and Astrid remembered that Ingrid had said that he was also the lawman. 'You are welcome to our house.'

'Thank you.'

'You have nothing to thank me for,' said Einar, and she remembered then that she owed him her life. 'If there is a fate in this, no doubt we shall discover it.'

'You saved my life.'

'I was there.'

Their conversation seemed to be over. She wasn't sure whether to go or wait. When Einar stood up he wasn't as tall as she had expected. Bjarni was a much more impressive figure. But she liked Einar better. Perhaps there was some fate that lay between her and him. He seemed to think so. She thought Bjarni less fierce than he looked, but she wasn't at all sure that he wanted her here.

Einar nodded to her and left the hall. When Ingrid came forward, Astrid realised that she had been standing behind her all the time. Ingrid caught Astrid's hand impulsively. 'I'm glad we shall have you here. But I'm sorry . . . What happened, I'm sorry.'

Astrid managed not to pull back. She liked Ingrid, but not sympathy.

'Company for you,' remarked Ingrid's father. He turned to Astrid. 'We miss Gudrun still. It's lonely for Ingrid. She minds the kye herself now, and there's the poultry. We need another young woman in this house.' He nodded to his daughter. 'Take her about, now she's on her feet again. No need to be idle. It's winter soon enough.'

'He means kindly, you know,' Ingrid whispered, as he left them.

'Yes. Who is Gudrun?'

Ingrid stared. 'Gudrun? My sister? But didn't you . . . it's so hard to remember you don't know anything. She's been asking about you. She'd have been over, but she's not supposed to walk too much.'

'Is she ill?'

'Gudrun? No, no. She's pregnant again. So this time we're not taking any chances. But we could go over to Byrstada tomorrow afternoon. Do you think you'd be well enough?'

'There's nothing wrong with me.'

Chapter 4

The next day Ingrid took Astrid to Byrstada. It wasn't quite raining, but the air was damp and salt. When Astrid stopped to listen she could hear the sea sluggishly breaking over the skerries. Clearly there was to be no escape from it in this place. As soon as they had skirted the knowe behind Shirva, she saw the eastern coast of the island, where the land ended abruptly in the cliffs behind the Byrstada land. So the island was barely half a mile wide. Astrid's heart sank. But she had been thinking in the night, and there were several questions she had prepared to ask Ingrid.

'Where will I find your priest?'

'Priest?' repeated Ingrid. 'What priest?'

'You must have a priest here.' A terrifying thought occurred to Astrid. 'You are Christians, aren't you?'

'Of course we are!' said Ingrid. 'What else could we be? But there isn't a priest here.'

'Then is there one somewhere else?'

'Listen,' said Ingrid, exercising great patience. 'There isn't anywhere else. Not that you can get to, anyway.'

'There must be priests in the Orkneyjar.'

'Of course. And in Hjaltland. But there'll be no more boats now before spring.'

'But what do you do when you need a priest?'

Ingrid shrugged. 'We don't need a priest, I suppose.' She looked Astrid over. 'Does that make us worse than anyone else? I hope you haven't had reason to think so?'

'Of course I haven't,' said Astrid.

She followed Ingrid across a stretch of marshy land, thick with cotton grass. The harbour came into view as they walked. A gaggle of children were playing on the beach, throwing stones into the sea.

'There's the smithy,' said Ingrid, pointing to a low turf-roofed building beside a burn, just above the beach. 'That's where you should go. Snorri can tell you about priests and things like that. He used to stay in Kirkjavagr. Ask him sometime, that would be the best thing.'

Astrid was little comforted. She could hear the surf more clearly than ever. Sea everywhere, and nowhere to turn for help. She decided to grow accustomed to the waves. Her life had not been destroyed by a sound, and she could not hate the wind and the sea forever. If there were no priests or nuns, she would have to rely on her own knowledge and memory, for she had been well instructed at home.

'Anyway, you must be glad,' remarked Ingrid, breaking across her thoughts.

'Glad of what?'

'That they gave you your freedom. The whole island is talking about it. There's no precedent. But Einar is the lawman, a better lawman than any lord ever was. So he won.'

'Won what?'

'That's true, I didn't tell you, Gunnhild said not, when we came home. I waited with her while the Thing met. You know what a Thing is – a meeting.'

'Of course I know that. But surely there's no Thing here?'

'This island has its own,' said Ingrid proudly. 'That's my uncle's doing. He set it up twenty years ago. He goes to the Thing in Hjaltland every summer. But he's our lawman, and we've had peace here ever since the Earl's Wars. Do you realise, there hasn't been a killing here for sixteen years?'

'No,' said Astrid, unimpressed. 'So why did the Thing meet?'

'About you, of course. That's what I said. Einar insisted that you were free-born, and cast up by a miracle at his feet.'

Astrid stopped and gripped Ingrid's arm. They stood still between two puddles on the track, where cattle had churned up the mud. 'What would have happened to me if he had not?'

'There have been none in this generation. But they all say the precedent is the same. Free-born or not, if the sea gives them to us they belong to us. There aren't many thralls on this island. We can't support them, and slaves and cattle eat more than their worth on a thin pasture. My father said that. On some islands, they would throw shipwrecked people back to sea if the harvest was bad. But Einar said we never did that here.'

'They would have made me a slave?' Astrid was furious, not frightened, as Ingrid had expected her to be. 'Me? My father was one of the best craftsmen of Dyflin. That's what I'd have been, if I wasn't a girl. There's nothing of a slave in me!'

Ingrid looked at her curiously. 'Are there many slaves in Dyflin?'

'Of course. That's how Dyflin grew rich. The church doesn't like it, but there are still slaves.'

Ingrid's eyes hardened. 'This is not so poor an island. My uncle brought you out of the sea, and gave you your freedom. My father said it was unnecessary. The Thing never meets between the hay and grain harvests. My father said, she'll grow into a woman. She'll never starve.'

Astrid was so angry she didn't trust herself to speak. She bit her lip and thought of Bjarni Thorvaldsson, smiling at her and saying she was welcome. She wouldn't trust him, ever.

The hall at Byrstada was set on the eastern slope overlooking the south harbour. Unlike Shirva, it had a clear view of the beach, and for the first time Astrid could see the island boats, lying in their noosts above the tideline like basking seals. The smithy was in full view at the bottom of the hill. To the west, she could just see the yard at Shirva. The whole south part of the island was dominated by the headland, towards which every dwelling faced. From Byrstada Astrid could see its sheer green slopes rising in front of her, the sea dark blue on either side.

The door was wide open, and Astrid followed Ingrid inside. There was a babble of voices, and for a moment Astrid shrank back. It was beginning to be an ordeal, being so totally among strangers.

There were more weapons hanging on the walls than at Shirva. The place smelt of baking bread and human beings. Peat reek filled the air with blue haze. Someone called out, 'Ingrid, is that you? Gudrun! it's your sister!'

It was a girl's voice, sharp and penetrating. Astrid peered through the smoke at its owner. She looked about Astrid's own age, but was taller and sturdier, with thick brown hair and pronounced features. 'Oh,' she said, looking Astrid up and down. 'So it's the selkie, is it? Well, you don't look that uncanny to me. Does she, Gudrun? If she was bewitched she'd be beautiful, wouldn't she?'

'Leave her alone, Ragna,' said Ingrid. 'How would you like it if someone talked like that in front of you?'

Ragna tossed her hair back. 'They wouldn't,' she said simply.

Another woman had detached herself from the group, and stepped round the hearthstones. She was dressed like a married woman, her hair tied back and hidden by a scarf. 'Ingrid,' she said. 'Let's get out of here. Ragna, you stay and see the baking gets done.' Ragna seemed about to protest. 'I mean it,' said Gudrun. Her eyes strayed to Astrid. 'Who's this? Einar's nixie is it? Come out quick, or they'll all be wanting to look at you.' She pushed Astrid and Ingrid towards the door.

She led them to the bench on the south side of the hall. It was cold and damp, and the wind caught them. Ingrid sat down by her sister, and Astrid, after a moment's hesitation, sat down on Gudrun's other side.

Gudrun was not unlike her father Bjarni, but his features were softened in her. She couldn't be twenty yet. Her eyes were as blue as Ingrid's, but looked colder. Astrid suspected that her hair was as red as her father's. She looked stronger than Ingrid, and she had an air of authority about her.

'You're Astrid,' Gudrun remarked. 'I hear that you now have the protection of the Thing, and my uncle is besotted with you. But he's not in love with you.'

'I should think not! He might be my grandfather!'

'Why should that stop him?'

Astrid stared at the sea. The view was not very different from the one from Shirva. It depressed her. She was just beginning to absorb the fact that there was nowhere else.

'There were more spars at Swarza geo yesterday,' said Gudrun. 'Still no bodies.'

'What, right round there? Already?'

'Rolf reckons they're coming through the tunnels. They couldn't have been washed round the coast already. It's hardly a week. Have there been any more on the west side?'

'Father saw a long spar yesterday near Hundi Stack. He thought it might be the mast. He went back this morning with Thorvald.'

'He's not gone down there with Thorvald? Suppose one pushes the other off the cliff?'

'You don't think it's a good idea for them to work together? I did. They'll have to speak to each other, doing a job like that.'

'I don't think that boy can speak.'

'Oh come on, you used to play with him, same as I did. And ordered him about all the time, I remember.'

'That was before he grew up.'

'I thought it was a good idea,' reiterated Ingrid. 'Their quarrel is getting out of hand.'

'I suppose Einar thought of it?' Gudrun pulled at a loose strand of red hair. 'Maybe Thorvald is improving a little,' she admitted. 'He may not push him off. Just loosen the rope a little.'

'Gudrun, don't. You know he wouldn't.'

'Please, who is Thorvald?'

The sisters stopped short and stared at Astrid.

'Thorvald is one of our cousins,' said Ingrid.

'We don't need to explain all that now,' said Gudrun abruptly. 'He knows about you of course. He goes to the Thing now.'

'It's like this,' said Ingrid. 'My father's younger brother Eirik was drowned. But before that Ingebjorg persuaded Eirik to leave the household at Shirva. They went up to Setr eight years ago, when I was eight.'

Gudrun frowned. 'And now Ingebjorg still stays at Setr and keeps her household to herself. It's ridiculous. It's an insult to Bjarni and Einar, after they offered to foster the boys. You'd think after Eirik died Ingebjorg would have the decency not to quarrel with his family. But no, as soon as she knows her husband's dead, she says she's having nothing to do with his brothers. She'd rather starve than keep the family together.'

'That's not fair,' said Ingrid mildly. 'Einar and Eirik had already made the settlement. It was their idea that Eirik's family should have their own house and lands.'

'But why do you think Eirik and Einar made that settlement?' said Gudrun. 'It was because Ingebjorg couldn't stand the way we work together, because we don't have a rich place like her father's in the Orkneyjar. So, she went on at Eirik until the only thing he could do was to ask for his part of the inheritance, and go to live at Setr.'

'Sometimes you sound just like Father. I don't blame Ingebjorg. She'd just lost her man and then Father comes along and says he'll take her sons off her hands too. I can just imagine how he said it. And she's a foreigner. I think it was brave of her to insist on staying over at Setr, and bringing them up herself.'

'That's all very well. But for a woman to take the matter to the Thing! It was a family matter, and she should never have opposed her husband's brothers in public.'

'All the men voted against Father,' said Ingrid. 'That's why he's never forgiven her.'

'She's split the place down the middle.' Gudrun swung round at Astrid. 'Can you imagine what it's been like, having cousins on our doorstep who won't have anything to do with us if they can help it?'

'They're not hostile,' said Ingrid. 'Olaf isn't at least. And Thorvald does his best.'

'How old is your cousin?' asked Astrid. It was good to think of something that had nothing to do with herself.

'Which one? Thorvald, he's of age now. That's why he was at the Thing to decide about you. He was fifteen this year.'

'Olaf will be fifteen too next year.'

'Have you thought?' said Gudrun. 'We'll probably have one of those two for lawman before we're dead. God help us.'

'Don't, Gudrun. Listen, we ought to go home now.'

'You'll be there tomorrow, when we bring the cattle across the hill dyke? You'll bring her, won't you Ingrid? The island ought to see her.'

'Why?' asked Astrid.

'You should be seen, better they talk about something real than just imagining you. Some still say it was devil's work.'

Within a few days, Astrid began to feel less uneasy at Shirva. True to his word, Bjarni made sure she was given work to do, but it was made clear that her task was to help Ingrid, and that she was to be treated on the same footing as a daughter of the household. There was plenty to be done, but Astrid had been well taught in Dyflin. It was easier to be busy than to contemplate her situation. About ten days after her arrival, she found herself alone when Ingrid went to Byrstada.

Astrid stared at the headland that reared itself up in full view of the doorway, and remembered that Ingrid had said the Orkneyjar were sometimes visible from the summit. Astrid dreaded even going to look. The only land she had seen from Shirva was a distant island, sometimes visible through a gap in the western cliffs. She hated to think that Fridarey was as small and isolated as that, a mirror image of the remote blue hump on the horizon. She didn't want to see how she was surrounded by the hateful sea, that she could never leave here again without once more confronting it.

It was only a short distance across the empty rigs to the foot of the slope. Just where the headland began, she came to the edge of the cliff, and saw stacks in the bay with white water round their feet, and further out, a great slab broken off from the headland, where shags perched above the waves. Hjukni geo was only five minutes' walk from Shirva, but Astrid didn't want to identify it. A wave broke on the shingle below her, and drew back, scraping the pebbles with a sound like falling spars. She turned to flee, but there was a shout behind her.

'Astrid!'

A moment later Ragna from Byrstada was at her side.

'Where are you going?' demanded Ragna. 'Shall I come with you?'

Astrid only hesitated for a moment. Although Ragna had been less than polite the only time they'd met, Astrid was ready for any distraction.

'If you like. But I'm not going anywhere.'

'You looked as if you were going up the headland.'

'I was. I wanted to see if I could see land.'

'See land! What's this, if it's not land?' asked Ragna, stamping her foot on the ground.

'Ingrid said you could see the Orkneyjar on a clear day.'

Ragna snorted. 'It's not a clear day. A few times a year you might see it. Hardly ever.' She looked at Astrid. 'Why do you want to anyway? You get a good view of the island up there though. I'm surprised Ingrid didn't take you. Why don't I show you?'

Astrid followed as Ragna led the way back to the shore which Astrid had so carefully avoided. As soon as they reached the top the wind met them. Ragna led Astrid up to a cairn, and pulled her down in the lee of it.

'This is one of the medes,' she told Astrid, touching the stones.

'What's a mede?'

'They line them up when they go fishing. Surely you know that? Look now!'

Astrid located Shirva at once, at the foot of the headland. 'See Byrstada?' said Ragna. Astrid followed her pointing finger. At Byrstada, just as at Shirva, she could see the turf-roofed hall and the outbuildings round it. There was one other large group of buildings at Leogh, but across the width of the townland there were low huts, all facing south-west, so that from where she sat she could see the doorway of every one. The houses had been built in the shelter of the small knowes that dotted the townland, on the south-facing slopes.

'There's the smithy,' said Ragna, 'just below our house, at Gaela; it's part of the Byrstada land. Snorri was wounded, and being our kin, we helped him find a living.'

The smithy lay tucked into a sheltered hollow by the burn that flowed into the Sudvik. Ingrid had told her to seek out Snorri smith, when she had asked for a priest. Ragna was directing her attention halfway up the hill between Gaela and Byrstada. 'See that level space just south of our house, under that knowe? That's the Thing place. Not many islands have their own Thing, but without one, every dispute has to be referred to the Earl. We don't have any of the Earl's retainers living here, not since the time of the beacons. Since then we've been the Earl's own farmers. Einar says it's better when all men are subject to their own law.'

'Do you ever get ships coming here?'

'We have our own, the Sula. She's my brothers' ship. But she's at the Nordhavn. You couldn't beach a trading ship anywhere else on the island.'

So there was a ship. 'Where's the Nordhavn?' Astrid asked eagerly.

Ragna waved vaguely north, beyond the townlands. 'See the hill dyke? The Nordhavn's over there, beyond the hill.'

The townlands north of Shirva were interspersed by undrained bogland, and the houses were more thinly scattered. Beyond them towered the familiar shape of the Seydurholm, a great cliff with bird droppings all across its lower face. To the south of the hill dyke there were pastures and shorn rigs, but to the north of it a succession of fierce cliffs, running east to west, bit deep into the island. 'Is there nothing else? I mean, are there no more settlements, no more people?'

Ragna stared at her. 'Where?'

Astrid pointed north, at the blank face of the hill. 'Beyond there?'

'No. There's only the Nordhavn. No one lives on the hill. How could they? Nothing human, anyway.'

'You mean other things do?'

'If you go out there, you'll see the trowie mounds for yourself,' said Ragna. 'The place is full of them, and old dykes and cairns. Someone built all that, and some say they're there still, or if they're not, their ghosts are. There are folk who've seen such things, even on the townlands.'

'Who?'

'My mother, for one. She saw the ghosts over at Bunes, where we put the kye for the summer grazing. But there are other places too, even between Byrstada and Shirva, that aren't canny.'

Astrid wasn't surprised. After all, the island had no priest, and no church. She crossed herself and changed the subject. 'What's that house away from the others, up against the hill dyke?'

'There? That's Setr, of course. You've not met Ingebjorg yet?'

'No. But Ingrid told me she was Eirik's wife.'

'Well, you're not likely to meet Ingebjorg at Shirva. You'll see Thorvald and Olaf there, though. Much good may it do you.'

'Don't you like them either?'

'Oh, they're not so bad. There isn't much choice on an island, you know. You look them over, and tell me what you think.'

Astrid had no wish to look Einar's nephews over, but she didn't say so.

'I know Thorvald very well,' Ragna told Astrid. 'We've always been friends. Don't believe everything they tell you at Shirva. Now, look at this.'

They were standing at the very edge of the cliff. Far below, in a yeasty sea, stacks rose like daggers out of the foam. There were skerries all along the western shore, in the lee of the cliffs. It was the wildest coast she had ever seen. Its deep indentations reached halfway across the island, to the foot of the highest hill.

'That's the Vord,' Ragna told her, 'where the beacon was lit for Earl Paul. We have our midsummer fire up there.'

Astrid wasn't listening. Somewhere down there, in that broken sea, her father's ship had come ashore, and Kol had drowned. In the geo directly below them, the rocks and stacks ended in a stony grey beach. The rocks were a curious colour, grey tinged with pink. Astrid looked away. She knew the place was called Hjukni geo.

Before Ragna could speak again, Astrid was running back downhill towards the townland.

Chapter 6

 It seemed to have forgotten to be winter, and Einar and Bjarni had taken advantage of the fine weather to get the autumn slaughter done. The women helped them drive the animals into a small pen at the end of the Shirva yard. While the men were preparing the pulley, Astrid and Ingrid leaned over the wall and considered their winter supplies. The dozen or so beasts were restless and frightened, eyes rolling, heads brushing one another's backs, leaving long trails of saliva. They seemed thin and puny under their thick black coats, even after a summer's grazing. In Dyflin the beasts that were brought in for the autumn market had been fattened up in the green water meadows that surrounded the city.

'Hey, Ingrid!'

Astrid looked up and saw two young men not much older than she was, both dressed in undyed tunics and woollen trousers. They were barefoot, although the ground was cold now, and most of the islanders were wearing winter boots. The elder boy was the fairer. His hair was bleached almost white on the top by wind and sun. His face was broad and freckled, with a turned-up nose. The younger had thick shaggy curls that fell to his shoulders, and looked as if they'd never seen a comb. His features were finer than his brother's; under all that hair he might possibly be goodlooking. Both carried axes, and wore knives in their belts. Both stared brazenly at Astrid with bright blue eyes.

'This is Astrid,' said Ingrid, but she didn't introduce them to Astrid. She didn't need to. These must be the cousins, Thorvald and Olaf.

The boys pushed in beside them, and peered over the wall. 'Not bad,' said Thorvald, poking the haunch of the young stirk nearest to him with the handle of his axe. The beast started out of the way, causing a surge of commotion in the pen.

'Why weren't you here to bring them in?' asked Ingrid. 'Father was furious.'

'Busy,' said Thorvald. 'But we're here now.'

'In at the death,' said Olaf. He slapped the sweating rump of a skinny heifer. 'Kill, kill! That's what we're here for! Wait till Bjarni sees us!'

'You should have been here.'

Thorvald made a derisory noise. Olaf leapt lightly on to the wall, and began to jig along it, his dirty feet on a level with their faces. 'Should, should, should!' chanted Olaf. 'Wait till you see us at the kill:

"That was something like butchery!
Christ helped us crimson the carrion, the . . . the . . ." '

'. . . black cattle,' finished Thorvald for him. 'Piled in the byre . . .'

Olaf gave a mock war cry, and jumped along the wall, landing in front of Ingrid's nose.

'Don't be blasphemous!' she shouted, crossing her fingers.

'Huh!'

'Thorvald!' Astrid had never heard Bjarni roar like that, and she jumped. So did Olaf, right off the wall, to stand sedately by his brother.

'So you're here at last,' said Bjarni. 'We've work to do.'

By midday, the yard was a mess of churned up mud, and rivulets of blood ran from the byre door across the brigstones. The kye kept up a constant bellowing, huddled together in their confined space, as one by one they were dragged out to slaughter. The yard was a confusion of struggling beasts and men. Once their throats were slit, the animals were swung up by the pulley in the byre and gutted. Soon the smell began to overpower the peat reek in the house. The women's job was washing out guts and offal ready to make puddings and sausage.

When the kye had been slaughtered, Astrid and Ingrid had to help drive the sheep into the same pen, a difficult job even with the dogs, now that the scent of blood was in the air. Once the killing was done, the men swilled down the brigstones with buckets of water.

Thorvald and Olaf stayed to supper. They had washed at the well and removed their tunics, but their shirts were still blood-spattered, and there were bloodstains round Olaf's wrists, showing just how far up he'd cleaned his hands. Both boys ate a large supper very fast, and said not one word throughout the meal. Every time Astrid looked at them, she found their eyes on her. Neither had addressed any remark to her throughout the day's work. When she caught Olaf's eye, he flushed and looked down. When she met Thorvald's glance, he stared blankly back. No one talked except Einar and Bjarni, who were discussing the extent of the winter supplies. It was a hurried, strained meal, held among the debris of the day's work, and Astrid was glad when it was over.

A couple of days later she and Ingrid were busy indoors all day making puddings. She saw Thorvald and Olaf once, when they came over to borrow a pony, which they loaded with their share of the meat.

'Tell Ingebjorg we can make her puddings here,' said Ingrid. 'You can come back for them.'

'All right.'

'He might have said thank you,' said Ingrid, returning to the hearth when Thorvald had gone. 'Why should we make their puddings, except it would be awkward to walk up to Setr with a bucket of blood.'

'Doesn't Ingebjorg come here?'

'No,' said Ingrid. 'At least, not recently. You see what it's like, trying to run a farm with family that won't speak to us?'

The slaughter seemed to have left everyone out of temper, except the men, who were quite satisfied with the year's crop of meat. 'We'll have a good winter,' remarked Bjarni to Astrid in a rare moment of expansiveness. 'You won't go hungry here.'

When Astrid went out to collect the eggs, the yard was quiet, and only mud and the red stains between the brigstones suggested that anything had happened there. She stopped on the threshold with her eyes half closed, feeling the warmth of the sun on her face. For a moment she might have been at home, in the stuffiness of wattle houses pressed against one another in steep narrow streets. Smells teased her memory: wood fires, drying fish, baking bread. She opened her eyes, blinking away sunspots, and saw the island. There was only the smell of salt, wet grass, and the midden, where the chickens were having a feast after the slaughter.

There was a footfall behind her, and Gerda began to scold before Astrid had time to turn round. Gerda always did her best to assert the authority of an old servant over the upstart whenever she and Astrid were alone. 'I said collect the eggs, not sit and lay one yourself!'

'Sorry.'

'Water! Where's the water? How do you expect me to get cleaned up in there without it?'

'I don't. Do you want the eggs first?'

When she came back Gerda was trying to unhook the chain from the tripod over the hearth. She could hardly reach; she was bent almost double, and the fire was too hot for her to get close enough.

'Shall I do that?'

Gerda sniffed. 'I don't suppose you can reach.'

But she let Astrid try, and Astrid unhooked the chain without difficulty.

'You can take it to Snorri and get the link mended there where it's weak. I was worried about it yesterday, when we were doing all those puddings. Take Gunnhild this as well. She said they needed a cure for worms, though whether it was for themselves or the beasts she didn't say. She thinks I've nothing better to do than run messages all over the island. What are you standing there for?'

Astrid was glad of an excuse to visit the smith. She hurried down to the Sudvik, where she saw Olaf on the beach, picking winkles off the rocks for bait. He waved as she passed, and Astrid waved back. She soon found the smith's house. The smithy was where she would have expected the byre to be, under the same turf roof as the house. It had a wide double door made of heavy slats of tarred driftwood. The door was wide open, and dark smoke belched from the chimney hole. She could hear a pumping sound which she recognised at once, familiar from the smiths' street in Dyflin.

There, the smoke hung like a pall, and the hammering of metal on metal rang out from one end of the street to the other. Here, there was only the noise of one pair of bellows, but it still sounded an echo of something homelike.

The smithy was pitch black inside, with a red glow in the middle of the darkness. Her eyes began to adjust. The smith had stopped working the bellows, and was standing before his fire, raking the glowing charcoal together, a black silhouette against red flames. He was very tall, and his hair shone fair in the firelight. Only when the daylight fell on him did she see that his hair was grey, and sparse on top. He wore baggy trousers and a sleeveless leather shirt. Sweat shone through the dirt on his skin. When he moved she realised he was crippled. There was a wooden bar nailed to the wall behind him, and he leaned his weight on it and lurched into the darkness, where she could dimly make out a shelf, stacked with a welter of blackened objects.

Astrid stepped forward so she stood in the middle of the door-way, and her shadow fell across the floor. He looked up and saw her. She couldn't see his face, as he had the fire behind him, but she guessed he was remembering who she must be.

'Fine day.'

'Yes.'

'Shame to be working, eh?'

'Yes. I've brought this. The link is wearing at the end.' He reached out, so she had to step right up to him to give him the chain. He took it and looked down at her. Her dark hair was coming unplaited, and there was pink in her cheeks from running. She wasn't pretty, not like the island girls; her face was covered with brown freckles, and her features were rather sharp. There wasn't much of her either, but maybe she was still growing. She stared straight back at him. Snorri didn't normally invite women to disturb his work, but this one had news from the world outside; besides, she was hardly old enough to matter.

'We've not met,' he said. 'You'll have a drink.'

It wasn't a question. He kept ale in his smithy, in a barrel behind the stacked up peats. He drew her a generous measure. Astrid blinked, but took it.

Snorri went on raking his charcoal together, while she watched. He didn't seem to expect her to talk. While he was looking away from her, she tried to work out which was the lame leg, and saw that he kept all his weight on his right side. Astrid wondered how he had been hurt.

She found part of an answer hanging on the wall that divided the smithy from the house. A round shield hung there, blackened with smoke, and beside it an iron sword in a decorated scabbard. Red light glinted on the bronze inlaid hilt. She had seen nothing so fine since she came here. The weapons at Shirva were of good quality, but not like this.

'A long way from home for you.'

She started, having grown used to the silence. 'Yes.'

'Dyflin, wasn't it?'

'Yes.'

'Fine city that.'

'It was.'

'A great city, with real craftsmen. Everything from churches to ships. You'll find no better than the tradesmen's streets in Dyflin. Never seen anything like it, and I've seen a few.'

'You know it? When were you there?'

He turned back to his fire. 'It was a long time ago.'

She glanced up at the sword. 'I suppose you used to go to sea?'

'You might say so.'

'In a longship?'

'One or two.'

There was a pause. 'Did you forge that sword yourself?'

He was shocked out of his reserve. 'No, no. That's a Frankish sword, well over a hundred years old. I had it from my grandfather. He was a Snorri Hakonsson too. He had the runes engraved on it. He gave it to me when I joined Svein Asleifarson. The blade is Frankish, but the hilt was made in these parts. It was the usual thing to do then.'

'You mean Svein Asleifarson of the Orkneyjar?'

'There's no other.' So she'd heard of him. They couldn't have much good to say of the Orkneyjar pirates where she came from. 'The hilt is probably Norse,' said Snorri.

'You sailed with him for a long time then?'

He shrugged. 'A goodish while.'

'And I suppose that's when you went to Dyflin?'

'Yes. But we didn't raid Dyflin that time. It was just a friendly visit.'

'I see.'

'We used to go to sea in the spring. Then we'd come back at harvest and in the autumn we'd go away again. We wintered in Gareksey, where he has the greatest feast hall in the Orkneyjar. I've been in Katanes with him, in the Earl's wars, and in the Sudreyjar and Irland and Monige. East to Noreg and all over Hjaltland and the Orkneyjar. He keeps eighty men in Gareksey all winter, and when he goes to sea he mans at least four longships. And nearly everywhere we went we raided, and never came home without treasure, enough to support us all like chieftains if we'd kept it.'

Smoke from burning houses is thick and yellow. Fire travels faster than a horse galloping. More people die of the smoke than of the burning. Yet Ingrid had sent Astrid to this man, when she had asked if there were a priest on the island. There was nowhere else to turn. 'Ingrid said I should come to see you,' said Astrid aloud. 'She thought you might be able to help me.'

Snorri looked startled. 'How could I help you? I'm not much use now to any man, unless you were wanting metalwork.'

'There's no priest here on the island.'

'That's true,' agreed Snorri.

'I wanted to find a priest. I've nowhere else to turn, you see. I don't belong to anyone here.'

Snorri bit his thumb, and frowned. He knew Einar's reputation well enough. But this was a child, and quite obviously a maid at that. If Einar hadn't meant well by her, why all that fuss at the Thing, insisting on her rights? No, it couldn't be that. 'Do they not treat you well at Shirva?' he asked aloud.

'Oh yes. But I can't stay here for ever.'

'Why not?'

Astrid spread her hands. 'I can't. It's not . . . this is not my island.'

'So how can I help you?'

'I don't know. Ingrid said I should speak to you, because you'd been abroad, and would know what I meant, when I said I needed to find the priest.'

'Priests!' said Snorri. 'I don't look forward to the day we have a priest from Hjaltland coming here, taking a tithe of our goods and giving us a prayer in return. I'd rather whistle for a wind any day.'

Astrid stared at him. He saw in her face that he'd shocked her, and relented. She was Irish, after all, and the Irish had been a priest-ridden nation for centuries, even before the death of the old gods. 'Don't worry, though,' he reassured her. 'This is a Christian island, and if you do no wrong no harm will come to you. If Einar means none by you, you're safe enough.'

'My father's drowned,' Astrid burst out suddenly. 'There should be a mass. I should make an offering; there should be someone to pray for his soul. How can I do that, just myself, the way it should be done? Do you have no mass, no confession, no sacrament on the island? What do you do then, when you need these things? What am I supposed to do?'

He frowned into the heart of his charcoal fire. 'I don't know,' he said at last. 'I don't know why Ingrid sent you here. I served my apprenticeship in Kirkjavagr. I'm not a godly man, but Rognvald's cathedral certainly made an impression on me. In the spring you could ask Dagfinn to arrange a mass there, if the Sula sails to the Orkneyjar. I've worked on that building. My master was commissioned to do the metalwork for the west door. There's nothing like that here. The nearest there is . . . but no, that wouldn't mean anything to you.'

'What wouldn't?' He was silent. 'Tell me, please,' begged Astrid.

'You know Raiva?' He saw her wince. 'You climb down there one day. It's dark on the beach, with the arch over you. The sun comes in shafts, just like through the windows of Rognvald's church. The sea has a different sound down there. Maybe you don't like to think of that coast. But the Cathedral itself was built to atone for bloodshed. It's the shrine of St. Magnus, remember. There are martyrs everywhere, it seems to me, whether to men or to the elements. Maybe you think that's blasphemy, but that's the nearest to a church I can offer you on this island.'

It was an extraordinary answer, asking her to face the sea she hated, and likening a cave to a consecrated church. Snorri was raking his fire together again. 'Take it or leave it. Perhaps you'll be in Kirkjavagr yourself one day, and then you can have your mass, if your heart's set on it.'

He seemed embarrassed, and she was just as keen now as he to change the subject. 'So you became a smith there,' asked Astrid, 'after you stopped fighting for Svein Asleifarson?'

'First I became a cripple. After that, a smith.'

'I'm sorry.'

'It's a long time ago. I didn't even bother to keep the treasure I'd won, which was foolish.'

'I suppose it didn't seem important at the time.'

'No. So you were travelling with your father?'

Astrid hesitated. She wasn't sure she wanted to talk about that any more. 'He was in the ship. But they didn't find him.'

'It was a bad night.'

Kol might have said that, with the same dry intonation. She felt a sudden warmth towards this stranger. 'I don't hate the island so much now,' she told him.

'It'll get better. You'll feel like yourself again after the winter.'

It was a promise of hope. She'd been wanting someone to say that this grief would end. One day she would get over it and belong, and be like everyone else again. She looked at him eagerly. 'Is that how long it takes?'

Chapter 7

The worst thing was the dark. At midwinter, it stayed dark until after the morning meal, and there was just a dim twilight in the middle of the day, often clouded by rain.

At night Astrid lay huddled in her blankets listening to the wind hammering against the walls. The noise entered her dreams, taking her back to that unbearable sea. In the morning she would see the waves crashing over the skerries. The whole of Sudvik was a cauldron of surging white water, and from the west coast white spray swept in over the fields right up to the house. Salt made its way into hangings, clothes and bedding, so that everything was sticky, and never quite got dry.

There were two young heifers in a stall by the byre door, and it was Astrid's job to feed them hay, sparingly, because some of the harvest had been wet and had spoiled, and sometimes give them clean straw. She became quite fond of her charges. At night they shifted in their stalls just beyond the hangings and coughed, and she was glad of their presence. She, Ingrid and Gerda slept at the far end of the hall nearest the east gable. The men were further along. Sometimes Bjarni snored, and when that happened she stuffed a sheepskin round her head, pressed tight over her ears. Occasionally Einar would leave the hall late at night, and return before dawn. Then the dogs would stir and whine, begging to be let out into the night.

Sometimes at night the weather was her ally; when she cried no one could hear. It was a relief to cry, but very difficult not to sob aloud. Astrid would lie on her back, her body racked by deep silent sobs, while the tears flowed down and soaked the blanket under her head.

Her main task at first was to help with the spinning. To her surprise, everyone in the household took part. There was a great deal to be done. The wool had been cleaned after the shearing, and was stored in the byre in sacks, far more than seemed necessary for one household.

'Of course we don't use it all ourselves,' was Ingrid's answer to her question. 'But first we need our share in the Sula's cargo, and then when Einar goes to the Thing in June, he takes the Earl's tax to Hjaltland in wadmal. After the Sula goes there won't be any time for weaving. It all has to be done in winter.'

'The Sula?'

'The ship. The Byrstada ship. Rolf and Dagfinn's. They sail to Biorgvin first in spring, and everyone on the island who can afford it puts in a share, so they have a full cargo. Then we get the same share back when they come home after harvest. We take ours in timber mostly, and charcoal and iron for the smithy. Last year we got a barrel of clay, that's how we got those new mugs. It was much better than the stuff they sell in Hjaltland. Rolf bought it abroad.'

'So you make your own pots?'

'Snorri made those. He has a good kiln.'

The spinning seemed endless. At first they put Astrid to combing and spinning wool until her hands ached. Ingrid sat at the loom, her back to the others in the room. When the men were there she was silent. On the days when Astrid, Ingrid and Gerda were left alone, Ingrid sang as she worked. The island songs were long ballads about family histories, or seal and whale hunting, with no variety in the tunes. Astrid found them tedious. It wasn't until after Yule that she mentioned diffidently that in Irland they had other songs. Then Ingrid wanted to know every song and every tune that Astrid could teach her. After that the work seemed easier. Astrid enjoyed having something to give; in exchange, she even began to learn some of the long ballads.

It helped even more when Ingrid discovered how well Astrid could weave. Astrid had been taught by the women who'd looked after her in Dyflin, and now it seemed worth all those long winter days of being kept indoors. The first time Astrid suggested that she should take a turn at the loom, Ingrid had been doubtful.

'Your tension will be different from mine.'

'When you start the next length, perhaps?'

'Maybe.'

Ingrid let her take over when the next length of coarse woollen cloth was completed. It wasn't interesting work; the wadmal had to be of standard length and width, and of unvarying weave. It was rough undyed cloth, which could be put to almost any use by those who were not particular. It could be greased or dyed later, now it was just basic material. But the weaving soothed Astrid, and it made a change from endless spinning.

When the last roll of cloth for the tax was finished, they were able to turn to their own needs. Satisfied by now that Astrid was neat and consistent, Ingrid let her do some of the household cloth herself. Given the chance to use her skill, Astrid's interest was fully engaged for the first time. Ingrid was impressed, and that spurred Astrid on. Using yarn dyed in the wool, she began to weave patterns, wishing she had paid more attention to the women in Dyflin. But the more she worked the more she remembered, and Ingrid went so far as to show off her work to Gudrun and to Snorri's wife Gunnhild, who was a frequent visitor.

'Astrid made it.'

'Did she?' Gunnhild looked at Astrid with something like respect. 'Well, I always heard the best cloth came from Irland. Can you weave linen?'

'I could if I had any thread.'

'We must ask Rolf to bring some. We've only ever had it in the cloth here.'

'I'd need the right loom, too.'

'Then the men of Shirva must make you one,' said Gunnhild.

After that, it no longer seemed to matter that Astrid had never tended livestock, or that she couldn't make horn spoons or fashion tools from driftwood. In Dyflin there had been workshops where all these things could be purchased. Now she could prove to the islanders that there was something she could do.

The days when the weather was worst were in some ways the easiest. Then everyone, both men and women, sat close to the hearth working, and told stories. Many of the stories were the same as at home. The ones Astrid hadn't heard before were mostly funny ones, tales about stupid farmers, unfaithful women, fishermen who outwitted giants. The islanders also told heroic tales, sometimes in verse, and often these were identical to those recited in Irland. Here they told more tales from Island than Astrid had heard at home, but then they had fewer Irish stories to fall back upon. They didn't even know the story of Cuchulainn, and when Astrid mentioned it, they demanded that she tell it.

Their request had seemed impossible at first. It was from Kol that Astrid had learned to tell stories, when he and his friends swopped tales. But the islanders, hungry for a new story, insisted, and it had been a strange release to find that she could do it. Once started, she did her very best, and gave the story as accurately as possible. They wanted it again. Then she gave them Niall of the Nine Hostages, and the Three Sons of Lir. Nothing could have delighted them more.

'You're a treasure,' Einar told her. 'A gift from the sea which will last us through all the winters of our lives.'

Their approval warmed her. She racked her brains, and gave them all the store she had.

There were feasts too, of course. When these happened away from Shirva, Astrid asked to stay behind. They did their best to persuade her to go, but did not force her. So at Yule she was left alone with Gerda, who never left her own hearth. The two of them hardly spoke. Astrid huddled by the fire, her feet tucked up in the sheepskin on her sleeping platform, and occupied herself with memories. She reconstructed the past inside her head, and set herself tasks. She had to remember every street, every workshop, the inhabitants of every house, in complicated imaginary journeys across Dyflin. Then there were the ships. All the ships she remembered in the making, half finished in Kol's shipyard. There were also ships in the harbour, arriving and unloading, then departing again. She remembered their cargoes, and where they came from. Timber from Noreg, wine and weapons from Valland, wool from Englaland. She went over it all in her mind. There was nothing else to think about.

When the feasting came to Shirva, she was forced to be present. Slowly the other islanders became familiar to her. She wasn't shy, merely indifferent. The most frequent visitors outside feast times were Eirik's sons. Thorvald and Olaf were always hungry, and she soon learned that the way to find favour with them was to give them bannocks or dried mutton whenever they appeared, whether it was close to a meal time or not. Olaf was the friendliest, though none of them said very much. The youngest, little Eirik, was completely silent. He had sores round his mouth, and a continual cold. When Eirik visited, attractive titbits of food were liable to disappear.

Astrid had chilblains which itched unbearably at night. Her feet were always damp, from going out on to the wet grass. Olaf's boots had strong cowhide soles, but even when plastered with grease the water came through the stitching. As in Dyflin, they all wore pattens, but the yard was so muddy it made very little difference.

One day when it was not raining Astrid left the house, and found her way at last to the beach at Raiva. It was less than five minutes' walk from Shirva. Whatever Snorri said, it wasn't like a church. Far above, she saw dead heads of the summer's thrift still clinging to their dried-out stalks. Waves pounded on the cliff beyond the arch and funnelled in under the cliffs, spouting up through two tiny gaps, then breaking on the shingle in a crash. God was not here. Devils, perhaps, or pagan spirits, but nothing she had been taught to revere. Astrid was about to cross herself, but dropped her hand as the impotence of the gesture struck her.

She couldn't pray here. She was too angry with God. God had forsaken her, and Mary the Mother of God was either useless or else had betrayed her. Hadn't Astrid prayed to them from this very sea, and been given nothing? Maybe Mary had heard her pleas that night, but failed to turn back the judgement of a cruel God. Astrid hated her, and despised the saints who had turned their backs.

She seized a rock from the beach and hurled it into the sea.

'I spit on your churches. I hate your God!'

No one could help her. The islanders told Christian stories, certainly. They had some of the parables, and a few of the lives of the saints and martyrs. But she knew far more than they did. Even the news of Thomas of Cantwaraborg was unknown to them. They knew of the troubles between King Henry and his one-time

Chancellor, and how Thomas had been in exile in Valland for over six years. They knew of his return to Englaland a year ago, and that he had been killed on Henry's order. But they did not know that he had been murdered in Cantwaraborg Cathedral itself, victim of the King's treachery. Nor had they heard of the miracles performed at his shrine since his martyrdom. Astrid had told them all about that. She also told them about the voyages of St Paul although they grew frustrated by the vagueness of her geography.

'Did he reach Mikligard?'

'I don't know. This was in Phrygia and Cappadocia.'

'Never heard of them. Do you have sailing directions?'

'No.'

But they had been kind to her. Sometimes, after Yule, tempers grew short, and on more than one occasion Bjarni threw down his work, and strode away into the night. But he never raised his voice to her, and when he wanted her to wait on him, he always phrased his needs as a request, not an order. He was less careful with his own daughter.

'Is the meal not ready yet? By Christ, do you realise what it's like out there?'

'Yes father,' Ingrid would say. 'Shall I take your wet clothes?'

'Are there any dry ones?'

Ingrid would feel the clothes where they hung on the line over the hearth. 'Well, nearly. They're only a bit damp.'

'Oh yes? And am I supposed to be grateful for that?'

'We had to keep the fire smoored last night. You know we did.'

'Oh yes,' he'd say. 'I know I know. I know.'

Kol had never spoken to Astrid like that. But they were never cooped up for months together. Kol would have hated that.

Very slowly, Astrid came to know them and to like them. By Epiphany, it was better when they were all there than when they went off to feast in another household. At Candlemas, she almost thought of going with them the night the feast was at Byrstada. But they had got used to her refusals, and so they did not ask. The night alone with Gerda had never seemed so lonely.

Astrid lay down, but she couldn't sleep. After an hour or two she could bear it no longer. She slipped off her sleeping platform without waking Gerda, put on her boots and cloak, and crept outside. At least she could walk a little way if the moon were still out.

She saw no moon, but the sky was bright. Astrid remembered
Ragna's talk of evil spirits. The whole southern sky was pale, but
there was neither dawn nor moonlight. With her fingers crossed,
Astrid stole as far as the gable end and looked round. In the north
the sky was white. Pillars of light flickered up and down the sky,
changing from white to green and back again. The lights had
shown like that from time to time all winter, but never as much as
this. Over the white columns the crown of the sky was red,
changing as she looked from dusky pink to the colour of blood. At
the zenith, right above her head, the veil of red drew back and
revealed a brightness which seemed to her to be that of heaven, a
direct glimpse into the other world. Astrid stretched out her arms
towards it. The island had revealed itself after all. There was a
heaven here, not in the sea or land, but far above, a light beyond
imagining. She saw it as a message that both her parents were safely
gathered in, and there was a place one day for her too, when this
long exile should be over.

Astrid watched, tears pouring unheeded down her cheeks. Mary
Mother of God, thank you for your answer to my prayer. For the
saints who did not cease to watch over us after all, I give you thanks.

The bright light began to dim. The crown of the sky was pale as
dawn. But the shafts of light below were dancing and changing,
like strings being plucked on a harp. As the red light faded, the
stars began to show through the torn curtain. She looked at the
Seven Sisters overhead, and slowly the familiar sky began to
re-form around them, telling her that on earth nothing had
changed. But Astrid no longer minded. The clouds drifted in, and
she felt the first drops of rain on her face. She crept back to the
doorway, her heart lighter than it had been since she had arrived
here. The island no longer seemed a prison. The sea might shut her
in, but she knew now there was a way out.

Part Two

The Islanders

Thorvald stood on the narrow causeway of crumbling stone which joined the Seydurholm to the island, with nothing around him but the sky. The cliffs, washed at their feet by a slow swell, were still empty of birds.

The path had suffered in the winter storms. Every year a little more crumbled rock was washed off the causeway, and now the narrowest part was scarcely a foot wide. There was no handhold. On either side the cliff fell sheer to the sea. Thorvald picked his way across the stone arch, waves breaking two hundred feet below him.

On the far side the gales had done even more damage. Whole chunks of gravel had fallen away during the winter. Thorvald trod carefully, testing every step. He couldn't see the top, but the climbing grew easier. There were patches of grass and dried out thrift. Sunlight shone straight into his eyes as he emerged from the shadow of the cliff on to a crumbly slope. As no one was watching, Thorvald wasn't ashamed to scramble up on hands and knees. When he reached the pasture he sat up, blinking in the sun. It was warm after the chill of the cliff.

He was at the foot of a stretch of turf, so steep it seemed ready to tip any intruder over the edge. The far end was way above his head to the south; to the north the lower edge curved like a bow over hidden slabs of rock. He could hear the sea funnelling into the caves beneath him. The sun had only just lifted itself above the highest point of the Holm, and every dip in the ground was accentuated by shadow. There was no shelter at all, just the sheer slope and the short green turf.

This was the best pasture on the island, the richest asset of the Shirva farmlands. Now that the grass was growing, the sooner the sheep were put up the better. But the crumbling causeway was becoming a problem. His uncles said it had been getting worse in the last few years; before that the causeway had changed every winter, but the path had never been threatened. Thorvald was here to see that the way was still accessible for the sheep. Bjarni was waiting on the island side of the causeway with ropes and stakes. Thorvald turned and signalled to him, and Bjarni waved.

Thorvald knew he mustn't keep Bjarni waiting, but the Holm fascinated him. He could even remember a time when he'd never been up it. Each time his uncles had gone over to the sheep he'd begged to go too, and each time Einar had said, 'Next year'. When Thorvald was eight he'd had enough of broken promises. One summer day he'd tackled the Holm for himself. It was the first time he could remember being on unknown ground. He'd sat at the cliff head, looking for a long time at the new view. He felt like doing the same now, though he was a grown man, and here with a job to do. He stood for a moment, looking back at the island.

Grey cliffs rose opposite him, indented by geos and broken by tumbled rocks. Above were the winter rigs, stubble among yellow grass. The newly lifted cattle dotted the empty land. At Byrstada Dagfinn was already ploughing; the tiny figures of man and oxen were followed by a mass of gulls, and behind them an ever-increasing stretch of bare brown soil. Someone was walking along the track to the smithy. Away to the north he could see his own home, apart from all the other houses on the island, snug against the hill dyke. Smoke rose from the roof. North of the hill dyke, patches of water gleamed on the saturated ground. Due north of the Seydurholm, a thin ayre of land separated the north and south havens. There was the turf roof of the shed which housed the Sula in winter, but Thorvald's own noost, where he and Olaf kept their boat, was out of sight behind the ayre. His uncles made a fuss when he'd insisted on using a noost there. They thought he should beach his boat in the Sudvik, with everyone else. But Setr was nearest the Nordhavn, and Thorvald liked a harbour to himself.

But he was supposed to be telling Bjarni about the state of the path. Thorvald slid across the loose gravel and edged his way down. While he was on the broken stretch he looked for a new way round. There was a slab of rock which would do if they cut steps, without having to haul the sheep up with ropes.

Bjarni was standing at the end of the causeway. 'You got up, I see.'

'You saw the broken part?'

'Yes. And I saw the speed you came down at too.'

'It's the only place that's loose. We can make a way round. I'll show you. We won't need the ropes.'

Bjarni grunted. 'I'd better have a look.'

As always, when Thorvald and Bjarni actually had to work together, they were unexpectedly pleased with each other. There was no need to talk much. Bjarni agreed that the dangerous place could be got round in the way Thorvald suggested, and they knocked out rough steps for about six feet. Bjarni insisted they rope themselves to a stake while they worked, and Thorvald didn't bother to argue. When they climbed up to retrieve the rope, they stood for a while looking down on the causeway.

'Mind you,' remarked Bjarni, 'It's not solved for ever. The whole cliff face is falling away. It'll be somewhere else next.'

'We could always haul them up from a boat on the other side.'

'Rather you than me. I don't like that path though. Let's get back to Shirva and have something to eat.'

Thorvald would have preferred to go home. This was the best day they'd had this year, and first he'd had to spend it with Bjarni repairing sheep paths, and now, when the sun was good for a long while yet, he was expected to go and sit indoors listening to the usual talk about the farm while his uncles ate with maddening slowness. At least the food at Shirva was always plentiful. Today it was salt herring with fish liver bannocks, which Thorvald particularly liked. Ingrid was making cheese when they arrived, so it was Astrid who waited on them.

His uncles were talking about the weather. Thorvald sighed. He had heard it all before.

'Dagfinn's ploughing today,' said Bjarni.

'I know,' said Einar, 'I've been avoiding him. He wants to have all the beasts across the dyke and the gates hung before the rest of us have even got the cattle lifted.'

'Don't let him bully you. If he sows too soon he'll probably lose the lot. Then he'll blame us for it.'

'I'm afraid his heart's not in his land.'

'His heart's in Biorgvin harbour these days.'

'Seems like he brought a choice piece of Biorgvin harbour back with him.'

Thorvald shut their voices out by repeating sailing directions in his head.

From Hern Island off Noreg due west to Herjolfsnes, passing north of Hjaltland close enough to see it on a fair day, south of the Faereyjar half sunk below the horizon. Three days' sail from there to the south of Island. Thorvald and Olaf had a boat of their own anyway. She wouldn't sail to Island, but she was a boat, and his own. He realised that Einar was speaking to him.

'I said,' said Einar, 'how's your boat coming on? You've been working on her, haven't you?'

'Yes,' said Thorvald. He paused. 'She's all right.'

Bjarni looked at his brother, but Einar avoided his eyes and tried again. 'You'll be able to do a bit of fishing with your brother.'

'If I'm here.' Better to fish in his own boat than with his uncles, but he knew he and Olaf couldn't catch enough for winter on their own. He didn't want to go fishing anyway. He wanted to go to sea with Dagfinn, and Einar knew it. Biorgvin, Kirkjavagr, Hjaltland.

'You'll do better in Einar's boat,' said Bjarni. 'You can't take that boat Dagfinn gave you into deeper waters. And there's no better fisherman to learn from on this island.'

'I must go,' said Thorvald. 'Olaf will be waiting for me. We have to launch the boat.'

'What, today? Isn't it a bit late?'

'Thank you for the meal,' Thorvald said to Einar.

His uncle nodded at him. So the boy could smile. After Thorvald had gone Bjarni turned to Einar. 'It's a pity we can't keep him up there,' he said.

When Thorvald ran into the yard at Setr, Olaf called him from the open byre door. 'In here! We're to dig the top rig tomorrow. All of us. Mother said.'

'But we'll be getting the plough, won't we, when Einar brings it over?'

'She doesn't want to wait. She said we can do it ourselves.'

'Forget it. We're taking the boat out.'

'Now? She'll be furious.'

'Nothing to do with her. It's my boat.'

'But we have to start digging first thing.'

'That doesn't mean we have to sit looking at the spades all night.'

'Aren't we going to tell her?'

'No.' Thorvald thought for a moment. 'I mean yes. Why not?'

Thorvald went into the house and tripped over a broken trace. 'Mother?' He went back to his brother. 'She's not there.'

They ran most of the way to the Nordhavn. It didn't take long to launch the boat and row out. They rounded the ness to port, where an arch overhung a big cave. There was no wind, so they kept on rowing below red cliffs. Beneath them the sand, green under the water, was interspersed by forests of weed. More red cliffs rose opposite, where the sea had bitten a deep cove out of the island, gouging out caves and tunnels. Thorvald and Olaf made for the skerries, where shags perched above the tideline. There was a shallow bar under water, where the sea washed over half-submerged rocks. They shipped their oars close by, and unwound their fishing lines. The tide was almost at the turn, so they rocked gently. Presently they caught the touch of a cold breeze moving landward. Thorvald righted the boat with one oar to stop it drifting. They had barely caught half a dozen piltocks. Thorvald didn't mind.

'You're not going to sea with Dagfinn then?' said Olaf presently.

'No.'

'Didn't Dagfinn offer to take you?'

'He would have done. It was my bloody uncle.'

'What's it got to do with Bjarni?'

'Not Bjarni. Einar.'

'What's wrong with Einar?'

Thorvald turned and faced his brother. 'Einar thinks we're too isolated at Setr. Einar thinks it's time we went back and learned to work all the Shirva lands together. Einar thinks if we try hard we can have an excellent partnership with uncle Bjarni. Einar thinks if he keeps me at home I might turn into a farmer. Then if I'm a good boy and Bjarni decides he could bear to share the farm with me he might let me go to sea. For a treat.'

'But we've been farming all our lives. Years and years.'

'That's nothing to him. He reckons in centuries.'

Thorvald turned back to his line. They sat silently, back to back. Olaf caught a dogfish, which thrashed and struggled in the basket. At last its gills stopped working, and it lay still. A breeze wrinkled the sea, and a moment later they were in the shadow of the cliffs.

'Sun's behind the island.'

'And we never did tell her. We'd better start rowing.'

It was twilight when they grounded on the beach. A small figure rose from their noost, and slithered over the stones towards them. Olaf cocked his head, listening.

'It's Eirik,' Thorvald told him.

'She sent me to see if the boat was in,' said Eirik. 'I didn't want to have to go back and say it wasn't, so I waited. It's nearly dark.'

'You needn't have bothered,' said Thorvald. 'Now you're here you can help carry all the fish.'

'What fish?' Eirik peered into the basket and made a derisory noise. 'She's cross with Olaf,' he said.

'Why me?'

'You left the byre door open.'

Gudrun opened her eyes. For the first time in days there was no sound of water on the turf above her head. She pulled back the hanging that separated the recess where she and Rolf slept from the main hall. A shaft of sunlight shone down from the chimney hole, lighting up the dust in the stuffy air. On the far side of the hearth the beams were splashed with chicken droppings, but the hens had left their roosts at dawn. The other sleeping platforms were empty. She was usually first awake, but lately there had been nothing to get up for. Since she had not woken, Rolf had not either. It was irritating to be depended on for that. She wished she could get away from him even for a day. From all of them. There were voices outside.

'Lovely morning, Ragna.'

'Just as well,' came her sister-in-law's voice, penetratingly, 'if I'm supposed to do all the milking myself.'

'Be the first time ever if you are. Shall I come and help?'

'No you shall not.' There was the clatter of a bucket falling on the brigstones. 'Let go of me, Skuli Hedinsson, or I shall scream, and my brother Rolf will hear me.'

'Not him. Sleeps through anything. Even at sea. I should know.'

Gudrun sighed. She didn't like Skuli much, but she had to agree

with him. She sat up. Rolf rolled into the space she had left, and
grunted. She pushed him away. Rolf Erlendsson, farmer, ship-
owner, trader. An honest and reliable man, respected by his neighbours and known as a shrewd merchant from Kirkjavagr to
Biorgvin. A very sound sleeper, and when he lay on his back he
snored. He was considered handsome, but Gudrun could see nothing of him now except tangled brown hair. He was ten years older
than she was, and when he was at home he was always very kind
to her. Gudrun reached for her clothes.

It might as well be raining. It was cold enough. She pulled her
tunic over her dress, then went outside to brush her hair in the sun.
Her hair was dark red, but the sun caught the light in it, and made
strands of it gleam like gold. Men had admired Gudrun for her hair,
and now that one of them had married her, no one ever saw it but
him. She pulled hairs out of her comb, and watched the wind carry
a little knot of them away across the yard. The sun made the
puddles so bright they hurt her eyes. Time to get the cattle lifted.
Gudrun began to plait her hair. This was the fourth spring she'd
lived here. The fourth time he'd leave her since she married him.
The fourth summer she'd work his land and wait for him to come
home at harvest. He always brought back gifts for her. He had never
raised a hand to her, and he never forgot anything she asked for
either. Gudrun picked up her scarf, and tied it round her head so
that her hair was all hidden. She fetched her pattens from just
inside the door.

For the first time this year she could smell new grass. Just as well,
there wasn't much hay left. She pushed the barn door open. The
place stank of hay, vomit and stale drink. The sleeping bodies of
the Sula's crew were huddled together on the remaining hay, more
or less covered by their cloaks. Someone had been sick just inside
the door. Gudrun stepped round it. They would sleep on the hay
now the straw was gone, pressing it down till it spoilt and it was
hard to find any without shoving one of them over. There was a
big empty space where the winter fodder had been. The crew's gear
was piled up; shields nailed to the wall, swords thrown in a corner.
They'd brought in seats, a bench of driftwood and an upturned
bucket. There were empty flagons, and a puddle of what she hoped
was spilled ale on the floor. Six of a crew, who stayed here all winter
with nothing to do, eating their heads off, drinking every night into
the small hours. When they were evicted from the hall, they just

carried on in here. They'd quietened down for a few nights after she lost the baby; Rolf had seen to that. Dagfinn wouldn't have bothered. Dagfinn's foreign crew was causing trouble on the island. Questions had been raised at the Thing, and Gudrun had experienced the sudden cease of conversation when she entered a house, so that she knew the affairs at Byrstada were on everyone's lips. Whatever she felt for Rolf, she wasn't sorry when they launched the boat after the sowing. These foreigners made trouble, and when the islanders complained it was she who had to deal with it. Sometimes the chief complaints only came to light months after the crew had left. Gudrun roughly pulled a bundle of hay from underneath the nearest. He groaned and rolled over.

Ragna wasn't in the byre, and the two cows in milk waited reproachfully. Gudrun filled the mangers, grabbed the bucket and stool, and sat down crossly. The cow shifted under her hasty hands. This particular beast was old and patient, and now her backbone was ridged and gaunt, her ribs showing through her tired hide. Gudrun paused and started to milk more gently. Skuli Hedinsson had been up, anyway. It would serve that girl right if he did seduce her, though he might have waited till they'd done the milking. Her sister-in-law was sixteen, and thought she knew everything. The byre darkened as a tall figure filled the doorway.

'Ragna?' said Gudrun.

'No, it's me.' Rolf came in, sunshine flooding in behind him.

'I didn't know you'd got up.'

'Don't sound so surprised.' He came over and touched the back of her neck.

'Stop it,' said Gudrun. 'Can't you see I'm busy?'

'That's why I don't get up early. Where's Dagfinn?'

'I don't know. I haven't seen Ragna either. For the same reason probably. I'd throw a bucket of water over the lot of them.'

'Where is she?'

'Not here. That's why I'm doing all the milking.'

He watched her for a minute. Then he picked up a stool and bucket and sat down to milk the other cow.

Gudrun looked up, startled. 'You don't have to do that!'

'Thank you,' he said, and went on milking.

There was quiet except for the shifting of animals in their stalls and the splash of milk into the pails. The floor was high with the straw that had been laid down layer upon layer over the winter.

Presently Gudrun stood up. Rolf took her bucket from her and poured the milk into the big churn. Gudrun strained off yesterday's buttermilk into a bowl, and took down a fresh cheese.

She would have gone outside again but he stopped her. 'What's the matter?'

'Your sister is the matter. I'm going to wring her neck. It's not the first morning it's been like this.'

'Wring her neck by all means. What else is wrong?'

'What a bloody stupid question. I suppose you've no idea. Or perhaps you've forgotten.'

'Of course I haven't. Come here.'

'Why should I? It's nothing to do with you. It was your baby, that's all.'

'Oh Gudrun, I'm sorry. It was my baby too, but we have to go on living.'

'Is that supposed to help me?'

'What else can I say? We've been through all this already. I want a child just as much as you do. I'm as disappointed as you are. Surely you know that?'

'Disappointed!' Rage overwhelmed her. 'Disappointed, you say? Oh, yes, I know you're disappointed! I know you wanted a child, an heir for Byrstada I suppose, or something to prove you're better than your brother. No I'm not disappointed. I'm hurt. I'm unhappy. It was that child I wanted. That one. The one that's dead. He wasn't just an accident that got in the way of what you want. He was a person. Now he's dead. Haven't you even begun to realise that?'

'Gudrun, I understand. It was my baby too.'

'You never even looked at him!'

'What do you mean?' For a moment Rolf looked frightened. 'There wasn't anything to look at, was there?'

'Nothing that would matter to you.'

'What do you mean?'

She could hear in his voice that she'd panicked him, and that fanned her rage. 'You care, do you? But you can go to sea and forget all about it. I've got to stay here. He should be here, and he's not. Nor are you. All summer. You won't have to give it a thought, you won't miss him. Any more than you did the other. I had them both baptised too. There was time for that. You never even asked. Never even asked what their names were.'

'Names? I wasn't thinking about names. If I could do anything, I'd do it. You know that.'

'You'll not do a thing, and you know it. You'll go to sea. Forget all about it. Forget I exist!'

'I never forget. You know that! I have to go to sea. I have to! What can I do but go with my ship?'

'Your ship! Your ship! I wish your bloody ship would sink!'

He went white and stared at her. She realised what she'd said and looked at him aghast. She would have run, but dared not move. He crossed his fingers against her.

'You ill-wished my ship!'

'I didn't. Not like that. I didn't mean it!'

'You ill-wished her.'

'No!'

'How dare you ill-wish a ship? Before a launching too. To lay a curse on her. That's wicked! Wicked!'

'Don't preach to me. Just forget your ship for one second. I wasn't even thinking about it.'

'You laid a curse on her!'

'I did not! I wasn't even thinking of it!'

'You ill-wished her!'

She was shouting, and didn't care who heard her. 'I wasn't talking about your ship! I'm talking about your baby! Yours!'

'Quiet. For God's sake be quiet! You'll be heard in the house.'

'So what?'

'Please stop. I'm not trying to hurt you. I'm the last person who'd do that. Please! You know I'd do what I could. How can I help the way it is?'

There was a little colour in his cheeks now, but she knew he'd not forgiven her. 'You don't understand,' said Gudrun in a low voice. 'I'm scared. If another one dies I think I shall go mad.'

'Of course you won't. I've never met anyone less mad in my life. But you can't say things like that. Do you want to destroy us?'

'No. I want help.'

'What more can I do?'

'Nothing. I'm going to see Gunnhild this morning. Maybe she can help me.'

'To raise a north wind?'

'I hate you! I wish I'd never mentioned the ship.'

'My God, so do I!'

'I want something to protect me.'

'I doubt if she can do much.'

'If she can't nobody can.'

'Come here. Don't cry.'

'I'm not crying,' said Gudrun furiously. She would have pushed him away but he was the stronger.

There were quick footsteps outside and Rolf let go of his wife at once.

'Oh there you are,' said Ragna at the door. 'I wondered what had happened to you. What's the matter?'

'I'm going out,' said Gudrun savagely. 'You'll have to see about feeding all those bloody men.' She swept out of the byre.

Ragna looked at her brother. 'Is something the matter?'

'What the hell do you think you've been doing? I've better things to do than milk the cows for you, just because you choose to lie in bed half the morning!'

'I was up before any of you! And I never asked you to do the milking.'

'I hope you wouldn't dare. Where were you? There's no reason why Gudrun should be left with all the work.'

Ragna looked at him coldly. 'Dagfinn's looking for you.'

'Whose fault is that?' Rolf controlled himself and went on. 'Listen, Ragna, I'll be at sea again soon. She has quite enough to do here. Naturally she's upset. She needs you to help.'

Ragna looked him in the eye. 'If you care that much, how come she keeps getting pregnant?'

Rolf lunged towards her, but she ducked, and was out the door. 'Dagfinn wants you in the barn,' she called, and ran.

Chapter 10

Dagfinn and Rolf cast the seed from baskets hung against their chests. The sun shone on to exposed brown earth, bringing out the smell of the soil. Gulls flocked screaming over the sown furrows, while children clapped and shooed them. This was the first sowing, in the oat rigs. The barley would come next, then the men would be gone.

As the sown furrows increased behind them the brothers drew nearer together. Dagfinn stopped and threw down his tunic, and presently Rolf did the same. Their younger sister Thorhalla shouted across the rigs. They took the blaand she had brought, and sat down on the turf bank above the ditch.

'We'll get the barley in early too at this rate,' said Rolf.

'Soil's warm enough. Two weeks, maybe.'

Rolf took a long drink. 'We could be on our way to Noreg in three weeks then.'

'Sooner. This weather will bring all the ships out early. I'm not spending the whole of May waiting my turn in Biorgvin harbour.'

'We've never waited more than three days.'

'Three days in spring is too much. I don't trust them to keep their contract either, if someone gets in first and offers a better price. And we'll sell the first cargo of timber for more in the islands too.'

'Fair enough.' Rolf put down his mug. 'Dagfinn?'

'Yes?'

'I don't like leaving Gudrun so soon.'

'We've been here all winter.'

'There was the baby.'

'I suppose so. Nothing much to be done about that.'

'She needs me.'

'You know best, but the way you get bairns on her, she might be better alone for a bit.'

'There's no danger of that just now,' said Rolf, through gritted teeth.

'What you do in bed is nothing to do with me. But you obviously didn't waste much time after harvest.'

Rolf's hand clenched into a fist. He stared out to sea and said nothing. Dagfinn looked the same way with oblivious cheerfulness. 'We could easily launch Sula if this weather would only last.'

'You know it can't,' said Rolf sourly. 'It'll be storms again by Friday.'

'You don't have to say so. No tact.'

'Tact!' Rolf made a sound that might have been a laugh. 'Ragna doesn't do anything to help Gudrun, you know.'

'Ragna will do a lot less to hinder when the ship is gone.'

'I wish we could raise a crew on the island. I don't think you've any idea what those men have done for our reputation here.'

'That's the island for you. We give them a ship. Can you imagine where they'd be without our trade?'

'Yes I can, but they can't. As for Ragna, I said before we shouldn't allow it.'

'Oh, Ragna will look after herself. You can preach to her if you like.'

Dagfinn stood up. He was vaguely sorry for his brother, but he had more important things on his mind. He hung his basket round his neck again, and returned to his furrow. Rolf frowned as he began to sow again. He had suggested to Dagfinn before that the sooner Ragna was married the less likely she was to get into trouble. 'It depends what you mean by trouble,' Dagfinn had said.

Dagfinn was not thinking about his family at all. Gulls swept across the sky above him, screaming at the bird scarers. His ship was ready; in three weeks he'd be gone. He'd sail to Biorgvin first, then back to Kirkjavagr with a cargo of timber. He'd have liked to take it further west, to the Sudreyjar even. Halfway to Dyflin, where Einar's girl had come from. So Dyflin was an English city now, but knowing the English it would still be a city with a market. If ever he had a big enough ship he would go there, and after that perhaps he'd go on south, past Bretland and Sylingar, and on to Armorica. Last year in Biorgvin he had bought wine from Valland and linen and sold them in the Orkneyjar. If he only had the right ship he could get as far as Nordmandi, or maybe to the south of Englaland, and buy goods like that at source. He wondered what Rolf would say, and grinned. Rolf would do sums all winter and conclude it wasn't worth it. Dagfinn thought about the green tree-clad hills of Armorica, long yellow beaches suitable for boats, the girls and youths his drinking companions in Biorgvin had been so eager about. He was a thousand miles away, running before the wind round Finnisterre, when he came face to face with his brother.

'I didn't know we'd got as far as that,' said Rolf. 'Is there any seed left?'

Dagfinn felt in his basket. 'No.'

Chapter 11

'I hate them!' said Gudrun, striding up and down.
She was almost in tears. Astrid, embarrassed, bent over her bowl,
in which she was kneading together oatmeal and warm water.

Ingrid didn't answer at once either. She set a pan of dripping on
the edge of the fire. 'Are you ready for the livers?' she asked Astrid.

Astrid nodded, and pushed the bowl over. Ingrid emptied a small
bowl of chopped fish livers into the mixture, and watched critically
for a moment, as Astrid began to mix them into the oatmeal with
her hands.

'I wish they'd go to sea and drown themselves!'

Ingrid stopped, petrified. Astrid's sticky hands went to her
cheeks, and she gasped. They both crossed their fingers, and stared
at Gudrun. Gudrun stared back defiantly, her hands behind her back.

'You'd never forgive yourself!' said Ingrid. 'You can't say that!'

'I have said it.'

'If anyone heard . . .' Ingrid backed against the wall. 'Take it
back, Gudrun. We won't say anything. Take it back!'

'Don't be stupid. I didn't mean it.'

'But you can't say it! However bad it is, you can't say that. Think
what it was like when Eirik didn't come home.'

'Don't I have reason to think of things like that all the time?'

There was a sucking of air towards the doorway, and the peats on the fire suddenly glowed.

'Who's that?' called Ingrid. 'Come in!'

Someone pushed back the hangings. A woman appeared, stooping under the lintel. Astrid thought she had met everyone on the island, and then she realised who this must be. Ingebjorg was talked of everywhere, but seldom seen – at least not at Shirva. She didn't look nearly as old as Astrid had imagined. She was tall, a big, strong-looking woman, who stood as upright as a girl once she was in the room. She was broader in the hips than a girl though; after all, she had three sons, two of them grown. Moreover she had brought them up herself, which might account for her commanding presence. Even Gudrun seemed to be momentarily silenced.

'Ingebjorg,' said Ingrid, as calmly as she could. 'Sit down. I'm glad to see you. Were you looking for my uncle? They were fishing this morning, and then they went back to mend a line.'

'It doesn't matter. Einar can come over to Setr, perhaps. So how is it with you, Ingrid?' She nodded to Gudrun.

'I didn't expect to see you here,' said Gudrun, 'or I'd have brought the butterwort. It's waiting for you at Byrstada.'

'Perhaps I'll call on the way home.'

So Ingebjorg did visit elsewhere. Astrid began to set her bannocks out on a tray, but kept her eyes on Ingebjorg. Like Astrid, Ingebjorg did not belong to the island. Like Astrid, she was stranded here. Her man had been lost at sea, and she had heard that Ingebjorg had never got over it, although that was not the impression she gave now.

Ingebjorg turned round before Astrid had time to lower her eyes. 'Astrid?' she asked.

'Yes. How did you know?'

Ingebjorg smiled. 'Who else could there be here, that I didn't know?' She looked her over. 'I'm very sorry about your father.'

No one else on the island had said that. Nor could Astrid think of an answer. But her heart warmed to this stranger, who possibly understood what the winter had been like.

'You must have had a hard winter,' said Ingebjorg. She seemed quite at ease with a one-sided conversation. Knowing her sons, Astrid wasn't that surprised. 'Olaf told me he'd met you. He talks of very little else, in fact.' Ingebjorg could have been laughing. 'You must come to Setr and visit us.'

'Thank you.' Astrid was startled, and wondered if Bjarni would approve. So far as she knew, only Einar went to Setr from Shirva.

Ingebjorg looked round the kitchen, as though taking in every detail: the baskets hanging on the walls, the blackened pots, the flour and oatmeal barrels. 'It's a long time since I was here.'

'You should visit more often.'

'It's been a busy winter.'

None of them could think what kept Ingebjorg busy all winter, alone with her sons up at Setr.

'They'll be launching the Sula soon?' said Ingebjorg to Gudrun.

'Yes,' said Gudrun, sitting down. 'I can't wait for the crew to go,' she added abruptly, 'And yet I don't want Rolf to leave.'

'Come over and visit me again, when they leave,' said Ingebjorg. 'Stay if you like.'

'Thank you. It would have been much worse before, if you hadn't let me come then.'

'I hope Rolf didn't mind.'

'No, he understands. I wouldn't tell my father.'

It seemed that Gudrun, free of Shirva, made allies where she chose, in spite of the cousins.

'I saw Olaf this morning,' said Gudrun. 'He was helping Snorri with the new band for the mast step. I think they were going up to the Nordhavn.'

Astrid began licking her fingers. For a moment she was unreasonably jealous. If she'd been a boy, maybe Snorri would have had her to help.

'So that's where he went,' said Ingebjorg. 'He was off the moment the rig was finished. It wasn't weather to work this afternoon anyway.'

'Maybe he could be a smith,' said Ingrid, buttering a bannock.

'Anyway, I shall have to go,' Gudrun said.

'I'll walk back with you, and pick up the butterwort.'

'Would you have believed it?' Ingrid said indignantly after Ingebjorg and Gudrun had gone. 'Gudrun never told me. Staying at Setr! What would father say? What am I to say if he asks me about it?'

'I expect that's why she never told you.'

Ingrid pushed back the hangings and went back into the hall.

'Why did she come?' asked Astrid, following. 'Ingebjorg, I mean. What does she want Einar for?'

'Oh, that's obvious. She always calls him in when she has a row with Thorvald. And they're just about to launch the ship.'

'What's that got to do with Thorvald?'

'You may well ask.'

I t was difficult keeping a trading ship on the island. The Nordhavn was a more treacherous anchorage than it appeared to be. If the island had had a safe harbour it might have been more important, being in the centre of the main trade routes. Eirik's ambition had brought a ship here in the first place. Eirik had gone to sea, and not come home for several years. When he returned, he was master of a trading ship, and the husband of a farmer's daughter who was cousin to one of the Earl's retainers at Orfjara in the Orkneyjar. Eirik didn't tell his family that Ingebjorg's family had cast her off when she married him, but allowed them to believe that he had wealthy connections in the Orkneyjar. He took his inheritance from his father in money, and beached his ship in the only possible place, the eastern end of the beach at the Nordhavn. In spring, it took every man on the island to launch the ship. Most of the islanders supported Eirik. It was true that he took all the young men away in summer, but he bought welcome trade goods to the island every winter.

It was Eirik who had first taken Dagfinn to sea. But Dagfinn left him in Biorgvin one year, to sail to Island with one of the biggest trading ships. When Dagfinn came back three years later, Eirik's ship had not returned. Dagfinn mourned his patron, but he now had money of his own, though he never said exactly how he had come by it. The next year he sailed with his brother Rolf to the Orkneyjar in the Byrstada boat, and ordered a ship of his own to be built in the yard at Kirkjavagr. Many of the islanders objected that after the loss of Eirik and his crew, there were not men enough left to crew and launch a boat. But Dagfinn raised a crew of his own in Kirkjavagr, from men who had no island of their own, because of land hunger or outlawry. The Thing had told Dagfinn what it thought about such men, but Dagfinn brought money into the island, and so he was able to have matters his own way.

Today Dagfinn walked to the Nordhavn, and crossed the beach to Sula's shed, where he found Olaf scraping the bottom of a barrel of whale's grease.

'Snorri rode back,' said Olaf. 'He wanted you. Did he find you?'

'No, I didn't come by the path.'

'Oh well. I have to carry his tools back when I've oiled them.'

'Helping him, are you?'

'Yes. We've fixed the bands round the mast step.'

Last season one of the timbers of the mast step had opened up along the grain, and during the winter Dagfinn had asked Snorri to make a pair of iron bands to fit around it. The crack should never have happened; the mast step was of seasoned oak, very expensive, and Dagfinn blamed the shipwright at Kirkjavagr for not treating his wood properly. He was going to demand a replacement this summer, but meanwhile Snorri's repair would have to serve. Dagfinn examined the work carefully, aware of Olaf's eyes upon him. Had he known it, Olaf could hardly see him, six feet away in the dim shed, and the blank look meant that he was listening.

'Are you walking back now?' asked Dagfinn.

'Yes.'

'I'll come with you.'

Olaf shouldered Snorri's tools, and they set off. The wind had died with the evening, and rays of sun shone golden across the grass. The slope above the cliffs was dotted with pale primroses. A lark sang overhead. Dagfinn glanced at the boy beside him from time to time, but Olaf said nothing. He was sweating under his burden, and his thin shirt clung to his body. There were sprigs of heather in his hair. Give him a good wash, thought Dagfinn, and some better clothes, and he'd be a fine boy. Not strong enough to take an oar along with the men though; there was no muscle on him

yet. But Thorvald had grown sturdier in the last year. Dagfinn
cleared his throat. 'What's become of your brother these days?
We've not seen much of him this winter.'

'He's busy.' Olaf didn't meet Dagfinn's eyes.

They passed the burn at Finniquoy, and walked into the shadow
of the hills. Olaf stared ahead, and dropped behind Dagfinn,
treading in his footsteps. 'Are you coming back to Byrstada?' asked
Dagfinn. 'After all that work, I should feed you, at least.'

'No, I must find Thorvald.'

There was no getting round him. He would be loyal to his
brother. Dagfinn felt a pang of conscience. He was going to sea
within the week, and leaving Thorvald behind for yet another year.
Dagfinn knew he should have spoken to him. He had promised
him a place, just as Thorvald's father had done for Dagfinn.

The year after Eirik had died, Dagfinn had taken Thorvald out
rowing in the Sula's old flit boat, which was lying at the Nordhavn.
By the time he left in spring, Thorvald was quite proficient, and
when Dagfinn came back at harvest, Thorvald had taken him out
again. He was rowed right outside the haven, under the rocky cliffs
of the northeast coast.

'Have you been out here before?' Dagfinn had enquired.

'Only when it's weather.'

'With your brother?'

Thorvald must have caught something in his tone. 'You aren't
going to tell my mother?'

Dagfinn could not bear to lose an admirer. He had praised
Thorvald lavishly, and had given him his own ancient thorshammer to hang around his neck. The sea had been as flat as a pool,
transparent down to the green sand and seaweed-covered rocks.
Dagfinn and Thorvald looked down and saw fish flickering over
the sea bottom. Unlike Olaf, Thorvald had always been quite
willing to talk to Dagfinn.

'Olaf and I have been catching piltocks.'

'From the boat?'

'We just say at home we were fishing off the rocks at Bunes.'

'You do know when it's not weather?'

'Course I do.' Thorvald had added, 'It usually isn't.'

'I have the same problem.'

'When I have a ship,' Thorvald had told him, 'I shall sail to
Groenland and bring back a polar bear.'

'That's a good idea. What will you do with it? Give it to the King of Danmark like the man in the story?'

'No. I shall keep it in the byre and catch fish with it.'

'Or you could keep yourself in the byre and send it out to catch fish for you.'

'It might get lost. But I could train it to roar at Gudrun and Ingrid.'

'You might find that Bjarni would come and roar at you.'

'My bear would roar better.'

Olaf and Dagfinn reached the turning to Setr.

'Goodbye,' said Dagfinn. 'Thanks for your help. Tell your brother I'd be glad to see him.'

'All right.'

Dagfinn knew very well what he had promised Thorvald that day. 'Five seasons from now I shall take you to sea.' That was seven seasons ago. Last year it had been Thorvald's mother who prevented it. No doubt if Dagfinn had insisted he would have persuaded her, but Ingebjorg was a strong woman, and Dagfinn had avoided a confrontation. This year it was Einar, who wanted the boy to resolve the quarrel between Ingebjorg and Bjarni, and to take more part in the farming of the Shirva lands. Dagfinn had had enough of all of them. A westerly breeze was all he needed once the ship was launched. It was the end of the winter, and no time for brooding. Dagfinn came back into his house and found Rolf sitting by the fire, chewing the nail of his left thumb.

'Thorhalla said Olaf was at the ship,' said Rolf.

'He was. Full of chatter as usual.'

Rolf looked round in surprise. 'Really?'

'No.'

'Have you talked to Thorvald yet?'

'No. I've not seen him.'

'Don't you think you should?'

'Einar explained to him how things stood. It's nothing to do with me.'

'The boy's fifteen. If you ask him he's free to accept.'

'Look, I have to live on this island. I can't afford to have Einar, Bjarni and Ingebjorg all after my blood.'

'I still think you should speak to him. Just so he knows why.'

'I'll talk to him at harvest. It won't hurt him to wait.'

Down by the burn it was almost hot. Around a pool enlarged by a small dam, the turf was cropped close, and the banks were studded with primroses. Here the women of Shirva and Byrstada came to do their annual wash.

They piled all the washing into one great heap on the turf. Then Ragna, apparently worn out by the effort, lay down in the sun and shut her eyes.

'Get up!' said Gudrun. 'Shall we sort it out then?'

Gudrun and Ingrid argued as they sorted, Ingrid insisting that they should do the blankets first so they had longer to dry, and Gudrun saying it would be better to start with the linen, as there was so little of it anyway. The heat, and the familiar task, made Astrid feel homesick. In Dyflin the women crowded round the wells and stopped to talk each morning. Astrid had always avoided women's work before she came to the island. Now, she was glad to be treated as if she belonged.

Thorhalla was also silent, but there was nothing unusual about that. She was the same age as Astrid, a pale, thin girl with a runny nose and a habit of chewing her hair. Thorhalla was considered too young to be taken seriously, both by her sister Ragna, and by

Gudrun and Ingrid. Since they treated Astrid as an equal, Astrid took care to avoid Thorhalla.

They shook clouds of dust out of the blankets first, raising a sour smell of dirty wool. There was a big heap of woollen clothes: cloaks, tunics, trousers, socks, then in softer wool, dresses and shirts.

Gudrun took her knife and sliced a chunk of turf away. There was a ring of whitened stones where a fire had been before. Gudrun took a glowing peat from a pot, and Ingrid crumbled black peats to add to the embers. She and Gudrun built up the fire, and called for the empty pot to be filled with water.

'Put all the socks in and let them heat up.'

'Ragna, do something, will you?'

'Me? I'm not touching Rolf's socks. Nor Bjarni's either.'

'How about his blankets then?' Astrid jumped as Ragna was pushed past her. The next moment, Gudrun was shoving Ragna's face down into the heap of blankets. There were muffled screams as Ragna kicked out wildly, catching Astrid on the shin. Gudrun shook her hard. The heaps of clothes were scattered over the grass.

'Mind the fire!'

Ingrid kicked Ragna's flailing legs out of the way. 'Stop it, both of you!'

Gudrun let go, and stood up. Her scarf was askew, and now she pulled it right off, so her red hair fell down. Ragna lay sprawled, showing bare white legs. She was red in the face and laughing.

The air was thick with the smell of winter. But tails of wind eddied into their hollow, and swept the staleness away to sea. Water heated in the pot and slow bubbles drifted to its surface.

They took their tunics off, and kilted up their dresses. Soon their feet and shins were numb, red with cold and then white. They spread the blankets over the stream-bed and trod them in unison. It was noisy with Ragna there, but still possible to talk.

'So they'll launch the ship tomorrow?'

Gudrun nodded. She didn't seem worried any more. With her skirt tucked up and her hair hanging to her waist, streaked wet where she had pushed it out of her eyes, she looked more like a water spirit than a Norse trader's wife. 'They'll launch her in the morning,' she said, treading vigorously. 'I can't wait.'

'Hey!' Ragna shoved her, and the splash wet them all. 'I'll tell my brother you said that.'

'Tell tale tit, tongue shall be slit,' muttered Thorhalla.

'Trouble is,' went on Ragna, 'it leaves us without a single proper man on the island. Not unmarried, anyway. It's all right for Gudrun. She's married, and obviously glad to see the back of him. But what about us? All summer, and nothing but animals doing it all round us. It's not fair.'

'Some of us aren't doing anything.'

Ragna turned and looked at her sister, as if she found the reason too obvious to mention.

Thorhalla understood her very well. 'Well, Ingrid isn't. And she's older than you, and better looking.' She dodged out of Ragna's way.

'The problem is,' remarked Ingrid peaceably, 'there isn't anybody. Not eligible to marry anyway. Not on the island.' She turned to Ragna. 'Seriously, you must have thought about that?'

'Have I not? And yet they blame my brother for bringing in more men. Well, what do they want? There are only about three men on this island who aren't fourth cousins or something closer. So what happens? They go away to sea and marry. And where do we end up?'

'Like Gerda.'

Ragna crossed her fingers. 'You don't mean that! I'll swim to Hjaltland first.'

'No you won't,' said Thorhalla from dry land. 'You'll go on kissing Skuli Hedinsson behind the barn.'

Ragna jumped out of the burn, giving the others another soaking, and then came back again. 'It's no use,' she said. 'The one thing that girl can do is run. And she takes every advantage of it.'

'You don't allow her many others, do you?'

'Skuli isn't bad,' said Ragna. 'What am I supposed to do?'

'He's too old for you, isn't he?' said Ingrid.

'And too evil,' said Gudrun.

'I wouldn't look twice at any of the others, would you?'

'I hadn't thought about it,' said Ingrid.

They all looked at her. 'Oh yes you had,' said Gudrun and Ragna aloud, while Astrid thought the same thing. 'How could you not have?' said Ragna reasonably.

'I don't know.' Ingrid turned to Astrid. 'What do you think?'

'It's all right for her. She's not related to anybody.'

'She can have her pick,' said Ragna, and chuckled. 'Who do you fancy, Astrid?'

'You could have our cousins,' said Gudrun, laughing.

'Tell us the truth, Astrid,' Ragna challenged her. 'Have you seen any men on this island you could call handsome? Any single one?'

Gudrun was intrigued. 'If you had to pick a man on this island, Astrid, who would you choose?'

Astrid crossed her fingers behind her back. It would never, never come to that, but she wasn't going to say that to them.

'Go on, choose!'

'I can't.'

'If you don't,' Ragna grabbed her shoulders. 'I'll make you sit down in the burn, so I will.'

Astrid looked at Ingrid for help, but Ingrid just looked interested.

'All right. Not that I want him, mind. Only if I had to choose, which I don't.'

'Go on.'

'Not an island man at all.'

'One of the crew, then?'

Suddenly she was enjoying herself, having all their attention. No one had ever shown much interest in her thoughts. The women were flushed and laughing; the burn chuckled past them. Astrid's feet weren't cold now, and the blankets felt soft, half floating in the wet. The sun warmed her back, and glinted on hair and faces and clothes. She felt as though she had never seen these people properly before. Astrid laughed back at them, as she had never done since she came here. 'Promise not to tell.'

'Promise!'

She trod her blankets lightly, almost dancing in the water.

'I saw him at Byrstada, and then when I was at Snorri's. Snorri told me who he was. He only came this year. His name is Leif.'

'Leif!'

'Leif Asbjornsson?' asked Gudrun.

'There isn't any other.'

'My brother took him on in Biorgvin last year,' said Ragna. 'That's why he's here. A man left him, so he was short of an oarsman. That's the only reason.'

She sounded put out. Astrid, surprised, looked at her.

'He is very handsome,' said Ingrid. 'But I don't know . . . maybe
he won't come back again.'

There was something they were not saying.

'Well, I don't care,' said Astrid. 'I never wanted him anyway.
You asked me, and I do think he's the handsomest.'

'He is,' said Gudrun with conviction. 'Oh yes, indeed he is.'

'What's that supposed to mean?' Ragna was suddenly aggressive.

'Hush,' Ingrid nudged her. 'She's coming back.'

Thorhalla edged down the bank, keeping a wary eye on her
sister. Ragna turned her back.

They wrung out the blankets, winding them into tight coils.
Then they spread them out on the heather, facing the sun.

'They won't be quite so heavy when it's time to go.'

'So long as it stays dry tomorrow,' said Gudrun. 'I can't stand
tubs of wet washing indoors everywhere.'

'It'll stay dry. It has to, for the launching.'

For the first time Astrid thought of the launching with a degree
of personal interest. Now she had named Leif Asbjornsson, plucking him out of the blue like that, he had become real to her in a
new way. She had never before admitted aloud that she had noticed
any male. He had very fine gold hair that reached straight to his
shoulders. He was tall for his age, and pale, with an almost unnaturally clear complexion. His eyes were dark and solemn, and when
she had seen him, he had paid no attention to anyone around him
at all. He had sat by the fire at Byrstada, tying fishhooks on a trace,
ignoring the preparations for supper, and the jokes that were
inevitable whenever Ragna and her eldest brother were together.

'The problem about Leif,' said Ingrid, as though she could
restrain herself no longer, 'is that it's rough on Thorvald.'

'Thorvald? Why, what's he complaining about now?'

'Gudrun, you know he doesn't complain. All I'm saying is, that
place should have been for him. Dagfinn said he'd take him years
ago.'

'It's not my brother's fault!' said Ragna in a flash. 'He would
have, if he'd promised. It's Ingebjorg. Won't let her little darling
out of sight, that's what it is.'

'That's not true,' said Gudrun. 'It's my uncle. But he's wrong.
Father and Thorvald should be kept apart, and that's all there is to
it.'

'Does Thorvald really think Leif took his place?' asked Ingrid.

'Who knows what Thorvald thinks? He won't talk to anybody.'

'Except his brother.'

'And that's the same as talking to his shadow,' said Ragna. She laughed suddenly. 'Wouldn't you prefer one of them, Astrid? There's no one else on the island that isn't too closely related to them, except me. One each, how about that?'

Astrid was aware of Thorhalla, all ears and looking sulky. Ragna seemed determined to ignore her existence. 'Or Thorhalla,' said Astrid. 'She's just as eligible as you, isn't she?'

Thorhalla scowled and turned her back. Gudrun and Ingrid looked out to sea with blank faces.

Astrid had no idea what she had done.

It was Ingrid who enlightened her, when they were spreading clothes out among the heather. 'She's our cousin. And Thorvald's and Olaf's. She can't marry into our family. Only officially she's not. So she can't marry any of the Byrstada cousins either. In fact, she can't marry anybody. If she'd been a boy, she could have left the island, and it would have been all right. Einar's not a bad man, not really. He would have seen to that – he's her father. Don't stare like that. Einar's a man, isn't he? And as for Erlend – Ragna's father – they always said her mother should never have married him. He was too old. She was only fourteen when Dagfinn was born. She didn't have any choice about Erlend. But no one speaks about Thorhalla. I thought I should warn you.'

Astrid sighed. For a short time she had felt like one of them, and now she felt an outsider again. It wasn't fair. She could not possibly have known. It was too difficult, this island. She would never understand what they were really like.

'Don't wring wool out like that! It's good cloth, that.'

'I know.' Even in her own ears Astrid sounded sulky.

'Hey, Astrid? I'll bring you a lock of golden hair if you like,' said Ragna. 'Do you dare me?'

'Golden hair?' asked Thorhalla. 'Whose?'

'Ask no questions. I'll do it tonight before they sail. Do you dare me?'

Astrid grinned. 'I dare you!'

Chapter 14

A farmer.

Thorvald huddled in the corner of the empty barn among the last of the straw.

A bloody farmer. Always scratching away in the soil. Same thing, same time, every year. Same harvest, nothing varying but the weather. An island three miles long, two broad. After fifteen years he knew every rock. Every face too. Sheep. Cows. Uncles.

'Thorvald! Time to go!'

He got up, rubbing his cheeks with his hands, scratched himself hard, and pulled his tunic straight. This would be the worst day of his life, but no one must see that. No able-bodied man could stay away from the launching. Thorvald pushed the door open.

It smelt very fresh outside after the barn, and he took a deep breath and pushed his hair out of his eyes.

'Your hair's all straw,' said Olaf.

'I don't care.'

'It doesn't look right.'

Olaf would never say Thorvald looked as if he'd been hiding in the barn, weeping with rage and humiliation. He didn't have to. Thorvald washed his face in the water butt, and Olaf brushed him down.

'That's better. But we're late now. We'll have to run.'

'No. If they want us they can wait.'

Olaf sighed. This was going to be a hard day. If Thorvald got into an argument, Olaf would have to support him. Naturally he thought Thorvald had been miserably treated, but loyalty was becoming more and more arduous these days. Olaf would be quite happy to see the ship go, but of course he did not say so.

'There's still our boat,' he said, as they climbed the hill dyke.

'Fishing.'

'Fishing!' said Thorvald.

'And you'll go to Konungsborg again with Einar.'

'Einar!' Thorvald spat.

Olaf tried to quicken their pace without Thorvald noticing. He wanted to ask if there were still any figures on the path ahead of them. If there were not, everyone would be at the Nordhavn already. Olaf opened his mouth, thought better of it, and shut it again.

Valland, thought Thorvald. From Jaeren in Rogaland three days' sailing – two with an easterly wind – to Spurn near Grimsbaer where Egil was shipwrecked. Then two days round the coast of Eastengle to the Foreland of Cantland, and half a day across the sea to Ruda in Nordmandi. Nordmandi. Rich cloth, thick glass, red wine, great fairs and markets under the southern sun. And the best weapons in the world.

To Olaf's relief, no one had started work when they reached the Nordhavn. The men were gathered on the beach, and the crew were carrying down the skids, which had been tied down all winter at the back of the Sula's shed. Olaf saw his uncles, but they had their backs to him. No one seemed to be looking out for them at all. Perhaps they had not been missed.

'Hallo, Olaf!'

It was Leif, standing at the top of the beach smiling at him. Olaf's heart sank. This wasn't going to make things any easier. He was painfully conscious of his brother at his side.

'Hallo,' said Olaf, wishing the sea would come and swallow Leif up.

He should never have talked to Leif in the first place. When it happened he had known that Thorvald wouldn't like it. Thorvald hadn't even wanted Olaf to visit Byrstada this winter, when he himself had stayed away. Olaf had very seldom gone, because he was always loyal, but once or twice there had been no choice. His mother had sent him with messages for Gudrun, or else he had been looking for Snorri smith. When he met Leif, Leif had been sitting by the fire with a cloth over his head, a bowl of steaming herbs in his lap, and Thorhalla beside him. Presently she had gone away, and Leif had ripped off the towel and looked at Olaf.

'Got a cough?' said Olaf shyly.

'Yes,' said Leif, and coughed.

'Been at sea long?'

'Three years.'

'Travelled far?'

'Noreg, Hjaltland, the Orkneyjar.' Leif paused. 'The Faereyjar.'

'Trading ships?'

'How else?'

'Don't go home in winter, then?'

'No.'

They had met again at Dagfinn's Yule feast. Everyone was talking about sailing directions to the Faereyjar.

'We can ask the expert,' said Dagfinn. 'Leif knows that coast.'

They asked him out of politeness, and when they found that he actually knew, they went on talking to him. Bjarni asked him about the north coast of the Faereyjar, and though Leif admitted he spoke from hearsay, he could answer the questions. 'There you are,' said Dagfinn. 'Keeps his ears open.' Olaf had looked at Thorvald. Thorvald hadn't eaten his dinner.

So now Olaf was caught between his brother and Leif, his brother's supplanter, whom he couldn't help liking. Olaf nodded to Leif, and hurried on to the beach. He wished Snorri were there; it would have made things easier, but of course Snorri would stay away today. A crippled man was unlucky at a launching.

The heavy beam that barred the seaward end of the shed had been taken down, and the doors swung wide open. The Sula smelt of fresh caulking, and her prow was newly decorated. She was not very big for a trading ship, but she was strong, clinker-built, full-bellied with high sides, for carrying as much cargo as possible.

Einar inspected her and said to Bjarni, 'I wouldn't be ashamed if she were mine.'

'I wouldn't know,' said Bjarni. 'Nor do you, come to that.'

Dagfinn gave orders sharply, and the crew, unlike the island men, leapt to obey. Dagfinn never took his eyes off his ship, as they fitted the ropes, and prepared to haul her.

The greased skids were set in place across the beach. The crew stood to the ropes, and Dagfinn called for the islanders to join them. They came in a leisurely fashion, for they were free men, in nobody's pay, who had come to do their neighbour a favour. When they were all ready Dagfinn gave the signal. Very slowly the ship began to move. She came forward on to the first skid. The men hauled with all the strength they had.

Sula dipped, as her weight came on to the first skid. Then she gathered a little momentum, and slid on to the next. Each skid was pressed hard into the sand as she came down.

'Keep her upright,' shouted Dagfinn. 'Smoothly, now, gently!'

Bjarni glanced up, the sweat pouring down his face. 'For God's sake,' he muttered. 'Gently!'

It was a high spring tide, and when Sula was nearly down the short beach, Dagfinn shouted to them to bring down the used skids from the top and have them ready at the bottom. Thorvald and Leif took one and waded into the sea. They had to hold it steady where the waves were breaking, one at each end. Thorvald slipped, and the greased wood slithered from his grasp.

'Hold on, can't you? This isn't a ploughed field.'

Thorvald's hands moved before he had time to think. He had a glimpse of Leif, neat and conceited, golden hair to his shoulders, his homespun cloak fastened unexpectedly with a silver pin. Then Thorvald jerked the spar upwards. There was a great splash, and Thorvald was drenched with spray.

The sea was icy. Leif gasped and choked on salt water. He fought for a hold, but his hands clutched only water. There was sand under his back. He struggled to his knees amid the breaking waves, pushed his dripping hair off his face, and shook the water from his ears. He could hear shouts of laughter from the men on the beach.

Others were wading into the water now. Sula was just above them. They held the skids steady, then splashed out of the way as she came down.

Thorvald waited for Leif, ready to fight. But just as Leif turned to face him Rolf shouted an order.

Leif looked at Thorvald once, then ran, dripping, to where Rolf and the crew were launching the boat into the breakers. They boarded her, grabbed the oars, then set out sharply towards the near skerry.

'Here, Thorvald!' It was Einar. 'Don't dream! Help keep her steady.'

Sula was poised between shore and sea. Thorvald, on the port side, hands on the gunwale, was soaked to the waist by breaking waves. They must have just about reached the stack. The hauling-off rope was fixed between ship and stack, a block halfway along its length. Thorvald inched along Sula's side, and saw the rope. It was tightening, dipping into the water and out again as it went taut. Slowly it took the weight. He felt Sula stir under his hands.

'Now!' Dagfinn signalled to the islanders. They heaved. Sula shifted, and stopped.

'Now!'

Another heave. The ship was free. Then the boat was alongside her, the men scrambling aboard. Two oars were shipped, and Rolf appeared at the steerboard. They brought her round sunwise, until she faced into the wind. Leif flung a line ashore and Einar caught it and made it fast to a mooring at the top of the beach. The anchor went over the stern with a soft splash.

'Not looking bad, is she?' said Einar to Dagfinn.

'She'll do.' Dagfinn looked at Einar as if seeing him for the first time that day. 'Thank you,' he said.

Einar brushed the sweat out of his eyes. 'Don't mention it. Break my back for you any time you like.'

The tide was on the turn, and there was still the mast to be stepped, and all the cargo to bring aboard. The islanders' contributions, mostly of wadmal, but also barrels of butter, seal and fish oil, feathers, and a couple of live hawks, had to be stowed as cargo, and there were the crew's supplies and sea chests to be shipped. Some of the islanders stayed to help flit the cargo from shed to ship, while the crew stowed it. When that was done, the island men sat down at the top of the beach, passing round flagons of Byrstada ale. Most of them seemed in no hurry to depart.

'Are you staying?' Bjarni asked his brother.

'No,' said Einar. 'Lambs won't wait for a wind. I'm off to the hill.'

Bjarni shrugged, and went back to Sula's shed.

The crew were rolling barrels down the beach to the shore.

'Five months,' said Skuli, turning a barrel upright as it threatened to roll into the sea. 'Five months without. Time we went.'

'Speak for yourself.'

'No he isn't, he's done all right.'

'I mean five months without much choice,' said Skuli.

'Not much choice in the Hjaltafjorden either.'

'No. He'd better take us ashore with him this time.'

'Three days!' Skuli snorted. 'While he takes the pick of the market.'

'Timber market. Very respectable.'

'I'd even buy that for him,' said Skuli, 'if I could get at some of the other.'

'Boys? Is that what you want?'

Thorvald, who was waiting with the boat, heard. He thrust the rope into his brother's hand. 'I'm going home!'

'Why?' called Olaf after him.

'To shovel muck,' said Thorvald savagely.

He had just reached the top of the beach when he heard footsteps behind him, and turned, just in time. Leif's fist crashed into his face below the eye. Thorvald kept his feet, reached out, and had Leif's wrist under his hand. Leif twisted and struggled, but Thorvald kept his hold. He wrenched the wrist sideways and heard Leif gasp. Leif broke free, hit out, missed, and staggered. Thorvald felt blood on his tongue. He flung forward and brought his knee up hard into Leif's stomach. Leif gave a sort of croak, and fell, pulling Thorvald with him as he went. They rolled over stones and sea poppies. Leif was on top, his wet tunic pressed against Thorvald's face. Thorvald's hands found Leif's hair and pulled it hard. Then Leif was gone. Rough hands seized Thorvald too and dragged him to his feet.

Thorvald pushed his hair back, and felt his nose. His hand came away covered in blood.

'What the hell?' Thorvald tried hard to bring Bjarni into focus. He had never seen him in such a rage.

'Nothing,' said Thorvald.

'Nothing! To launch a ship with brawling and bloodshed. Nothing! To cast ill luck on a whole season! And you Eirik's son! To curse a ship like this!'

Leif didn't speak. He was kneeling on the ground, breathing in gasps, and he didn't look up. Thorvald jerked himself from Bjarni's grasp, and for the first time in his life turned and swore at his uncle. Bjarni grabbed at him, but Thorvald ducked under his arm, and ran.

When he was out of sight he slowed down. Blood from his nose splashed on to his tunic. He wiped it with his hands, then found a lump of moss and held it against his nostrils. He flung himself down in a sheep shelter on the hill. It was soft and lined with green. The cliff was twenty feet away. If he threw himself over it, he would be dead in a moment. He wondered briefly what that would be like, and picked more moss. He couldn't get at his boat because it was beached in the Nordhavn and they'd hang around there drinking half the day. Tears trickled down his cheeks and mingled with the blood. He would run away. He and Olaf could take their own boat to Hjaltland, and he would find a trading ship, and never be heard of more. But what would Olaf do, left behind in Hjaltland?

The sun was dropping, and the breeze off the sea was suddenly chill. They would be lighting the fire on the beach. Thorvald thought of roasting mutton, and realised he was hungry. His hand went to the thorshammer, hanging round his neck. If his father were still alive it would not have been like this. His father too had launched his ship with a sacrifice to forgotten gods, and to the Christian saints, neither of whom had saved him. 'I want you,' Thorvald whispered, and clutched the silver hammer in his fist. 'I want my father back.'

He had thought all that was finished years ago. Ashamed, he let go of the amulet. His hands were streaked with blood. He tried to wipe them on the heather but the blood was already drying.

Tomorrow the ship would be gone, if the wind stayed westerly. He willed it to do so.

Bjarni sat at the top of the beach with the sailor who had helped him to break up the fight. The man seemed in no hurry to return to his work, but that was none of Bjarni's business. He seemed quite serene, in spite of ill omens, and hummed irritatingly. Bjarni refreshed himself at intervals from the flagon, and eventually spoke. 'The other boy, the one who was winded,' he asked. 'Where does he come from?'

'Leif?' said Skuli. 'He's been here all winter. You must have met him.'

'I've seen him. Who is he?'

Skuli shrugged. 'Just a seaman.' He paused. 'You're not the first on the island to ask me that.'

'I dare say.'

'He's been with us since August, but I couldn't tell you where he's from. The islands of Noreg, to judge by the accent. But he keeps to himself, that one.'

'He must have joined you somewhere.'

'Biorgvin.'

'But he's not from there?'

Skuli leaned back comfortably, his eyes on Rolf's back. He never minded telling a story, and he had had considerable success with this one already. 'It was odd. We came into the Hjaltafjorden after the hay harvest, and had to wait to get into the harbour. Everyone was turning up for the last run to the islands. Dagfinn went ashore first to see to the business. We waited two days, then came ashore. Dagfinn had the cargo down already, and it didn't take us long to load. We were moored offshore again, waiting for a wind. I can't remember, but we had to take the boat back again; there was time to buy more fresh food. It was Magnus and I, and we were just about to cast off again when he – Leif – came along. He didn't say much, never does, but he asked us, was our captain Dagfinn Erlendsson, and were we from the Sula? So we said that was right, and he said, "Tell your captain, please, that Leif Asbjornsson changed his plans and is still in Biorgvin, and if your captain's offer of a place still stands I'm willing to accept it."'

'Well, we knew Dagfinn had spoken of taking on another man, as we were short; we'd heard Rolf nagging him as to why he did nothing about it. So we said to the boy to come along with us, for we'd soon be sailing. He wouldn't do that. He said, "I'd rather you gave him the message first. I'll wait here." So we went back without him. And it was just as we'd thought. Dagfinn said what the hell did we mean wasting everyone's time, we should have brought him back at once. So he sent us straight back again. Sure enough, there he was, waiting on the beach, sitting on his sea chest.'

'So you took him aboard?'

'That's right,' Skuli was about to say more, but Bjarni seemed unresponsive. 'I suppose I'd better get on,' said Skuli, 'or they'll think I've deserted.'

When Olaf came home that night, he was slightly drunk, and feeling guilty that he had not followed Thorvald sooner. He climbed on to the barn roof and recited a prayer to St Olaf to raise a west wind. It seemed the best thing he could do to help his brother. Then he went to bed and slept soundly. Thorvald never stirred. Olaf was awake early, and he climbed over Thorvald and crept to the door. Outside the sky was grey before the dawn, the grass bent over to the east. Olaf stepped out of the shelter of the house and the wind tugged at his shirt, and lifted his hair across his eyes. Two clouds cast a brief shadow over the island. Then the wind took them, sailing east towards Noreg.

Part Three

The Farmers

A lamb dropped on to the turf in a small wet heap, and the ewe turned to lick it. Then she strained again, and another followed. Ingebjorg moved round them and began to rub the second lamb with a rough cloth. Then she put it to its mother, and the lamb searched for the teat and began to suck. Ingebjorg stood up.

Dew shone coldly on the grass. The sheep stood huddled in the enclosure, lambs white against the dirty fleeces of the ewes. Ingebjorg spoke to the patiently waiting dog, who trotted stiffly over, wagging her tail, then they walked back over the island, their feet leaving long marks in the grass. Ingebjorg blew her nose on her fingers. 'Cold,' she remarked to the dog. The dog pressed its nose against her skirt.

In a hollow behind an ancient turf wall they found four more sheep and another lamb. The lamb suckled steadily, its tail wagging. They were Shirva sheep. Ingebjorg looked them over, and went on.

The western cliffs fell to the right, lost in the shadow of the island. The ledges were splashed white with droppings, lined with birds almost down to the sea's edge. A wash of foam rose and fell below them. Something showed brown down in the water, but there was no way of retrieving wood from there. The boys might have tried it, but they were still at home, sleeping.

The spar of wood reminded her of Einar's child from the sea. She had meant to see Astrid again, but that was not easy. And now that they were into spring, there was little time for anything. It must be very difficult for the girl. Of all the people on the island, perhaps only she, Ingebjorg, could have any real idea. The other women knew nothing of the kind of life Astrid had left behind, and the men who had been abroad had no idea what it would be like to be forced to stay here, perhaps for ever.

Ingebjorg had once found it difficult too. Sometimes she felt that evil luck had hung over her from the beginning. When she first met Eirik life had promised to be fair, but promises were precarious. There had been excitement once, the possibility of good fortune to come. Now that had all passed, and there was nothing greater than Bjarni Thorvaldsson to contend with. In the early days, it had been different.

Ingebjorg was the daughter of a man called Grim Erlingsson, who had been one of the Earl's retainers at Orfjara, the Earl's great hall in the Orkneyjar. Under Earl Paul's patronage Grim prospered, and he bought himself a farm which he renamed Grim's town, on the shores of Heradvatn. But Paul was dogged by an evil fate, for he was one of the sons of Hakon, who had killed Earl Magnus the Good on Egilsey. Hakon's punishment fell not on himself, but upon his sons Paul and Harald, between whom the Earldom was divided at his death. Harald died of a poison that was meant for Paul, and so Paul ruled alone.

Ingebjorg was born the year after Earl Paul was betrayed and killed by his former retainer, the pirate Svein Asleifarson. In that year Rognvald became Earl of the islands.

Grim retired to his farm, since he was unlikely to find favour with the new Earl. The times were dangerous, and the Orkneyjar were full of landless men. Rognvald gathered many round him, who later went with him on his Crusade. Throughout Ingebjorg's childhood there were plots. Men gathered in her father's house at night, and she and her brothers learned not to speak of it. There were many killings, and often they saw bands of armed men passing on the road by the stone circles on the other side of Heradvatn. These were the great years of the Orkneyjar pirates, of whom Svein was the chief. Sometimes there was money in the house, and foreign luxuries. In other years there were meetings in the dark, and confinement to the farm.

Ingebjorg played pirates on the loch with her brothers, on a home-made raft. In their games they enacted the killings which were never far from home. At home they avoided their father, who was heavy-handed with his children, though less so with Ingebjorg than with his boys.

She and Erling were the eldest. Ingebjorg grew into a very attractive young woman, and her father hoped to marry her well. Erling was sullen at home, and secretive about his life outside. He stayed away more and more, but he never lost touch with his sister. He would have taken her to Orfjara, but Grim kept her strictly at home, although reports of her beauty began to spread among Rognvald's retainers. Ingebjorg relied on her brother to tell her what was happening in the world.

When Ingebjorg was fourteen, Erling quarrelled with his father. Earl Rognvald was preparing for his great Crusade, and Erling, now sixteen, was determined to go. He had been getting into wild company among the warriors who were assembling that winter at Orfjara. One night he and some friends broke into the great trows' mound Orkahaugr, and spent a whole night there, as a dare, in spite of the evil spirits that dwelt inside. Two men had been stark mad next morning, but not Erling, who thought himself a fine warrior, and cared nothing at all for his father's ancient loyalty to Paul. When Grim heard that Erling was planning to go on Earl Rognvald's expedition, he forbade Erling to come home again.

Ingebjorg would have run away too, if she could. Her father had quarrelled with all his neighbours, and no one cared now about the faction he represented. The islands were more peaceful, but with the best of the young men gone, there was nothing interesting happening. Ingebjorg saw almost no one but her family, and she had no sympathy for Grim's determination to ruin himself in support of a dead cause.

She was seventeen when Erling returned, having won honour for his family in the Crusade, so that Grim forgave him and ordered him to come home. Meanwhile, Erling had made a friend in Kirkjavagr, someone who had had nothing to do with Rognvald or his Crusade. This young man's name was Eirik Thorvaldsson. He was having a ship built in Kirkjavagr. He was handsome and ambitious, although he had an outlandish Hjaltland accent, and his island was apparently a poor place, lying on the very edge of the Orkneyjar. Erling persuaded Eirik to come home with him to Grimstown.

When Eirik arrived, even Grim was glad of the diversion. He encouraged Eirik to stay at his house. Eirik had time on his hands, and came as often as he could.

When Grim realised that this young friend of Erling's was after his daughter, he would have sent him packing, but by that time it was too late, for Eirik had already seduced her. In a fury, Grim sent Ingebjorg in shame from his house, without her dowry. Ingebjorg didn't care. Eirik might be a Hjaltlander, but he was handsome and brave, and she loved him. She trusted him too, ignorant of the world as she was, and luckily he treated her as well as he had promised.

He took her to Kirkjavagr, where his ship lay in the boatyard. They stayed there three months, until it was time to sail in spring. Ingebjorg had never known such freedom. She had a husband, more or less, and her favourite brother. The township was buzzing, with the building of the church, and all the traders and pirates. It seemed to Ingebjorg like the centre of the world.

Eirik made love to her at every opportunity, and told her that he would take her home to his own island, where his family would welcome her. He and she would have sons, and perhaps daughters too, and he would go to sea and bring her home a fortune. Unlike her father, he never raised his hand to her. He was pleased with all that she did, and among his friends he made it clear that he was proud of her.

Just before they sailed, he took Ingebjorg to a priest, and married her. Then Ingebjorg had boarded a ship for the first time in her life, and he had brought her to the island.

Where she had remained ever since.

Ingebjorg started out of her memories. She was nearly at the hill dyke, and Setr was just below her. Smoke rose out of the chimney hole, so the boys were up. When she reached the steps in the hill dyke she climbed lightly over. She might be over thirty, but she still walked like a girl, and there was no grey in her hair. Other women were grandmothers at her age, and looked it. And yet they had men, and were not alone every night at their own hearth. Not that she was solitary, with three strong sons of her own, but of all the fates she might have guessed at, loneliness would have been the last to occur to her in earlier days.

She could not hate the island now. Although she was shocked by their outlandish habits, Eirik's brothers treated her at first with a courtesy she had never known at home, and her sister-in-law, Bjarni's wife, welcomed her with delight. Ingebjorg had never known a house with no quarrels. Even though Eirik had to leave her at once, she had not been unhappy. He left her pregnant, and she and Bjarni's wife, whose second baby was nearly due, had worked together as if they had been sisters.

But Eirik had been gone less than a month when Ingrid was born, and her mother died in giving birth to her. Then Ingebjorg's own pregnancy began to terrify her. She had seen Bjarni's wife die, and sometimes she thought she would rather kill herself than die the same way. But there was little time to mourn, with two orphan babies to look after.

Thorvald was born at Michaelmas, two weeks after Eirik came home, and he thrived from the first day. Eirik was delighted with him, but he hid his pleasure out of respect for Bjarni's loss. That winter Bjarni had taken no notice of his daughters, and had left Ingebjorg to manage them. It was only later that he began to interfere with her arrangements for the children. Luckily Eirik was at home, and he had smoothed things over, for the time being.

Ingebjorg reached the door at Setr. The warmth of the house struck her as she entered. Peat reek filled the room, and under it the fire glowed red.

'Mother?' said Olaf.

Ingebjorg hung up her cloak to dry. 'Where have they gone? Did you have your morning meal?'

'Porridge in the pot. We left you enough. To the boat. How was it?'

'Four. One pair of twins. I'm cold.' Ingebjorg sat down and tugged her boots off, then scraped the pot, while Olaf squatted by the hearth and piled on fresh peats. Ingebjorg put the bowl down and closed her eyes. There was a strong smell of wet dog. Wind eddied down from the chimney hole and made the peats glow. The strings of drying fish swayed as the draught caught them. No weapons hung on the walls in this house, for Eirik's had been lost with him, and his sons had no others. Instead there were baskets full of kitchen implements and pots, and one nearer the door with fishing gear. There was a low table of scrubbed driftwood by the hearth, and a full bucket of water beside it. The room was clean and swept. Olaf came in again with a full peat bucket, and kicked the door shut behind him.

'Did you see Einar yesterday?'

Olaf nodded. 'You were asleep when I got back. I had supper there.'

'How's Astrid?'

Olaf took a moment to answer. 'She's all right.' There was a pause. 'Einar brought back a caddy lamb. Gave it to her to rear.'

'Does she know what to do?'

'Einar showed her how to feed it from a skin. He thought it might cheer her up a bit.'

'Did it?'

'I don't know. She said it was better than a baby.'

Ingebjorg laughed.

'Seems a funny thing for a lass to say,' said Olaf.

'She sounds quite sensible to me.'

Chapter 16

'Take him to the Thing this year,' said Bjarni. 'It'll do him good.'

'You don't mind?' Einar still looked anxious. 'It'll mean more work for you.'

'I doubt it.'

'No, at Setr. You'd have to keep an eye on things at this time of year. Olaf and his mother can't do it all.'

'Ingebjorg won't thank me for interfering.'

'That's what I'm afraid of. But if I take the boy, someone has to do his work. You've done the same for me all these years.' Einar paused. 'Bjarni, wouldn't you prefer to go to Hjaltland?'

'Me? Instead of the lawman? No, thank you. I'm not the man for that kind of business.'

'Better than most,' said Einar. 'They ask for you, you know, the ones who remember the old days. You've not been off the island for over ten years, Bjarni.'

'Seventeen.'

'There you are. Why don't you go?'

'With Thorvald? No, thank you.'

'Yourself. Thorvald and I will look after the farm.'

'We go through this every year. You go. I have no business there. If anyone wants to see me, bring him back to the island. And take the boy with you. Time he saw more of Hjaltland than the quarries, anyway.' Bjarni swallowed the last of his meal. 'I don't mind working with young Olaf anyway. No harm in that boy. I'd take it as an opportunity, if you take the other one off for a while.'

'That would be the best of all, if you got to know Olaf, work with him a bit. He'll be left when Thorvald goes to sea. The future may well depend on how we work things out with him.'

'He'll be loyal to his brother.'

'Yes, Olaf will be loyal, but when Thorvald's at sea he'll trust Olaf to make the decisions at home. Get to know him, Bjarni. That's the best thing you could do. It may depend on him in the end, to bring the farms back into one family.'

'You'd have to get his mother out of the way first.'

'There's nothing she can say, once they're of age.'

'Thorvald is of age.'

'Once Thorvald gets away from here, he'll grow up. All right, I'll admit he should have gone with Dagfinn. That was my fault. He won't work with us. But Olaf's a good worker. If I take Thorvald away, you see what you can do with Olaf while you have the chance.'

'The boy will be loyal to his brother,' repeated Bjarni. He stood up, and brushed the crumbs off his tunic. Outside the house he found Astrid, dressing crabs with a hammer and a knife. He watched her carefully extract the pink meat from one claw and put it in her mouth. Then she picked up the other claw, and ripped it apart at the joint. She was about to break the shell with the hammer, when she saw Bjarni, and stopped, looking guilty.

'I don't mind what you eat,' he told her.

Astrid flushed, and pushed her hair out of her eyes with one crab-stained hand.

'You should tie it back.'

Ingrid would have looked hurt, but Astrid regarded him stonily. 'There was a message from the smithy,' she said.

'From Snorri?'

'Gunnhild. She said she'd be at the peats herself, and thank you for yesterday.'

'Ah.' He turned to go, then added, 'If Ingrid asks, I've gone to the hill.'

Out of the shelter of the hall, the wind whipped into his face, doing its best to slow him down. Bjarni strode north to the hill, head down.

Seventeen years. He hadn't thought of it, until Einar started talking. He had been twenty, with a wife and baby at home. It had been no fun living in a small booth at the Thing with Einar for two weeks when he didn't want a woman himself. He had had nothing to say at the Thing, but Einar had spoken concerning a point of law, and Bjarni had been proud of him. Something to do with an inheritance case. Bjarni had never been much of a lawman, and he hated the idea of speaking in public, especially away from his own island. Every year since then Einar had offered to stay at Shirva and have Bjarni go in his place. Every year Bjarni had refused. Seventeen years ago they had laughed at him, for his stolid faithfulness to his wife at home. He had no wife now, but he had all he needed from a woman on his own island, and he was more discreet than his brother. Faithful too. Bjarni stopped, and frowned into the peat bogs below him. Faithful after a fashion. He felt a familiar pang of something like guilt, but he dismissed it. What was a man to do? If he had wronged a friend, at least he made sure no one knew of it, and no one was shamed. He would have taken another wife if that had been possible. But even if there had been anyone on the island, there was little he could fairly offer. The farm was not large; he had two daughters already, and the threat of an inheritance case between the future heirs. Besides, he had no love to offer but what was already given.

The few sheep on this part of the hill were from Setr. He had automatically checked them in passing. But now he saw a patch of dirty white that didn't move, below an outcrop of rock. Bjarni hurried back down the slope.

The crows had had the sheep's eyes. It had been in labour. The body was distended by the unborn carcass, hind legs thrust apart and rigid. The fleece was matted with mud and blood.

Bjarni turned back towards Setr.

He found Thorvald and Olaf coming up the hill together, with ropes, baskets and a snare. Going after eggs, without even bothering to do their hill round first. Bjarni ran to intercept them. When they saw him coming they stopped and waited. Olaf shifted the basket on his shoulder, and moved closer to his brother, standing just behind him. Thorvald folded his arms. The gesture seemed insolent. Both boys had blue eyes just like his brother Eirik's. The same blank gaze.

'Thorvald,' said Bjarni, struggling to catch his breath. 'You've a dead sheep up there. Not today's either. Don't you do your round?'

'What?'

'You heard me. A dead sheep. On the hill. Died in labour. Where were you?'

'It happens every year,' said Olaf. 'To everyone. Who can be there all the time?'

'Accidents, yes. That sheep's been there two days. Three maybe. That's an offence. Affects us all. In the middle of lambing, too.'

'A late one,' said Olaf. 'Lambing's done, more or less.'

'I'm asking your brother. It's his responsibility.'

'And mine.'

Bjarni looked them both over. 'You need to look to your sheep every day,' he said to them. 'You know that as well as I do. It does the island no good. I could bring it to the Thing, if I chose.'

'They'd laugh at you,' said Thorvald.

Bjarni's fists clenched. Eirik's sons. No, he must not do that.

'Listen,' said Bjarni. 'It was one thing when you had no man at Setr. But if you will keep to yourselves you'll have to do it well like the rest of us. One bad farmer hurts us all. Thorvald, you're a man grown. You'll have to behave like one.'

Suddenly Thorvald began to shout. 'Any man can lose a sheep and take a little while to find it. I do look to my sheep! Einar knows that if you don't! My farm is nothing to do with you!'

'Dead animals on the hill are very much to do with me! I've my own flock out here too. A bad farmer is a bad neighbour. I won't take this from my brother's son. You'll have that sheep off here by nightfall, or I'll take the matter to the Thing. That's the law, and you know it.'

'Law!' sneered Thorvald.

'I've nothing more to say to you.'

Bjarni strode away up the hill. Two boys. He could have beaten them. Eirik's sons. Leaving anything dead to lie, that was an offence. They'd have to bury it by nightfall. Ought he to check? There were the smithy peats, waiting. He had cast them for years, first when his friend Snorri was at sea, then after he came back crippled. Gunnhild was the only woman on the island who could cast peats like a man. Eirik's sons. It would be better if Ingebjorg had never come to the island. But Eirik had brought her home, and Bjarni's own wife had loved her.

Thorvald took the rope off his shoulder and thrust it at Olaf. 'Take the things home,' he said. 'Then come back here with a spade.'

'We're doing it then?'

'Gravedigging? Yes.'

Thorvald walked parallel to the hill dyke until he reached the sea. He retraced his steps, taking a line further north, until he reached the spot where they had first seen Bjarni. Then he cast back again, further up. A few yards further on he found the sheep. No wonder he hadn't seen it from above. The hollow would have been hidden by the outcrop. Bjarni must have realised that.

Olaf was waiting with the spade when he got back to the hill dyke. 'I'll come with you.'

'No point.' Thorvald shouldered the spade, and plodded back uphill.

The ground was stony under the turf. Thorvald dug viciously, breaking up the stones. Sweat dripped into his eyes. He stripped off his tunic, and the wind cooled his wet skin through his shirt. The spade rang on stone, half buried in reddish soil. He found an edge, and tugged at a slab till it came free. It was rectangular, like a brigstone. There was another next to it. A floor, two feet down. His skin prickled. There were trowie mounds not far away, but it was daylight, and he had a sheep to bury. He went on digging. His spade struck something pale grey. He picked it up. It was a smooth light stone, a kind he hadn't seen before, with the sharp edge shaped to a point. He crossed himself over his thorshammer, picked it up, and slipped it in his pocket.

Chapter 17

Ingebjorg leaned on her hoe. The hills cast long blue shadows, but it would be light enough to work for a couple of hours yet. She didn't want to waste this weather. She bent over her work again, scratching between the rigs, leaving the weeds lying. It was mostly chickweed, as they had kept well ahead of the weeding this year, with both Thorvald and Olaf able to do a man's work. But now they had quarrelled with Bjarni, after all her efforts to keep the peace.

Her back ached. She knew she should stop, but she had nearly finished the row, and tomorrow the gold light might all be turned to grey.

'You're not still working?'

'Gunnhild!' Ingebjorg stepped across the onions, and looked over the bean rows. 'I'll stop now. You'll have a drink with me?'

'I saw you'd cast your peats.'

'The boys finished yesterday. And yours?'

'All done.'

'Pity,' said Ingebjorg. 'How will you manage now?'

'Only Freya knows. Anyway,' said Gunnhild, 'it doesn't solve anything. I'm too old for sprawling on a cloak behind a dyke. It's not dignified.'

'Is that what Bjarni thinks?'

Gunnhild looked at her, then laughed too. 'You're so hard on him, poor man. And I hear your boys have taken to confronting him as well. No, he doesn't like it either. But what can he do?'

'Do without. Some of us have to.'

'Try suggesting it to him.'

'Me?' Ingebjorg laughed. 'Can you imagine it?'

Gunnhild chuckled, cradling her mug. She was the same age as Ingebjorg, but had no children. She had always been pretty. Every eligible man on the island had once wanted to marry her, but she had chosen Snorri Hakonsson, although he had the least land. She had had no father to advise her, but perhaps she had been right, for Snorri had made money at sea, and kept her well. He had made a good husband, they all said, when he had been at home, though in the early years that was seldom. He had become a pirate, and didn't often come back even in winter. When he did appear he brought treasure with him, such as had seldom been seen on the island. But that was all over now. It was Bjarni Thorvaldsson who saw the longship that brought him back to his own island in the end, and he brought Snorri ashore. His shipmates thought they had brought him home to die. When Snorri had been lowered into Bjarni's boat, the longship had slid away into the twilight like a ghost. Bjarni took Snorri back to his wife, and Snorri had not died, for all his wounds.

Gunnhild pulled back her scarf, and rubbed her head. She had thick brown hair, which curled at the ends. There was a touch of grey at her temples.

'Seriously,' said Gunnhild. 'I do wonder what I should do. It isn't easy.'

'Two men at once. It's hard enough to be private with one.'

'I never knew my luck before. It wasn't hard at all. I had my house to myself half the year or more, and when Snorri was home, well, we were younger anyway. I knew Snorri wasn't faithful to me. How could he be? You know the Orkneyjar pirates. But now . . .'

Ingebjorg looked at her friend. 'Why go on, if it's that difficult? Are you just sorry for Bjarni?'

'No.' Gunnhild sat up. 'No, that would be an insult. I tell you, you don't know Bjarni.'

'I believe you. But you still don't need to get cold and wet, making love to him among the peats.'

'I'd rather do it in a bed.'

'Why do it at all? You've got Snorri, haven't you?'

'Yes, but with Snorri it's all over in two minutes flat.'

'Is it really that much better with Bjarni?'

'Oh yes, he can go on for hours. At least he could if only we had a bed.'

'Well, I don't know. Ever since Snorri came back, you've been going to give Bjarni up. Then you're going to tell Snorri. Then you're going to tell Bjarni you won't see him. One minute it's no good, the next it's the only thing that's any good. Snorri's been home for four years now, and you're still going round in circles. Perhaps Bjarni should have married again.'

'There's no one on the island he could marry.'

'I know the feeling.'

Gunnhild laid her hand on her friend's knee. 'Ingebjorg, I wish I could give you one of them. It's not that easy, I promise you.'

Ingebjorg laughed. 'If only you would go off with Bjarni, that would make life much easier for both of us.'

'No one will ever get Bjarni off this island now. And if I did, what then? I'd leave you my husband, would I?'

'Two minutes flat, you said. No thank you.'

'It's probably all those years at sea,' said Gunnhild ruefully.

'Eirik was always at sea, and he never had any problems like that.'

'Well, maybe Thorvald's sons are the best lovers, and that's all there is to it. Look at Einar. He's slept with just about every woman on the island.'

'Except me,' remarked Ingebjorg.

'And me, now you mention it.'

Ingebjorg stood up. 'Another drink?'

'Yes, why not?' Gunnhild followed Ingebjorg inside. It was dim and stuffy indoors after the evening air outside. The blankets on the sleeping platforms were huddled and untidy. 'Where are the boys?'

'I don't know. I didn't think they'd stay in on an evening like this. I hope they took Eirik.'

Gunnhild watched Ingebjorg pour two measures from an earthenware jug, which she replaced in its bucket of cold water. 'So Thorvald didn't go to the Thing with Einar?'

'You know he didn't. I wanted him to go, but he wouldn't. He said Einar had thought of it to get him out of the way, because he'd quarrelled with Bjarni. I should have let him go with Dagfinn.'

'Why didn't you?'

Ingebjorg didn't answer.

'They all go in the end,' said Gunnhild. 'Snorri came back, and Eirik didn't. That's fate. You needed Eirik. It's not fair. But at least you and I can support each other.'

'Perhaps you needed Snorri too.'

'Perhaps. But Thorvald's being a fool. He needs to see the world. Next year he'll go, one way or another. You'll still have the others.'

'Not for ever.'

The sun sank behind the hill, and they were sitting in blue dusk. Stars showed faintly in the bare sky.

'You know Einar's girl? Astrid?' asked Gunnhild.

'I've met her.'

'What did you think of her?'

'A little waif. But Gudrun says they treat her well.'

'Meaning Einar hasn't seduced her? I know that. She came to me.'

'What for?'

'She wants to get to Papey Stora, in Hjaltland. Her father had a friend there. She thinks he would help her, if she could only get a message to him.'

'Why does she need help?'

'To get away from here.'

'Why should she want to do that?'

'Ingebjorg, you of all people. How can you ask?'

'If she's lost all she had, she's probably safer here than anywhere.'

'That's probably true,' said Gunnhild.

'It's what Einar thought. He wouldn't take her.'

'Is that why? Astrid said something quite different.'

'What did she say?'

'That Einar told her she was sent here by fate, and he could not be the man to alter it. She said he frightened her. She thought he meant her to stay for ever. "But I don't know why," she said. "What could he want me for?"'

'At least he hasn't made it obvious.'

'Oh no, you're wrong. He doesn't want that. He regards her as a child. But think, he has no legitimate child of his own, and he found her out of the sea. He sees it as a miracle.'

'Does he indeed? Well, it's not what he told me.'

'He talked to you about it?'

'He said he knew she wanted to go, but he couldn't in all conscience send a child like that into the unknown. He said he knew of this man, Amundi Palsson. Apparently he's one of the richest and most ruthless landowners in Hjaltland. Einar said he wouldn't trust a young girl to him unless he swore to do right by her, and he doubted very much if Amundi would be willing to declare himself Astrid's legal guardian.'

'I see. Then why did he tell her a different story?'

'How should I know? I don't know what men think about.'

Chapter 18

Ingrid was plucking an eider duck. She collected the down into a bucket, tearing the soft layer off like wool, against the way it grew. When the bird was stripped she put it ready for the pot. Next to it lay half a dozen puffins, ready plucked and drawn, their striped beaks gleaming.

She wiped her hands on her apron. She had been sitting long enough not to notice the fishy smell. Small curling feathers had escaped and caught in her hair, where they clung like petals. She dumped the rejected feathers in the bucket with the guts, crossed the yard with it, and tipped her bucket over the yard wall on to the midden. Hens, foraging above the rigs, responded in a squawking flutter.

She leaned on the wall. A breeze lifted her hair, and out at sea she saw the same wind fill the fullspread sail of the Leogh boat. Ingrid could recognise every boat on the island. She'd never wondered how until Astrid had asked her. The question had confused her; she didn't know how she knew. Today Astrid had gone to the peats with Gudrun and the others. Ingrid missed her; it was surprising how quickly she had got used to having a stranger around. If she had been warned of it beforehand, she would have hated the idea. Ingrid watched the boat come about, and frowned.

I wish I could leave home, she thought, for the first time in her life. Gudrun is herself, at Byrstada. Astrid is herself. She's lucky. That's a wicked thing to say. She's lost everything. Ingrid crossed her fingers. But I want something to happen to me. I hope that's not wicked. She looked up at the sky as if expecting a vortex of storm clouds among the limpid blue. The sun was hot on her flushed cheeks. Please, thought Ingrid, let it be my turn. Let something happen to me. It didn't seem a very Christian prayer, so she kept her fingers crossed.

She picked up the bucket off the wall and collected her birds. She dumped them in her apron, and held it together with one hand, while she collected her knife and bucket.

Suet, she thought, crossing the yard. Stuff the puffins with suet, and roast them on the spit. The dunter can go in the pot, or there won't be any stock. There should be enough suet to stuff six puffins. Ingrid came round the corner.

There was a stranger there.

A man. A tall young man with curly hair.

Ingrid gave a small scream and dropped the birds.

'Good afternoon,' he said. 'Is this the house of Einar Thorvalds-son?'

Not a raid then. No danger. Ingrid's hands had gone to her face. She let them drop, leaving an oily smear across one cheek. She had never seen him before in her life.

'I hope I didn't startle you.'

He spoke with almost no accent. Astrid's accent was so strong it was sometimes incomprehensible. His hair was very thick, even more curly than her cousin Olaf's, and much fairer. He was thin, like a boy still growing, but as tall as her father. He had no sword.

'Arne Helgisson,' he said. 'Is this the house of Einar Thorvalds-son?'

'How did you get here?'

'I came with Einar.'

'With Einar?' She began to understand. 'You mean he's back already? Were you at the Thing then? Where is he?'

'We beached the boat just now,' he told her, without taking his eyes off her. 'We had an excellent voyage, with a good wind all the way. That's why he's back early. He's seeing to the boat. He told me to go on ahead, and tell his brother Bjarni we were back. Am I at the right house?'

So he was meant to be here; Ingrid's thumping heart settled back to normal. He was young. She had thought of the men at the Thing as old, like Einar. Some of Dagfinn's crew were young, but they were landless men. She had forgotten this man's name already. She looked down and saw dead birds all round her feet. Her apron was filthy, and she must smell of fish.

'This is Einar's house. I'm Ingrid Bjarnadottir. You are welcome to our house.'

'Thank you.'

She bent to pick up the birds. The puffins looked pale and naked on the brigstones. Ingrid kept her eyes lowered.

Two brown hands reached into her line of vision, and helped her collect the puffins. The birds' heads sagged on broken necks as he dropped them into her apron. 'Thank you.' Ingrid stood up. 'It's just that I wasn't expecting anyone. I didn't know the boat was back.'

'You can't have many strangers here.'

'That's not true.' It seemed like an aspersion on the island. 'We have the crew in winter, and last year there was Astrid. Please come in.'

He followed her into the house, where Ingrid emptied the birds on to the table. 'Are you hungry?' she asked.

She gave him oatcakes and cheese, and a mug of ale. He sat and watched her as he ate. Ingrid in her turn observed him covertly, while she washed the birds in a bucket of clean water, then knelt by the hearth, pulling the peats apart so they blazed up. She began to lay fresh fuel over them. Her hands were shaking. It was extraordinary to have a strange young man in her own house, watching her go about her work. She longed to ask him questions, but she didn't want to seem curious.

'Where are you from?' she managed to say at last.

'From Papey Stora, in Hjaltland. But I was at the Thing this year. That's how I met Einar. He must be your uncle, then?'

'Yes.' She looked up at him. He was friendly, and well-spoken, but not exactly good-looking. He had round cheeks and a freckled nose, and the beginnings of a beard. Perhaps he was older than Thorvald, who had no hair on his face as far as she had noticed. 'You hadn't met my uncle before then?'

'No. I never went to the Thing before. But my father knew Eirik Thorvaldsson. They were at sea together once, and were sworn to friendship, so Einar said I should come back with him to meet Eirik's sons. He said it was a shame to lose touch with a friend, who might give support if ever one should need it.'

'So you've come to find Thorvald and Olaf?'

'I'm not looking for support, you understand,' he said hurriedly, as if she might suspect his motives. 'But Einar thought it a good idea. And to see another island – it was a chance, you see. In the end my father agreed, and so I came. I have to be back before the hay harvest, so it's not for long.'

'No,' she agreed. He must be about her own age. Sixteen, seventeen, maybe. If his father had been sworn to friendship with Eirik, it would be safe to assume he was a man of substance. Ingrid had only been eight years old when Eirik was lost, but the whole island had known of his ambition.

'Wait a minute. I have to fetch the suet.'

It only took a moment to get it from the dairy shelf in the byre. Arne was presumably too young to be married. He might be betrothed.

'You're not related to us, then?' she asked, dividing the suet.

'No. Your uncle and my father were sworn to brotherhood, but not by blood. Had Einar been kin, my father would have seen more point in my coming.'

'Why?'

'We're a large family,' he said at last. 'It's too many to divide the farm among, and my sisters must have portions. I have to go abroad. But there's land hunger everywhere, and no one would take a man on outside their own kin.'

'I know. So will you go to sea?'

'If I have to, I suppose. But a man must have land behind him, and there's little to be had these days.'

If he had no land he couldn't be betrothed already, and he wasn't a relation. Ingrid thoughtfully laid the puffins in a row. There was enough suet for dumplings in the stew as well as stuffing. With a guest, the meal today would need to be in the nature of a feast. It was a pity the kale wasn't ready for harvesting. She didn't dare take up some thinnings, for fear Bjarni would accuse her of improvidence. It would just have to be dumplings, and thyme to flavour the duck.

'This is a good farm,' she remarked. 'Eirik's sons are the heirs, and me and my sister. That's all. Would you like some more ale?'

He held out his mug, and she poured ale from the jug, noticing his hands again. They were thin and brown, roughened with work and salt water, but still delicate compared to the men of her family. His eyes were a greenish hazel, rather like Astrid's. The hay harvest would be in about three weeks, assuming the weather played no tricks. By now the whole island would know he was here, so they could expect visitors at Shirva.

'And what brought you to visit us?' asked Bjarni, gnawing the leg bone of the duck.

Arne wiped his plate with barley bread before he answered. 'It was a chance to see another island.'

'And how does this compare to Papey Stora?'

It would not be tactful to say that this island was small, the soil poor and the anchorages disastrous, with no beaches suitable for boats. 'Our island has red rock,' said Arne at last. 'The farmlands are bigger, and we have good beaches.' He searched for a complimentary comparison, and found none. 'The fishing here must be good.'

'Exposed,' said Bjarni. 'You need to know this sea.'

'Our coast is very treacherous.'

'I've heard about that,' said Bjarni. He made it sound ambiguous, as if perhaps the men of Papey were not to be trusted. Arne looked uncomfortable.

'So you were at the Thing with your father?'

'It was the first time,' said Arne.

'Did you find it instructive?'

'They talk a lot.' Arne helped himself to another dumpling. 'Lawsuits. After the first day it's not so interesting.'

Bjarni smiled at him, and suddenly ceased to be intimidating. 'What would you rather be doing?'

Arne looked round the table. Everyone was chewing their bones, and no one seemed to be listening. He felt less shy now, in spite of being quite alone among strangers. 'The trouble is,' he said quietly to Bjarni, 'I don't know. I just like fishing, and making things, working the land. My father wants me to have more ambition. I have to do something, anyway.'

Bjarni picked up a puffin carcass, and tore it in half. He handed one piece to Arne.

'So you have to seek your own fortune?' he asked, as he pulled the bones apart.

'I know I'm useful,' said Arne. 'I've been doing a man's work since my brothers went away. My father knows that. But he talked to me before we left. "Arne," he said. "There's ten of you. Six younger than you to feed and clothe and provide with a living. The others can help me run the farm quite easily now. You're strong and able; you should find it easy enough to get work." That's what he said. I suppose I should have been expecting it. "It's not that I love you any the less," father said. "In fact, the opposite. But there just isn't enough here to go round. You'll find it easier to seek a living than your young brothers. And I must keep dowries for your sisters." '

'So what did you say to that?'

'I just said I wished he'd told me sooner. I'm nearly eighteen, with no trade at all but farmer. I don't want to be another man's labourer. It's a bit late now to learn anything else.'

'That's a fair point,' said Bjarni.

'So then we came away to the Thing. There's land in Hjaltland, but it's all taken. My father said it would be a good idea to talk to people. There are lords at the Thing with plenty of land. But no one wanted to talk to me.'

'Except my brother, it seems.'

'It was my father who fell in with him, but father didn't want me to come here. "Fridarey," he said. "There's nothing there." ' Arne suddenly realised what he had said, and blushed. 'That is to say . . . I didn't mean that. This is a very good island. But not large.'

A jug of ale was passed along the table, and Bjarni signalled to Arne to hold out his mug. 'No, not large. So why did you come?'

'It was something to do,' Arne said. 'I did want to see another island. And my father did say he'd like me to find Eirik's sons. It's good to have friends among the islands.'

'Yes, indeed, Eirik's sons,' said Bjarni. 'My brother will send for Thorvald and Olaf to meet you tomorrow.'

'I thought they'd be living here.'

'No, they don't live here.' Bjarni leaned back against the wall, and looked at Arne over his mug of ale. 'Tell me about your farm at home. How many head of cattle do you have?'

Chapter 19

'So you'll support me?' asked Ingrid, four days later.

No one on the island had ever shown real need for Astrid before. She shifted the basket of food on her back, and skipped from foot to foot. She wanted to run with the wind behind her, but Ingrid walked steadily beside her, not wanting to catch the others up. They had almost reached the hill dyke.

'I'll support you,' said Astrid joyfully, smiling at her.

'It's not going to be easy.'

'I'm glad you want my help.'

'Astrid, you look happy.'

Astrid stopped short. The others, Gudrun, Ragna and Thorhalla, and the women from Leogh who felt like outsiders in their small group, were over the stile. Astrid stared at the hill dyke in front of her, across rigs of young barley, surrounded by meadow grass. 'Yes,' she said slowly. 'I suppose I am happy.'

Today, she thought. Not yesterday. Not through all the months behind. Not through the long winter and the endless dark, the twilight in the middle of the day. But today it was summer, sharp and bright. They were to be away from home all day, raising peats. Ingrid wanted her support. The cold months were over.

Astrid climbed the stile, and jumped. Peewits tumbled in the wind. The waterlogged track gleamed in the sun. The little boy from Leogh splashed in every puddle, while the women walked in a huddle, drab in their undyed shawls, some with straw baskets on their backs. Only the boy seemed to have noticed it was summer.

'So what are you going to do?' Astrid circled Ingrid as she spoke to her, skipping so that the basket jigged on her back.

'I'm sure he likes me,' said Ingrid.

'It's obvious he does.'

'How do you know?' asked Ingrid eagerly. 'How can you tell?'

'It's the way he looks at you like a cow waiting to be milked. With big eyes. Oh, he likes you. I don't know why you should be surprised about that.'

'Do you realise, I have never in my life before met a man the same age as me, whom I had not known all my life?'

'That's not true. What about the crew? They look at you too, I've noticed.'

Even this did not divert Ingrid. The crew no longer held the slightest interest for her. 'Never mind that,' she said impatiently. 'Arne is different.'

'You could marry him, you mean?'

'I want to marry somebody.'

'Of course,' said Astrid. 'I don't see why you shouldn't. But if not, you can always find someone else.'

'Find someone else? Who? Where? Don't you see, a chance like this may never come again? There's never enough men on an island. And Arne arriving now, it's like a fate, isn't it? But he's going after the hay harvest. I don't have very long.'

'Then you'll have to do something quickly.'

'But what? My father mustn't know.'

'Why mustn't Bjarni know? He likes Arne. What's more,' Astrid had a sudden insight, 'He might be thinking just what you're thinking. He must want you to be married. After all, he's your father.'

'I can't tell him,' said Ingrid. 'And that's that.'

Astrid shrugged. The wind was beginning to irritate her. It blew her hair forward round her face, and her skirt flapped against her legs. The little boy had abandoned the puddles, and was running ahead up the highest hill, the wind helping him on his way.

'Don't you think about it?' said Ingrid. 'Being married, I mean. After all, you belong here now. There are several people you could marry.'

The wind tugged at the basket on Astrid's back, trying to knock her sideways. Married. Not married. Land. No land. A man. No man. She kicked a stone off the track into the heather.

'I know Einar's thought of it,' pursued Ingrid. 'When you turned fourteen he said, "She's of age now, we should be thinking of the future." My father said, "Time enough, we'll see them all settled yet." He's wrong though. There isn't time. I'm sixteen now. Astrid!' Ingrid seized her by the arm to make her keep still. 'Don't you see what happens? Here I am: you're right, men do look at me. But what use is that, if no one suitable ever sees me?' She was almost crying. 'It just seems such a waste.'

Astrid wasn't listening. So they had talked about that, had they, without even telling her? Well, they were right, she was of age, and no one was going to order her life without even asking her. She pushed Ingrid's hand off, and began to run.

She passed the group of women, who trudged on, slow and incurious as a herd of cattle. She hated them. The track went steeply up, but still she ran. Her hair was coming unplaited, blowing in her eyes. Round the Vord now, sea in front of her, framed by the cliff edge; her feet thudded on the turf. She was sick of them all. Her breath came hard. Wind tore over the cliffs. There were ripples blowing over the peat pools. The land swept up and down like a wave, demanding that she follow. She saw the boy, slithering down, sometimes on his feet, sometimes on his bottom. She slid, her skirt rucked up round her knees, and passed the little boy just above the peat cuttings, where she flopped down on her back, panting.

Walls of cast peats stretched across the dale. The opened banks lay in lines across the grass, changing the level of the ground in sharp angles. At the bottom of the banks water had collected in brown pools. Astrid rolled over on to her front, and let the wind cool her hot face. Curlews called across the moor.

She heard a thump, and Ragna landed beside her, panting.

'You can run,' she said, gasping. 'You're as fast as Olaf, I shouldn't wonder. Pity you're a girl, or you could have challenged him to a race. Bet you'd win.'

'So Olaf's a good runner?' said Astrid.

'Best on the island.'

'Better than Thorvald?'

Ragna spat, and looked scornful.

'I see,' said Astrid.

'I hate this,' went on Ragna, who was getting her breath back. 'Bent double all day, peat getting in my eyes, sitting on a soggy hill with a load of women who do nothing but gossip about sex and babies. And no men.'

'There's that little boy from Leogh.'

'Kari? Yes. And Hilda brought the other one on her back.'

'I saw.'

'It dribbles down her neck. My sister likes babies,' said Ragna bitterly. 'Hilda says it only wakes twice a night now.'

'Einar gave me a lamb to rear. It had to be fed in the night too.'

'Don't tell me.'

There were voices coming down the wind. 'Here we go,' muttered Ragna.

'Since you've come all this way,' said Gudrun, 'perhaps you'd like to raise a peat or two?'

Ragna rolled over. 'Not much.'

'Get up. You look quite abandoned.'

'Pity there's no one to appreciate it,' said Ragna.

Raising peats was not as bad as Ragna had said. Astrid managed to tie her hair back again, and if she took care to face into the wind it didn't get in the way, except that then the wind blew bits of peat into her eyes. Tormentil flowers were scattered across the grass like sparks of flame. She built up the peats among them, one flat, two against it, two at each end, one over the top. She stood up to stretch her back. The little boy was climbing up an old bank and slithering down it. The baby, wrapped in a shawl close by, began to cry. Its mother straightened her back slowly, and went over to it. Astrid bent to her work.

'Don't you want any morning meal?'

Astrid looked up. The sun was high to the south. 'Yes please.'

They huddled under an old bank, the wind impotent above their heads. Ingrid unwrapped a cloth, and handed Astrid a bannock with curds.

'Of course we can manage,' Ragna was saying. 'Even I can't raise the peats wrong.'

'The question is,' said Gudrun, 'whether you're likely to raise them at all.'

'What do you think I've been doing for the last four hours?'

'Scheming,' said Gudrun. 'I'll go home.'

'Do you want me to come with you?' asked Ingrid. 'Are you sure you'll be all right?'

'No. I expect the trows will take me. That might be fun.'

'Gudrun!' gasped Ingrid, and even Ragna crossed her fingers.

Gudrun looked white and haggard. She turned away abruptly, and began to climb the hill.

Astrid sat down next to Ingrid. 'What's the matter with her?'

'Oh, Astrid.' Ingrid sighed. 'She didn't want me to tell anyone, but you're the only woman who's come near her who hasn't guessed. She's pregnant.'

'That's my brother for you,' remarked Ragna. 'He promised her he wouldn't, and then he did. Well, what can you do? We're a passionate family.'

'Shut up,' said Ingrid. 'I shouldn't have mentioned it.'

'We don't need you to tell us,' said Ragna. 'Anyone with half their senses could see what the matter was a mile off.'

'She didn't,' said Ingrid, jerking her head towards Astrid.

'Her? She should have been a boy anyway. Did you see her run?'

'I don't want to talk,' said Ingrid.

'That's all right,' said Ragna obligingly. 'We know why. Who's looking after young Arne today then? Do you think he'll be all right without you?'

The little boy came and sat down beside Astrid. 'You came off a ship,' he said.

'Yes.'

'But the ship was broken at Hoini.'

'Yes.'

'That was a silly place to bring a ship.'

'It was an accident. The ship was never meant to come here at all.'

'They must have steered her wrong.' A moment later he said, 'I've got a sword. My granddad made it. I found the wood though, at Hjukni geo.'

Her throat felt tight. 'This winter?'

'Yes. I shall go on a ship one day.'

'What's your name?'

'Keri.'

Before they went back to work, Astrid climbed on to the top of the bank and looked out to sea, remembering something Ragna had told her. Ragna herself appeared at her side. 'Lost something?'

'In a way. Do you remember telling me you could see Hjaltland from here?'

Ragna glanced back at the others. 'I'll show you,' she said, and ran downhill, crouched low so that the others, in the shelter of the bank, couldn't see her go. Astrid followed. As soon as they were out of sight Ragna slowed down. She led Astrid the short distance to the cliffs at the very north of the island. The stacks were like sharp triangular teeth breaking out of the foam. The cliffs were almost vertical; grass slopes interspersed with overhanging slabs of greyish pink rock.

Ragna led her across a narrow causeway above a sheer rock wall. Astrid took one look at the white sea below, and followed. Sea surrounded them on three sides. The pinnacle of a skerry was visible below; it looked sharp enough to impale a body. A beach of grey and pink boulders lay in the shadow of the cliff, lined with basking seals. There was a thread of a path across the face of the opposite cliff, and someone had dragged a whitened tree trunk up above the tideline. Two skerries lay offshore, each tailed by lines of foam. Beyond them lay another blank wall of cliff.

'What are you looking for? I thought you wanted to see Hjaltland.'

'Can we see it?'

'You tell me.'

Astrid scanned the horizon. To the east she saw the same island that was sometimes visible from Shirva. 'That's not Hjaltland, surely?'

'No, that's Fugley. Look north.'

There was a faint rounded shape in the distance. 'Is that land?'

'That's the Fitfugla Head. You can't see the Svinborg Head today. But yes, that's Hjaltland.'

Astrid stared at it. It was just a dim grey shape that might have been a cloud, but at least it was there. She was aware of a weird wordless singing from the rocks, like a call out of another world. 'What's that noise?'

Ragna listened. 'It's just seals.' She looked mischievous. 'So they say. But I told you before, there's more things out here than I'd dare swear to.'

Astrid crossed herself covertly. Swimming birds, auks and gulls, drifted along the lines of foam. A line of white extended from the outermost stack like a warning, daring anything human to approach the shore.

'You should see it in winter. It's dangerous then. Dagfinn's been blown right off his feet out here. He was lucky not to go over the edge.'

Astrid drew back. 'Hadn't we better go?'

When she and Ragna went back to work, the little boy was playing close by. 'Who is Kari?' asked Astrid.

'What? Kari Solmundarsson?'

'No, I'm not talking about tales from Island. I mean that little boy.'

'Kari Njal's son-in-law was here, you know. He stayed a whole winter at Byrstada with David, my ancestor. David went to the Orkneyjar with him, when the Burners were at the Earl's hall. Kari killed Gunnar Lambason, and the Earl would have killed Kari, only he had been his retainer, and not one of the Orkneyjar men would lay hands on him. So they let him go, and he came back here to Fridarey that winter. The name Kari has been common here ever since.'

The boy Kari was breathing hard as he struggled up the slippery peat, then slid down fast. His clothes were streaked with wet peat, and his feet were stained brown from the pools. He had reddish brown curls and a straight freckled nose.

'I know what you're thinking. He's another.'

'Another what?'

'Come on, you should know one of Einar's by now when you see one. The baby isn't, though. Einar arranged a marriage for Hilda after Kari was born. He had to, her father took him to the Thing about it. I think he still sees her though.'

'But he's old!'

'And Hilda isn't? It's usually like that, isn't it? What do you expect?'

Astrid was silent. Thorhalla appeared at her elbow.

'The others are getting ready to go.'

'Thank God,' said Ragna. 'Tell Gudrun I was the last to leave, will you?'

Thorhalla sniffed. Astrid stood up and looked over the slopes. The neat brown walls had gone, and in their place rows of little

mounds were spread across the grass. There were only two walls of
cast peats left, just beyond the Shirva banks.

'Aren't they ours?' asked Astrid, pointing.

'Setr,' said Ragna. 'Ingebjorg and Gunnhild usually come with
the rest of us, but if one doesn't, the other doesn't either. Thorvald
must have cast those. See how crooked they are.'

'They're not crooked.'

'Aren't they? Well, maybe it was Olaf.'

Astrid fetched her basket, and swung it on to her back. Her arms
hurt. There was a slight movement beside her, then a small hand
slid into hers. She was flattered and held Kari's hand carefully, as
if it were an egg that might be easily broken. He was clutching a
large round stone against his chest with his other hand, and he
looked sunburned and sleepy. The wind had dropped. A lark broke
into song above them, and she screwed up her eyes to see it against
the sky.

Chapter 20

'Those are the trowie mounds,' said Olaf. 'If you hear music from there you should beware. It can enchant you away, and when you come back hundreds of years have gone by, and your own time is lost to you for ever.'

Arne looked down at the green knolls scattered across the marshy valley. Pools of water spread over the valley floor and the grass was very green. There were mounds like that on his own island, more dwellings of the older races than anything Fridarey could boast of. They couldn't frighten him this way.

'It sounds quiet enough to me.'

'You mean you can't hear it?'

Eirik's sons made Arne uneasy. It was not that they had been uncivil, but merely that they continually reminded him that this was not his island. He was fairly sure that this expedition had been Thorvald's own idea, not Einar's suggestion. Possibly Eirik's sons had never before entertained anyone from another island.

Thorvald and Olaf were already halfway up the next hill. Like Arne, they carried straw baskets on their backs. Thorvald wielded a long bird snare as if it were a lance, and Olaf had a coil of rope over his shoulder. Arne ran after them, above a wild coast of cliffs and stacks. The cliffs here were grey, not red. The heather was dry and crackled under his feet, and the ground was uneven and treacherous. Arne tripped, and fell.

His wrist hurt. He wiped a smear of blood from a scratch on his face. On his own island, he could have kept up with Thorvald, but he couldn't have outrun Olaf anywhere. Arne walked slowly on.

He saw them sitting side by side on the next hill, waiting for him. Arne refused to hurry. He would not have treated a stranger this way. He thought about his brothers, whom he missed much more than he expected. The elder ones had teased him when they were at home, but they had taught him how to fish, and snare birds, and taken care of him when he was small. Leaving his family might be harder than he thought.

Ingrid Bjarnadottir. Arne began to climb faster. Unless he had read the signs completely wrong, she liked him. At meals he would catch her eyes across the table. She didn't say much, but she was close to him more often than she had to be. Yesterday her hand had brushed his twice, and Arne had felt an unexpected rush of desire. He wondered if she felt the same. He was nearly at the top of the hill, and the two brothers were just above him. Suddenly he didn't mind their hostility. Ingrid Bjarnadottir. He wondered if she guessed how ignorant he was.

'Are you ready to go on?' asked Thorvald, as he reached them. 'Yes.'

Olaf smiled at him, and Arne, surprised, smiled tentatively back. Perhaps they didn't dislike him. He followed them, rolling up his shirtsleeves as he went. The sun was getting higher. The sky was blue as blackbird eggs, and there were curlews calling across the hill. They crossed a burn and climbed yet another heather slope.

At the top, Thorvald spoke to him. 'Gullvatn,' he said.

There was a lochan in a hollow. The grass round it was wet, and endless drops of water caught the sun. A small cloud drifted across its surface. A rain goose swam low in the water, and the sky vanished in a mass of yellow ripples. The cloud left the loch and passed over green slopes as a small shadow.

Arne realised Thorvald wanted him to like this place. That was why he had brought him here.

Arne still felt warm inside from thinking of Bjarni's fairhaired daughter. He smiled, and looked round. 'There's been a lot of rain,' he said.

'Yes,' said Thorvald. 'Come on.'

'Watch out,' said Olaf presently. 'There's a bit of a hole just here.'

At the same time Thorvald grabbed Arne's sleeve, and halted him. 'Look.'

The ground fell away in a great gulf at his feet. It was like a cauldron, with the sea boiling within a circle of cliffs. A little light filtered through from far below, where the sea entrance must be. The ground where they stood was damp and crumbly.

'Can you reach it from the sea?'

'When it's calm enough.'

'You've been down there in a boat?'

'Of course.'

'We have tunnels too,' Arne told him. 'Some you can row into. Some are only just wide enough, so you have to make speed, then ship your oars to get through. There's one where my brother and I pushed our way right through against the rock at low tide.'

'If it's weather,' said Thorvald, 'we might show you something like that.'

'There are tunnels that go right under Papey Stora, more than two miles. My father's been through one of those.'

'There's one like that under the house you're staying in now,' said Thorvald.

'Yes,' said Olaf. 'On bad nights you can hear the waves breaking underneath you at Shirva. Any night now it'll fall through, just like this hole here.'

'Tonight, perhaps,' said Thorvald. 'Don't forget. It would be a shame to miss it.'

'In that case maybe I'd better stay,' said Arne lightly.

Thorvald and Olaf regarded him with eyes of an identical blue. He couldn't tell what they were thinking.

When they reached the cliffs along the north coast, they saw guillemots feeding offshore, along a line of white that marked the tide rip. Thorvald led them to a place where the island dwindled to a thin headland high above the sea. In front of it the ground was broken and slippery where the sea was gradually wearing it into a separate stack.

'The guillemots are down there.'

'I see them.'

There were two wooden stakes in the ground above a cliff face in dark shadow. Arne heard the distant thud of waves. The smell of birds wafted up to him, fishy and pungent. He could see tightly packed rows of black and white, the lowest just out of reach of the tide. He had never climbed an unknown rock like this, although long before the day when his father had announced that he too was allowed to go birding, he had scaled cliffs with his brothers. His uncle had been killed on the cliffs when he was twelve, but Arne wasn't worried. He knew he was good, and that he was being challenged by these strangers, and would be judged. He gauged the unfamiliar rock spangled with clumps of sea campion, searching for cracks and gullies that would make a way down, and picked out a long fissure, less than six inches wide, where mayweed grew in sheltered cracks.

Thorvald wound the rope round the stakes, so it could be pulled up short at once if it had to bear a man's weight. 'Olaf will mind the rope,' he said. 'Arne, if you stand the other side you can watch me, see the way down. I'll signal when I'm coming up.'

Thorvald strapped the basket round his waist, tied the rope over his belt, and took the snare on its long pole. He took the way Arne had guessed, picking his way from hold to hold across the cliff face, following the line of the crack in the rock. He held the snare away from the cliff with his left hand. Arne watched intently. He'd seen a man almost lost by hooking his snare against an outcrop.

Olaf's hands were on the rope as it uncoiled over the cliff, his head cocked as though he were listening hard. Thorvald had rounded the vertical face, and had disappeared from sight behind an outcrop. The rope stopped moving, shifted, and stopped again.

'That's it!' Olaf had felt the signal. He began to wind the rope in cautiously, never quite letting it pull tight.

'I can see him. He's coming up!'

'Any birds?'

'I can't see. He's moving as if there's a weight. Yes, it's full.'

There were scraping sounds, and presently Thorvald's head appeared. He crawled up beside them, untied his rope, and un-strapped the basket. Arne looked at the pile of black bodies, with their strongbeaked heads dangling.

'I'm hot,' said Thorvald, pushing back his hair.

Olaf was tying the rope round himself. He strapped the other basket round his waist. 'I'm ready.'

'There's no hurry. I told them to wait for you.'

'Shall I take the rope this time?'

'No.' Arne went back to his place.

Olaf was over the edge in a moment, climbing rapidly across the crag, straight on to the overhang. Arne bit his lip and clenched his fists apprehensively.

'Slower, you bloody idiot,' roared out Thorvald, from the rope.

Olaf made an obscene gesture and began to descend more gently. He didn't go as far round the overhang as Thorvald had done, so Arne could see him until he was almost above the waves. He was standing on a ledge, if you could call it a ledge, parallel to the massed guillemots. Arne saw the pole reach out, thin as a thread against the white of the waves below. Thorvald stood braced, holding the slack of the rope.

Olaf came up more slowly. The basket was full: Arne could see black feathers gleaming. Olaf reached the edge, then he was on the slope, then on the grass beside them, the basket tumbled over, black bodies gleaming on the turf.

'What the hell were you doing, going down so fast?' Thorvald was really angry. Arne would never have guessed it, all the time Olaf had been on the cliff. 'What were you thinking of?'

'Sorry,' said Olaf. 'Here I am, anyway.'

Arne looked down at some shags skimming the water below. Thorvald had stopped ranting. They were both regarding him steadily.

'My turn?' asked Arne.

Thorvald nodded, and handed him the rope and snare.

Arne wiped his hands on his trousers, knotted the rope deliberately, and strapped his basket round his waist.

'Ready?'

'Yes.'

'I'll take the rope. Signal when you're coming up.'

Arne edged himself over the crumbling cliff edge. There were scrape marks in the soil where the others had gone the same way, then rock, solid under his feet. Handholds. Going down, remembering the holds, slowly, feeling his way. New rock. Greyer than at home, with streaks of pink. He could hear the sea. There should be a ledge below his feet, the way Thorvald had gone.

Arne wedged himself into the end of the ledge, and pressed his body against the rock. He was facing inwards, and looking down. The water was white below. He crept along the crack, like a fly across a wall. The rope gave as he moved further down.

Then the birds were on the ledges beside him. They were agitated, but they didn't fly away. Guillemots stayed put. Arne wedged himself tight, and when he was quite sure of his balance shifted the pole to his right hand. Then he reached out.

He looped a bird, pulled tight, strangled it. He blinked away the sweat running into his eyes, brought the pole back, unhooked his bird, and edged it into the basket with his other hand. Then he reached out again. Another. He was absorbed now in his hunting. There was nothing in the world but the cliff and the guillemots, and his own skill. Reach out, drop the noose, hook the bird, strangle it, pull back, loose the knot, body into the basket. Balance, aim and drop. The pole had become part of himself. The basket was nearly full. He didn't want to stop. One more. Two more. They were as thick on the ledge as when he started. He edged his way along, feeling with his feet. The overhang was lower, pushing him out from the cliff face. Slowly he ducked under it. It was only just possible to balance. A little further along he could stand straighter, and wield the snare. He caught a bird, brought the snare back. One more, two more. The basket was full to overflowing, the strap biting into his middle.

Unable to turn because of the basket, he inched back blind. The overhang was harder this way. Flat against the rock like part of the cliff itself, very slowly he ducked and passed the curve. Then he could turn his head. He rested his cheek against rock, and cautiously pulled at the rope. A gentle tug replied.

Arne began to climb slowly. The birds were a dead weight dragging at him. Maybe Thorvald and Olaf could see him now. Grey rock here, not red. For a short time it had been like his own island. Himself and the rock.

The sun was in his eyes, crumbled soil under his hands. Arne scrambled, and the rope went taut. He came on to level ground on hands and knees, the basket twisting round him.

He sat up and pushed back his hair. His face was wet with sweat.

'That's not bad. That's more than either of us!'

'They must be good climbers on your island.'

They respected him now. The sun was hot. Arne leaned back, resting on his elbows, took a skin of water from Olaf, and drank.

They were the cousins of Ingrid Bjarnadottir. Kin. That was how a man found kin. Thorvald was idly splicing the frayed rope end.

Olaf stared out to sea, his eyes as blue as the sky behind him. Ingrid had eyes that colour too.

'You have good cliffs,' said Arne. 'I'm glad I came.'

'We'll do more hunting before you go.'

That must be an invitation. 'You'll keep my birds, anyway.'

'No, take them back to Shirva.' Arne saw Thorvald catch his brother's eye. 'Give them to Ingrid, with her cousins' good wishes.'

'That's right,' said Olaf giggling. 'And any other messages you like.'

Gunnhild sat crosslegged, with a wooden tray across the hearthstones in front of her. Rain beat against the roof, and the wind whistled under the door. The board was pulled across the chimney hole, so it was as dark as if it were autumn, in spite of being nearly midsummer.

She might as well have been alone. She had withdrawn into a realm of her own, one which had grown upon her with the years. An evening with these two men would once have been fraught with excitement. Now, she was thinking about Gudrun. Yesterday, Gudrun had come to her. Today, Gunnhild had visited nearly every house on the island on her behalf.

Salt at one end of the table, an open knife, blade turned inward, at the other. Holy water from the shrine of St Magnus at Byrgisey. Earth in the floor beneath her, fire in the hearth. Gunnhild set out small contributions wrapped in cloth: bere meal, eggs, a skin of milk and some precious honey. Nine offerings from nine households. Everywhere she had visited, a woman of the house had given something. She began to mix her ingredients. There were words to be said, but not out loud, with the two men across the hearth. She whispered them, and they were hidden in the noise of wind and rain.

'Check!'

The voice startled her.

'Check,' said Snorri again.

She stirred her mixture until it was smooth, and put the bowl aside. Tansy to keep a baby safe in the womb, to stop bleeding and soothe anxiety. Gunnhild took the knife and began to chop the herb.

'Checkmate,' said Snorri.

She dropped her herbs into the mixture, and invoked the blessings of the three wise women, Sunniva, Mary, Bride. May Gudrun Bjarnadottir bear a live child at last. Free her from this curse, I beseech you. From this cruel fate, wise ones, deliver her. Amen.

'I didn't see that knight,' said Bjarni. 'That was clever.'

'I thought you'd notice.'

'Old age. I was after that queen.'

'I know.'

'Canny,' said Bjarni. 'Too canny. You'll come to a bad end.'

'I already have.'

Gunnhild greased a cooking pot. They would ask for ale in a moment. She had finished now, anyway.

'Gunnhild?' said Snorri, peering into the shadow where she sat. 'Is there ale?'

He'd be surprised if she said no, thought Gunnhild, and got stiffly to her feet. She took mugs from a basket on the wall, and stooped under the hangings, to where the ale barrel was set at the cool end of the room, behind the piglets' stall.

When she came back, they were re-arranging the chessmen, discussing the point when Bjarni had failed to take Snorri's queen. When she held out Bjarni's ale, he looked up; she held his gaze; Snorri was still bent over the chessboard. When Bjarni took the mug, his hand brushed her fingers. She touched his wrist, and turned away.

He still never failed to move her. Now, when she looked back on the days when Snorri first came home, she was astonished at the risks they had taken. She had all but made love to Bjarni under her husband's very eyes, and yet the friendship between the two men had never cooled, and Snorri had never given any sign that he had noticed. Sometimes she thought that it was his deliberate choice to remain ignorant.

'You had that pawn in the way,' said Snorri. 'And you never brought up your rook.'

The first winter she was married, Bjarni Thorvaldsson used to come in the evening and play chess. She would sit at her loom, with her back to them, while they played their game, and discussed it afterwards. It was always Bjarni who came to the smithy. His own house, at that time, was full of women and babies.

Gunnhild drew herself a measure of ale, and knelt by the fire to build up the peats around her baking pot.

'I must introduce you to our guest sometime,' Bjarni was saying. 'Arne Helgisson, from Papey Stora.'

'Too late, I've met him. A pleasant boy. Not ambitious, but no doubt he'll make a good man yet.'

'We don't all have to be ambitious.'

'You know what I think. You were wasted, Bjarni, on this island.'

'I was sick every time I went to sea.'

'So are the best pirates of all.'

'Not as sick as I was, or they'd have gone home. As for the boy, he'd make a farmer, but he lacks land. The old story.'

'We don't have much here,' remarked Snorri.

'He didn't come here for land. He came because his father swore oaths with Eirik, and sent Arne to seek out Eirik's sons.'

'Yes. It was Olaf who brought him to visit me.'

'With a basket of guillemots,' put in Gunnhild. 'Olaf's a generous boy.'

'He said they were from his mother,' said Snorri.

'Well, Ingebjorg's a generous woman. I liked Arne, Bjarni. Is he going to stay here?'

'He has to go home for the hay harvest. Einar will take him as far as Konungsborg when they go for the soapstone. Then he can make his own way back across Hjaltland.'

'Has it occurred to Einar . . .' said Snorri slowly, and paused.

'Yes?' prompted Bjarni.

'The Irish child. That ship was on its way to Papey Stora, where there was a man called Amundi Palsson who owed Astrid's father a favour. I know that Einar was going to speak to him about it at the Thing.'

'Amundi Palsson was not at the Thing this year. He went to Starnevegr, on account of some killings. My brother thinks him a dangerous man, and didn't want to put the child into his hands, unless we had guarantees that he would look after her properly.'

'So he doesn't want to let her go?'

'Not without an agreement. What do you think about it?' said Bjarni to Gunnhild.

'I think at least Einar should send this man a message, now he has the chance to do so. Bjarni, will you keep a secret?'

As if she needed to ask him; he had kept their secret for fifteen years without telling a soul, which was more than she had done.

'You're going to tell me that Astrid asked Arne to take a message for her to Papey Stora.'

'He told you?'

'No, but it was obvious she'd speak to him about it, when she knew where he was from. Astrid came to you for advice, did she?'

'She came to Snorri.'

'I know her city,' put in Snorri, as if that explained everything. 'She said Arne told her he wouldn't take any messages behind Einar's back. She lost her temper with him.'

Bjarni was mildly surprised. 'I've never known her do that. What did she say to him?'

'She said he'd win no favours from Bjarni by sucking up to him.'

'She's a clever girl, Astrid. She's right, he won't.'

'So Arne's to be disappointed?'

'In what way?'

Snorri glanced at Gunnhild, who said, 'Bjarni, don't pretend you don't know. You must have thought of it at once, when Einar brought him here. Everyone on the island is wondering if you're planning for Ingrid to marry him.'

'Arne? He has nothing to offer her. A man needs land, and work before he can take a wife. Arne knows that as well as I do.'

'A man often finds land and work by marrying.'

'You know how the Shirva lands are. There's nothing I can say to him.'

Snorri and Gunnhild looked at each other.

'So that's what she said.' Bjarni chuckled. 'Astrid, well, well. She will be provided for, you know. We've discussed it. Einar speaks of visiting this Amundi himself, if he doesn't come to the Thing next year.'

'I don't envy you,' said Snorri, 'with all these unmarried girls on your hands. You'll have no peace for years.'

Over the smell of peat came the smell of fresh baking. Gunnhild stooped over the fire and raked back the peats.

'Is that something for us?'

'No, but you can have bannocks. Wait a minute.'

She set the cake upside down to cool, between the salt and the knife, aware of Bjarni's eyes on her still. She should have guessed that he had the affairs of his own household in hand. She did love him. She had the memory of all those years when Snorri had been gone, when Bjarni used to come late at night, after everyone in his own household was asleep. All that time she had not had to share herself with anyone else, except when Snorri occasionally spent the winter at home. Snorri never asked how she managed without him. By now, he must be aware of what had happened during his absence. She was almost sure he didn't realise how it still was.

She had hardly seen Bjarni alone this year. There had just been that one time in early spring, when Snorri had gone to fix the iron bands round the mast step on the Sula. That had been a risk: if anyone had come to the house and found the door barred, they would have suspected.

Bjarni was watching her, even while he and Snorri talked about hay. His hair still gleamed red in lamplight. In daylight it was getting grey and thin on top. She remembered when it was thick dark red. The hair on his body was more copper coloured.

'Are there any more bannocks?'

'There are oatcakes and honey.' As she prepared more food for them, she thought about her husband too. He loved her still. Before she married Snorri, he and Bjarni had sworn oaths of loyalty to one another. They were born in the same year, and had been friends all their lives. She would always have to protect him from the truth.

The tansy cake for Gudrun had come out smooth and even. That was a good sign. Gunnhild moved round the earth into the shadow, and drew a sign in the ashes at her feet.

Sunniva guardian of women, Mary Mother of God, Bride of the islands, watch over Gudrun Bjarnadottir. Deliver her from this doom that hangs over her. Deliver her from evil. The blessings of the saints, Jesus Christ, Magnus our holy martyr, watch over our island. Freya, guardian of women, bring this child to a safe birth. Protect those whom we love. Amen.

Chapter 22

The sun was setting in the northern sky, and an
answering blaze flickered red on the top of the Vord, where the
islanders were standing round their fire. To their flame-dazzled
eyes, the land below was deep in shadow, with only the north-
facing slopes lit pale gold, each stalk of heather standing out from
its shadow.

This was midsummer, once the feast of Baldur the god of light,
now the mass of John the Baptist. It was also the feast of lovers.
Everyone had collected bunches of dried heather stalks, and that
morning the boys had gone round the household demanding as
much peat and driftwood as they could carry, and brought them up
to the hill. This year the glowing peat had been brought from the
hearth at Shirva, and Ingrid had set it in the centre of the fire,
where the heather stalks had blazed up at once. It had been a dry
year. The hay was ripening, and the corn was beginning to turn
from green to gold.

There was no sense of uneasiness this year. They followed the
usual rituals with the indifference of long habit. Bones were burned,
one from each household. Skins of ale were passed round, and
lumps of meat skewered and roasted in the ashes.

The centre of the fire grew solid red. Some years the weather was wild, some years there were fights, or flirtations, an excited rowdiness. This year there was hardly a breath of wind. They could talk in ordinary voices, sitting round the fire as if at their own hearths.

It was a good night for stories.

First of all, because it was a feast for lovers, Einar gave them the story of the king, who, after trying every other method, cured his retainer of unrequited love by agreeing to listen to him every day, talking of the one woman whom he would ever love, whom he had lost forever.

'But what about her?' said Gudrun, when Einar had finished. 'Didn't she mind being married to the wrong brother? Was she forced? She had no king to listen to her troubles, had she?'

'It's not her story,' said Bjarni. 'If she was fool enough to take the wrong brother, she doesn't deserve sympathy. It was probably all the same to her.'

'You don't know that! What choice did she have?'

'If you don't like that story, Gudrun, give us another.'

'All right, I will then.'

She gave them the story of the death of Gudrun Osvifsdottir. When she had finished they were quiet for a moment.

' "I was worst to the one I loved the most",' repeated Gunnhild. 'Does that always have to be true?'

'I think we've heard enough about love,' said Bjarni. 'Who'll give us something else?'

'It's the feast of Odin,' said Einar. 'We should have poetry.' His eyes lit upon his nephew. ' "Thorvald! Have you anything to say about love?'

'No,' muttered Thorvald.

'Then give us poetry!'

That was easy enough. Thorvald, relieved, stood up, and began to recite:

'I know that I hung
On the windy tree
Nine whole nights
Wounded with a spear,
Given to Odin,
Myself to myself;
On the tree

Of which no one knows
From what roots it came.'
The poetry seized him, as he repeated the verses they all knew
by heart. No longer shy or angry or separate, Thorvald gave them
the song of the wisdom of Odin, and the words he spoke echoed in
every mind, the same story.
'Hail to him who sang!
Hail to him who knows!
May he who has learned profit by it!
Hail to those who have listened!'
In the distance they could hear waves wash on rock. The sun
was low over the sea, dipping into the water, half sunk.
'It's going!'
The sun was red as fire, the northern sky streaked orange. Faint
lines of cloud were etched on the horizon. The sun's rim seemed
to blaze the sea away as the water swallowed it. Then it sank,
leaving a thread of gold linking the horizon to the island. The air
turned chill, the gold light drained away, leaving the sky blank, the
hills flat and cold without their shadows.
There were no more stories after that. The older people began
to go, wandering in twos and threes towards the hill dyke. Gudrun
went with them. The younger ones edged forward into the warmth.
Ingebjorg had a brief argument with Eirik, who didn't want to go
back with her. Other mothers were gathering their children. Eirik
hung back just out of reach.
'Please!'
'Oh, let him stay,' said Olaf at last. 'I'll mind him.'
'Please!' said Eirik.
'All right,' said Ingebjorg, 'but make sure you don't bother him.
It's not a feast for children.'
'I'm not a child.'
As she passed them she touched Olaf lightly on the shoulder.
'Thank you. That was kind.'
Thorvald didn't see her go. He was talking to Arne, sitting in
the space his uncles had left. Arne peeled a heather twig, and gazed
into the fire, his shoulder touching Thorvald's.
'So you see,' Thorvald was saying, 'I won't be here another
summer. I'm of age, my uncles can't stop me, and Dagfinn promised
me a place when my father died.'

Arne pulled off another piece of bark, and examined the exposed stalk. 'You and your two brothers, you're the only heirs to Shirva, besides Bjarni's daughters?'

'That's right. But it would be a poor living for us all, if no one from the family goes to sea.'

'Will your brothers go to sea?'

'Eirik might. I don't know what Olaf wants.'

Olaf wanted only one thing. Thorvald knew the one real terror that the future held for his brother. He would never betray Olaf's secrets to one who was no kin, but he gave Arne a slight hint. 'His sight's not that good,' he said, and tossed a fragment of peat into the fire.

'He seemed to see well enough when we went hunting.'

'That was different. He knows the cliff.'

Arne changed the subject. 'I'm not ambitious either. I don't want to go abroad.'

'You are abroad.'

'I'm beginning to feel quite at home here.'

'My father swore oaths of friendship to yours,' said Thorvald after a pause.

'That's why I came. My father regretted Eirik's death very much. He valued his friendship.'

'I was too young to know much about my father's friends.'

'But you don't lack kin.'

'Nor you.'

'No, but I have to seek my living.'

'And I want the chance to seek mine. We should have been in each other's places.'

'That's what alliances are for,' said Arne. 'My father has many friends. But I'm of age now; I respect him, but I have to make my choices for myself. Do you understand what I mean?'

'The choices that are made for the future,' said Thorvald, 'it's we that will have to live with them, whoever has the authority now.'

'That's what I think.'

A dark figure stood between them and the fire.

'Thorvald!' said Ragna's voice, 'Stop gossiping, and pay attention to the rest of us.'

'Why, will it be worth it?' Thorvald leaned back, his arms behind his head, squinting up at her. Arne was aware of the challenge between them. He thought of Ingrid.

Ragna took a skin flask from under her cloak. 'I challenge you first, to drink this right down to the bottom without stopping.'

'Ragna, don't.' That was Ingrid's voice. 'He's had quite enough to drink already.'

Thorvald held Ragna's gaze. She hadn't spoken to him since winter; in fact she had gone out of her way to insult him at every turn. He knew exactly why, but now Skuli Hedinsson was hundreds of miles away.

He stood up and took the skin from Ragna. The wind shifted and they were caught in the smoke. Then Thorvald raised the skin to his lips and drank. When he held the skin upside down, and only a few drops trickled out, they cheered. The others produced skins of ale and challenged each other to do the same. Someone threw a fresh bundle of heather on the fire, and a shower of sparks engulfed them all. Under cover of the smoke, Thorvald grabbed Ragna by the arm and pulled her into the shadows. 'Satisfied?'

'Don't pull me about!'

'Don't you mess me about then. You've not spoken to me since Candlemas.'

'Don't talk about that!'

'Why not? Ragna, why not?' He was laughing. 'I've been waiting to do it again ever since.'

'I don't need your kisses, Thorvald Eiriksson!'

'Not Skuli Hedinsson's either?'

He didn't know if she'd hit him or laugh at him. He got his arm round her, and walked her away from the fire.

'Where do you think you're taking me?'

'Nowhere you don't want to go.' He faced her to him. 'Be friends, Ragna! Haven't we always been?'

'Of course, before you changed it all at Candlemas.'

'Not against your will, I didn't.'

'I'm not going to marry you, Thorvald.'

He was so startled his arm dropped. 'I should think not! Whatever made you think of that?'

She grabbed him and shook him hard. 'If I hadn't known you all my life I'd hate you for ever.'

His hand was back in hers. 'Come and hate me then. Come on, just for a minute.'

Astrid watched them disappear round the hill. Suddenly she felt cold. There were only a few people at the fire now. The heather twigs had left whitehot ashes. She threw in more peats.

It wasn't her island. She was no kin of theirs. This feast had been all right to begin with, but the poem had unsettled her, almost to tears. She'd never heard Thorvald speak out loud before. Kol had made poems sound the same way; he used to recite them to her, as if she were a good enough audience, all by herself, to have nothing but the very best. Thorvald's verses had been for her too, whether he knew it or not.

Then Ragna had gone off with Thorvald, in spite of all the things she'd said about him, and Ingrid had vanished in the opposite direction. Astrid felt desolate. A breeze sent the smoke shifting straight into her face, and she moved round to where Thorvald and Arne had been sitting. There was a rustle from the hill behind her, and two figures came into the firelight.

Olaf sat down next to her. 'I want to go after the others,' said Eirik.

'Sit down and shut up. You can share my cloak if you're cold.' Olaf turned his back on Eirik and spoke to Astrid. 'Ever been to a midsummer feast before?'

'Not like this.' He was flushed, as if he had had quite a lot to drink, and he was smiling at her very warmly.

'This is nothing yet. Wait until the sun comes back.'

'How long will that be?'

He pointed north, out to sea. 'Is it growing any lighter out there?'

'No.'

'It will. An hour or two, maybe. Tell me when it does.'

She wasn't sure they'd still be sitting here in two hours' time. 'You'll see it for yourself, won't you?'

He didn't answer.

'Won't you?'

'Listen,' said Olaf, 'do you know that if you went down to the beach just now, you'd see the selkies come ashore, and shed their skins to dance in the moonlight, this one night.'

'There isn't any moon tonight.'

'Sunlight, then. This is one of the nights of the year when they come ashore, and dance until the sun comes back. Do you want to see?'

'No thank you. I'd rather stay by the fire and keep warm.'

'You might not get the chance again. It would be a perfect night for it.'

'Possibly.'

'Don't you have selkies in Irland?'

'Not in the river at Dyflin.'

'I'll tell you a story if you like.'

His shoulder was touching hers. Eirik was silent on the other side of him. 'Go on, then.'

He moved so that his left arm was behind her back, not exactly round her, but she was aware of its pressure. This was no public story-telling. It was just for her, almost whispered in her ear. She had to lean forward to catch the words. She couldn't tell if he were serious or not. Olaf was staring into the fire, his profile clearly lit. She had thought of him as just a boy, but from this angle his features were sharply defined, almost stern. For the first time she saw a family likeness to Bjarni.

'Once upon a time there was a young man from an island not far from here. He heard that the selkies came ashore at midsummer, and he made up his mind to go to the place where they gathered and watch the dancing for himself. So in the evening he crept away from the feast and hid among the rocks at the top of the beach.

'Sure enough, as the light began to fail, and the sun went down, lots of seals appeared and swam towards the shore. They came up from the foam at the edge of the sand and their skins fell away from them. They stepped on to the sand as people, more beautiful than any he had seen before.' Olaf cleared his throat, and shifted his weight off his arm so that it was free. 'They didn't have any clothes on.'

'I'd have been very surprised if they did.'

'They laid their skins on the rocks above the tide. As they did so his eyes fell upon one, a beautiful girl with long dark hair, and . . .'

'And what?'

'Freckles. She laid her sealskin very close to where he sat. She didn't have . . .'

'You said that before.' His hand was touching her shoulder.

'All night long they danced, winding and twisting on the empty shore, and all night long he watched them. But at last the sun rose and at once they turned to take up their sealskins.'

'They can't have been there long then, if it was midsummer night.'

'It was long enough. The girl looked for her skin but she couldn't find it. As the seals slid back into the sea she stood naked in the rising sun, trapped upon the shore.

'The young man stood up, and she saw him with her skin under his arm. She begged him to return it to her, but he wouldn't, and so she had to go with him. They lived together for many years and had many children, but he always had to take care that his wife should have no chance of getting hold of her sealskin. He kept it locked up in a chest, and wore the key on a chain round his neck.

'One day he went out to the fishing, and as he sat in the boat he realised that the chain was gone, and he had left the key at home. So he called out to the others, "Today I have lost my wife." They pulled up the lines and rowed home as quickly as they could, but when they reached the house she'd gone. Only the children were left. She'd put out the fire and put the knives up high so they wouldn't hurt themselves. The children had run after her down the beach and seen her put on her sealskin. They had seen a great bull seal waiting out in the bay. He'd been waiting for her all that time. The children watched them swim away.'

'I'm glad she escaped,' said Astrid. 'I've heard a story nearly the same as that in Dyflin.'

'Ah, but that's not the end.'

His arm was definitely round her shoulder now, but she didn't mind. He smelt of peatsmoke and fish, which she did not find unpleasant.

'It was years later, and the man decided to go sealing with his friends. The night before he set out he dreamed that his former wife came to him, and told him that if he went on the hunt, he must take care not to kill the great seal at the mouth of the cave, for that was her mate, nor the two young seals at the back of the cave, for those were her two young sons. And she described to him the colour of their skins.

'He remembered his dream in the morning, but he thought it was foolish and forgot it again. They went out and caught all the seals they could lay hands on. Then they divided the spoil. The man got the head of the big seal, and the hands and feet of the two young ones. He brought them home and they cooked them for supper. They were just sitting down to eat when there was a great crash and the seal wife came in. But now she had become huge and ugly, a great troll woman. She sniffed at the dishes and cried, "Here lies the head of my mate, the hand of Harek and the foot of Fredrik, but it shall be avenged on the men of this island. Some will perish in the sea, some fall down the cliffs, some die by the sword, until the number of the dead is so great they will reach around the whole island, holding one another by the hand."

'She vanished then, but the curse came true. There is not an island in the sea where young men do not die. Some perish in the sea, some fall down the cliffs, some die by the sword, and so it must ever be, until the number of the dead is so great they reach around their whole island, holding one another by the hand.'

White ashes were heaped where the fire had been. Astrid slipped out of Olaf's arm, and piled on the last peats. The stirred ashes floated upwards.

When she sat down again, he shifted closer, and stretched his legs out to the fire, wriggling his feet. 'I've got pins and needles,' he explained.

'Maybe you need to walk about a bit.'

'I can't move. My brother's gone to sleep.'

Peering round him, she saw Eirik, his head fallen against Olaf's tunic, fair hair tangled in Olaf's belt buckle. 'He's not used to being up all night,' said Olaf, taking her hand.

His hand was warm and rather sticky. He gazed into the fire again.

'Do you hunt seals?' she asked presently.

'Of course. In the autumn, when they come to pup.'

'You don't worry they might be selkies?'

He giggled. 'I've never done it with a selkie yet.'

Someone threw a heap of driftwood on the fire, which burst into a blaze. There were shouts, and Olaf started as he heard his brother's voice. 'Give it back, will you! Come here!'

'Shan't!'

Two figures shot past the flames on the other side, then tumbled together. Ashes went flying. There was a scream. 'Let go! Thorvald! Get him off me! I'll be in the fire!'

'So you will, Ragna Erlendsdottir, if you don't give me back my knife!'

'Watch out!' There was a shout from behind them. 'I'm coming over!'

It was one of the boys from Leogh. He hurtled down the slope towards the fire. When he reached the ashes at the edge he leapt, and just cleared it.

'That wasn't over the middle!' jeered Ragna, her hand on Thorvald's shoulder.

Another boy came thudding over the turf, but at the last moment he skidded sideways and jumped wide. Bombarded with catcalls, he fled away into the dark. Someone threw on a knot of driftwood, and fresh flames leapt up. Olaf had gone, and Eirik was sitting up with his hair all in tangles. Astrid stood beside Thorhalla and Ragna, out of the way of the runners.

'Come on then if you're coming!'

Thorvald ran more heavily than the others. He didn't seem that fast, but he jumped clear over the middle, where flames from driftwood blazed up green and gold.

'Now that was over the middle! Dead centre!'

'Best yet!'

'My turn!' Olaf's voice rang out high treble. He cleared his throat savagely.

'Wait, it's getting too high.'

'That fire's bigger than you are.'

Olaf ran lightly up the slope.

'He's drunk.'

'Wait till it goes down a bit. Stop him, Thorvald!'

When Olaf looked at the fire he saw shifting red, glowing like an eye at the bottom of a dark pool, surrounding by flickering shadows. He'd counted his paces, so he knew the distance.

When he was ready he ran. The mass of red grew huge, then for one second focussed, as he leapt. There was a rush of hot air, sparks and smoke, then the brightness was gone.

He landed hard and would have fallen, but Thorvald caught him against his chest. The ground was warm under his feet. The others surrounded him, suddenly laughing and noisy. They held an aleskin and half poured it down his throat, so it flowed down his cheeks, but he managed not to choke. The ale was warm and tasted of leather. He looked round for Astrid. She smiled at him. Olaf held on to Thorvald and drank to her.

'What about the stranger?'

'Yes, where's your friend, Thorvald?'

'Where's Arne?'

They scanned the twilit slopes.

'Shame to his island then!'

'Arne, we challenge you!'

'Leap our fire, Arne Helgisson, or we spit on your island!'

Arne heard their shouts, but he never knew they were meant for him. In a sheep shelter, among lush grass, with nettles crushed under his cloak, Arne and Ingrid huddled under Ingrid's cloak. Under her dress she was naked. He explored her with his hands, kissing her hard. When she pulled up his shirt and undid his trousers, he gasped like a man thrown into water. Dimly he was aware that she was supposed at some point to stop him, as every girl had done before. But she didn't stop him, she encouraged him, and touched him just as he had wanted. He hadn't thought she would be so fearless. He pressed himself against her, skin to skin. She rolled over so he was on top, fumbling, scared, aware of his own clumsiness.

But she was not clumsy. With one hand she guided him, and then he was inside her. The cloak slipped, and there were nettles under his cheek. He never felt them sting. He couldn't stop. Arne gasped and shuddered. The nettles were stinging him, everything was dissolving all around him. Her body under him was soft and slippery.

Slowly he raised his head. Ingrid was looking into his eyes. The whole thing had happened so quickly she didn't know what she felt. Gudrun had told her it hurt, but it hadn't. Arne seemed so vulnerable in this state, she thought it would be quite easy to love him. She had got exactly what she wanted, and her father would have to accept it.

'I love you,' said Arne hoarsely. He could hardly see her face.

'And so do I love you.'

Twenty minutes later they were back at the fire. Arne was red with self-consciousness. Their absence must have been noticed. 'They won't mind,' Ingrid had said. 'No one will tell tales tonight.'

The others were huddled round the fire again. Ragna glanced at Arne and Ingrid and smiled knowingly, but no one else spared them any attention.

The fire was dying, and they all had their cloaks pulled tightly round them. The hills were grey shadows. At a point above the low cloud on the horizon the sky was pale yellow. Only Eirik hovered and wandered about. He was so cold and tired he was almost crying, but Olaf couldn't make him sit still.

'That's the sun now,' said Eirik fretfully. 'Look, it's brighter.'

'Not yet,' said Olaf. 'You won't miss it when it comes.'

The sky began to show a faint tinge of orange.

'That must be it now! It is lighter. It is!'

Olaf sat close to Astrid, his hands clasped on his knees. His eyes were shadowed, and his face was drawn with tiredness.

'I can see it now,' said Eirik, his teeth chattering.

'No, you can't,' said Olaf wearily.

'I'm cold.'

'You'd better share my cloak then.'

'I'm not a baby,' snapped Eirik, but he sat down beside his brother, and almost at once he was asleep.

Thorvald passed one of the last skins of ale along to Arne. Astrid glanced at Ingrid, who seemed as remote as the queen of the icefields in the story.

Deprived of either light or dark, the island looked quite bare, with its bony rocks breaking through its thin cover of soil. The sea was a cold sheet of grey. To the north-west the square hump of Fugley reared into an empty sky. Thorvald's voice sounded strange in the silence, like someone half woken. 'Sun's coming up now. Look.'

A flicker of light shot like a flame across the horizon, and the sun was there, a solid sphere of red. It cleared the clouds and rose in the pale sky, which responded in a flush of pink. Everyone came to life, seizing and hugging each other around the embers of their fire. On the hilltop it was as clear as day. Only in the valleys below them did the night linger, hidden among the soft folds of the hills.

Part Four

The Pirates

Chapter 23

The Shaldur was bigger than the other island boats, nearly thirty feet long, though little more than six feet wide, rising to a point at prow and stern. A south-east wind for the trip to Konungsborg had come at last, heralded by wispy clouds the previous afternoon, when they had taken Shaldur round to the Nordhavn, and loaded the ballast. They'd left in the small hours of the morning, as soon as the tide began to ebb. The wind being on the starboard quarter, there was little work for the crew to do, until they reached the edges of the Svinborg rost. Kalf of Leogh stood at the helm, and Einar sat at the foot of the mast, by the halyard, ready to let the sail down if necessary. Every few years they made this trip to the quarries at Konungsborg. This year they had a crew of six going out, but Arne would be left in Hjaltland, leaving Thorvald, Einar and the three men from Leogh to sail home with the cargo of soapstone.

When Thorvald had last made this trip it was the first time he had been away from his own island. To him, aged twelve, the bare shore of Hjaltland might have been Vinland itself, it held out such promise, and the settlement at Konungsborg could have been the city of Mikligard, it was so full of new sights and smells. At first the strangers had bewildered him, and he had turned to stare at each

one who passed, trying to see who these unknown people were. 'It
helps if you don't look at them,' Einar had advised him. 'You'll wear
yourself out. Just greet them and walk past.' At night Thorvald had
dreamed of scores of unknown folk with empty faces, for whom he
had no names. But when he got home again he had been restless
and the island had never been quite enough for him again.

At least now he would have one friend abroad. Thorvald
glanced at Arne, who sat by the rail, aft near the helmsman. One
moment Thorvald had to look up to see him silhouetted against
the sky, the next he was a dark shadow against the sea, with
Thorvald looking down on him. Arne stared eastward, now at the
breaking light, now at the dark water. Strange that someone who
took to the sea so easily showed no ambition. It would suit
Thorvald if Arne came back to settle on the island. He must speak
to him about it again before they parted.

It was a long way from Fridarey to Papey Stora. If I were to live
on Fridarey, Arne was thinking, I would very seldom be able to go
home. Perhaps I'd see the Papey men sometimes at the Thing. But
I'd never see my mother, or my sisters. Fridarey is poor compared
to Papey Stora. At home, I know the name of every rock, every
stack, every rig. If I stayed on Fridarey, I would have to learn all
that, and even then I'd never know it as Thorvald and Olaf do. I'd
have to learn the medes for the fishing, the sheep marks, maybe
they even have different words for things, different words you have
to say at sea. I shall never be at home again anywhere, if I leave my
own island, and if I marry, I'll have men I can call cousin, but not
my own brothers.

If Ingrid's pregnant there's no going back. How can she know
so soon? I have to tell my father. If I tell him I can marry a girl with
land, he'll surely be pleased. It's what he wanted. If I tell him it has
to be done before winter, I don't know what he'll say. The others
will laugh at me, but he won't. He'll be scared that Bjarni
Thorvaldsson will take him to the Thing. He can't afford a fine.
So he'll have to help me marry her. But he'll be angry. I don't want
him to come back here to arrange the settlement. My brother Jon
must do that. He won't quarrel with Bjarni.

I never meant to make love, not the first time. I thought she'd
say no. Anyway there've been enough times since. I bet she is
pregnant. Was it worth it? She has land. If I marry her we can sleep

together as much as we like. I'll have Bjarni as my father-in-law. I
like him. I'll have kin.

Arne glanced at Thorvald. Thorvald had land, and kin, yet all
he seemed to think of was giving it up to go to sea. Easy enough to
want that, thought Arne, if you had property at your back. I'd be
happy to call him cousin. Olaf too. Thorvald doesn't seem to mind
that I have Bjarni's favour, but I'll have to tread carefully. There's
nothing worse than feuds within a family.

At the foot of the mast, by the halyard, Einar glanced at the sun,
which hung in the pale sky like a coin. It was past noon already.
They would soon reach the rost of Svinborg, keeping well east to
avoid the tail of it. Once the rost was passed they would have to
work their way north-west up the coast, which would be harder
sailing. Before the afternoon was out they could be at Konungsborg.

Kalf had kept the helm without a break since they left. Einar
wouldn't have minded a spell himself, but he would wait to be
asked. Kalf was a humourless man, but it was no good making
quarrels on the island. Einar's only feuds had been over women,
and these he had mended with money and fair words. He was the
lawman. He wanted no blood shed on his own island.

The young didn't see it like that. Boys who had grown up
without violence didn't understand the benefits of law. Thorvald
looked happy enough now. The sulky look which had dogged him
for months was gone. I should have let him go before. I hope to
God no harm comes of my mistake. He's safer off the land. It's this
that makes him happy. All I can do now is keep a watch on things
this year, and let him go next spring. He's his father's son, after all.
I'll love him better when he's gone.

When Thorvald looked up, Einar beckoned him over.

'Glad to be away now?'

'Yes.'

They sat either end of a thwart, the oars lashed down between
them. It was easier to talk here than on the island.

'You should have come to the Thing in Hjaltland. It'll be a long
time before you have the chance now.'

'I don't mind.'

'I don't suppose we'll see much of you after next spring.'

Thorvald grinned. 'No, maybe not.'

'But a good trader knows his politics too.'

'I'll be home in winter,' said Thorvald. 'You can tell me what's happening.'

'Law is important,' said Einar. 'The rule of law. That's what the Thing is for. Not piracy, not violence. I hope as a trader you'll live by law, though you'll have to defend yourself too.'

Thorvald ducked his head, and did not reply.

'I wish you could hear the law recited at the Thing. You know what Njal the Islander had to say about the law, Thorvald?'

' "By law shall our land be built up, and by lawlessness laid waste." Everyone knows that.'

'But does everyone act on it? You've never known trouble in your time. At most times in most places, in this world, men live in the fear of violence. It's a privilege to have peace. I know you're tired of your island. I know it's small and poor, and out of the way of adventure. But you'll live to be glad that's so. To keep your own land and support your own family in peace, that's all most men would ask for, and more than most ever get.'

'I don't want my family to suffer. But if there was only peace, where's the adventure in that? There are other things than peace.'

'That's what they said at the Thing this year. It's something everyone must learn for himself.'

'What did they say?'

'Apparently Magnus of Noreg has complained to Earl Harald again. He feels something should be done about the pirates.'

'He should mind his own business. We're not his subjects.'

'Yes, but the earldom has been divided too often. There are some who look to Noreg.'

'For what? Subjection?'

'It wouldn't do to offend the King. Hjaltland is closer to him than the Orkneyjar in more ways than one. We've had too much civil war. If there were war in the Orkneyjar again and the King of Noreg were called upon again, we might find he brought more than promises.'

'He'd have no right to attack us. He's not our King.'

'No. Perhaps he finds that frustrating.'

'He's no right even to think about it. The islands are nothing to do with him.'

'You're not the first to say so. But then, no king has ever conquered the islands. You know why?'

'Because the islanders would never let it happen.'

'The islanders, you think? What do you see there?' Einar pointed over Thorvald's shoulder.

Thorvald looked puzzled. 'Nothing.'

'Nothing?'

'Only the sea.'

'There you are. You remember what Knut told his retainers in Englaland, when they called him the ruler of the seas?'

'Yes,' said Thorvald impatiently. 'He needed a boat. The English aren't clever enough to build good ships. The King of Noreg has several.'

'The King of Noreg also needs an excuse. He thinks there are too many pirates in the islands and something should be done about it. Many in Hjaltland agree. So the men of Hjaltland decided at the Thing this year that it would be in their interests to act.'

'Against the pirates?'

'They think it would be sensible.'

'Don't you?'

'It depends whether you see the King's influence as the greatest threat. There are fewer ships in the islands. Trade is declining. The smaller islands get cut off because there's no money in visiting them. Apart from the Earl, there's only one class of men sailing longships in the islands.'

'The pirates. So what did they decide?'

'The same as last year. To discuss the situation again next year. To compare our situation with the Orkneyjar, the Sudreyjar and the Faereyjar, and to refrain from piracy in cases where to do so would not conflict with our own interests.'

'I see.'

'Do you? You should have come with me. But Thorvald, remember the law. Nothing else protects the innocent, nor ever will.'

Chapter 24

'I wondered where you were,' said Astrid.

Ingrid threw down a full basket smelling of wet rushes and soil, and hung her cloak over the hearth. The hem was soaked through, and drops hissed in the fire. 'It took a while. Einar can tell just by looking, but I have to count each lamb.'

'I'm glad you're back. I tried to give the crab medicine to the grimet cow, but she wouldn't drink it.'

'I'd better look at her. Where's Gerda?'

'She went to Leogh. Hilda wanted medicine for the baby's teeth. The cow seemed all right. Just restless.'

'That baby never stops growing teeth. The cow'll be missing her calf. Here,' Ingrid nudged the basket with her foot. 'Can you tie the moss in bundles and hang it to dry?' She lifted the lid off a pitcher. 'Is this today's?'

'I just skimmed it.'

Ingrid dipped the ladle. 'I'm thirsty. That moss should last a while. I'll not be needing any more myself this year.'

Astrid was searching one of the baskets hanging on the wall. 'Do you know where the twine is?'

'There's rush twine in the other basket. I said, that moss is for you. I'll not be needing any.'

'All right,' said Astrid. 'Shall I use this?'

Ingrid dropped the ladle back in the milk. 'You don't take a hint, do you?'

'What hint?'

'I've tried. I've said things any woman in the world would understand. I don't know what you think about.'

'Have I done something wrong?'

'Astrid.'

'Yes?' Astrid squatted by the hearth and emptied the moss out of the basket.

'You don't make it easy, do you? Listen . . .' Ingrid stopped. 'Is that my father?'

'No, it's just that gull on the roof again.'

'Listen, Astrid, you'll have to know. I think I'm pregnant.'

'How can you tell? It's only about five weeks since you met him.'

'Six and a half. Four and a half since the first time it could have happened. But I know. I kept trying to give you a hint.'

'Why didn't you just say?'

'Oh Astrid. You don't seem very surprised, anyway.'

'No.'

'You guessed I'd made love with him?'

Astrid didn't like to say that everyone who had been at the Midsummer Feast had been talking about Ingrid and Arne ever since. 'I noticed you both kept going over to the hill,' she said tactfully.

'My father mustn't know.'

'He's going to have to know sooner or later, isn't he?' asked Astrid, pulling bundles of moss apart.

'I'm going to marry Arne.'

'Bjarni will have to be told about that. Does Arne know? He shouldn't have just left you.'

'He'll be back before winter. He promised. He has to go home first, to speak to his father, and get one of his family to come and discuss the marriage settlement for him. There wasn't any other way to do it.'

'But how can he get back before winter? Will you wait for the Thing in Hjaltland? It'll be born by then. In fact,' said Astrid, calculating, 'August, September, October . . . it'll be four months old. You'll have to marry him before it's born, or it won't be legitimate.'

'I tell you, he's coming back before winter. He'll bring one of his brothers who can propose the marriage to my father. My father won't refuse when he realises there's a child.'

'I think Bjarni would approve of this marriage anyway.'

'Do you? But Arne's landless, at least, he won't inherit.'

'Bjarni likes Arne. He must know there's no one else. And you have land. Mind you, I suppose he might be angry when he realises you're pregnant.'

'Angry! He'd kill him! He mustn't know, not until Arne and Jon come back, and the settlement is made.'

'But he'll notice sooner or later.'

'Not before they get back. Arne will come before the end of September; after that it won't be weather. Jon will be back from sea before the corn harvest.'

'What will Arne's family say?'

Ingrid shrugged. 'They'll be glad to see him marry where there's land. He says they'll support him.'

'But can you keep it secret until September?'

'Why not? It won't show. You won't tell on me. Nor will Gudrun. No one else need know.'

'But what if you start being sick? Isn't that what usually happens?'

'Whatever happens, father's not going to know. You will help me?'

'Of course. Is Arne pleased?'

'He's frightened, but he loves me. I suppose I'd better look at the cow.' Ingrid pushed back the hangings, then let them fall again. She came and stood over Astrid. 'Arne will come back,' she said firmly. 'Even if he didn't care about me he'd come back. He needs land. He's looking for a place in the world, and that's what I can give. He knows that. I can trust him to come back.'

'I think he will.'

'Even if he didn't, what have I lost? I wouldn't be the first on this island. My father might never forgive, but he'd stand by me. If Arne goes away I don't much care what happens. What choice had I? I'd rather suffer for having had something, than live my whole life without so much as a crumb.'

Astrid watched needles of rain vanishing into peat smoke. 'I don't know about marriage,' she said. 'I don't know whether I'll ever marry anyone now.'

'Whatever happens, I'll have Arne's child.'

If it lives. Astrid drew a cross in the cold ashes, where Ingrid couldn't see. 'He'll come back,' she said. 'I know from the way he was always looking at you. Your father must have noticed that too.' She glanced up. 'Bjarni isn't going to be that surprised.'

'Hush! Who's that?'

The outer door slammed, and the hangings were pushed roughly aside. Eirik came in with such a rush that the smoke whirled upwards, and a flurry of ashes blew across the newly swept floor.

'Eirik! Is anything the matter? What do you want?'

'Where's Bjarni?' Eirik's shirt was streaked with wet, and his legs were splashed with mud. 'The ship's back!'

'Shaldur or Sula?'

'Sula. I have to find my uncle.' He turned to the door, but Ingrid grabbed him by his tunic. 'Wait! You say the Sula's back?'

'Yes.' Eirik wriggled. 'Rolf said to fetch my uncles. Let me go!'

'Why? What does he want them for? Does he need help with the ship? When did they get back? Answer me, or I won't let you go!'

'I have to tell Bjarni!'

'Bjarni's out fishing. You tell me! Is Rolf all right?'

'It's not Rolf, it's Dagfinn. Let me go!'

Ingrid jerked him round and made him face her. 'What's happened to Dagfinn?'

'Lost,' muttered Eirik.

'Lost?'

'There were pirates. He hasn't come back. Rolf wants to tell the story to witnesses. He sent me to fetch my uncles. Let me go!'

'I shall come,' declared Ingrid. 'Hold him, Astrid. I need my cloak.'

'Let me go! You can't be a witness!'

'Shut up. Nor can you. I'm going to my sister. Hold him, Astrid.'

Astrid twisted Eirik's arm behind his back so he couldn't struggle.

'What else do you know?' demanded Ingrid. 'You can tell us as we go. When did the Sula get back?'

'I saw her.' Eirik was sullen at first. 'I had to go to Bunes. To look for the pony. I got to the big grey stone, and I climbed up so I could see across the hill. She broke her tether. That's where she usually goes. So then I was looking out to sea. That's when I saw

Sula, beating north, past the Seydurholm. So I went to the Nordhavn. I helped bring the rope ashore so they could moor her. Leif rowed ashore and he and I fastened the mooring. They sent the anchor down as well, aft. That was her moored. Then they all came ashore, but not Dagfinn. I said to Rolf, "Where's Dagfinn?" '

'Come on,' said Ingrid. The rain had thinned to drizzle, and the mud in the yard oozed between their toes. 'Will they be at Byrstada?'

'Yes, but they don't want you.'

'Shut up and go on telling. Hurry, now!'

Astrid kept hold of Eirik's wrist as they picked their way across the yard.

'Rolf said to run for my uncles, and send them at once to Byrstada. He sent Leif to the smithy. He was giving orders about unloading the ship. He didn't listen to me at first. I kept saying, "But Einar's not here! Nor Thorvald neither. They went with the men of Leogh two days back to get the soapstone."

' "Hell!" said Rolf. Then he said, "you must fetch Bjarni then. Quickly now! Tell Bjarni to come to Byrstada. Tell him I have to report the loss of my brother to witnesses." So I came.' Eirik tugged against Astrid's grip, 'To speak to Bjarni, not you. Now I have to get back.'

'You're getting back,' said Ingrid curtly.

Long grass drenched with rain soaked their skirts. Eirik, compelled to keep abreast of Astrid, had to wade through rushes and campion, a mass of brown seeds clinging to his trousers. The strong scent of dried fish and smoke that hung about him reminded Astrid of Olaf.

Ingrid stopped where the path forked to the smithy. 'We'll go to Snorri first. We'll see what he knows.'

'Then let me go!'

'Listen you! You want to fetch my father? You can. Run down to the Sudvik, and wait at his noost. When he gets back, give him the message. He should be there any time now.'

Astrid let Eirik go, and he ducked away from them and ran.

Ingrid and Astrid found Snorri and Olaf outside the smithy door. 'Did you know the Sula was back?' Ingrid asked them.

Olaf smiled at Astrid. He didn't seem troubled by the news. 'We did,' said Snorri. 'Leif was here.'

'Are you going to Byrstada?'

'There's no hurry. Rolf can't leave his ship yet, and he'll wait now until Bjarni gets back.'

'I sent Eirik to tell father as soon as he gets back.'

'And I sent Leif to do the same. They can entertain each other while they wait.'

'Did Leif tell you what had happened?' asked Astrid. They all looked at her as if they had not expected her to speak. It was not her island.

Snorri led them to the bench outside the smithy. Ingrid spread her cloak and sat beside him, while Olaf flopped down on the brigstones at his feet. Astrid hesitated, then knelt beside Olaf. The stones were cold and wet.

'Olaf, do you want to tell them what Leif said?'

'No,' said Olaf, startled. 'I didn't even see him. Anyway, I can't tell stories.'

'That's not true,' whispered Astrid. He didn't look at her, but he grinned.

'This is what Leif told me,' began Snorri. Then he paused and Astrid realised suddenly that he was moved. Did he care that much for Dagfinn? She wouldn't have expected it.

'They were boarded by pirates in the Sudreyjar,' said Snorri. 'Pirates from the Orkneyjar. It was Svein himself. Svein Asleifarson.'

Ingrid gasped. 'Him! Has he killed Dagfinn?'

'There was no battle. Dagfinn went with him. He'll never be content with trading now, if he lives.'

'How did it happen?'

'Did he know Sula was from your island?' Astrid asked.

The question obviously pleased Snorri. 'Dagfinn must have told him by now.'

'So there wasn't a fight at all?'

'Leif said . . . But wait, here he is.'

Leif's wet cloak was thrown over his shoulder, and he was flushed from running. Olaf embraced him as if he were his own kin. Astrid was surprised. She had heard there was a quarrel between Leif and Eirik's sons.

Leif let go Olaf's shoulders, and smiled at him. 'I found your little brother at the Shirva noost, so I set him to watch for your uncle. He wasn't pleased.'

'Do him good,' said Olaf.

Leif sat beside Snorri and ignored Astrid and Ingrid completely. Astrid found him too attractive to know what to say to him anyway.

'So now you can tell us your story,' said Snorri.

'Very well.' Leif began to speak formally, as if he were giving them a story at a feast.

'We were back in Biorgvin by the middle of June. We got a commission to sail to the Sudreyjar with a cargo of hardwood, some church ornaments and a communion set. Dagfinn showed it to me. We took a mason from Dumferlin and two carpenters along with us, to build a church on the north island of Uvist. The man who put up the money made his fortune as a pirate. He lives in Biorgvin now, but he wanted to endow the church on his own island. It's to have panelling, and a rood screen, and a carved font; just like the Cathedral in Nidaros. Only not so big.'

'The Cathedral in Kirkjavagr is like that too,' observed Snorri. 'You didn't have to take the priest aboard though?'

'No, there's a priest already on the island. Just as well, there was an ill fate, as it was.'

'Go on,' said Ingrid impatiently.

'The voyage to the Sudreyjar was one of the best bits of seamanship I've ever seen, and that's saying something. Dagfinn knows exactly what he can do with Sula. When the wind came it was northerly, and we came south-west out of Biorgvin through the channels until we were due west of here. We saw the cloud over Fridarey when we were still half a day's sail away. We passed to the south but we couldn't stop. We couldn't have sheltered in the haven with that wind anyway.

'We were only one and a half days out of Biorgvin. Rolf was worrying about the shoals off Rinansay. He always does. We made for that anchorage we use at Rappisnes – you know the one, Snorri – it's the best place when there's a northerly wind, and we wanted to avoid going round Vestrey.

'In Rappisnes we anchored and waited for the tide. If we'd stayed overnight the folk at the hall there would have feasted us. But the wind was still fair for Ljodhus, so we sailed on all night, north of Rolfsey, and along the north shore past Byrgisey. That was our last sight of land. We set a course just south of west, which Dagfinn said would raise Sulaskaer. Rolf would rather have kept the coast in sight, even though it was a lee shore all the way.'

'That would have been foolish,' said Snorri.

'Anyway, we stayed in the open sea. I was asleep for most of that stretch. There was just a bit of broken water off the Cape at Katanes. We could see the Sulaskaer for a while, and we could see the hills of Katanes, so we weren't worried. As soon as we were well past, we brought the wind round to the quarter and made straight for Starnevegr. We had the wind until we were coming down the Ey ness. We just managed to drift around the skerry there, with the wind on the beam, then we had to row into Starnevegr. There's an anchorage on the north shore, at Mol Sandvik – do you know it?'

'If it was a northerly you were sheltering from, I think I know. You made good time then?'

'Three and a half days, just, including a few hours at Rappisnes. We'd have done it in even less if we hadn't lost the wind.'

'Go on,' said Ingrid.

'After that it started to blow from the south, so we couldn't leave Starnevegr. We shifted across to a bay on the south side. It's one thing carrying treasure when you're safe at sea, but it's a worry when you're lying close inshore and you can't move.'

'Did anyone know you were carrying treasure?' said Olaf.

'They'd guess,' said Snorri, 'Once the word got around you had craftsmen and wood for a church.'

'That was it. So Dagfinn went into Starnevegr and hired a pilot. The weather was turning. As we had warning that there'd been raids further south, so everyone was getting edgy. Dagfinn was desperate to get out, and Rolf was saying it would be mad to go on. The wind had shifted westerly as far as we could tell, tucked in there, and Dagfinn gave the order to leave. The wind was coming on the beam. Once we were clear of the harbour it was plain sailing down to Seunta. But the land trends south-west . . .'

'I know it.'

'It began to look as if we were going to have to go east of Seunta. The pilot said we wouldn't clear the shoals on the west side. I was thinking we'd have to run for shelter. You know what that place is like.'

Snorri turned to Olaf. 'Those stacks at Seunta, they stand out of the sea like teeth, with shoals on both sides, and a lethal tide rip. If you miss the channel you're in trouble.'

'That's it!' exclaimed Leif. 'We did it with the tide rip. They all said "Turn back!" These stacks were coming closer on the port side, and there was a reef right ahead, I could see the waves breaking.

The wind was blowing us right into white water. And Dagfinn was saying, "The spring tide's with us. We'll make it." We had the sail close-hauled, with the foot right round to the stern. And there was Rolf shouting, "Turn back, for God's sake turn back, we'll never clear that reef!" Then we were swept past, just in time. It was a brilliant piece of sailing, best I've ever seen.'

'Good God,' said Snorri.

'So then what?'

'The wind did shift northerly, just as Dagfinn said. We were able to work back towards the shore. We anchored off the settlement. Dagfinn and the craftsmen went ashore. One of them couldn't even walk.' Leif laughed. 'He'd never stopped being sick since we left Starnevegr; I don't know if he even saw that reef. But his friend did. He was praying out loud all the way.'

'I'm not surprised.'

'We unloaded on the top of the spring tide. We floated the wood on to the beach, and got the other stuff off as fast as we could. We had Sula over shingle, and if we weren't quick enough and we missed the tide, we'd have been stuck on a hard beach for a fortnight. The tides round there aren't predictable, so we hauled out as fast as we could, and anchored in deep water.

'We stayed until the Sunday, and then they had a procession and a service at the site of the church. Dagfinn ordered all of us to go to the service, and the priest blessed us. Most of us thought it was a good omen. The priest offered us confession before we left, and when I told him as well that I had no family, he gave me an amulet. Look.'

Leif unhooked a chain from round his neck, and held out his hand.

'A cross,' said Snorri. 'I wouldn't want that at sea. You don't want to tempt fate.'

'May I see?'

Leif dropped it into Olaf's hand. Astrid looked over his shoulder. It was a small enamel cross, four square, with a ring at the top. When she looked closely at the carvings on it, she could see the figure of a man.

'I think you'll do very well with that,' said Olaf.

'I think so too,' said Leif. 'Anyway, we left with a south-west wind, but we'd got no further than the sound between the islands. That's when we saw the longships.

'They came out just as we were crossing the sound north of Uvist. They rowed us down fast. Five. We hadn't a hope. There was no point unlashing the oars, although we did. Dagfinn said, "They won't take us without a fight."

'They used two ships to cut us off from the open sea, and they drove two more up against us, one on each side. We only carry three bows. So we drew our swords and waited. One man was forward, with an arrow strung. When the longship rammed us he shot, and we saw a man fall on the other ship.'

'I bet that was Skuli Hedinsson.'

Leif's surprised glance fell on Ingrid. 'I wasn't going to name names.'

'So what did Dagfinn do?'

'They were right on us. He couldn't say anything. We stood still, and waited for them to board us.'

'A man came to the gunwale, below us in the longship, and called out: "You call yourselves Norsemen? Will you make me a gift of your ship and her cargo?" Dagfinn said, "I will make the ship as dear a gift as I can. For the cargo, take it and welcome. I'll deny you nothing in my hold that you could wish for. It seems a waste of good men's lives to defend it, for you see we're outnumbered."

'We were lined up facing each other, us on the deck above, but outnumbered five to one.

'Then their captain laughed and leapt aboard. He was old, with white hair. But he jumped aboard easily, and stood there with his sword drawn. He faced Dagfinn. "So you are the captain of this ship?"

'"I am," said Dagfinn. The tide was turning. The three ships, locked together, were drifting into the shoals. I thought we would have to fight until we died. It was evening, and the breeze was just starting to come in off the sea. The islets were bright green, and the sea reddish with weed. I could see white sand below. If there had been a fight, it would have been a short one.

'Dagfinn said, "You must be Svein Asleifarson of Gareksay in the Orkneyjar. In other circumstances, I would count this meeting an honour." "Why's that?" he said.

'"I come from an island where your name is well known," Dagfinn said. "I am from Fridarey in Hjaltland, and Snorri Hakonsson is my kinsman. I have learned to speak well of you, and think the same."

'Svein laughed. "Very well," he said. "And now this cargo, with which you are so generous. What do you carry?"

'Of course, we had nothing to show but ballast, stones off the beach at Uvist. Svein looked at our stones, and there was a long silence.

'At last, to our great relief, he laughed, and kept on laughing. Then he said, "So, you're Snorri Hakonsson's cousin? You have killed one of my warriors with your arrow."

'Dagfinn said, "We can kill more, if necessary."

'Svein laughed again. "Snorri's kinsman, if that's who you are, I won't molest you, but I will have recompense for my warrior. I'll let you all go on your way, to sell stones wherever you please, except for the one responsible for the killing. He will come with me. He can sail with us to Dyflin, and win glory there and English treasure, if he dare." '

Snorri slapped his sound leg. 'I see it! I see it now!'

'Dagfinn said, "I'm the captain of this ship. I will come." And he stepped within range of Svein's sword, and sheathed his own.

'Then Svein said, "Can a captain so easily abandon his ship?" Dagfinn said, "I can trust my brother Rolf as I do myself." '

'Did Rolf make a successful voyage?'

'Oh yes,' said Leif. 'Then Dagfinn and Svein boarded the long-ship, and we lowered Dagfinn's sea chest after them. They pulled away, and rowed west, then vanished among the inlets of the sound.'

'Did you hear nothing more of them?'

'In Starnevegr they spoke of nothing but raids. Rolf said we'd lose business if we talked. There were all kinds of rumours.'

'What were they?'

'That a great raid is planned next year on Dyflin. I heard in Starnevegr that the English have repaired and strengthened the defences.'

'Henry of Englaland's troops against Svein of Gareksey,' said Snorri. 'That'll be a battle worth seeing.'

'There's been no news from the Orkneyjar?' asked Leif.

'No boat from the Orkneyjar since you left. Einar's at the Thing in Hjaltland. He may hear something.'

'There's father!' cried Ingrid.

Bjarni came up the path with Eirik half running behind.

'We must be off to Byrstada.' Olaf stood up as Snorri spoke, and helped the smith pull himself to his feet.

'What's this then?' asked Bjarni, as he reached them. 'The boy says Dagfinn's away with Svein Asleifarson, and Rolf is anxious to report the loss of him.' He spoke to Leif. 'What happened?'

'He's told his story,' said Snorri. 'He can tell you again while we walk to Byrstada. Olaf, can you find my stick?'

Bjarni looked at his nephew. 'You're coming to Byrstada?'

Olaf looked surprised. 'Rolf won't want me.'

'I don't see why not. Rolf must report Dagfinn's loss at once, so we can legally witness that the Sula is his, until Dagfinn turns up again.'

Olaf shook his head. 'No. I don't have the right.'

'I'll walk with you,' said Ingrid to her father.

'Very well,' Bjarni nodded to Olaf. 'If you're not coming with us, you can see the lass home.'

Olaf didn't look at Astrid until the others had set off, Eirik tagging behind them. 'Do you want me to come back with you?'

'I don't mind.'

Fresh rain blew against their backs, and slowly penetrated Astrid's cloak and hood. Olaf's hair turned straight and dark as it got wet, and drops of water trickled down his fringe on to his nose.

Astrid broke the silence. 'Was Rolf ever jealous of Dagfinn?'

Olaf squinted at her through the rain. Her cheeks were pink, and her hood framed her face in soft folds. 'Of course not. Dagfinn's his brother.'

'That might be why.'

Olaf looked worried. 'I don't think so. Sometimes they've quarrelled. But Dagfinn gave a splendid feast for Rolf's wedding.'

When the path narrowed Olaf walked ahead of Astrid, leaving his footprints in the mud. She deliberately set her own feet in his prints.

'It's not usually like this when Sula comes home,' said Olaf abruptly, when they could walk side by side again. 'Usually everyone goes to meet her, and after the hay's in we have a feast at Byrstada before they leave again.'

'We used to meet my father's ships too.'

'Did your father own ships?'

'No, he built them. We always kept track of their voyages.'

'What kind of ships did he build?'

It was raining harder now, so she had to raise her voice so he could hear. 'They were mostly ocean going trading ships, much larger than the Sula. The biggest he ever built was forty or fifty tons, I think. About seventy feet long, anyway. How big's the Sula? She looked about forty feet to me.'

'Forty-two,' said Olaf, trying not to show that he was impressed.

'I don't know,' said Astrid. 'Watching the ship grow is the interesting bit, seeing what she's turning into. The Sula has nice lines, I think.'

'He'd see it in his mind, I suppose,' said Olaf. 'Then as he built it he'd make it come real, as near as he could to the way he saw it. Did your father have his own shipyard?'

'In the end he did. He started as apprentice in the biggest yard in Dyflin, where they made longships. He rose to be a journeyman shipbuilder, though he had nothing to begin with. When I first remember it he was already building trading ships, and his name was known in every guild. They were mostly commissioned in Irland, but not all. In fact there was a man in Hjaltland . . .' She paused. Since Arne had refused to take her message, she had thought a good deal about that man in Hjaltland.

'Where did the ships sail to?'

It fascinated Olaf to hear Astrid talk. He had never seen her so animated, and there was a lilt in her voice which was quite unlike any other speech on the island. When she smiled he could see a gap between her two front teeth. He wondered what it would be like to kiss her.

'Everywhere,' Astrid told him, 'Englaland, Skotland, Valland, Danmark, all over the Norse lands. One man sailed a ship of ours to Marsilia and beyond, just like they used to do.'

'Not to Mikligard?'

'No one goes there by sea. But he reached Romaborg, and when he came home to Dyflin a crowd went to the harbour to look at the ship. It was right at the end of summer. There were so many people we could hardly get through. Then Kolbein saw us and called out: "Here's the man who built her", and everyone cheered. Kolbein showed us some of his treasure: bales of real silk, and lapis lazuli from the far east, and jewels set in gold. If Romaborg is like that, then the whole north must be pale grey beside it.'

Olaf looked at her sideways through the rain. He remembered holding her hand, how small and cool it had felt. He wondered what she would say if he tried to do it again. Astrid wiped her nose on the back of her hand and sniffed. Her wet hair hung in little tails where it had escaped her hood.

On Snorri's brigstones he had sat within a foot of her, and noticed how smooth the skin was on her neck, and how her breast curved under her dress. Olaf had never seen a woman naked. All he knew were the crude drawings made with a hot poker on the walls of the barn at Byrstada, where the crew slept in winter. The drawings didn't tell him much. The reality was beside him now, but he didn't know how to get any nearer to it. They were almost at the Shirva turning.

'What was your father's name?' asked Olaf. He wanted to imagine her now, to get some grasp on who she really was, and he wasn't even sure what he needed to know.

She hesitated for a moment, then said, 'Kol Sigurdarson. But in Dyflin they called him Kol the Shipbuilder.'

G udrun sat at the end of her sleeping platform, with a sheepskin behind her to keep the cold of the wall off her back. She wore only her shift, which revealed the swell of her pregnancy. The baby seemed to have got suddenly larger in the last week. Rolf's return had brought a sense of coming to rest at last, that she would never have expected. Something had changed between them, although they had had no chance to speak alone until now.

He had drawn the hangings across as if it were December not July, so that on the platform it was like being inside a cave. A soapstone lamp was set in a bracket on the wall, its wick floating in a pool of pungent seal oil. There were other smells too: thrift, bedstraw, meadowsweet and thyme, from the bunches of herbs amongst the flock pillows. Voices from the hall came faintly, muted by the thick hangings.

She was astonished to be so glad to see him. One of them must have changed, or perhaps they both had. She had been relieved to see him go in spring, but while her pregnancy advanced, and the child still lived, there had been time to feel a tenderness that had been too long suppressed. Perhaps she had grown to love him after all. For the first time in two years there was no sorrow to come between them.

Rolf sat crosslegged at the other end of the narrow platform. He had been out in the yard washing himself in fresh water, as he always did when he came home from sea. His hair was still wet from rinsing out the salt, and now he was combing it through slowly. The worst tangles he cut off with his knife. His hair was much longer when it was wet, reaching halfway down his chest. His clean shirt was still unbuttoned.

Gudrun watched him hack off a lock of hair. 'Do you want me to do that for you?'

'It's easier if I do it myself.'

Gudrun began to unplait her own hair. She knew he liked it loose. 'Go on telling me. What was it like, this church?'

'It was only half built, bare walls, and the sky for a roof. Like a ship upside down it will be, when it's finished. You know how they build those new German merchant ships, on solid frames? No, you don't, but the roof is designed just the same way. No resistance to the water of course; for a ship I mean.'

'But good enough for a roof?'

'And it had a stone floor, swept clean, and a high round window. It'll be quite bright inside. The Cathedral at Nidaros has windows as well. They make a lead frame for the window, and put glass into the spaces. In Valland I've heard they use different coloured glass. The light shines through and makes patterns on the floor, like a rainbow.'

'We should have a church here,' said Gudrun.

'Maybe.' He smiled at her. 'One day I'll take you to see the cathedral in Kirkjavagr. Would you like that?' He started to trim his beard, as if he had said nothing out of the way at all.

'You'd take me to Kirkjavagr?'

'Why not? When the little one is big enough. I'll have a ship. I can take both of you there in a year or two.'

Gudrun crossed her fingers. 'Don't! The child's not born yet. If our fortunes have turned we must look the other way and not yet speak of it. And even if you have your own ship now, you don't want to wish any evil fate on your brother.'

'Of course I don't. But I think he'll be happier where he is.'

'And you're pleased too, aren't you, Rolf? Aren't you much happier?'

He glanced towards the hangings. Then he dropped his knife, to come and sit beside her, clutching both her hands between his.

'Gudrun, I can't say so. If our fortunes have turned, I don't know why, or what can last. You know I can't say so.'

She took him in her arms, and held him to her awkwardly. 'Rolf, it's all right. You've done nothing wrong. What is it?'

He didn't raise his head, but she could hear his whisper. 'It is a fate. I have to tell someone. I made it. They had the service of dedication, in that church. It moved me. I thought priests brought an ill fate to sailors. But there – all those people in the church, and seeing the sky where the roof would be, imagining it, as you imagine a ship that's not yet built. Gudrun, it moved me. Can you understand?'

She held him to her breast, reassuring him. 'There's nothing to be afraid of.'

'But there is. You don't know what I did.'

'Nothing wrong, I'm sure of it.'

'I prayed. He said – the priest said – that's what we were to do. I understood that much, "Oremus." In Norse that means, let us pray. So I made my own prayer.'

'That's not wrong.'

'I asked that I might have a ship of my own.'

'A ship?'

He looked up, terror in his eyes. 'Gudrun, you don't know what it's been like. Everything I say or do, all my life. He mocks at me. Makes out I'm a fool, or an idiot. He takes the most appalling risks. That voyage off the Sudreyjar, with the Seunta rocks under our lee – I still don't know how we got clear of that reef. He said it was the tide, he was so pleased with himself, he said he knew exactly what he was doing, but it was sheer luck. He could have killed us all. The pilot was begging him to turn back, but Dagfinn wouldn't listen. It was madness. The passengers were sick to death. He spares no one, nor his ship either. And when I speak, he laughs at me.

'In Starnevegr they told us there'd been raids this year in the Sudreyjar. We should have sent scouts, waited for an escort, or for news. We had the richest cargo we've yet carried. Treasures for a church. It was pure chance they didn't intercept us on the way down.'

'Dagfinn has his own luck.'

'But it's not *my* luck. I've had no chance in my life to prove anything. On the voyage back I was my own man for the first time in my life. I bought salt whale meat, and hide and oil in Starnevegr, and sold it at Byrgisey; I thought the earl's own household would give me a good price, and I was right. There've been no successful hunts in the Orkneyjar this year. And the rest of the whale oil and meat I brought back here, to help us through the winter. Isn't that success?'

'It is, Rolf.'

'I feel I'm free at last. Can you imagine it?'

'I don't need to. I see it in you.'

'Gudrun!' He had her by the shoulders. 'God forgive me, I prayed I might be rid of him, and by Christ that's what's happened, and I don't want him back.'

She pulled him down and held him. 'Don't cry. It's all right. You've not done wrong. You haven't.'

She'd never seen him weep before. Soon he sat up, and wiped his nose on his fingers. 'You think not?'

'I know not.' She picked up her comb. 'Let me finish this.'

He let her comb out the remaining tangles.

'I still have to trim my beard.'

'There's no hurry. Oh.'

'What?'

'The baby. It's awake. It usually begins about now. Put your hand there.' She guided his hand on to her belly, over her shift. 'That's it moving. Can you feel?'

He didn't speak, but she watched his face.

'At first I wasn't sure what it was. At least, I dared not believe it. I still dare not think too much.'

'You must take care.'

'I do take care, and . . . Gunnhild did something for me. It was strong. I think it helped.'

'That's all that matters. Do you feel well?'

'I'm beginning to. After you went I was sick all the time.'

'I would have looked after you if I had been here.'

'Easy to say,' said Gudrun, breaking through a knot in his hair.

'Today, when I told them what had happened,' said Rolf, his hand still resting on his unborn child, 'they said that the ship was legally mine, until Dagfinn should return.'

'You needn't have been so worried about making a formal statement. Everyone knows you had a half share in her.'

'I did it to ease my own mind. It seemed very important to clear up the matter at once. Whatever I feel, I've only done what was right.'

'No one need know how you feel.' She turned his face up so he had to look at her. 'I think you're a very patient brother. And brave too.'

'Do you think he'll come back?'

She shrugged. 'Not for a long time, unless something happens to him.'

'Like what?'

'Like Snorri perhaps.'

He crossed his fingers. 'God forbid.'

'You wouldn't be responsible.'

Rolf picked up his knife, then set it down again. 'Do you like Dagfinn?' he asked.

It was a while before she answered. 'Yes, but I married you. It's you I love, not him.'

On summer nights Ingebjorg worked on long after the evening meal, and tonight Gunnhild was with her. There was only one patch of hay still to cut before the dew fell. Ingebjorg swung her sickle, and the grass fell before her feet in flower-studded swathes. Gunnhild piled the hay into strips with long sweeps of the wooden rake. Her back ached from stooping, and midges settled on her eyes and forehead. Suddenly she threw down the rake. 'That's enough. These midges are driving me mad. The boys can finish that corner in the morning. Come on.'

It was dark inside the house. Ingebjorg lit the lamp, and laid a pile of dried seaweed on the fire. Blue flames shot up. 'That'll keep the midges out.' She took bannocks out of the crock by the wall. 'I'll pour some blaand.'

'So Thorvald has his wish,' said Gunnhild. 'I didn't ask you what you thought in front of him. It's easy to see he's happy.'

'I know. He's been himself again, ever since Rolf came over.'

'It was Rolf's idea?'

'Oh yes. Thorvald would have been too proud to speak to him. He felt Dagfinn had let him down. It was my fault. But I'm not standing in his way now.'

'So how do you feel?' asked Gunnhild, cutting open a bannock.

'Relieved. I knew he should have gone with them last time, even before Sula left. But I couldn't raise the matter again. Dagfinn hadn't spoken to me, and you know how it is with Shirva. Thorvald needs to be away.'

'He'll be quite different when he gets back.'

'I know.' Ingebjorg stared into the fire. 'I've done my best, but it's not been good enough. I've been a mother to them, but I couldn't be a father.'

'Thorvald knows he had a father to be proud of. And a mother too. That's more than many get.'

'I'm angry with Bjarni still,' said Ingebjorg. 'My boys are his brother's sons. Einar would have been willing to know them better, if Bjarni hadn't kept them apart.' She added, 'I know I shouldn't speak against Bjarni to you. Thorvald will be fine with Rolf.'

'Would it have made a difference if it had been Rolf two years ago?'

'Instead of Dagfinn? Well, I trust him more, but of course I quarrelled with Dagfinn.'

'Do you think you wouldn't have quarrelled with Rolf?'

'I hardly know him.'

'You've known him sixteen years.'

'I don't think any of us know Rolf, Gunnhild.'

'What do you mean?'

Ingebjorg bent over to replenish the fire. The smoke was hardly rising, and the reek was so strong it caught their throats. 'No one on the island has ever considered Rolf without his brother. Dagfinn's shadow. Yesterday was the first time I'd ever really heard him talk. Not that he came to discuss the matter with me.'

'He ignored you?'

'He had the right. It's nothing to do with me now. He said, "Thorvald, I couldn't talk while we were unloading the Shaldur, so I've come to speak to you now. As you know, I'm captain of the Sula while Dagfinn's away. We'll be leaving straight after the hay harvest. Will you sail with me?" '

'Straight to the point.'

'That's Rolf. Thorvald was as offhand as if Rolf had offered him a mug of ale. "Thanks," he said, "I'll accept your offer." '

'And that was all they said?'

'No. They talked about Rolf's plans for a final trip to Biorgvin this year, fetching timber to sell in Hjaltland. Rolf wants to make a regular run, importing timber. He says it gives insurance against a bad season.'

'Snorri has changed his mind about Rolf,' said Gunnhild. 'He used to think he lacked ambition. Now he says he's the kind of man we need.'

'They could be gone in a week,' said Ingebjorg.

'It's a short voyage though, from now till the corn harvest.'

'But a tricky time of year.'

'Rolf won't take risks.'

'No. I saw Gudrun yesterday. She'll be all right, won't she?'

'If the birth goes well. I hope she'll be happier with Rolf now.'

'I hope she'll have reason to be.'

Ingebjorg was silent, remembering another summer day, when they all still lived at Shirva. She had been washing a sheepskin on the grass beside the well, and Gudrun and Ingrid were playing on the bank above her. Their shrill voices had suddenly stopped, and she looked up to see what was the matter.

It was Dagfinn, just back from his last voyage with Eirik. He stood in the sunlit Shirva yard, with his long hair falling in curls to his shoulders. He wore a fine cloak embroidered with scarlet braid, and a gold bracelet shone on his arm. He even had a sword in an ornamented scabbard. There was a long sigh from behind her.

'Look at him,' Gudrun had said. 'That's the one I'm going to marry. Ingrid, you can have his brother.'

'No thanks,' Ingrid had replied. 'Rolf has spots all over.'

'You don't know they're all over.'

'All over his face, anyway.'

That was ten years ago. Ingebjorg shook herself out of her daydream, and took another bannock. Rolf had no spots now. Instead he had a ship of his own, and Gudrun's child was due in November.

'It's strange how things turn out.'

'Not just strange,' said Gunnhild, who was still thinking about Gudrun's child, and how an evil fate had been averted. 'Luck comes when God wills it.'

'And goes the same way. It seems hard to believe God could be cruel enough to order an ill fate deliberately.'

'Fate was never kind.'

'Gudrun thinks we ought to build a church.'

'I heard about that,' said Gunnhild. 'Perhaps we should have the priest from Svinborg to visit us as well. It would cost something, though.'

'It might be worth it.'

'In the Cathedral at Kirkjavagr, you can light a lamp to protect a man at sea, and the Holy Virgin herself will watch over him. Snorri told me that.'

'I know,' said Ingebjorg. 'And you can light a lamp without a church too, but it doesn't always work.'

Thorvald and Olaf moved slowly along each side of a drainage ditch, turning the hay that lay drying on its banks. The blue sky of high summer arched over them, and the breeze brought the faint call of kittiwakes from the cliffs.

Turning hay was an easy job, shaking out the half dried grass and spreading it again. They had left the steep banks until last, but this was where the best grass grew, sheltered from every wind, and watered by the stream below. When the meadow gave way to rushes and cotton grass, they stopped and sat cooling their feet in the peaty water.

Olaf caught a trail of chickweed between his toes, and picked it up. He lay back, the sun full on his face, chewing.

'Don't go to sleep!'

'I'm not,' said Olaf lazily. Am I in love with her? he wondered. Am I?

'Next time,' said Thorvald, 'you'll go instead of me.'

'Go where?' The sun was red on Olaf's closed eyelids, and its warmth was miraculous. He didn't want to go anywhere.

'To Konungsborg,' said Thorvald. 'Isn't that what we were talking about?'

'I was thinking about something else.' Olaf wished he were alone; his body was insistently telling him something that had nothing to do with Konungsborg.

'I'm telling you, you'd like it,' said Thorvald. 'But you'll go to the Thing with Einar next year. I was a fool not to go this time. I may never have the chance now. Olaf?'

'Mmm?'

'I'll be gone in a week. I know what I want, and I'm on my way to getting it. But what about you? What do you want?'

No one had ever asked Olaf that before. He sat up reluctantly, spat out a chickweed stalk, and considered the matter. 'I don't know. I like making things. I'd like to travel, yes. I'd like to see how things are done elsewhere.'

'You'd have liked Konungsborg. Not so much the quarries, but the harbour, with boats from Katanes and Noreg, and even further: you'd like that.'

'Hard work though. I'm glad Sula was back before you. I wouldn't have wanted to unload all that soapstone without the Byrstada men to help. I'd rather go to the Thing, I think.'

'It was easier than the quarrying. And the loading; getting all those blocks balanced securely – you can imagine. If you go to the Thing you'll sail with Einar to Skalavagr.'

'Isn't that where Rolf wants to sell timber?'

'If Rolf has his way, that's all Sula will ever do. Biorgvin to Hjaltland, four times a season. Timber and iron in exchange for wool and sealskins. Dagfinn had greater ambitions than that. But it's a start for me, at last.'

Olaf picked more chickweed. 'And now Dagfinn's just a pirate. I'd rather make things than break things.'

Thorvald didn't want to argue. He started to pull seedheads off the grasses, and stared up at the Vord, where the islanders had once lit the fire that deceived Earl Paul, in the days when Fridarey mattered.

'Our father wasn't a pirate,' observed Olaf.

'He was a trader. But he could defend himself if he needed to.'

'You don't have to tell me. I'm his son too.'

Thorvald stared at his brother. 'Are you angry with me?'

'No.' Olaf picked a plantain, and shot the seedhead at his brother. 'But you shouldn't think it's a disappointment sailing with Rolf. Snorri says he's the better sailor.'

'Snorri hasn't been to sea for years. He's never sailed with either of them!'

'You haven't been to sea at all.'

'So? I know what they say. I was at Byrstada again yesterday. I heard how Dagfinn sailed the length of the Sudreyjar, when no other man would have dared.'

'Dared, yes. He nearly killed his passengers from exposure, nearly smashed Sula to bits on a lee shore, and it was just luck they didn't meet the pirates while they still had that cargo. With Rolf you'll live till you get your own ship, anyway.'

'Do you think I will ever have my own ship?'

Olaf shrugged. 'If you want it. If you can do what we've done with a two-oared boat, you can learn to sail a trading ship to Island, or wherever you fancy going.'

Thorvald let his breath go in a long sigh, and stood up. 'I suppose we should just do the little meadow.'

'Soon. You go on. I want to rest for a bit.'

Thorvald was startled. Olaf never rested.

'I'll catch you up,' said Olaf.

Thorvald's eyes were on the southern headland. 'In that case I might just go up the hill. I won't be long.'

Looking for a longship, thought Olaf. Dagfinn won't be home this week, or maybe ever.

Thorvald left in the direction of Shirva, and was lost in a blur of green and sunlight. Olaf stopped watching, and wriggled down in the grass, out of sight.

Little strands of cloud, high and white, were coming in from the south. Thorvald reached the coast at Hjukni geo. Seaweed rose and fell round Astrid's rock, like hair being washed and combed by the surf. Thorvald skirted the Shirva land, where the spread hay was bleaching in the sun. Two ravens flew up as he passed and flapped away over the rigs. He climbed fast, not pausing for breath until he stood on the headland.

He could see everyone out cutting the hay at Leogh. At Byrstada the first round coles quartered the ground like draughtsmen on a chessboard. Rolf had the whole crew out there, besides the women. If the Byrstada Lammas feast were to be tonight, word might come for him to be ready to sail tomorrow. Thorvald turned south and looked out to sea.

To the south-west where the Orkneyjar lay, the sky was turning milky grey. Thorvald sniffed the beginnings of a wind. There would be rain tomorrow. He ought to make straight back to his hayfields, but he stood still, eyes narrowed. The ripples reflected the sun so brightly it was difficult to be sure, but there seemed to be no ship as far as the eye could see, which was almost to Rinansay on a day like this.

Someone else was here, on the slopes below him. Someone else was gazing out towards the Orkneyjar. Thorvald moved closer.

It was Leif Asbjornsson.

Thorvald would have retreated, but Leif turned and saw him. They were within half a dozen yards of each other.

Thorvald came three paces nearer. Leif clenched his fists.

They had to meet sooner or later. The ship might sail tomorrow, and Leif must know by now that Thorvald was to sail with them. Something had to be done about their quarrel before they left.

Leif's tunic was still fastened with a silver pin. He seemed cold and aloof, pale in spite of his weeks at sea. There were sores on his face, but he still looked neat, and very conceited. He wore a knife at his belt.

Thorvald had thrown his knife down in the meadow with his belt and tunic. He wore only an unbuttoned torn shirt, and patched trousers. He must be covered in hay, the very image of what Leif had mocked at him for being.

If there was going to be a fight, it must be now. The harvest was almost in, and a fair wind coming.

Thorvald met Leif's wary eyes, and came six feet nearer.

'Do you think,' Leif asked him, 'that we really did bring an evil fate to the voyage?'

Thorvald stared. Were Bjarni's words being used to mock him, or was Leif serious? Thorvald remembered how Leif's fist had smashed into his face. The bruise had only recently faded.

'Because if we did,' said Leif, 'I for one am sorry.'

Thorvald lowered his hands. 'You were there. You should know.'

Leif shrugged. 'Who knows?'

Thorvald looked towards the Orkneyjar hidden beneath growing cloud. 'If Dagfinn means to come back before we sail again, he'll know he's only got a day or two.'

'I know that,' said Leif, 'but if he did want to join us, he couldn't have sailed from Gareksey until today, even if he'd got that far.'

There was nothing arrogant in Leif's tone. He was very serious; perhaps he was unhappy. His hair was straight and fair, and he had only the beginnings of a beard. He couldn't be more than seventeen. Alone of all Dagfinn's crew, including Dagfinn's own brother, only Leif had come to look for a ship from Gareksey.

'I doubt if he's intending to come back,' said Thorvald.

Leif shot a swift glance at Thorvald. 'He gave you his thorshammer, didn't he?'

Thorvald's hand went to his neck. With his shirt unbuttoned, the thorshammer hung there in full view. 'That was a long time ago,' he said, as if offering an excuse.

'Maybe you need to keep it safe for him.'

'Snorri thinks it's the best thing that could have happened to Dagfinn, and he was one of Svein's own men.'

'Until he was wounded.'

'He came back with honour, anyway. Svein gave him rich gifts. He wasn't just a sailor, he was a warrior.'

'Every seaman has to be that. How else would they get their cargo home?'

'How long have you been at sea?'

'This is my fourth season.'

Perhaps he had a right to talk as if he knew it all. 'You were lucky that they let you go so young. I wish it had been like that for me.'

The remark struck Leif as silly, but it wouldn't do to say so. He didn't want to fight. When he heard that Thorvald was to come on the next voyage, Leif had realised that inevitably, being of equal strength, they would be expected to row opposite one another, and so become messmates for the entire voyage. So Thorvald was envious of him. What did he know? Leif thought of what his life at sea had been like. It had started with a conversation that he remembered very clearly. For a moment he seemed to hear their voices again: "Send that boy to sea? You might as well kill him outright!" "He has to learn a trade, he has nothing of his own." "But a child like that, who's been ailing every winter since he was born? He'll not survive one season!" "Possibly. But what did Asbjorn ever do for me, that I should be called upon to rear his bastard?"

Leif turned to Thorvald. 'There wasn't anyone to stop me,' he said.

No uncles. Thorvald gave Leif a look of undisguised envy. 'Will you stay with Sula now, after this voyage?'

Leif hesitated. No one, least of all Thorvald, could have any idea of the situation that Leif had to face. The burden of guilt was almost more than he could bear. If Thorvald could only guess what demons Leif had to wrestle with, he would never have dared to call him lucky. Thorvald's life must be so simple. Leif wasn't sure whether he despised or envied him, but suddenly he felt desperately weary of his loneliness. For now, he had to patch up some kind of alliance with Thorvald. By tomorrow they might be living together on the deck of the Sula, in the space between two sea chests.

'Why don't we sit down?' said Leif. 'We need to talk about ship's rations.'

'Do we?'

'It's the custom to share with the man on the opposite oar. They'll put us together, you realise that?'

'I suppose they will. I'll share if that's what's done.'

'You don't have to, but it's the custom. Two can cook better together if we get the chance to go ashore. It's easier for collecting wood and everything.'

Thorvald realised he was being offered a truce. 'That's fair enough. I have dried fish mostly, and some dried mutton.'

'That's good. I couldn't get anyone to sell me meat at this time of year. They give us a grain ration from Byrstada, but you'll need to bring your own. Put it in an oiled sack, though it'll get damp anyway. Gunnhild sold me a cheese. This being a short voyage, we might make it last the month.'

'I could bring cheese too.'

'You supply meat, and I'll put in cheese. That's fair. We get water on the ship, and whey, and ale sometimes, so you don't need anything to drink.'

'Bread?'

'Bring enough for a day or two. After that it goes mouldy. Then it's porridge, and we can make enough to keep some cold for a few days. I have a sleeping bag you can share. That's what most men do. It's warmer. If we sail at night, we'll be on alternate watches. So then we only use it one at a time, and the other man keeps it dry for you.'

'I've got a good blanket too.'

'I'm glad to hear it, because I haven't.'

'Get one of the islanders to weave a new one for you next year.'

'I should have a woman,' said Leif, smiling. He turned serious again. 'If Dagfinn doesn't come back, will you stay with Rolf?'

'I've nowhere else to start.'

'He's a fair captain. He takes trouble to discuss things with us, but it's his word that counts, and you know it.'

'So you'll stay with him yourself?'

'No, I don't think so.'

'What ship were you on before?'

Leif leaned back, his hands behind his head. 'Audumla. She's one of the best trading ships. That was my second season. We went to the Faereyjar from Biorgvin. We dropped some of the wood in Thorshavn, and the rest was for a settlement at Kvivik, on the Vestmannasund. Then we picked up sealskins and oil, and took them east, right back to Gotland. Audumla was much bigger than Sula. The following season she went to Island. There was a man from Island who'd made his money in Vindland who wanted to go back home. He hired the ship for the season, to take all his goods back with him, and his family.'

'My father knew a man who'd done the voyage to Island,' said Thorvald. 'The mountains are very high, cold and dangerous. But underneath they're on fire.'

'In Island they have no overlords, and pay no taxes,' said Leif. 'The land is poor, and trade is going down, but I think one could still live well there.'

'So why didn't you go if you had the chance?'

'I didn't have the chance. They turned me off in autumn, and I had to spend the winter in Biorgvin. They had no trouble getting a crew in spring, for men still pay to get to Island. There aren't that many ships, and there's always travellers waiting for a passage.'

'How did you live alone in Biorgvin all winter?'

'Not well.'

'Couldn't you have gone home?'

'I wouldn't call where I came from "home".' Leif looked away, and was silent.

'What was the first voyage you made?' asked Thorvald, trying to change the subject.

For once Leif allowed himself to tell the true story. 'My first voyage was a short one,' he said, not looking at Thorvald. 'Not all ships are good to sail on, you know. This one was trading with the Finn men. That's against the law of Noreg. The crew were not just landless men, but outlaws. The man who bound me to their captain was my kin, but I'd never call him cousin if I saw him again. He knew what that voyage would be like for me. I ran away on the coast of Norrland, and bribed some fishermen to take me to Birka. Then a ship took me back to Hedeby, and from there I found a boat to Biorgvin.'

'How did you manage to live?'

'There are always ways.'

'And then you met with the Audumla? You were lucky they took you on.'

'There are ways of arranging that too.'

'I don't think I'd know how to be landless, but I'd not want to stay on the island all my life.'

'No,' said Leif. Some burden seemed to have lifted, for he suddenly smiled. 'You'd rather go to Groenland. It's a rough trip, and getting worse these days. I wouldn't want to do it.'

'I think I'd like to try.'

'And there's nothing in Groenland anyway, except ice, and a fortune in hunting. So they say. If you ever got home again you'd be rich. You can sell there at whatever prices you like – grain, timber, iron, cloth, they don't have anything out there. But you'd pay for it in trouble, and rheumatics for the rest of your life probably.'

'West of Groenland,' said Thorvald, looking out to sea, 'there's supposed to be a sound where the inner sea meets the outer. A passage going north-west that must lead to the outer sea. They know it must go through, because sometimes the current between Groenland and Markland reaches seven knots. That comes in the story of Thorfinn's voyage. Do you know it?'

'Old stories,' said Leif. 'No one goes further west than Groenland now, even if they ever did. I'd rather go south. The English lands are some of the richest in the world. In Birka I met a man from Aquitania. They have castles and forests, and drink wine every day, and the sun shines all the year round. He gave me this.' Leif indicated the silver pin in his tunic. 'You want to look south and east. That's what the Baltic merchants do. They take all our trade routes, and they build strange ships like tubs. Forget Groenland. It's not worth going west any more.'

'Well, I'm starting by going east. Maybe tomorrow.'

Leif grinned.

Chapter 28

They were working as fast as they could at Shirva, stacking the hay into coles. The sky was dull grey, and the wind was strengthening. Until today the raking had been quite pleasant work. The good weather had made everyone cheerful, and even Ingrid had stopped saying, whenever she and Astrid were alone, that she was missing Arne.

But this morning there were no smiles, no jokes, and no breaks. Even Gerda, who did no outdoor work now, was wielding a rake. It was all Astrid could do to rake fast enough to supply the men as they built the round coles. They had had nothing for the morning meal except yesterday's porridge, and Astrid dared not stop even to help herself to a ladleful of skimmed milk.

The first drizzle came in just before noon, when they were on the final strip. They built their last cole, and it was no sooner done than the skies opened. In five minutes they were all soaked to the skin, and the shorn meadow had turned from bleached yellow to sodden brown. The only thing they still had to do was to weigh down the last cole and collect their tools. Rain and sweat mingled and dripped into Astrid's eyes. Her skirt clung dripping to her legs. There was hay down her neck and hay in her hair; her arms had turned red and itchy with the stuff. But the field was bare, studded with neat coles, each one netted over and weighed down with stones. The harvest was in.

There was a visitor at Shirva, coming out of the empty house where he had been looking for them, a sack over his head and shoulders to keep the rain off. He didn't see them; they were upwind of him, and he was keeping his back to the rain.

'Thorvald!'

He turned round at Einar's shout.

'We just finished the hay.'

'Just in time,' remarked Thorvald, looking warily at Bjarni. 'I've brought you some mackerel.'

'Mackerel? Already? The first this year. Good luck to you.' Einar led the way into the house. 'We've not had the chance to fish. There were none two days ago.'

Ingrid began to uncover the fire. Astrid was sent to fetch more peat. Bjarni stripped off his wet tunic, and hung it over the hearth.

'You've been fishing this morning?' he asked Thorvald.

'Yes. They're in that basket.'

'You've finished your hay, then?' Whatever Bjarni said to Thorvald, it sounded like an accusation. 'When did you do it?'

'Today, as soon as we got back. We were fishing all night.' Thorvald sat down, and warmed his feet on the hearthstones. Gerda sat down without a word and began gutting the fish, so Astrid only had to skewer them and set them over the fire. They gleamed blue and green in the firelight. Thorvald's tunic and trousers glittered with fish scales, and he smelt of the sea. Under his sunburn he looked tired. Astrid wondered if Olaf had been up all night too.

'You kept some mackerel for yourselves?'

'Oh yes. It was a good catch. I won't have another chance. We leave tomorrow.'

'You had word?'

'Last night.'

'Where did you fish?'

When the men began to talk about fishing medes Astrid could never understand where they were referring to. Ingrid had explained to her that they were obscure on purpose, but there was not much Astrid could do with such knowledge. At first their secret language had made her feel indignant, but now she accepted it.

The fish were beginning to smell good. Astrid turned the skewers and wondered why Thorvald, who hadn't been there for weeks, should spend his last day on the island visiting Shirva.

'Those fishes are done. Give them to me, and start the next lot.'

Ingrid served the men, and they began to eat. Astrid caught a drop of oil off a sizzling fish to taste, and burned her finger.

The men were ready for more before she had even had a bite. She had just turned the third batch, when the door opened, and the wind stirred a flurry of ash, turning the fishes white.

Before they had peered through the smoke to see who it was, Ragna's voice rang out. 'Are you all there? Did you get your hay in in time? I've come to bid you a feast at Byrstada tonight, before they sail tomorrow.'

'You should have waited for Lammas,' said Bjarni.

'They'll be halfway to Biorgvin by then. Come tonight, and make the most of it.' Ragna spoke to the men of Shirva with an offhand equality which Astrid would never have attempted. She swept up to the fire. 'I can smell mackerel. Who caught that?'

'I did.'

'Oh, it's the sailor. I didn't see you there.' Ragna was standing between Thorvald and his uncles. Astrid watched him stick his tongue out at her, then mouth a word she couldn't catch. 'How come you've been fishing?' asked Ragna. 'What about your hay?'

'Done.'

'It wasn't done last night. I was on the hill, and I saw it all still spread.'

'Well, it's done now.'

'Did the trows do it for you in the night?'

'That's right,' said Thorvald, but Astrid saw him cross his fingers at her words, in the shadow of the hearth where Ragna couldn't see.

Ragna turned to Einar. 'You'll come to our feast then? That smells like good fish.'

'Were you waiting to be asked?' said Einar easily. 'You surprise me. Help yourself.'

Even Bjarni looked benign, and Astrid wondered how Ragna got away with it. When she helped Ragna to her fish, she took the chance to serve herself too.

'So Rolf reckons to be away tomorrow?' said Bjarni to Ragna.

'To Biorgvin,' she announced. 'With the summer's fish. Then to Kirkjavagr with timber. They have to bring us more grain from the Orkneyjar, and then they'll come home for the corn.'

'I wonder if he'll get news of Dagfinn.'

'In the Orkneyjar, he hopes. There should be news of Svein's campaign by then.'

Thorvald wiped his greasy hands on his trousers, and yawned. 'I must go.'

'To get some sleep before the feast?' said Einar. He stood up. 'We have that other matter to attend to first.'

'I'll see you tonight,' said Ragna, licking her fingers.

Thorvald winked at her behind Bjarni's back, and raised his thumb. Astrid saw Einar watching him. Then Einar stepped up on to the bench next to the high seat, and took down the shield that had hung on the wall ever since she had come to the island. He passed it to Thorvald. The stone wall showed paler where it had hung. Einar unhooked the scabbarded sword that hung from a nail above the shield, and passed that down too.

Ingrid and Ragna had stopped talking, and watched with as much interest as Astrid. Thorvald balanced the sword in his right hand, holding the shield and scabbard in his left.

'It's heavier than the ones Olaf and I practised with.'

'Those were just for boys to learn with. You can give yours to Eirik now.'

Einar stepped down from the bench, and Astrid realised that Thorvald was almost a head taller. Thorvald swung the blade.

Einar motioned him out to the byre. 'We'll have a word outside.'

The three young women looked at each other.

'Are there any more fish?' asked Ingrid. 'We might as well cook the rest. Father, do you want any more mackerel?'

'He's gone to sleep,' said Ragna.

Bjarni's head had dropped across the sheepskins, and his mouth was open. He snored gently.

'He was out doing the hay this morning when I woke,' said Ingrid.

'Can we finish the fish then?' asked Ragna in a low voice.

'I don't see why not. It'll be nothing but mackerel now for weeks. But don't wake him.'

Astrid, Ragna and Ingrid gathered close around the hearth.

Chapter 29

'Byrstada feasts are the best,' Ingrid told Astrid. 'Keep still! I can't do all these little plaits if you move.'

'I feel like a hedgehog.'

'What's a hedgehog? You look nice though,' went on Ingrid, not waiting for an answer. 'Ingebjorg used to do our hair like this when we were little. I wish you could see yourself.'

'I used to, at home.'

'In water, you mean?'

'No, it was glass, from Venice. You can look at your face in it and see yourself, just like everyone else sees you.' Astrid was examining the cracks on her fingers, made by peat and cold water.

'It sounds dangerous.' Ingrid crossed her fingers. 'There. That's done.'

'Shall I do yours now?'

'Yes, just plait it the ordinary way. One day we'll get Ragna here, then I can teach you how to plait hair Ingebjorg's way. There'll need to be three of us for that.'

The hall at Byrstada was decorated with patterned hangings which Astrid had never seen before. They were creased from being folded in a chest, and they smelt of the herbs that had been used to keep moths away. Trestle tables had been put up the length of the hall on both sides of the hearth. The one above the hearth had the Byrstada high seat as its centre. The one below reached to the door, and the chickens and store barrels had been moved into the byre to make room for it.

Gudrun, wearing a fine linen scarf and a blue dyed tunic over her dress, came to greet them, and to take the basket containing dishes from Shirva. It was not like a feast in Dyflin. Here, men and women were mingling and talking to one another, sitting at the same tables. Einar and Bjarni moved across to the high table, but Astrid could see Ragna by the byre door, holding a full flagon to her chest, exchanging comments with the crew. An unmarried girl would have had to behave very differently in Dyflin.

Ragna set her jug on the table, and came over. She looked uncannily like her brother Dagfinn. Her long hair hung down loose, and was tucked into her belt at the back. She looked Astrid over.

'Did Ingebjorg do your hair?'

'No, Ingrid.'

'Well, what do you think of this? Is it as good as a feast in Dyflin?'

'I didn't go to many feasts in Dyflin. When I did, they were very long, and I had to sit still and behave well. The women took me home early. I like this better.'

Ragna opened her eyes wide. 'You mean you're beginning to like us? Well, I'm sure we're honoured.'

Thorhalla tapped Ragna on the shoulder, ignoring Astrid completely. 'You're to pour the wine at the high table,' she said sulkily. Astrid wondered if she had wanted to be the wine bearer. Ragna was looking over Astrid's shoulder. 'I must go,' she said suddenly.

Astrid looked round, and saw Ingebjorg come in, ducking under the hangings. Her three sons trailed behind her, looking remarkably washed and brushed. By the time Ingebjorg reached Gudrun, only Eirik was still with her. He looked bored. Children were running up and down the length of the room in the narrow space between the tables and the hearth, skidding in the fresh straw, and getting under everyone's feet. Eirik watched them, and as soon as one of the boys came within range, he dived at his legs and brought him crashing to the floor. Skuli sauntered in, his hands on his hips, and tripped over them. He swore, and picked Eirik up by his tunic. 'Want to fight, do you?' he said softly.

'No,' said Eirik, wriggling.

'Too bad. Have a drink instead.' Skuli held his leather flask to Eirik's mouth and tipped it up. Eirik choked, and struggled free.

Ragna was at her side again, slightly breathless. 'Stay with me,' she commanded, to Astrid's surprise. 'You can protect me from Thorvald. He keeps following me about.' She seized Astrid by the wrist, and led her to the high table. 'We'll stay here. They'll all sit down in a minute.'

Rolf sat down in the Byrstada high seat. Gudrun's place was beside him, but she was still supervising the serving. The islanders seemed to know from long habit where they should be. The crew took their places at the lower end of the second table, among the lesser folk from the island.

'I'll be back,' said Ragna. She stood up, fetched a flagon, and began to fill the drinking cups, beginning with Rolf's, and working her way round the high table.

'What have we here then?'

Rolf leaned back in his seat and grinned. 'You like it?'

'Wine!' said Einar. 'Wine at an island feast! We are going up in the world. I drink to the host who can provide it. Where did it come from?'

'I bought it from Rhenish merchants in Biorgvin. Good, is it? I wish there were more, but there's a measure for everyone. And then as much ale as any of you can drink. So drink!'

The wine was rough and red. Astrid would have preferred hers with water, as they drank it in Dyflin, but she didn't like to ask. They marvelled over it, and discussed it, and the men reminisced over wines they had tasted before, in places far afield.

'Can you move up?' said a voice in Astrid's ear. 'I need a space to sit down.'

Olaf squeezed in beside her, and set his mug on the table. 'This is going to be good,' he told her. 'They killed a calf yesterday, and last night they were out after puffins.'

'Is that so?'

'Meat,' said Olaf. 'That's the thing. In the middle of summer too. Better than fish.'

Astrid wondered if he could be drunk already, but he was right about the food. There were ducks and seal meat, as well as beef and puffins, enough for everyone. As soon as the first pot was set on the table, Olaf became absorbed in his dinner, leaving her free to look round.

She was sitting at the foot of the top table. Opposite to her, on the end of the bench at the lower table, she saw Leif listening to a story Skuli was telling further down. Leif was dressed for a feast, with new braid embroidered on his tunic. She wondered if he had sewn it on himself. His tunic was fastened with the silver pin he always wore at the shoulder. The yellow lamplight made his hair gleam like pale gold silk. He was drinking steadily, and his normally pale cheeks were flushed red.

When he looked up and saw her, she let her eyes drop at once, and turned back to Olaf. In contrast to Leif's his hair was an indeterminate brown. He had obviously washed it, and it was standing up all round his head in wild curls. He smelt of something astringent which she couldn't identify. His eyes were clear and more focussed than usual, looking straight into hers. Astrid turned hurriedly back to her plate, and waited for her cheeks to grow less hot.

Thorhalla came round the table with a dish of roast birds. She set it down with a look that suggested she hoped it might poison them, and Olaf helped himself. 'Want some of this?' He tore off a puffin leg and gave it to Astrid. He was pressed right up against her, now that so many people had squashed on to the bench, and suddenly she recognised the smell. He had drenched himself in lotion of thyme.

At last the dishes were removed, but the ale kept coming round. Ragna had never returned. Astrid saw her sitting next to Thorvald at the other end of the table. She was sharing a drinking cup with him, insisting that he take measure for measure with her. When she saw Astrid looking at them she waved.

'A story!' The cry came from behind her. 'A story,' the crew echoed, and banged their mugs on the table.

Einar rose to his feet rather carefully, and thanked Rolf for his harvest feast. 'And if there's to be a tale,' he went on, 'as I hope there will be, and many of them, for it's early yet . . . We've all heard rumours, everyone's heard something, but we don't know all the details. We'd like your own version, Rolf. The story of Sula's adventure, and how Dagfinn went to sail with Svein, and the saving of the ship.'

Rolf told his tale in the formal way, as if he himself had had no part in it and his audience were listening to a well known story. He held them enthralled right up to the raid on the Sula. When they heard how Dagfinn had saved his ship by sheer audacity, they cheered, and when Rolf spoke of the past deeds of Svein Asleifarson, and Snorri's part in the Earl's wars, they hammered on the table again, and raised a toast to Dagfinn and to Snorri.

When he had finished everyone started talking at once. Only Leif, at the end of the table opposite Astrid, remained silent. His cheeks flamed scarlet now, and he was still drinking.

The islanders round Rolf were passing round the long Byrstada drinking horn.

'The tale of the Sula deserves to take its place in the annals of the Orkneyjar,' said Einar.

'The only annal now is that of Svein,' said Snorri. 'It'll be all too soon that campaigns like his are history.'

'It would improve trade to have less piracy,' said Rolf.

'Trade!' scoffed Snorri.

Bjarni laid his hand on Snorri's shoulder. 'We should have another tale, this time of past deeds. You're the one to give us that, Snorri.'

Snorri downed his draught of ale and began. 'This is the tale of the feud between Earl Thorfinn of the Orkneyjar and Rognvald his nephew. You all know how it was that they fought over the Earldom . . .'

'Was there ever an earl that didn't?'

Astrid hadn't heard this story before, but the islanders, who knew it by heart, were as absorbed as she was. They began to argue about it as soon as Snorri had finished.

'I'd support Thorfinn,' said Astrid to Olaf.

'Because he won?' asked Olaf, smiling at her very warmly.

'Because whatever else he did, he saved his wife.'

'Leaving all his men to burn to death?'

'What would you have done?'

There were shouts from the lower table. Two of the crew swayed together, hands at each other's throats, until the others pulled them apart.

'Tales from the Orkneyjar always make them fight,' said Olaf. 'Better to stick to Island. Then they just sit back and say how noble.'

Rolf was banging on the table. 'Another tale! Let's ask the strangers among us for some new ones.'

'Preferably a long way from home,' muttered Olaf.

Ragna called out, right down the length of the hall as no girl in Dyflin would have dared to do: 'Skuli Hedinsson, you can tell us a story!'

'What sort of a story?'

'A love story!'

Skuli smiled easily, and came forward to the high table. 'This isn't a love story. This is the story of a man who lived by his wits, and prospered mightily. It comes from Island.'

'Let's hear it then!'

The story was about Stub the Islander, a man descended from Gudrun Osvifsdottir. It seemed a suitable story for Skuli to tell. Astrid thought that Skuli, like Stub, would have no trouble gaining a king's favour, and maintaining his position by means of insult and repartee. Skuli ended by singing Stub's lay in honour of King Harald Sigurdarson.

'A good tale,' said Snorri. 'Not noble, but worth telling.'

'You can have too many heroic stories,' said Gunnhild. 'At least in the common tales they usually show more sense.'

Snorri was slipping down on the bench, but he pulled himself up. 'We should think about the old stories,' he said. 'They tell us what kind of people we once were.'

'Or might have been,' said Rolf.

'Of course they do,' said Einar. 'That's why we're waiting to hear another.'

Rolf called down to his men: 'Who can give us something new? Svein, have you a tale from Danmark?'

The man he addressed was a tall Dane with a ring of thin curls around a bald head. He came to sit near the high seat, stooping under the rafters. 'I can give you a story from Danmark, yes, if you will listen patiently. This is another story about a quarrel in a family, just like your earls in the Orkneyjar.

'Long ago there was a king of Danmark called Rothgar. He ruled well for many years, and he had a very beautiful queen. He also had a nephew, the son of his elder brother. This young man's name was Rothulf prince of Danmark. The tale takes place at the king's castle, in Helsingor.'

His tale was already familiar to many of them. He told it well. The fire burned low and nobody moved to mend it. A lamp guttered and went out. When the story had moved to its tragic climax, nobody spoke. Then suddenly applause broke out.

'That was a noble story.'

'And well told.'

Svein took his applause and bowed. 'I have done my best, but truly it is a theme which deserves a greater poet than I.'

They rewarded him with ale and compliments.

'You should have been a skald, Svein,' called out Bjarni. 'Whatever took you to sea?'

He grinned. 'It was the only way I could get away from my family.'

The tables were all cleared. They pushed back the hangings and opened the outer door, to let the wind blow through. Two lamps went out. Some of the women got up to go home, taking their children with them, while other guests moved up to the pool of lamplight that still flickered over the high table, while others withdrew into the shadows. Ingebjorg found Eirik fast asleep on one of the benches. She picked him up, and carried him away, his head dangling over her shoulder.

'Can your mother walk all the way to Setr like that?'

'Like what?' asked Olaf, peering through the smoke.

'Carrying your little brother.'

'She'll put him to sleep at the smithy and he can walk back in the morning. That's what she used to do with us.' Olaf's voice sounded strained. A moment later he got up hurriedly, spilling his ale. 'Wait there, I'll be back in a minute.' Astrid watched him stagger to the door.

It was getting noisy again. Ingrid had gone; Astrid could see no sign of Ragna or Thorvald. Thorhalla was down by the hearth, stroking one of the dogs.

One of the crew slid along the bench beside Astrid where Olaf had been. He put his arm round her, and breathed ale into her face. Astrid jerked herself away. Someone shouted from the shadows. 'Leave the lass alone, Magnus.'

Skuli's voice rang across the hall: 'You don't need a lass, Magnus. Nothing you could do with one.'

Magnus was over the table, and after him. Astrid caught the gleam of a knife. Skuli's voice came above the din. 'We know what you need! And now there isn't any competition!'

There was turmoil and shouting in the dark. The islanders at the other table were on their feet. Rolf leapt over the table and across the room. 'Enough! This is my house you're in, and don't you forget it!'

The shouting died to a muttering. Presently most of the crew went out, bearing flagons of ale.

Olaf was on his way back to Astrid, but as he passed Snorri reached out to stop him. 'This is the one,' said Snorri to Rolf. 'Give him ten years and he'll build you a ship.'

Olaf hiccupped.

'You could be a shipbuilder, couldn't you, Olaf?'

Olaf seemed dazed. 'I'd rather be a smith,' he said as clearly as he could.

'Now there's a compliment for you, Snorri,' said Rolf.

'Then have a drink.' It was the Byrstada drinking horn Snorri passed to Olaf.

Rolf left them and went over to the door. He came back to the hearth and stood over Thorhalla.

'Where's Ragna?'

'She was with Thorvald.'

He seemed relieved. 'No one else?'

'She might be by now. But she went outside with him, after the crew went back to the barn.'

'Has she no modesty? Well, if it's only Thorvald she's with, it doesn't matter.'

Astrid could have enlightened him. Thorvald had not reappeared, but Ragna had been back, only to disappear shortly afterwards with Skuli and his leather flask.

Suddenly there was a new sound in the hall. A harp. Astrid looked up. Someone had begun to sing one of the long ballads the islanders preferred. The voice was deep and pleasant, and the harp reminded her of other times. She stood up to see who it was.

It was Bjarni Thorvaldsson. He was singing the story of two brothers, who were loyal and loved one another, until the younger accidentally killed the elder with a stray arrow from his bow. The song told of the misery of the king their father, mourning the one son, yet unable to avenge his death, for that would be to lose the other.

The lamps were all out, but the dying fire cast a red light that was reflected in the weapons on the walls. The few remaining guests sprawled in the half dark, some too drunk to notice anything, others listening to the music or talking quietly. Someone took a half burnt peat and stuck it up on a bracket where a lamp had been. Rolf sat near the high seat with his head resting on his arms.

Thorvald was there too, looking disconsolate. When Einar passed the drinking horn to him he drank without stopping. Someone had put chicken feathers in his hair.

Bjarni finished his ballad and passed on the harp.

'It's no use passing it to me,' said Rolf, 'unless you want me to make bowstrings of it.'

'If you're looking for someone to play perhaps I could take a turn?'

Leif took the harp and played a tune without words, like they played in Irland. Astrid felt unwanted tears come to her eyes, and rubbed them quickly away. She stood up. It would be better to go home.

Before she reached the door Einar took her by the shoulder.

'Don't go yet, my dear. It's still early.'

Astrid had never known him in this mood before. She didn't like to pull away, but she was frightened by the way he looked at her.

'My fate,' he said. His speech was slurred. 'A fate from the sea. A lass from Irland. What kind of luck is that, do you think?' His arm was round her, pulling her towards him.

'I don't know.' She tried to wriggle free. He had never touched her before. 'I'm going home.'

'A fate from the sea,' he repeated, 'An Irish selkie. Shall I come home with you?'

She was scared into a lie. 'I'm going with Olaf.'

'And what shall I do, then?' He laughed, and swayed on his feet. 'Go fishing? That's cold and comfortless, on a night as wild as this.' His arm tightened suddenly, and he reached to kiss her. He missed her mouth, but his lips smeared wetly on her cheek.

She pushed his arm from her shoulders and struggled to get away. 'Yes, if you like,' she said desperately. 'Go fishing!'

'A hard fate,' he murmured, as she fled.

Astrid hid in the shadows until she saw him leave the hall, supporting himself against the doorpost as he went.

She was shaking. She had never dreamed that Einar would touch her. All her peace was destroyed. Even if he had forgotten by tomorrow she never wanted to see him again. He was like her father, and now he had done this.

The music stopped. There were stumbling footsteps behind her and she backed against the wall, as Rolf lurched towards the door.

He stopped by the hearth, swaying, leaned forward and was violently sick.

Astrid ran for the door.

It was no longer raining, but the wind blew fiercely in a grey dawn. Astrid drew a deep breath, and set off running to Shirva.

'Astrid!'

She came back reluctantly.

'Where did my uncle go?' asked Thorvald.

'Bjarni? He's inside.'

'No, Einar. I saw him speak to you. I didn't think he'd go home tonight.'

'I don't know. Perhaps he went with Olaf.'

'Olaf went home. He was sick.'

'I don't know,' said Astrid helplessly. He seemed to be waiting for her to speak. 'Goodbye,' she said firmly. 'I won't see you till you get back. You're going to sea today, aren't you?'

He gave a wry grin. 'I doubt if anyone's going anywhere today. Besides, it's getting wild out there. Goodnight, Astrid.'

She was glad of the gale. She ran, fighting it, head down. In a strange way it satisfied her. She remembered going home from another feast, along muddy streets between dark houses, then across an open square by a church, where the moon cast square white patches between the shadows of the wattle buildings. Their torch had burned with a yellow flame, so the straw roofs shone and the water in the puddles gleamed golden as they passed. They had heard someone singing drunkenly, not droning a ballad, but singing a bawdy song with a proper Irish tune to it, as the singer lurched across the stinking gutters.

By the time Astrid was asleep at Shirva, the rain had come back, sweeping across the island before the gale. Cattle huddled behind walls and in hollows. The wind shuddered against roofs and walls, and tore over the boats that were lying in their noosts on the shore. It found one noost empty and seizing on a bailer that lay there, sent it bumping down over the boulders into the white waters of the Sudvik. It was the bailer from Einar's boat.

Part Five

Thorvald

Thorvald dreamed he was sailing outside the Nordhavn. His boat was tossed towards the rock, but the steerboard was heavy under his hand so he could not turn. Now the rocks were within an oar's length, and each time the sea fell he saw a slime of seaweed. The sail flapped uselessly. Still he sat inert, slouched over the steerboard. He should have oars but he could not rouse himself to search for them. The rock hung over him, and the wind was like a scream.

He woke in terror, his hand clutching his thorshammer. Only the wind was real. The rafters creaked as gusts struck the roof. He pushed his hair off his damp face, and half sat up. Laying his hand flat against the wall, he could feel three feet of solid stone shaking.

Thorvald staggered to the door and opened it cautiously, while the wind tried to snatch it out of his hands. The gale caught his shirt and hair, and swept round his legs. Blinded by the wind, he could hardly see across the yard. Wind stormed through the grass and nettles like the shadow of an invasion. No voyage today, or tomorrow.

It was a south-westerly, so Sula, beached in the Nordhavn, should be safe, but if the wind veered they'd have to haul her up much higher, which would mean calling out all the islanders. Rolf must be worried, up at Byrstada. He wouldn't have reckoned his wind would turn to a gale like this.

It flashed across Thorvald's mind that Rolf might have called up more than he bargained for. It was illegal to use sorcery to raise a wind, but Ragna had told Thorvald that Gunnhild had made a charm for Gudrun, and that was why Rolf's baby lived. Where one spell came from, there might well be another. Thorvald crept back to bed and lay shivering. He stretched out along the platform until he found Olaf's feet under his blanket, and warmed his own feet against them. Olaf didn't move.

Thorvald was woken again by Eirik shaking him. 'Thorvald! Thorvald! Wake up!'

When he had wakened the first time his head had not hurt. This time it did. There was a foul taste in his mouth, and Eirik's voice in his ear was as piercing as a seagull's. Thorvald groaned. His eyes wouldn't open. There was a banging inside his head, like hammers echoing round a quarry.

'Thorvald! You have to wake up! Bjarni sent me. You have to wake up!'

Thorvald rolled over and looked at his brother blearily. Eirik's face was white and frightened, and there were smudges of dirt mingled with tears on his cheeks. Thorvald reached out and took his brother by the shoulder. 'What is it?'

'Did you see Einar?'

'Einar? See him where?'

'After the feast. The Shirva boat's gone. He's not at any house on the island. He left Byrstada at dawn. He didn't go home, or to the smithy, or Leogh, or here, or anywhere. Then when Bjarni went to the south haven the boat was gone.'

Thorvald held his hands to his head. 'The boat? That's not possible!'

'He was drunk,' said Eirik, and began to cry.

'What's going on?' Olaf emerged from his blankets in a tangle of hair. He still had all his clothes on. 'Oh God, I think I'm going to die,' he moaned, and sank his head in his hands.

Thorvald went to the bucket by the door and splashed his face thoroughly. He wrung out a wet cloth, and gave it to Olaf. 'Put that round your head. Einar's not back, and his boat's gone.'

'Not back from where?'

'The feast.'

Olaf frowned. 'What's that got to do with a boat?'

'There's a gale blowing.'

Olaf was tying the towel round his brow. 'So?'

Eirik spoke in a frightened squeak. 'Bjarni thinks he took the boat out. He was drunk. Bjarni's been all over the island. He came to the smithy. We were having breakfast, me and Gunnhild. Snorri was asleep. He was looking. He said the boat was gone from its noost. And no one saw Einar at Leogh or Byrstada. Bjarni said run back here, and if he wasn't here wake you, tell you to come.'

'We could take the boat out,' said Olaf.

'Listen!' said Thorvald.

The wind howled above their heads. Eirik whimpered, and Thorvald took his hand.

'No one could go out in that,' whispered Olaf.

So many nights their mother had said that. Thorvald and Olaf used to hear her prayer, "From the fury of the tempest, good Lord, deliver him."

'Pray to God no one did,' said Thorvald.

Chapter 31

It was four days before they could launch a boat. The wind moved into the north-west and stayed there. After the first day the gale subsided enough for them to bring home the peats. Thorvald worked as hard as he could, to keep himself from thinking. When he could carry no more loads he walked the cliffs, going over the same ground again and again. The wind stung his cheeks and froze his fingers, and when he stared out to sea the fast driving waves blurred into a froth of white. Even when the wind blew itself out the sea would take days to subside. Shower after shower came over, turning the water dark beneath them and breaking the swell into foam. When the rain reached him Thorvald turned his back while it pierced his cloak and drove against his legs. Then he'd go on tramping the hills in useless watch. There was no evidence, only an empty noost, and a man who, when all the searching was done, was nowhere.

Einar's elusive passing affected the whole island. People seemed at a loss, like sheep when the white tailed eagles have killed their prey and flown. There was continual visiting from house to house. Thorvald watched them from the heights: groups of two and three following the well-worn paths. Several times he saw Rolf on the hill, walking his own section of cliff between the Sudvik and the

Seydurholm. Thorvald came face to face with him once, above Swarza geo.

'You've seen nothing?'

'Nothing.'

Thorvald knew from Olaf that rumour was rife. Rolf's feast, Rolf usurping Dagfinn's high seat, Rolf who had bound spells of witch-craft round his unborn child, Rolf who might even have bargained illicitly for a wind that had brought a cruel fate upon one of the best men the island had ever known. Einar, folk said, had abhorred lawlessness and witchcraft. Who knew what spells Rolf had set for Dagfinn on the notorious isles of the Sudreyjar, for all his talk of churches?

Thorvald, standing beside Rolf now and looking down into a yeasty sea, thought of rumour and dismissed it. Rolf's eyes held not guilt, but grief. Thorvald envied the grief, which would not touch him, although he longed to feel it. Certainly Rolf could not have done more, even though all action was useless. He had the crew posted round the island, looking for any signs of a boat, or of flotsam. They sighted nothing.

Thorvald often saw Bjarni north of the hill dyke, but he never approached his uncle, and was never certain whether Bjarni had seen him; if he did, he too made sure they never met.

When Thorvald went to Byrstada Ragna gave him little com-fort. 'I can't talk about it,' she said. 'I wish Dagfinn were here.'

'I don't see how that would help.'

'Nothing can help,' she said, and turned her back on him.

Thorhalla brought him barley bread and blaand. 'It's terrible for you,' she said maternally. 'And an evil fate that's come to Shirva.'

'It's nothing to do with the Byrstada feast,' he reassured her. 'It's nobody's fault. No one could have prevented it.'

'I'm not sure about that.'

'What do you mean?'

'It's only what they're saying.'

'What are they saying?'

'About the shipwreck, of course, last autumn. Einar said himself it was a miracle she survived. He called her a fate from the sea. Even before this happened they said he'd acted like a man be-witched.'

'What have you been listening to?'

'I'm only saying what I've heard.'

'Heard where?' She was silent. 'What's said of Shirva concerns me.'

'It's just what they've been saying.' She sounded aggrieved. 'It's nothing to do with me.'

He remembered then who Thorhalla was; how Einar was said to have seduced her mother. 'Are you very unhappy about my uncle?' he asked, as gently as he could.

'I just think justice should be done,' said Thorhalla, lowering her eyes.

'Justice to whom?'

'You didn't hear what happened when they told her Einar's boat was gone? Apparently she went completely hysterical. You know how quiet she's always been. Not any more. She was screaming for her father. She screamed out that it was all her fault. "I want to get out! I want my father back!" They could hear her from Leogh. She ran off to the smithy, still screaming. She's been there two days now, and hasn't set foot in Shirva since.'

'Astrid?'

'Yes. People said from the beginning it wasn't right. Now she's admitted it. She's possessed. Even Einar said it was fate, when he took her in.'

He looked at her in disgust, and pushed his ale away. 'I think you're mad.'

Thorhalla began to cry. Exasperated, Thorvald got up and left.

The next day he went to the smithy. Rolf had sent the crew to bring home the smithy peats. Thorvald found Gunnhild and Astrid in the yard, stacking the heap of peat that had been dumped outside the smithy door. Gunnhild was showing Astrid how to build a stack properly, laying the biggest peats lengthwise along the outside, their ends sloping outward so that the water would drain off them, keeping the peats inside quite dry.

Astrid looked ill and strained, just as she had when he and Olaf had first gone to Shirva to look her over. Then he had thought her a scraggly little creature, not worth bothering with, but perhaps she had simply been unhappy.

Gunnhild looked up. The peat had left black lines round her eyes as if they were painted, like the women who mourned at funerals in the old tales.

'Is Snorri in?'

Gunnhild jerked her thumb towards the smithy door.

Snorri was even less comfort. 'Have you been to Shirva?'

'No, not today.'

'Why not?'

'They don't need me there.'

'It's your duty. Out of respect to the dead, and in support of Bjarni. A man needs his kin when he's suffered a grief.'

'I don't think Bjarni needs me.'

'You owe it to him. If you don't go, trouble will come of it.'

In the yard, Gunnhild and Astrid were bent over their work with their backs to the wind. Rolf's men might have stayed to help build the stack. The day stretched ahead without hope. Without a word Thorvald began to help them. Gunnhild nodded to him, but didn't speak.

He worked at the stack as fast as he could. When they started on the top, he was up on the stack while they handed the peats up. He built the long peats in overlapping rows, to make a watertight roof. Then he helped them mark out the next stack. Every handful of peat he threw was a fight with the wind. Peat dust flew up into his eyes and nose.

At last the stacks stood in the yard like barrows for the dead, dark and smelling of earth. The women took a basket each, and began to pick up the scraps that lay scattered across the yard.

Thorvald and Olaf only visited Leogh once. Their arrival stemmed the conversation for a moment, but then it swept on, and they soon caught the current of it.

'I happen to know Gunnhild made a spell to save Rolf's child. She came here, and I gave her flour for it. She took food from nine hearths on the island, and cast a spell over it.'

'And Gudrun thrives with it. She's only got three months to go now.'

'If she bears a live child, everyone will suspect why.'

'The whole island knows that Gudrun Bjarnadottir could never bring a child to term by normal means.'

Olaf broke in, 'You can't know that.'

'That's what they say, boy. There are women who can never carry a child to term. And she has red hair.'

'What of it?'

'If Gudrun Bjarnadottir led Rolf into witchcraft, then that would account for that ill wind coming home to Shirva.'

Thorvald jumped to his feet. 'Gudrun is my cousin! What have you to say against her?'

'Nothing, nothing. If she married into an evil house, one can only be sorry for her.'

'What's this got to do with Rolf?' demanded Thorvald.

'Sorcery spins its own thread, and you'd need long sight to see the end of it. Who raised that wind? That's all I ask.'

Thorvald seized Olaf by the arm. 'I'm not staying to hear anyone speak against my kin, or the man I sail with!'

As they pushed their way out through the hangings, they heard comments break out behind them.

Thorvald stayed away from home as much as possible, afraid of his mother's silence. Since the news of Einar's loss first came, she had hardly spoken of it. One night he woke and heard her weeping. Her sobs were muffled as though she were holding her blanket over her face. Neither of his brothers showed any signs of stirring. The weeping grew louder, as if it could not be suppressed.

He knew he should go to her. When he was a small boy he used to climb off his sleeping platform and get in beside her where it was warm, to try to comfort her. Now he was a man, and he couldn't do it. Thorvald pulled his own blanket over his head. He couldn't stand hearing her.

During those nights long ago, she used to talk to him about Eirik. 'Eirik', she would say, not 'your father'. Eirik was my man, and there was no one like him. Eirik said goodbye in the spring and promised he would be back at harvest. I gave him four children, of whom three lived, and I loved no one more. When I was a girl I came back here with Eirik, and since then there has been no one else. For the nine years of my marriage I slept alone all summer, and never rested when a gale blew up and the ship was out at sea.

On the fifth day they were able to take the Leogh boat out. They forced a passage up the east coast, staying close under the cliffs to get the shelter of the land. Under the lee of the island the wind seemed to come from every direction, catching the boat in a down draught, blowing it back towards the rocks, or leaving it in uneasy calm. Once they were past the Burrian rock they were out of the swell, and able to go into some of the geos.

They kept as close inshore as they could, right round to the east side of the Seydurholm. The sea lifted silently against the cliffs, then fell in cascades like waterfalls. It wasn't until they left the shelter of the Holm that the wind hit them. They rowed across the entrance to the south haven, fighting with every stroke not to be carried out to sea. At the north end of Buness the swell was breaking badly in the shallows, and they stood out to sea to avoid it. For a moment the boat was exposed to both sea and wind, when a sudden squall broke over her. The port oars missed their stroke, and the starboard oars were caught by a heave of sea that threatened to drag them out of the rowers' hands. Bjarni put the steerboard over to turn back.

With wind and swell behind them, they fought their way back into the south haven. They beached the boat there and hauled her up. There was nothing to say of the search, except that they had survived it.

On the sixth day, Rolf came to see Thorvald.

'We could put to sea any time now,' he said, 'but I don't want to leave matters unsettled. Gudrun's worried about these rumours. She shouldn't be upset.'

'Of course not.'

'I can't stop gossip. Only time will do that. It would be better if you and I were here, but that can't be.'

'Me?'

'We're both being talked about.'

Thorvald put down the line he and Olaf had been mending, and stared at Rolf. 'Who's talking about me?'

'They're speaking as though there's a dispute now between the heirs of Shirva. They say you're not on speaking terms with Bjarni, and that you want to claim his inheritance for yourself.'

'But that's madness! What inheritance? I'd never thought about it!'

'But you haven't been to Shirva, have you?'

'I don't know what to say to Bjarni. But there's no quarrel.'

'Tomorrow is the seven day feast.'

'Seven day? You mean an inheritance feast? But . . . we don't know that! Who says that? Nobody told me.'

'I've just come from Shirva. I told Bjarni that I'd tell you.'

'Bjarni's having an inheritance feast, as if there'd been a burial?'

'Thorvald, listen. Put down that line, Olaf, you can listen too. It concerns all three of you. You brothers are all heirs to Shirva.'

'Eirik's taking Snorri's pony back to the smithy,' said Olaf. 'We borrowed it for the peats.'

'Never mind Eirik. Listen. Neither of you has been to Shirva, and that was wrong. You had a duty to Bjarni, and it would have shown respect for the dead. That can't be mended now. Bjarni has drawn his own conclusions. You can hardly blame him.

'Bjarni's my father-in-law, and it's my duty to support him. He knows quite well what's being said about the heirs to Shirva. He knows too that I have to leave before the week is out. I've a contract to fulfil and a lot of folk to support this winter. Also, the iron for the smithy is still in Biorgvin. So I suggested that we hold the seven day feast tomorrow, counting from the day Einar was lost.'

A seven day feast was held when a man had been buried a week. Thorvald had known there was no hope, but there was no body, no trace of what had happened. A seven day feast meant the death was real, sealed and ratified by law. Einar was dead.

Rolf touched Thorvald's shoulder. 'I know it's soon. But it's not as if there could be any doubt. There'll be no burial, you realise that.'

'There should be something.' Thorvald heard his own voice come out choked and hoarse. It was not yet time for an inheritance feast. Einar's death had not even been acknowledged.

'Something?' queried Rolf.

'He means a mass,' said Olaf. 'The bits we can have without a priest. There was one for father in Kirkjavagr. Prayers. And a runestone. There should be that.'

'There will be, of course. You can't think Bjarni would neglect anything necessary. Einar was his brother.

'We must deal with this before Sula puts to sea,' repeated Rolf. 'We can't leave, Thorvald, until we see the matter settled. That's what we can achieve tomorrow.'

Thorvald held his hands to his head. There was a knot inside him that stopped him thinking. He couldn't speak.

He heard Olaf's voice beside him. 'We understand. It makes sense. We'll come to this feast tomorrow.'

Olaf could deal with this, and he couldn't. With a great effort Thorvald controlled himself. 'Yes, we'll come.'

'We can also talk about prayers perhaps,' said Olaf, 'and a runestone.'

Rolf looked at him curiously. 'Is that so important?'

'It's the correct thing to do,' said Olaf. 'We did it for my father.'

Rolf had only been gone a few minutes when Eirik burst into the house, calling out for Thorvald.

'Sit down,' said Olaf, 'and tell us what happened.'

'It was the pony.' Eirik was half crying. 'It wasn't my fault! It was the pony!'

'What happened?'

'It bolted just as I was passing Shirva. I couldn't stop it! Something blew past. I don't know what it was.'

'I told you to lead her!'

'Don't shout at him, Thorvald, or he won't say anything. Eirik, go on! What's the matter?'

'Bjarni was there. He was in Shirva's end rig, by the mound, hoeing the kale, and the pony bolted straight into his oat rig. I couldn't stop her!'

'Oh God! That's all we needed!'

'He was shouting at me. I couldn't help it! I was right across the horse's neck, but I didn't fall off. He grabbed her halter. He was shouting at me. He said he'd beat me.'

'And did he?'

'I jumped off and ran. He was holding the pony so he couldn't chase me. He said, "Come here, you little coward!" I'm not a coward. I said, "Coward yourself!" '

'Oh my God!' groaned Thorvald.

'Was that all?'

'No. He said, "Get off my land!" I said, "Who says it's your land anyway?" '

'You what?'

Eirik looked defiant. 'Well, it's not! It's ours as well. That's what this meeting tomorrow is all about. I heard them saying so at Byrstada.'

'Oh no,' gasped Olaf. 'What did he say?'

'He was in a rage. He was shaking the hoe at me. That made the pony pull, of course. He couldn't get me.'

'I wish he had!' said Thorvald.

'He swore at me and I swore back.'

'What did you call him?'

'I remembered how angry you were before, Thorvald, about that sheep. I called him a sheep killer.'

Chapter 32

'I won't go,' said Thorvald. 'How can I go to this seven day feast? How can I? Bjarni's inheritance feast, and you expect me to make this wretched claim in public. He'll have nothing to do with it! He never even sent me word, except by Rolf. Everyone accuses me of not going to him but he never came to me! And then Eirik goes and insults him like that!'

'Don't be foolish,' said Ingebjorg. 'You have to go. If you don't, he really will have reason to disinherit you.'

'I don't care! He can keep his cows and his crops!'

'Now you're being thoroughly selfish! You've your brothers to think of too!'

'They've not thought much about me!'

Olaf was sitting at the other end of the hearth, tying fish hooks carefully to a trace. He didn't look round.

'If you let Bjarni seize your land now you're letting him drive you off the island,' Ingebjorg went on. 'This land isn't going to support all of you when you have families of your own.'

'I don't want a family.'

'Listen. Einar's land should be divided equally among his heirs. All you have to do is stand up and say so.'

'But Bjarni will say that when my father was given his ship, and came to live here at Setr that was his share of the inheritance, for himself and his heirs.'

'This land isn't a third of his father's lands. Setr was Eirik's home, not a land division.'

'So what do you want me to say to him?'

'You know what to say: that this part of the farm was given to Eirik as a home for his family, and that it was my right as his wife to keep it during mine. And that it's my right as your mother to bring up my own sons in my own house. That's what I fought for at the Thing and won. I can't help it now if Bjarni's never forgiven me for it. It doesn't alter the fact that you three are Einar's heirs. If Bjarni wants to deny that, he's a fool.'

'You expect me to tell him that?'

'I expect you to stand up for your rights, for your brothers' sake as much as your own.'

Thorvald finished polishing his knife, ran his hand along the blade, and sheathed it.

'Are you listening?'

'I don't want his bloody land. I want a ship.'

'And your brothers are to starve because you haven't the courage to stand up to Bjarni?'

Olaf looked round from his fishhooks. 'Thorvald isn't a coward, mother,' he said, 'ever.'

When Thorvald and Olaf arrived, Bjarni was already in his place next to Einar's empty high seat. His daughters sat opposite him. They were the only women present. Rolf sat at Bjarni's left hand, and Snorri next to Rolf. Kalf of Leogh sat on Bjarni's right, on the other side of the empty place. Thorvald and Olaf took the bench opposite Snorri.

It was Bjarni's inheritance feast and his hospitality was generous, but neither food nor drink did much to relieve the tension in the hall. The meal was soon finished, and the business of the day began. Kalf of Leogh had been chosen as lawman. When he began to speak, everyone fell silent.

'I request all the creditors of Einar Thorvaldsson to present their claims now and cite witnesses.'

It was as Thorvald would have expected. Einar owed nothing. He had been provident until the last day of his life.

'In that case I declare that Einar's debts are all discharged. If any claim is made in the future I ask you all to bear witness to this declaration.

'Now we come to the inheritance left by Einar. This has been assessed and consists of thirty ounces' weight in silver, in coins and ornaments, and six ounces' weight in gold. Also, he and Bjarni together owned this hall and everything it contains, and the lands and stock belonging to the farm of Shirva, together with fishing gear, lines and nets.'

No boat.

'Einar Thorvaldsson left no legitimate descendants. The rule that applies is that of the third law of inheritance, under which brothers may legitimately succeed to an estate . . .'

'Before you go on I'd like to mention another claimant.'

Kalf looked up. 'Who is speaking?'

'Magnus of Leogh.'

Snorri whispered to Rolf, 'If we start on this sort of thing we'll be here until morning.'

Magnus of Leogh came forward from his place near the door, stooping. 'I am here on behalf of my grandson, Kari Hildasson.'

Bjarni had obviously expected this, and it did not take long to reach a settlement.

Kalf continued. 'Now, concerning the main part of the inheritance, I will state the law under which Bjarni Thorvaldsson is heir to his brother's estate.

'The law is that of the third inheritance, under which a brother inherits from a brother. Einar Thorvaldsson left one surviving brother, Bjarni Thorvaldsson, who is thus the principal heir to the estate.' He paused, then continued less firmly, 'Under normal circumstances brothers' sons would also inherit. Einar's brother Eirik had three sons. But here a different case applies. Eirik Thorvaldsson received his share of udal land together with a large gift of money upon the occasion of his marriage . . .'

'No!' Snorri held up his hand.

'What is it?'

'The money was nothing to do with it. Einar gave him the money long before that for his ship. It was a gift.'

'Can you cite witnesses?'

'He has no need.' Bjarni's voice sounded weary. 'Eirik received his ship money four years before his marriage.' He briefly met Snorri's eyes.

'I'll proceed,' said Kalf. 'Eirik received his share of the udal land ten years ago, when he took his family to live at Setr. After his death this settlement was ratified by his widow at the Thing. Therefore Eirik's sons are not concerned with the present inheritance.'

Thorvald stood up. Their faces swam. He felt hot and confused, without a coherent thought in his head. 'That's not true,' he said.

There was a silence.

'Would you like to enlarge your argument a little?' said Kalf.

'Neither my father nor my mother ever agreed to a settlement that denied us our rights as heirs to Shirva.' Now that he had started it wasn't so bad. 'Einar gave Eirik the farm at Setr to be his home. When he died my mother wanted to stay there. Bjarni tried to persuade her to come back to Shirva to live but she didn't want to. He said he'd foster us and she didn't want that either. You all know they disagreed about it and the matter was taken to the Thing. Einar was in Hjaltland at the time. All of you voted for her. You agreed that she could live separately at Setr and have that land for her farm. Nobody ever said that the land division was permanent. Einar never thought so. He always said we were his heirs too. He told me so the day he died, when he gave me his sword. No one ever suggested differently until Bjarni started saying it this week.'

Thorvald sat down. Sweat trickled down his chest. He was sure he'd left something out, but he couldn't think of anything more. Olaf touched his knee.

Bjarni rose. 'I deny that entirely! The matter had certainly been discussed before that. Your mother rejected every offer we made. Why do you suppose we were so anxious to bring Eirik's family back to Shirva if not to secure your rights, and stop your mother taking a step that was in your very worst interests? You have no legal claim on Shirva, but I would never deny you your rights as my kinsmen.'

'We don't want your generosity. We want our land!'

'What does the law of inheritance say on this point?' Snorri asked Kalf.

'Very little. But I would quote you this, qualifying all the dispositions of inheritance: "Now this is called the order of inheritance, but the kinship of men can take so many forms that no one can draw up a complete order of inheritance, and those who apply the rules will have to do what seems most reasonable." '

'Very helpful,' muttered Olaf.

Kalf continued, 'There is still the question of the money paid out to Eirik Thorvaldsson for his ship. I can quote you the law on this:

' "If a man gives more to one – in this case brother – than to another, when they come to divide the inheritance the other shall take as much out of the property as the one who received the larger sum; then let them divide equally what remains." '

'We agreed that the money has nothing to do with it,' objected Snorri, 'and if a law says that Eirik's sons are to receive nothing minus the cost of a ship that has lain at the bottom of the sea for seven years, then the law is unjust.'

'In any case,' said Kalf, 'the only property in dispute is Einar's udal land, not his money or movable property.'

'No,' said Snorri.

'You dispute that?'

'Einar had a sword and shield, and he intended to give them to Thorvald when he went to sea. I can cite witnesses.'

'You have no need,' said Bjarni. 'Einar's weapons are Thorvald's by right of gift, and no one can accuse me of denying it. We are talking about the inheritance under udal law.'

'If a settlement is to be reached some tolerance is essential from both parties,' said Kalf. 'Do you have anything more you wish to say, Thorvald?'

'No.'

'Then it seems to me that nothing further is going to be achieved by this meeting. I propose that this case should be taken before the island Thing.'

The next morning Thorvald and Olaf killed one of last year's wethers, which Ingebjorg had decided was fat enough to be worth eating. Olaf held it down in the byre, and it lay quivering, its brown eye fixed and staring. Thorvald tested the newly sharpened blade of his knife against his thumb, grasped the animal firmly by the head and cut its throat. A pulley hung from the beam above, and they swung the carcass up at once, and shoved a bucket under it to catch the blood. Head down, the sheep kicked and jerked as its blood gushed out. Thorvald wiped his knife and sheathed it. Presently the animal stopped jerking, stretched out, and began to stiffen. Thorvald unwrapped the bloodstained sack he had tied round his middle. Last night, when they had come home from the inheritance feast, he had been sick, and he still could not think about Einar. In fact there were moments when he caught himself assuming that Einar would be able to solve everything. He had always known what to do.

'I know I'm not much use,' said Olaf, breaking across his thoughts, 'but there are two of us.'

'At least that's one thing we can take for granted.'

An hour later, Eirik's sons set out to the smithy. Olaf looked uncomfortable in his best tunic; Eirik was still clean from the washing he had had before the Byrstada feast, his hair shining almost white in the sporadic sunshine.

'Remember,' said Thorvald, 'you don't say anything, Eirik. Just look sensible and behave yourself.'

Snorri smoored his fire when they arrived, and invited them to sit on the bench outside. 'So. What can I do for you?'

Thorvald cleared his throat, and spoke formally, as Rolf had coached him. 'We've come to ask for your support in our claim as heirs to Einar's estate, when the matter is brought before the Thing tomorrow.'

Snorri considered the matter, while Olaf and Thorvald sat patiently on each side of him, and Eirik started drawing ships on the brigstones with a piece of charcoal. 'On what grounds do you propose to found your case?' asked Snorri at last.

Thorvald had his words by heart. 'That the settlement which gave Setr to my father didn't mean that we lost our rights as heirs to Shirva.'

'Thorvald's sons were all good friends of mine,' said Snorri at last. 'Einar and Eirik were honourable men. But Bjarni and I were born in the same year, and perhaps now that he has lost both his brothers I can claim to know him better than any other man.

'Which isn't to say we've always agreed.' He looked from one to another of Eirik's sons. 'Whatever settlement is reached you can trust Bjarni to abide by it. Could he trust you to do the same?'

'Yes,' said Thorvald.

'It would take a strong case to make me take sides against Bjarni,' said Snorri. 'I gave him my friendship long ago. When I came back from the wars he was very generous to me. But there are other things which I can't ignore. Did you know that Einar had discussed the settlement with me?'

Thorvald sat up. 'I didn't know that.'

'He reckoned you were his heirs.'

'Will you give witness to that?'

'He told me he was upset that you had little to do with your own kin, not just because you were Eirik's sons, but also because you were making life harder for yourselves. He said the division was causing too much hardship, and that it might cause conflict in the future. Bjarni told him he was a fool to do so much for you when you gave nothing in return. As far as I know you were the only cause of contention between them.'

'You mean they disagreed about the settlement?'

'They disagreed about the settlement that was made with your mother. Remember, Bjarni was at that meeting of the Thing, and Einar wasn't. They agreed to differ.

'Einar made it quite clear that you were heirs to Shirva. He wouldn't have had you at Setr a moment longer than you chose to remain there. Einar's intentions have the most significance in law, and I'm bound to make them known. I'll support your claim.'

'Thank you,' said Thorvald, feeling close to tears. He'd never really known Einar. In Einar's presence, he'd always seen himself as a boy; now, he would never meet his uncle as a man.

'I'll be there at the Thing tomorrow.'

Snorri limped back into his smithy before they could say anything else.

They found Rolf in the yard at Byrstada, supervising the unloading of the peats. The ponies stood patiently under loads that were bulkier than they were, and the crew looked less than happy.

As they approached, they heard Rolf's raised voice. 'Women's work, is it? And will it be women's work to keep you here all winter? Get to it!'

Olaf tugged his brother's sleeve. 'Maybe this isn't the best moment.'

But Rolf had already seen them. He ordered Skuli to see to the stacking, and took Eirik's sons inside.

Gudrun and Ragna were at the hearth, and a simmering pot of kale filled the hall with cabbage smells. Rolf hesitated, as if he would rather have gone somewhere else, then invited his visitors to sit down.

'What's this?' asked Gudrun sharply. 'A deputation?'

'It's not women's business,' said Rolf curtly. 'If you're staying, you must leave the talking to us.'

Gudrun was on her feet in a flash. 'You're asking me to be silent while you plot to betray my father? Is that it? You expect me to stand for that?'

'We have guests.'

'We have my cousins, who've come to ask you to turn against your own father-in-law. Is that the kind of loyalty you give me, Rolf?'

'We had all this out last night. I'll do what I think's right.'

Thorvald and Olaf looked at each other. Olaf jerked his thumb towards the door and raised his eyebrows. Thorvald shook his head. 'I'll not sit here and have you plot against my father!'

'Then get out!'

'It's my house! I won't leave it!'

Ragna was on her feet too. 'Don't you speak to him like that! No one tells us who to entertain here! Treat my brother with respect, or get back to Shirva where you belong!'

'Keep out of it, Ragna!' shouted Rolf.

Gudrun seized a soapstone dish and hurled it at Rolf. It smashed to pieces against the wall.

'Don't you dare!' she shouted at him. 'Who brought this on us? You'll ruin us! You'll betray us all!'

Ragna was shouting too. 'Make her stop! She's your wife! Why don't you stop her? Dagfinn wouldn't stand for it! You couldn't do this if Dagfinn were here!'

Rolf lashed out and sent his sister reeling.

'Get out!' said Rolf to Gudrun, 'Get out!'

'I'm going.' At the door she turned and yelled at him, 'And I'm not coming back!'

'She'll go to Shirva,' said Ragna, weeping with fury. 'Is that what you want? Off to tell her daddy she can't control you. I hope you're proud of her!'

When Rolf took a step towards her she too turned and fled.

Boiling water bubbled under the lid of the pot of kale, and sizzled on the peats. Rolf paced up and down the hall. 'I must apologise. The condition she's in, she gets upset.'

'You mean because she's pregnant?' Eirik thought it over. 'Then I hope I never marry anyone who is.'

'Anyway,' Rolf was still slightly out of breath, 'you've come to seek support from those who'll take your part, as I suggested?'

'Yes.' Thorvald told him how they had fared at the smithy. It was difficult to concentrate. The quarrel he had just witnessed had shaken him.

'Well, you have my support, though as you can see it's caused some trouble. My argument's quite simple, and it's not personal either. You needn't think I want a quarrel with my wife's father, but what concerns me is that there simply aren't enough men on this island. We lost our best seamen seven years ago. So now we rely on a foreign crew. That's expensive for the shipmaster, and the islanders don't like it. It would be easier for me if I just left, taking my wealth with me.'

'Leave?' The idea seemed incomprehensible to Thorvald.

'Has it never occurred to you that I could take the Sula and settle anywhere I wanted? I could sell Byrstada. There are always men seeking land. I'd do better in Biorgvin or Kirkjavagr; in fact anywhere's better than operating from an island with no safe anchorage and no market. Think about it! I've had Sula beached in the Nordhavn for two weeks now. She's only just above high water. I've had to keep men on watch there all the time. It's no place to keep a ship.'

'Leave the island?' repeated Olaf. 'Take Sula from the island?'

'What would happen if I did, do you think? In my father's time, we didn't need our own ship. Hardly a month went by all summer without a ship putting in here to buy supplies. Or we only had to take a boat to Svinborg to get all the trade we wanted. But all that's changed now.'

'But you wouldn't leave the island! What would Gudrun say?'

'Do you think I want to? But if this island wants to keep its ship, it must have men. We lost a generation of seamen. That was a disaster. We can't afford to lose another.'

Nobody had ever suggested such a thing before. 'You mean you'll support us, because we need our land if we're to stay on the island?'

'If you have to go, one day I'll have to follow. If I couldn't make enough money to support a foreign crew all winter, there wouldn't be enough men here now for me to launch or haul up my ship. No Sula – no timber, no iron, no salt, no imported goods except what a boat could bring from Hjaltland. What kind of life would that be?'

'My father had a ship,' observed Eirik.

'That's true,' agreed Rolf. 'And a fine sailor he was too. Do you understand me now, Thorvald? The living we have here is much more fragile than you think.'

'Do you think Bjarni's thought of that?' said Olaf suddenly.

'He's not been away,' said Rolf. 'Einar knew.'

'Did Dagfinn ever talk about leaving?' asked Olaf.

'Never. However long Dagfinn stays away, this is the only place he'll call home. He'll come back.' Rolf smiled at them with an effort. 'But we haven't all day. Thorvald, I'll be there at the Thing tomorrow, and for what it's worth I'll bring all the support I can.'

Yesterday Thorvald had not had the faintest idea how he would begin, yet in the small hours it had come to him all in one piece, and he had repeated it to himself until he knew it by heart. Now, Bjarni stood on the other side of the circle with Kalf of Leogh, where Einar used to stand. There was no sign of Rolf. Snorri sat on the wooden stool they always brought to the Thing for him, close to Thorvald and Olaf.

The murmur of talk died down as Kalf declared the Thing open, and he had no sooner done so when the men of Byrstada appeared out of the mist. Rolf wore a scarlet cloak that had been Dagfinn's. His hair was combed back and fastened with an embroidered headband. His men took their places at the circle. The islanders moved up. There was an uneasy silence. Kalf cleared his throat, and once again declared the Thing ready to act. He had a short speech prepared about the loss of the man who had been their lawman for over twenty years. The islanders took up the tale with fewer words, but less restraint.

'He was the best lawman this island ever had.'

'He'll be badly missed.'

'He was an honest man.'

'He deserved a Christian burial,' said Snorri, 'which the sea denied him.'

Rolf said, 'When I reach Biorgvin, I can ask a priest to say mass for him, and if we make an offering, they'll pray for his soul.'

Bjarni looked across the circle at him. 'I'll pay for it, however much it costs.'

'The island should pay,' said Snorri. 'He was our lawman, and has kept the peace here for more than a generation.'

It was agreed that all the free households on the island should contribute.

Thorvald was watching Bjarni. The only sign of feeling Bjarni showed was at the mention of a mass. Otherwise he remained grimly aloof. Kalf announced the case of the Shirva inheritance, and called upon Thorvald to state his case.

The mist swirled round Thorvald; the ground under his feet seemed not quite real. Then a voice started speaking, which was his own, although he hardly recognised it. Just say the words as they had been in the night.

'I have come to state my claim, and that of my brothers, as heirs to the farmland formerly belonging to my uncle, Einar Thorvaldsson.'

Thorvald forced his legs to stop trembling, and continued:

'You all know that Einar had two brothers, Bjarni and Eirik. If Eirik had lived, under udal law all the land would have been shared equally between him and Bjarni. Eirik left three sons, and we in our turn are the heirs to what would have been his share of Shirva. Under udal law there is no doubt about the matter at all.

'The cause of contention is the settlement made by my father, and later ratified by my mother, which gave a small part of the Shirva farm to my father for his home. The land that went with Setr was never intended to be Eirik's share of his father's inheritance.

'When my father was drowned my mother wanted to stay at Setr. Bjarni tried to force us all to go to live at Shirva with him and Einar. My mother took her case to the Thing, and the Thing confirmed her right to live at Setr and bring us up herself.

'Einar was in Hjaltland when the case came before the Thing. I have witness that he still thought we were his heirs. He several times tried to persuade us to bring our land back in with his, and to keep all the farms together. He said it was the best thing to do for the future.'

'And did you do it?' Bjarni broke his silence with a fury that made Thorvald step back. 'You did not! You insulted him in life and now you come like a raven after the pickings! Disloyal and lawless! Would he be proud of you now?'

'Quiet!' That was Kalf. 'Order! Let him present his case!'

The interruption had distracted Thorvald. If he had ever had more to say, he had now forgotten it. He stepped back, and it took them a few seconds to realise that he had finished.

'I thought you were going to bring witnesses?' Kalf said to Thorvald.

'Rolf will bear witness that Einar said we were his heirs,' Thorvald said loudly, 'and that the settlement made with my mother wasn't a permanent land division.'

'At another Thing seven years ago,' Rolf began, 'Ingebjorg Grimsdottir stated her own case, a case not concerned with property but with guardianship. Eirik was dead, Einar was in Hjaltland, and Bjarni was here. Bjarni put it to Ingebjorg that the guardianship of Eirik's sons should now revert to Eirik's brothers, saying she had no means of supporting her sons herself. She said that wasn't so; and that it would suit her best to keep the home she and Eirik had had at Setr. Bjarni told her it was legally within his power to take Setr from her, and compel her to come back to Shirva. That would seem to prove that there had been no permanent land division.

'Furthermore, Dagfinn had promised to take Thorvald on to the Sula last year, and Einar asked him not to. This was the reason he gave: that Eirik's sons were heirs to Shirva, and the disagreement between Bjarni and Ingebjorg hadn't been resolved. He said Thorvald was a man now, and he hoped he could persuade him to do what Ingebjorg had refused to do on his behalf, that is, to bring back Setr to the main farm. He hoped Bjarni and Thorvald would work towards a reconciliation without either being forced to act against their will.

'I don't want to take sides. Everyone in the dispute is my kin by marriage. I've acted as I have for the good of the island. If Eirik's sons lose their inheritance, they'll have no living on the island. Setr might just support one man with his family, but not three. We've lost too many of our men to the sea. Must we lose them by our quarrels too?'

Thorvald came forward again. 'I have another witness. I call upon Snorri Hakonsson to give his testimony.'

It did not take Snorri long to give his evidence:

'There was no suggestion that the settlement Ingebjorg made forfeited her children's rights as heirs to Shirva. All that was agreed was that she should live at Setr as long as she wished, and bring her sons up herself. No one suggested the natural laws of inheritance should be waived. Einar never said so. He said Eirik's sons were heirs to Shirva often enough in the last seven years. Sometimes he said it in front of Bjarni, who always disputed it.

'For seven years there has been a dispute inherent in the Shirva settlement. That's nobody's fault, but it fell out so, and could not be avoided. I hope we'll see it resolved.'

'Have you anything else to say, Thorvald?'

'No.'

'Bjarni, do you wish to state your case?'

'Very well. I will take the case back to its beginning.

'My tale begins sixteen years ago with Eirik's marriage. Until that time Einar, Eirik and I shared between us all that we inherited from our father. Six years after his marriage Eirik said to us that he wished to set up a household of his own, with his wife and three young sons, the two you see here now, and another who died young. We came to an agreement.

'Eirik had gone to sea as soon as he was a man. He was away several years, then one winter he came back, and said to us that if he had his own ship he could come home. He could make a noost for a trading ship at the Nordhavn, as there had been in my grandfather's time, and he could raise a crew on the island, which would bring wealth to other men as well.

'Eirik was ambitious and confident, and an excellent sailor. We trusted him entirely, and so Einar and I agreed that he should go to the Orkneyjar and have his own ship built, and the money for it should come out of our inheritance from our father as well as from Eirik's own wealth brought back from sea. We still had the treasure given to Thorvald my father by Earl Paul for his support in the Earl's wars.

'If our property were to be divided into three, the ship money would represent the most part of Eirik's share. He proposed that we should consider it to be so. Years later, when Ingebjorg wished to leave our house, he reminded us of our agreement, and asked that for the rest of his share he should now take a portion of land equal to the remainder. He said all he wanted was land enough for a house and yard, and enough of a farm for his wife to tend while he was away. What she could not grow, he could buy. The land was never intended to be his family's sole support. When Eirik had his ship he was by far the richest of us all.

'As regards proof, all I can do is give you my word that it was as I describe. Eirik is dead. Einar is dead. There is no one else to bear witness to it now.

'That is the way we lived for two years, and there was no contention between us. Eight years ago last spring my brother Eirik sailed to Biorgvin as usual. He never came back. In the spring my brother Einar went to Hjaltland to seek news of Eirik's ship. We did not expect Einar to return until after the Thing in Hjaltland.

'I went to Ingebjorg and told her that a woman with four young children couldn't maintain things as they were before. I said to her that it was only right that she should bring her sons to live at Shirva, and that her husband's brothers should be the ones to foster them. She refused; she said that she had managed at Setr when Eirik was alive, and she would do the same now, even if he were dead, which was not proven.

'I said to her that all that Eirik had was his ship, and if that were lost his sons had nothing. We would take them back to Shirva and foster them as our own, and by adoption all that Eirik had once shared with us would be theirs to share too.

'She refused again. In the best interests of us all I thought it right to try to insist. I feared just such a division in our family as has now arisen. Ingebjorg took the matter to the Thing. It was made clear there that Setr was part of Eirik's inheritance along with the ship.

'Einar came home in June. He had found no trace of Eirik, nor any news of his last journey. He was distressed at the way things had gone here, but the matter had gone to the Thing, and could not be resolved by the two of us. We discussed it more than once in Snorri's presence. We decided that all we could do was offer Eirik's children what support we could as kinsmen, and perhaps another settlement might be made with Thorvald and Olaf when they came of age. So far Snorri will agree with me. He is also willing to state that although Einar believed that Eirik's sons might still inherit Shirva land under udal law, I never believed it, and I have never hidden my opinions.

'Thorvald was fifteen last winter. My brother hoped that he might be willing to do what his mother had previously refused to do for him. I left Einar to reach an agreement. I believe Einar said to Thorvald that this was his chance of being accepted as one of the Shirva inheritors.

'Einar failed. Eirik's sons have been taught to range themselves against their father's family, and remain as independent of them as possible.

'That is all. Eirik is dead, and Einar is dead. There are six of my father's descendants left on the island. I never wished to stand like this against my brother's sons. It's too late now for them to be Einar's heirs, for Einar is dead, and the reconciliation he sought was never made. Thorvald and Olaf, you are my brother's sons, and it is as such that I would prefer to treat you. In law your father received and lost his inheritance long ago. As your kinsman I would do what is right, but my legal rights and the inheritance that I have shared with my father and my brother all my life, that I will not forfeit, for you or any man.'

The wind had dropped, and the sun shone hot and humid. Insects buzzed round the heads of the men.

'Bjarni, do you wish to cite witnesses?'

'You know that my brothers and I were not in the habit of demanding the presence of witnesses.'

'Then I shall attempt to sum up.'

Einar is dead, thought Thorvald. Einar as lawman had been quick, incisive, humorous. Kalf was none of these things.

'Thorvald, will you please answer me?'

'I'm sorry.'

'Do you agree to vote on this proposal?'

'Yes,' said Thorvald, and hoped that was right.

'You must vote yourself,' whispered Olaf. 'It's our case.'

He voted.

'In that case,' said Kalf, 'Those who believe that Ingebjorg forfeited her sons' rights as heirs to Shirva when she refused the offer made by Bjarni, stand forward and declare it.'

He seemed to spend a long time counting.

'Is anyone undecided on this issue?'

They were not.

Kalf counted again. 'The voting is divided equally.' He looked perplexed.

The circle broke, and men moved forward into the centre, talking excitedly. Thorvald and Olaf stared at each other with frightened eyes.

'I can't do more,' whispered Thorvald.

'They wouldn't ask you to fight,' Olaf whispered back, but he didn't sound convinced, and he clutched his brother by the sleeve.

'Fight Bjarni?' Thorvald looked aghast. 'He'd cut me in two!'

'He'd have to cut both of us.'

Kalf was still talking. 'As this meeting can reach no agreement on the exact terms of the two settlements, I rule that we can proceed no further. In such circumstances there is only one alternative open to us . . .'

His voice trailed away, as if he hesitated to pronounce it, then it gathered momentum.

'. . . and that is that the whole arbitration will need to be referred to a higher court, that is to say, to the Thing in Hjaltland when it meets next June.'

Chapter 35

It was Dagfinn who had told Thorvald the truth seven years ago, on a day when the snow was blowing so thickly that they had had to draw the shutter right over the chimney. Dagfinn had visited Setr often that winter, though not as frequently as when Eirik had been there. Thorvald had been talking to him while Ingebjorg did the milking.

'When my father comes home from Noreg, he's going to bring wood and make me a rowing boat for my own.'

Dagfinn hadn't answered at once. A few stray snowflakes found their way past the shutter, and melted over the fire.

'Thorvald,' Dagfinn had said eventually, 'I thought you understood. Eirik isn't going to come home.'

Now it was Rolf talking to him. 'Thorvald! Did you hear what I said?'

'Sorry. I was thinking.'

'I said,' said Rolf, 'that we must find a lawman who can present your case for you at the Thing in Hjaltland. You can't do it on your own. The best lawmen in the islands meet there, and they give litigants a hard time, just to show off their knowledge. They all know each other, and they make a game of it. They'd mash you to pieces if you tried to present your case without support.'

'But I don't know anyone who goes to the Hjaltland Thing!'

'That's what we've just been saying. There's no one on the island. Bjarni will go next year of course, and from what I've seen today, I'd guess that Kalf will help him present his case. There's no other lawman here. I'd give you my support, but I can't be in Hjaltland next June.'

Thorvald's eyes turned to Snorri.

'I'd be no use to you, even if you could get me there. I've no law to speak of, and they won't want common sense.'

'So what shall I do?' Thorvald still couldn't believe all this was happening.

'Eirik had friends everywhere; you're his son, there's many who'd be obliged to help you.'

'But I don't even know who they are!'

'Yes, you do,' said Olaf unexpectedly. 'Don't you remember what Einar said when he brought Arne over to Setr? He told us how Arne's father and ours swore oaths to each other long ago, and how Helgi had sent us a message that we could count on him for support if ever we should need it.'

'Arne's father?' Thorvald considered it.

'Who else?' said Snorri. 'Einar did you a good turn there. He always tried to keep in touch with Eirik's friends. Unfortunately we don't know who the others were now, but at least we know about Helgi, and Arne you know yourself. Helgi goes to the Thing, and coming from Papey, he's likely to have plenty of contacts.'

'I know Arne would support me.'

'Then he can persuade his father to do the same,' said Rolf briskly, 'which is more to the point. Arne may be an excellent young man, but though I've not met him myself I hardly think he could present your case for you.'

'I couldn't ask a stranger,' said Thorvald slowly. 'I wouldn't know what to say. But Arne would do his best, and perhaps he'd help me talk to his father.'

'So you have one ally of your own,' said Rolf. 'That's good. Others will act for your father's sake, but your own friend will have more of his heart in it. Then you'll need to discuss the matter with Arne as soon as possible.'

'I thought we were talking about next June?'

'Too late,' said Snorri. 'There's a case to prepare. That means enlisting support in plenty of time. By the time men come to the Thing they'll need to know all about it.'

'You'll have to go to Hjaltland,' agreed Rolf.

'But I can't! I'm going to sea.'

'You're going to have to resolve this first. You've six weeks at the most before winter. Better waste no time. I'll take you to Svinborg tomorrow, on our way to Biorgvin. Get to Papey as quickly as you can. There should be boats going up the west coast. Speak to Arne, speak to Helgi, get their support. Helgi may have other ideas. He'll know who Eirik's friends were.'

'Go to Papey? Now? Instead of coming with you?'

'No choice,' said Snorri. 'It's the best thing to do.'

'If you can be back by winter,' said Rolf, 'you can sail with me in the spring. I can drop you in Hjaltland next year before the Thing in June.'

Not to go to sea. Not to go with Rolf. To go instead to Hjaltland. Alone. Thorvald remembered seeing Arne off from Konungsborg. They had walked about two miles together, on to a long ridge that stretched the length of Hjaltland. Westward, there were low green islands, and, where Arne pointed to the north, the hills of Hjaltland lay hidden in a blue haze.

'I could go to Papey now,' said Thorvald. The idea came like a burst of sunshine. He could get away from everything: the island, the lawsuit, their serious faces, the business of mourning and facing loss; he could shake it all off and go. He instantly realised that there was nothing he wanted more.

'I'll do it. I'll go to Papey.'

Olaf made no fuss when Thorvald insisted that he was going on his own, but Thorvald knew he was hurt. Olaf went out, to look at his otter snare, he said. There was nothing to be done about it. Thorvald had to go alone, and that was that.

He felt more kindly towards his family than he had in years, but there was no way of showing it. Thorvald wandered restlessly through the yard and outhouses. Sula was to leave an hour before dawn, when the tide began to ebb. She was back on her mooring, and everything was ready. Thorvald kicked a stone across the brigstones.

In the byre he found the sheepskin he and Olaf had put to soak in a tub of urine. He took it out and rinsed it, for something to do.

He was stretching it on a wooden frame, when he heard a light footstep on the stones. Looking up, he was surprised to see Astrid; she had never come to Setr before.

'Do you want my mother?'

'No,' said Astrid. She came and stood beside him. 'I'm looking for you.'

Thorvald pulled a leather thong tight and knotted it. 'Me? What can I do for you?'

'Snorri was telling Gunnhild you're going to Papey, in Hjalt-land.'

He stopped what he was doing. 'You heard that? Do they know at Shirva?'

'I haven't been to Shirva.'

Relieved, he turned and made another hole in the sheepskin with the point of his knife. 'What of it?'

'My father knew a man on Papey Stora called Amundi Palsson, who was a friend of his and owed him a favour. That was where we were bound for, before the storm.'

He made another knot. 'You want me to take him a message?' He was thinking fast. This might be an excuse to speak to an influential landholder, and if Amundi were to regard such an errand as a favour, he would be in Thorvald's debt. 'That's easy enough. No trouble at all.'

'No, not a message.'

'What then?'

'I want to come with you.'

The knife remained poised over the place for the next hole. 'You can't do that!'

'Why not?'

He sat back on his heels, amazed at her cheek. 'I'm going by myself!'

'I don't mind.'

'I can hardly help you to run away from Bjarni.'

'You wouldn't be. I'm not afraid to tell him where I'm going. I owe it to him, anyway.'

'You can't tell Bjarni you're off to Papey with me! He's to know nothing about it!'

'Oh.' She thought that over. 'I'll tell Ingrid, and once we're away, she'll tell Bjarni that I went away with the Sula. After all, that's what we are doing, to begin with, anyway.'

'Yes, but once I get to Svinborg, I'll take passage on any boat I can find going west. It's not the sort of journey you'd be used to.'

'I don't care. What did you think I expected?' She squatted down on the brigstones. 'Listen, Thorvald. I don't know you. You don't know me. But try to imagine. This isn't my island. My father was drowned here. The man who took me in, the only person here I owed anything to, he's drowned too. I don't want to be here. It's like a prison. I feel as though I'm hammering at the walls. I've a place to go. I've friends. But I can't get out. I won't trouble you, I know how to look after myself. If I can get to Svinborg I'll walk, if you don't want to take me. Just let me tell Rolf I'm coming with you, and he'll give me a passage. He said he'd never take me if I had no man to escort me. He said ask you; you'd see at once that it would be to your advantage.'

'Why?'

' "Amundi Palsson?" Rolf said. "You don't mean it? That's better than any unknown farmer, however much he was Eirik's friend. You tell Thorvald that. If he doesn't see sense, I'll come and speak to him myself." '

Thorvald stared at her. 'Rolf said that? He thought I'd say yes? Who is Amundi Palsson, anyway?'

She shrugged. 'A man in Hjaltland, that's all my father said. But he must be rich. He bought two trading ships from our yard within a few years. He came to Dyflin, but I don't remember him. I was only about two at the time.'

'You can't come!' said Thorvald, and bent over his sheepskin. If he had said no to Olaf, he wasn't about to say yes to a girl who was nothing to him. He made the next hole, pulled the thong through, and knotted it. Astrid showed no signs of going away.

'Why not?'

'I told you.'

'Listen,' said Astrid. 'This isn't my island. This is the only chance I may ever get to return to my own people. Would you want never to see any of your own kin again, to be exiled for the rest of your life?'

He didn't answer.

'I'm only asking you to let me come with you as far as Papey. After that I can manage by myself. But if you want a word spoken for you by Kol shipbuilder's daughter, in a place where that might count, I'll do everything I can to repay you for your trouble. This one journey with you would give me back my freedom, and you need never think any more about me.'

'Why can't I take this man a message?'

'He might not act on it.'

'That's foolish.'

'No it isn't. If I arrive he won't have to send for me.'

'If you turn up with me he'll think I've seduced you.'

She was indignant. 'Then I'll tell him at once I wouldn't let you touch me if you tried!'

He turned his back on her, made the next hole, and threaded the thong through. It was his fate he had to think of, not hers. But Einar always used to say that chance could come in strange disguises, and you had to think what you were doing before you rejected anything unusual. Rolf saw this as an opportunity. He might be a fool to say no to it; he might regret it for the rest of his life. It wouldn't take that long to get to Papey. He pulled a loose knot apart and tightened it.

'Be at the Nordhavn an hour before dawn. The Sula won't wait if you're not there.'

Her whole face lit up, and she clasped her hands together, as if in prayer.

'I'll be there,' she told him.

Part Six

Papey Stora

Chapter 36

Hjaltland. They hove to in a sheltered bay on the east coast, after rounding the Svinborg Head. Today's voyage had been neither eventful nor dangerous, but Astrid had found it hard enough. Sula was the second ship she had ever sailed on, a much smaller, plainer ship than the first. Everything had been much too familiar: the captain shouting the same orders, the helmsman with his eyes fixed on the medes ahead, the crew working the sail, the haste and tension of departure and arrival, and the cold, weary hours between with nothing to do but watch, and remember.

They had made the journey in only six hours, which had seemed long enough to Astrid. She had only been frightened once, when they were tossing on the edge of the Svinborg rost. No one else had seemed worried.

Rolf was speaking to Thorvald. 'All right then? We'll put in before Michaelmas if it's weather. If there's no word from you here, we'll assume you're wintering in Hjaltland.'

Leif and Svein had the flit boat alongside. Astrid picked up her small bundle of belongings.

Rolf turned to her. 'I'm not coming ashore. We want to use this wind while we've got it. Skuli will put you ashore.' He hesitated, then awkwardly touched her shoulder. 'Good luck go with you.'

'Thank you,' she said. 'And thank you for the passage.'

'They'll bring news of you to the Thing next year,' said Rolf. 'I know my sister will want to hear what's happened.'

Astrid hardly knew Rolf, but for a moment he seemed to represent all that she had grown familiar with on the island, which itself no longer seemed a prison but a friend. Today she had watched it fade from solid land to a distant double hump. Then the Seydurholm had disappeared into the blue, and there was only the faint outline of a shape like a barley bannock on the horizon. She never expected to see it again.

The flit boat bobbed up and down, its gunwale hardly above the surface. She sat facing Skuli, who rowed with short quick strokes, while Thorvald sat in the stern. They landed among breaking waves, and when they touched sand she jumped ashore. Skuli tossed her her bundle, and gave her a friendly mock-salute as Thorvald pushed the boat off. She watched it dip up and down, vanishing between the short waves so that Skuli looked like a Finn man, without boat or oars.

Astrid and Thorvald had scarcely spoken during the voyage. Now they were set ashore together in a strange country. Astrid's hands and feet were numb, and the sun's warmth struck her like a benediction. Her stomach was knotted into a hard lump. Thawing out in the sunshine, she realised she was ravenous. The sand dunes rocked in front of her eyes, making walking difficult.

'I'm hungry.'

'Come on then. Rolf said it's this way.'

There was a sandy path through the twitch grass, wide enough for a cart, and rutted with distinct wheel marks. It was like coming back into the world again.

The path led them across marsh and meadowland, until they reached the settlement on the southern shore, on a small promontory above a long sandy beach. There was a large hall with extensions at each end, and byres, barns and a smithy grouped round. Peat stacks lay in the lee of one of the barns. The smell of smoke, drying fish, and middens rose to greet them, along with noises: a cock crowing, children playing, someone hammering. Chickens and a sow with piglets scavenged the yard. A net patched with new twine was pegged out in the sand.

Thorvald had halted.

'Shall we go up to the hall?' she asked him.

'I suppose we'd better face it. The man we're to ask for is Bergfinn of Svinborg.'

'That's easy enough,' she said, leading the way. Thorvald followed without a word.

A flock of children came racing out of the dunes and stopped dead. The biggest girl came up to them.

'Did you come off that ship?'

'Yes,' said Astrid. 'Can you take us to Bergfinn of Svinborg?'

'Grandfather? Yes, but he'll be annoyed that the ship didn't wait to see if anyone needed a passage. Not enough ships come here now.'

'We need to get to Skalavagr,' Astrid said. 'Do you think there'll be a boat?'

The child shrugged. 'I don't know. I'll take you to Grandfather.'

The youngest child could barely walk, but toddled after them, naked except for a scrap of blanket which he chewed as he watched them. Their guide scooped him up and carried him on her hip. He never took his eyes off the strangers, but he wouldn't smile.

They passed the entrance to the hall, where joints of mutton hung drying in the wind. The door had brightly painted wooden pillars on either side. Sounds of laughter came from inside, and the smell of fresh bread.

They found Bergfinn of Svinborg talking to a woman who was harvesting kale leaves into a basket slung round her neck. Bergfinn was old, bent with rheumatics. His hair was thin and white, and barely reached to his shoulders.

'Grandfather!'

Thorvald hung back, but Astrid walked straight up to Bergfinn and greeted him.

'We've just come ashore from the Sula, out of Fridarey,' she told him. 'I am Astrid Kolsdottir of Dyflin, and this is Thorvald Eiriksson of Fridarey. We were told to find you by Rolf of Byrstada.'

He looked her over. 'So that was Dagfinn's ship? What does he mean by heaving to like that, then setting off again without a word? What's the meaning of it, eh?'

'He was afraid of being trapped by the onshore wind. He had to get to Biorgvin. Anyway, Dagfinn's not there. It was Rolf.'

'Rolf? Why Rolf? Where's Dagfinn?'

'In the Sudreyjar. Rolf is captain of the Sula while he's away.'

'Is that right?' He looked at her, then turned his gaze on Thorvald. 'So what's all this then? An elopement, is it? Off to the broch on Mosey, like the Earl before you?'

'No, no,' said Thorvald. 'I'm taking her to her father's friend, on Papey Stora.'

'Oh, so you can speak,' said Bergfinn. 'Papey Stora, eh? And Dagfinn in the Sudreyjar. There've been raids there this summer so I've heard. You'd better come in and tell me what this is all about.'

He limped back to his hall, indicating that they should follow. As soon as they were out of earshot of the woman with the kale, Thorvald caught Astrid's sleeve and held her back.

'What is it?'

He glanced at the surrounding children, and whispered, 'Can I use your story? That we're going to Amundi? I hadn't thought before . . . He'll know Bjarni. I can't say what I'm here for.'

'I won't mention your affairs. If you want to say you've come with me, you can.'

The inside of the hall was finer than any house on Fridarey. Weapons hung the length of the walls, and a good fire blazed along the hearth between the benches. The place was almost free of smoke, with both the chimney holes unshuttered. It was warm too, and Astrid stopped shivering at last.

Bergfinn called for food to be brought to the guests, and a woman came in with bannocks and ale, and a big slab of butter.

As soon as Bergfinn had taken in exactly who Thorvald was, he asked after Einar of Fridarey.

'Einar died two weeks ago. He was drowned just after the hay harvest.'

'I'm sorry to hear that.' There was a pause. 'He always spoke good sense at the Thing, which is more than can be said of some. I've not been there for years, but my son speaks of him. What happened?'

Thorvald looked at Astrid, but she looked stonily away. She wasn't going to help him with this.

'It was after the harvest feast,' said Thorvald. 'He went fishing the same night, when that gale blew up.'

'Any of his kin are welcome here. You're the son of his brother, you say?'

'Of his brother Eirik.'

'I knew Eirik. An excellent sailor, and very ambitious. That was a fine ship he had. A sad loss. There's another brother, isn't there?'

Thorvald hurried into uncharacteristic eloquence. 'Astrid has been living at Shirva with my uncles, but now Einar's dead she's on her way to Papey Stora, to find a friend of her father's called Amundi Palsson.'

'Amundi Palsson?' Bergfinn stiffly turned his whole body to face Astrid. She saw Thorvald lean back and wipe his brow. 'You keep high company then. What connection have you with Amundi Palsson?'

'That wasn't fair,' said Astrid, as soon as Bergfinn left them.

Thorvald scraped the last butter off the plate and licked his fingers. 'I wouldn't have done it if I'd thought of any other way of diverting him. But it's a good thing. Now he thinks you're important. That means he really has gone to find out about a boat. If he thought we were just nobody he wouldn't have bothered.'

'I'm glad I can be useful to you.'

To her surprise he smiled at her quite warmly. 'Doesn't that old man frighten you at all?'

'No, but I wouldn't annoy him. I don't think he's dangerous.'

'Dangerous, no,' said Thorvald. 'That would be much simpler.'

They were interrupted by a boy carrying a puppy. 'My uncle wants you,' he said to Thorvald. 'You're to come and speak to the shipmaster.'

'Who's your uncle? What shipmaster?'

'My uncle Bergfinn. It's the boat from Vagr, they might take you back. They'll be feasting here tonight. You're to come and arrange it.'

When Thorvald returned he was among a crowd of sailors who seemed to be familiar guests. The women were boiling up meat and birds for the night's feast. Astrid and the girl who had met them that morning sat together chopping herbs. The girl was called Sunniva. There were always boats calling from different parts of Hjaltland, she said, though of course there used to be more. Presently the others joined in the conversation, and Astrid began to feel quite at home. She and Kol had sometimes stayed in other men's halls, so she was used to being left among unknown women, until the man she was with should reappear.

She saw Thorvald for a moment just before the meal. 'Is there a boat?' she asked him.

'Pure luck,' he said cheerfully. His shyness had fallen away, and she had never seen him look so animated. 'They're from Vagr, away to the west. They're on their way home from Konungsborg. They'll take us all the way to Vagr tomorrow, and then we're almost there. We leave in the morning, a couple of hours after high water.'

'Did Bergfinn arrange that for you?'

He grinned. 'Yes, and he says I must take care to remember him to Amundi Palsson. I didn't dare say I didn't know the man. So you'll have to see to that.'

'I'll try,' said Astrid.

Chapter 37

Someone was shaking him, speaking in his ear. Thorvald groaned.

'You don't want to miss that boat any more than I do! Wake up!' She was pulling him by his tunic. He sat up, pushing his hair out of his eyes.

'They'll go without us. Wake up, will you!'

His head ached and he was very thirsty. In the cold morning light Bergfinn's hall seemed vast and chilly. There were people sleeping on the benches round him, but empty spaces where the crew of the Vagr boat had lain. Thorvald forced himself awake.

'Is there any water?'

'Outside.'

'Where are my shoes?'

'Here. And your cloak.'

'I can dress myself,' he said irritably. 'Are you ready?'

'I've been ready for hours. Come on!'

As soon as they were at sea Thorvald felt better, and the captain of the boat put him to work at once. The launching had been difficult, as the wind was blowing from the south-west on to the beach, whipping up the waves as it came. They had to row into the wind until they had passed the long promontory that protected the beach on the west side. After half an hour at the oars, Thorvald was warm, and wide awake.

The Vagr crew obviously knew this passage well. As soon as they were past the promontory the helmsman laid the steerboard hard over, and with the tide slack, they rowed through the narrow gap between the ness and the islet beyond. Thorvald felt rough water under them, and five minutes later, as they emerged from the channel, he looked back and saw long slopes of rock stretching down to the water on either side, the waves running up them as if on a beach, and breaking at the top.

Once they were free of the shore, they shipped the oars and set sail. They were still close to the last islet, but well clear of the narrows. The great cliffs of the Fitfugla Head reared ahead; wind and tide together were pushing them that way. Thorvald and another man were ordered to the starboard oars again, to row while the boat sailed, to keep her closer into the wind. The rest of the crew had the tack of the sail pulled right round on to the bow, sailing close-hauled. Everyone but the rowers was ordered to port, while the starboard gunwale was only just above water.

It was difficult to row at such an angle. Waves slopped over the side, and one of the crew was bailing hard. Thorvald felt the shadow of the Fitfugla Head before he saw the cliff. He could tell they were close under it by the sound of waves crashing and echoing. Looking back, he saw open water, where birds and seals were feeding in the tide stream at the edge of the rost. The waters under the cliff were full of fledgling seabirds.

They passed the headland, a sheer wall of cliff with jagged skerries at its foot. The sea hurled itself against the rock in sheets of spray. The boat was passing very near, as close-hauled as she would go, keeping in the long lift of the swell where it was still smooth. The wind eddying against the cliff played tricks, and the sail shook, blown by the back draught off the cliff. Then the wind went quite dead on them, and only the tide kept them under way. But they were in deep water, and there was no sign of any swell breaking until it hit the cliff.

The sea settled into a long swell. Finally the sail was eased out, and the order came to ship the two oars. Thorvald sat up and stretched.

The crew spread themselves across the benches, and Astrid sat down beside Thorvald. He had forgotten all about her.

'All right?' he asked, friendly because he was enjoying himself.

'It's better now.'

'Better than what?'

'We were very close to those cliffs.'

'We were fine. There was plenty of water under us. If there hadn't been, you'd have seen it break.'

'It reminded me,' she said abruptly.

Fridarey must have looked like that the morning Astrid was shipwrecked. There'd have been the same long swell running towards the cliff, breaking against it to leeward, the same line of rock growing closer. No doubt they'd have tried the same tactics: the sail close-hauled and possibly oarsmen to starboard. There'd have been fluky winds too, no doubt, under the cliffs at Hjukni geo. No wonder she looked a bit white. 'It wasn't the same at all,' he told her kindly. 'The tide was with us, and we had all the water we needed. There wasn't anything to worry about.'

'No,' said Astrid, and made no more fuss. Because he felt sorry for her, Thorvald stayed with her for several minutes, but when the helmsman called him over, he slipped away at once.

'You've not been out this way before then?' the helmsman asked Thorvald idly. He had one hand on the steerboard, his eyes on the sail.

'I know the Fitfugla Head. We see it from Fridarey. I didn't expect us to pass so close. I was thinking we'd have to go about.'

'There's plenty of water there, under the cliff.'

The sea lapped under the keel. The man who'd rowed behind Thorvald was already asleep. Thorvald yawned. Astrid was looking happier now, staring out to sea at the line of hills that were slowly taking shape ahead. When one of the crew nudged her she started, then took the dried fish he was offering. The man came aft with food for Thorvald and the helmsman. Thorvald was too thirsty to be hungry. He took his flask of water from his belt and offered it to the helmsman, who shook his head, and handed Thorvald a skin of ale.

'Bergfinn doesn't send us away empty-handed.'

They were well out from land now, rising and falling in a gentle swell. Looking past the sail, Thorvald studied the faint grey hills ahead. Behind them, the southern ness of Hjaltland was receding fast.

'Nothing to see now till Vagr,' remarked the helmsman. 'Five hours maybe. Nothing to do till then.'

Thorvald was looking west. 'There's Fugley! My uncle told me it was like that from here!'

Fugley was no longer the solid hump it was from Fridarey, but a ridge of three sharp peaks that reached up to touch the small cloud hanging over them.

'Your uncle knew this coast?'

'He used to come to the Thing.'

The helmsman pointed north towards grey horizons. 'You won't see much today, but Skalavagr lies in there. That's where he'd land. There's a good harbour there with a big hall above it. It's one of the richest estates in Hjaltland.'

'Are those islands in front of it?'

'There are islands all along this coast. See where the cliffs fall away a bit there? St. Rinan's island lies there. You'll have heard of that, surely? There's a shrine there to the saint. North of that are the Borgarey islands, with good channels behind them if you need to run for shelter. Good fishing too, among the islands. The best approach to Skalavagr is west of the Borgarey. There's just one place where you have to watch the reefs, off the south of Oxney. That's the route your uncle would take, crossing some of the best fishing grounds in Hjaltland.'

'Tell me the names of the islands again.'

The helmsman obligingly repeated them, along with sailing directions which Thorvald recited back until he had them perfectly. All the time the hills on the west side were drawing nearer.

'Ah, now you can see the mede, young man. That means we're halfway home, more or less. Look back to the ridge behind us. Do you see a gap? That's Hvarfi. They use it as a portage when the weather's too bad for Svinborg. It's one of the most useful medes in these waters. The channel I was telling you about is due west of it.

'We should be home in a couple of hours now.'

The cliffs on the west side of Hjaltland were reddish. Spray had dissolved into a fine mist that hung along the shore, melting under the sun in rainbow-shot brightness. It was a wild coast, long lines of sheer cliffs with stacks and holms guarding every geo. A rocky headland reared to starboard with a great arch under it, the sea dark green at its feet.

'We go in east of Valey,' the helmsman told Thorvald. 'The western channel looks wider, but avoid it if you ever come this way; there's a shoal right across it.'

The water was black in the shadow of the cliffs that rose sheer on each side of the channel. A round tower, half ruined, stood at the cliff top on the starboard side. 'That's a Picts' castle!'

'That's right. It's a good mede for the entrance.'

As they passed a stack on the shore below the tower, the crew shipped their oars. The sail flapped, then drooped. As they came out of the channel the sea turned lumpy, and Thorvald realised the tide was against them now, running down the shoreline.

'It's deep water now all the way in.'

Thorvald nodded. If there had been one harbour like this on Fridarey, what a difference it would have made. Still under sail, they slipped quietly into a narrow voe, where a flit boat lay at a mooring.

'We'll land everything first, and put you ashore as well.'

Thorvald and Astrid waited on the beach while the helmsman and one of the crew moored the boat.

'I must say it's good to be on land again,' remarked Astrid. 'Do you realise it's only just after midday?'

The helmsman tapped Thorvald on the shoulder. 'Where're you staying, boy?'

'I don't know yet.'

'Better come with me. It'll rain tonight.'

Early next morning, Thorvald went to the shore as the helmsman had directed him, and, mentioning the man's name, asked if any boats would be going to Papey Stora.

The fishermen shook their heads. 'Not today. But the Tystie might go any day with supplies for the longships. Come this evening and ask again.'

'I've got a lass with me.'

The men winked at each other. 'Then you're a lucky lad.'

So that was all right. He'd been afraid they wouldn't take her.

Astrid seemed quite content to wait. Later that day Thorvald wandered along the shore with her, always keeping his eyes on the channel entrance for any sign of a boat.

'Are you in a great hurry to get to Papey?' she asked.

'The sooner the better.'

'I suppose it's too late to make any voyages before winter now anyway.'

'Voyages?'

'Isn't that why you've come?'

'I've come to see Arne. Did you think I was going anywhere else?'

She looked puzzled, and a little embarrassed. 'Maybe I just jumped to conclusions. I assumed you'd decided to go with a ship from Arne's island, to get away from all the quarrelling.'

'I wish you were right,' said Thorvald regretfully, 'but unfortunately it's not quite like that.'

'Do you want to tell me? I don't mind if you don't.'

A wren bobbed in and out of the cracks in the stone wall by the path. It occurred to Thorvald that he liked Astrid. 'No one told you exactly what was decided at the Thing?'

'I knew it was about who inherited Shirva, of course, and I knew the quarrel was between you and Bjarni. I thought you'd decided to solve it by going away.'

'Not exactly.' He sighed. 'Let's sit down. I'll tell you what did happen.'

The barley shook and rustled in the field, a sea of bristled corn dotted with scarlet poppies. It was a relief to share his thoughts. Astrid began to pick the grasses round her while she listened, absentmindedly stripping them of their seeds.

When he'd finished she was frowning. 'But Thorvald, you're not planning to ask Arne to support you in a suit against Bjarni?'

'Why not?'

'Because he can't possibly!'

'It was my father who made an alliance with his father, nothing to do with Bjarni.'

'That's not what matters now. Arne's got to ally himself with Bjarni now, because of Ingrid.'

A horrifying suspicion struck Thorvald. 'He didn't seduce her? She's not pregnant, is she?'

'I can't say. I promised not to tell.'

His whole plan crumbled into dust.

'I thought you'd have guessed,' said Astrid. 'But you can hardly ask Arne's family for support against Bjarni.'

'What do you think I should do now?' Thorvald asked her.

She looked at him sideways. 'Wouldn't it be a good idea for everyone, perhaps, if you did what I thought you were doing? You do want to go to sea, don't you? Well, just go.'

'I can't. I have to think of my brothers.'

'You don't think that if you weren't there, they'd soon make terms with Bjarni?'

'I owe it to them to pursue our case,' he said stiffly, not daring to consider that she might be right.

'So what will you do when you get to Papey?'

The awkward question irritated him. Who was she after all? She could hardly solve his problems, and now he was stuck with the burden of looking after her.

'I'll think of that myself.'

At last the rain was beginning to ease off. Astrid sat forward on a box of live crabs. Her clothes felt heavy and clammy, but the grey mirk was growing lighter. The men seemed to be rowing harder than ever. With no landmark to show their progress time seemed suspended. There was greyness everywhere, rain merging into sea. Astrid shivered uncontrollably. Two rowers spelled each other, and Thorvald scrambled forward beside her.

'Is it much further?' she asked.

'I don't think so.' He was as wet as she was. Drops of water and sweat dripped off his hair on to his shoulders. He was hot from rowing, and smelt of wet wool. 'We must be crossing the sound.' He waved vaguely east. 'We have to stand out to sea as far as we can. The tides here are treacherous. We don't want to get carried into the sound. The tide's pulling us east all the time. That's why we needed that wind.'

'But the wind's against us!'

'To give us a direction,' explained Thorvald. 'So long as we keep it on the port bow we're all right.'

She was looking east over his shoulder, and as he spoke she cried out. 'There's land there!'

At the same moment the helmsman saw it too, and called, 'Papey Stora!' The rowers bent over their oars, while Astrid and Thorvald stared into the mist.

Slowly the island took on form. The wind grew cooler and stronger, ruffling the sea. Small waves slapped against the bows. The swell was still on the beam, as it had been since they lost sight of the Hjaltland cliffs. Astrid could see the whole outline of the island now: a high knob of hill to the west, and ranks of cliff in front. The land ended in a tremendous rock arch, which supported a pinnacle, carved by the sea into a shape like the bow of a ship. 'See that rock? It must be the horn of Papey.'

The men rowed on through crowds of swimming birds. A long slab of skerry was rising ahead, and the swell seemed to be pushing them on to it. Astrid looked away into the sound. The sea was dark green, and seemed to be slanting uphill. The skerry seemed scarcely an oar's length away. She cried out in spite of herself, shutting her eyes, and clutching Thorvald's tunic with the hand that was not clinging to the gunwale.

She felt a wave surge under them, and heard it break with a roar. Then the sound receded, and they were floating on a gentle swell. She opened her eyes.

A beach lay to port. Seaweed gleamed golden on the rocks, and brushed against the boat's side. 'I'm sorry,' said Astrid shakily, letting go of Thorvald.

'It was quite safe. They know this coast.'

She nodded.

'Don't worry, we're here now. You don't have to do it again.'

Astrid smiled feebly and looked away. They were emerging into a wide voe, as smooth as a lake. The day was magically transformed. The wind had blown the last cloud away, and after six hours' cold and wet, the smell of the land was like a welcome. Green townlands were opening out to the west round a cluster of buildings. To the east the hill came right down to the shore. Basking seals on the opposite shore slid into the water as the boat approached the rocks.

The captain called to Astrid and Thorvald. 'I can put you ashore here. That's your direction.'

They grabbed their bundles, and climbed out on to weed-covered rock.

'Up there,' said the man, pointing east. 'That's where Amundi's hall is. Cross the hill and you'll reach the dyke.'

The boat slid away, and started across the voe to the settlement on the far side. Astrid and Thorvald climbed the hill behind the beach and crossed the dyke. The view that met their eyes was quite unexpected. Rich as the plains of Tara. Astrid had never thought Hjaltland could be like this.

The hay was cut, but rigs of oats and barley stretched down to the sea, interspersed with kale and beans. A herd of black cattle grazed on lush pastures, and in a voe to the north-east two ships swung on their moorings. The turf roofs of buildings were every-where, with cows tethered nearby. Smoke rose from many roofs, and here and there small figures moved across the townland, one with a pony, another with a huge basket on her back.

'No wonder they call Papey rich,' breathed Thorvald. 'No wonder!'

Amundi's hall was the largest building Thorvald had ever seen. It stood among many outhouses, and its peatstack alone was the size of the house at Setr. Ponies were tethered in the yard, and there were benches outside with room enough for twenty men to sit.

Astrid went up to the heavy oak door, which opened straight into the feasting hall. The chimney holes were unshuttered, and the fire smoored, so it was daylight inside, and very grand. The wooden pillars of the high seat were painted red and gold. The hangings on the wall were not plain weave, or even patterned, but showed pictures. There were men armed for battle moving across the narrow strip of material. Some of them rode horses. Thorvald had never seen horses as tall as men, but he had heard about them. He stared at the scene. The figures had been made so real, he seemed to have entered their country. He could imagine being there, just as if he were listening to a story. He felt the picture might swallow him up, and he crossed his fingers, and looked away. But there was another woven picture on the far wall, showing a tempest, with grey clouds, and a dark blue sea. A figure with a halo stretched out his arm over the water. There was a boat, but the figure wasn't in it; instead, he walked on the sea. Thorvald knew that story, but even so his hand went to his thorshammer.

A range of weapons hung opposite: swords, shields and axes. One sword curved like a scythe, and had a scabbard decorated with flakes of gold, and next to it there was a thing like a harpoon that must be a lance. The benches in the hall were wide, and covered with thick skins, some from strange animals he didn't recognise. Astrid looked smaller than ever, in her seastained brown cloak with her bundle on her shoulder.

'There must be somebody about,' she said.

Thorvald couldn't imagine any normal person living here. He would have liked to leave, having now done what he had promised, which was to bring her here.

A door opened at the far end of the hall, and a man appeared, stooping under the lintel so that he filled the entrance. When he stood straight Thorvald realised he was over six feet tall. He had a huge black beard, an impressive paunch, and was completely bald. Thorvald took two steps backwards.

'What's this? Who are you?' It was a voice suitable for outshouting a tempest, but overwhelming indoors on a fine day.

Astrid stepped forward. 'You must be Amundi Palsson?'

'I'm seldom challenged in my own hall,' he remarked. 'Who are you? I've heard of no one like you on the island. What do you want with me?'

'We've just arrived with some fishermen from Vagr. I am Astrid Kolsdottir. My father built you two ships, and I think he was a loyal friend to you when you were in Dyflin.'

Amundi looked her over. Thorvald admired the way she looked straight back.

'Kol shipbuilder?' said Amundi softly. 'Yes, I know him well. A little man no warrior would look at twice, yet he built ships that could sail from here to Holmgardr. I wondered about him when news came last year that the English were in Dyflin. You have a look of him, certainly. Isn't he here with you?'

'He was drowned. We were on our way to you a year ago, as soon as Dyflin was taken, but we were driven by a storm, and our ship was wrecked on Fridarey.'

He sat down on the high seat between the great carved pillars. 'He was a loyal friend, Kol shipbuilder, and a great craftsman. He is dead, you say. God rest his soul. Perhaps you'd like to tell me, then, what brings you to visit me?'

Astrid looked so small in front of Amundi, but she wasn't scared of him at all. Yet she was afraid of a few breakers when the wind was fair and the channel to the anchorage wide open. Thorvald had done everything now that he'd promised. There was nothing to keep him.

'My father was on his way to you,' Astrid was saying, 'after we had to flee from Dyflin. He knew that he could trust you to help him, because he'd done the same for you. He is dead, and I've been on Fridarey for nearly a year now, but I came here as soon as I could. That's what he'd have wished me to do. I've nothing to bring you. In the shipwreck I lost all that I had. I can only ask you to return the favour my father once granted to you.'

Amundi stirred in his chair. 'What do you wish me to do for you?'

He didn't sound eager. Thorvald would have forgotten anything he'd had to say, but not Astrid. She faced Amundi squarely, and said, 'To re-instate me as my father's daughter, to give me a passage to Noreg, and to help me find my relations there, as my father had planned to do.'

'Do you know these relations?'

'I know one or two names, and I know they live in Hordaland.'

Amundi sat staring at her. She didn't lower her eyes. Then without looking round he said, 'Who is this man you've brought with you?'

Thorvald flinched. He should have gone. None of this had anything to do with him.

'This is Thorvald Eiriksson of Fridarey. He was travelling to Papey, and he kindly agreed to bring me here.'

Thorvald tried to look disinterested. He feared that Amundi was about to accuse him of seducing her. After all, it was less unlikely than Astrid seemed to suppose.

'Is your business with me?' Amundi asked him.

'No.'

Amundi looked surprised, and appeared to be waiting for more.

'My business is with Helgi Sverreson,' said Thorvald.

'Helgi?' Thorvald was beginning to dislike Amundi's thoughtful look, it seemed to imply that everything was part of a plot. 'Ah yes, Helgi. Well, you'll find him easily enough.' Amundi turned back to Astrid. 'You won't find it very easy to get to Noreg. I'll think what is the best thing to do.'

Thorvald didn't like the sound of that. If Amundi wasn't to be trusted, then Thorvald would have to come back and check that

Astrid was safe. There was no end to responsibility, it seemed. Perhaps Helgi would advise him. Amundi spoke again.

'However, I will certainly not abandon the daughter of Kol shipbuilder. You must stay here while I consider the matter. The women will see that you're provided for.' He turned back to Thorvald. 'My folk will set you on your way. Will you be on the island for long?'

'I don't think so.' Clearly he was expected to go. He didn't feel comfortable about leaving Astrid. He didn't trust this man, and she had no one to protect her. He looked at her. Her cloak from Fridarey seemed very shabby in this rich hall. 'I'll come and see you again before I leave.' She gave him a doubtful smile.

Chapter 39

Astrid had a visitor the next morning. A plump young woman with a round face was waiting for her in the yard.

'I'm Signy. Signy Helgisdottir.'

Astrid saw the likeness at once. 'You're Arne's sister?'

'That's right. Arne's friend told us about you last night, so I've come over.'

'I'm glad. I need to see Arne as soon as I can. My friend Ingrid on Fridarey gave me a message for him.'

'But he's not here.'

'Not here? Didn't he get back?'

'Oh yes, he got back. Your friend's upset about missing him too. But he and my brother Jon have gone to Fridarey. One of Amundi's ships was going to put them ashore there on its way to the Orkneyjar.'

'You mean he's gone to marry Ingrid?'

'They went to arrange the settlement. Mind you, my father was furious at first.' Signy regarded Astrid speculatively. 'Do you know all about it?'

'Ingrid's a close friend of mine.'

'What's she like? Did Arne seduce her? I'd never have thought it of him. The girls on this island always said he was a bit slow, in that way, I mean; he's bright enough.'

'I don't think Ingrid found him slow.'

'You must tell me all about it.' Signy looked round cautiously. 'Amundi's not about, is he? That man gives me nightmares. Why don't we go for a walk? I'll show you the island.'

The wild side of Papey was as open and windswept as the sea. A pair of eagles soared over the cliffs. White rock, encrusted with lichens, stuck like bones from the thin soil underfoot. The heather was in bloom, sweet smelling on the wind. Signy led her up a grassy hill, and below them was the sea. The island was red under its thin covering of earth. Red cliffs faced the sea, and the rock like the bow of a ship hung over a massive arch, behind which Astrid recognised the two skerries they'd seen from the boat yesterday. There were sheep grazing on the holms, where grass grew to the very edge of the rock, and campion and stonecrops clung to the fissures in the cliff. Gulls swept in on the wind, wheeling overhead with raucous cries.

Astrid gazed westward, and for the first time recognised the sea as a possibility, or a challenge. It was like a glimpse into Thorvald's mind. He never talked to her about anything that mattered to him, but just for a moment she had a notion that this was the sea as he saw it. It changed her idea of him. He might be less clever and less kind than his brother, a peasant compared to her father, hardly even a friend, but even so she had not done him justice.

'Come down here!' Signy shouted above the wind. 'I'll show you something.'

It was a big pool among the rocks, like the pool at Hestigeo on Fridarey. The waves seethed below it, but here the water was calm and transparent. Fronds of green seaweed floated, and the rocks were stained pink with barnacles.

'Mussels,' said Signy, pointing across the rocks. 'Too small though. It's exposed out here.'

The pool was quite still, and the sun, trapped in the half circle of the cliff, warmed Astrid's face. Above her head the rocks had been scoured into curves by the sea.

'Do you like this place?'

Astrid nodded.

'We'll go back by the peats.'

The empty peat banks made long brown scars across the turf. The peats were gone.

'The banks are much deeper on Fridarey.'

'I've heard ours are shallow. That's why they're so long. We cut a lot of turf as well.'

Two oyster catchers were calling across the moor, and Astrid was surprised to feel a sudden rush of homesickness for Fridarey. They crossed the hill dyke, and Signy stopped dead, gripping Astrid's sleeve and pointing to the hill ahead. Astrid saw a puff of smoke, blown by the wind. She clasped her hands. 'Not a raid?'

They began to run. At the end of a stony beach they saw two little boys. All the noosts were empty. Signy called, 'What is it?'

The bigger boy cupped his hands and shouted back, before hurrying on, 'Whales! It's the whale hunt!'

'Come on!'

Astrid ran after Signy to the summit of the next hill. Groups of boats were converging outside Housa voe. She gradually began to see what was happening.

Some boats were still rowing out of the voe, others were spaced out in a line, sailing east before the wind. Two more came between the stacks on the far side. The line of sails began to turn, closing the mouth of the voe.

A patch of rough water was moving south into the voe. Sleek black bodies broke the surface, curving like part of the waves themselves.

As the two lines of boats converged, the whales dived and surfaced, swimming to and fro with no clear direction. Some turned northwards, and the men in the boats splashed their oars and shouted, until the whales turned back into the voe again.

The whales were moving faster now as the boats closed behind. With a sudden concerted movement they turned shoreward, away from pursuit. The water was so shallow that they formed a wave of their own, which rose right over the beach before it broke and crashed on the sand. The sea withdrew, leaving the sand littered with gleaming bodies.

Those whales left in the sea swam wildly, intermingling with the boats. The water was stirred like a whirlpool, the boats breaking line, whales struggling in the shallows in huge splashes of foam. There were men in the boats, hurling spears, and the water was changing colour. A pool of murky brown seeped outwards, and turned red.

'Come on!' Signy was pulling Astrid's sleeve. 'Come down to the shore! Come on!'

Chapter 40

The kill stirred Thorvald: the surge of men and fish, hurling his harpoon, striking the right place behind the dorsal fin. Cries of men echoed round him, the boat swayed, writhing bodies thrashed against wood. He tumbled into a heaving sea, blood and salt in his mouth, and stood chest deep, wielding Arne's whale knife. He found the blowhole and struck down, while the fish thrashed like a demon. Its spine cracked and broke. Then another whale, body against body, smooth skin slippery under his hand; Thorvald struck hard, and red blood welled into pink water. A straight wound this time, the resistance of bone, the spine breaking, both his hands soaked in blood.

Suddenly it was over. Men were scrambling on to the beach, hauling their boats up after them. Thorvald waded ashore through breaking waves, and saw the long line of bodies on the beach, wealth such as he'd never dreamed of. Still out of himself, dazed with the kill, he pushed his wet hair out of his eyes, and wiped his bloody hands on his trousers.

He wasn't left bemused for long. They were setting up a block and tackle, and he was set to work with a team hauling the whales up with ropes. Men waded through the bloodstained water, feeling for bodies, and as each whale was hauled up, it left a bloodstained dragmark behind it.

Then he helped with the gutting. Arne's whale knife was one of the best. The unwounded whales were killed first to stop them thrashing, then two men moved along the row with the whale measure, and a third read off the tally and made notches on a stick. Thorvald and Arne's brother split the first whale's belly open so that pink ropes of gut spilled out, hot and slimy to the touch. Helgi's fairhaired grandsons got in the way of the work, climbing and poking among the bodies, looking for the harpoon wounds.

The last whale Thorvald came to was a big female. As he ripped its belly open, Arne's brother made some remark he didn't catch.

'Eh?'

The young man pulled the guts aside, so they spilled out over their feet. He reached into the belly the length of his arm, and felt around. He pulled out something red, and thrust it at Thorvald. 'And good luck to you!'

The thing was a small red replica of the mother, its veins showing blue through transparent skin. Thorvald held it up by the tail, and flourished it at the measurers. The boys screamed with delight. Someone called out something lewd that he didn't catch, and the men laughed. The work finished, Thorvald climbed up the beach, and saw Astrid.

He waved with his free hand, but she didn't look round. He put down his trophy and sheathed his knife, and when he looked again she'd vanished into the gathering crowd.

The sun had dropped behind the hill dyke, leaving pale streaks of orange in the western sky. Only when the first lamps were brought down was Thorvald aware how far the daylight had drained away. The whales lay dead, and the island seemed to wait quietly, suspended between day and night.

Within the stone circle above the beach where the Thing met, a huge bonfire had been lit. Torches of flaming peat were stuck on poles. The sea sighed on the shore, and the autumn stars were bright, the Hunter and the Bear awakened from their summer sleep. An acrid smell of peat drifted over the dim fields. People were gathering like moths, making their way down from the houses. Their long shadows reached down and mingled with the bodies on the beach.

The whale recorders had retired with their tally to work out the shares, but the word had gone round already. Seventy whales lying dead on their shore. Enough for meat and fuel for everyone for the whole winter. The ghosts of hunger and darkness receded, banished for another year.

Thorvald and his hosts pushed their way into the crowd. Leather flasks were passed round. A stranger held his out and Thorvald drank deeply. He was hungry too, but there was no time to think of eating.

He handed back the flask, as a voice broke out in song behind him. It was the ballad celebrating the whale hunt. Thorvald only knew the chorus; they'd had no reason to sing it on Fridarey. Other voices joined the first singer. A circle began to form, stamping out the rhythm. As the dancers came past, Thorvald was grabbed by a blackhaired sailor, who pulled him in. The words went on and on, almost dying away as the leaders started each verse, then swelling up again with the chorus. Thorvald joined in. The sailor next to him was wearing clogs, and Thorvald had to move fast to keep his bare feet out of the way. When their section of circle came into the light, the fire was hot on their faces, then they moved on into the dark, and the chill breeze struck their backs.

The ballad ended at last and the ring broke.

'Have a drink.' It was Arne's eldest brother. 'You've earned your share of whale,' he told Thorvald. 'You'll have something to take home.'

'I've no way of doing that. But at least I'll have a proper gift for your father.'

Another ballad began, and they were dragged back into the dance.

Thorvald caught sight of Astrid on the opposite side of the ring. There was colour in her cheeks, and when the boy next to her spoke to her she laughed, and tossed her hair. When the ring broke again, Thorvald pushed his way through the people until he reached her side.

'Hey!' He grabbed her by the shoulder.

'I knew you'd be here somewhere. Were you in one of the boats?'

'Of course.'

'There's blood on your face,' she told him.

'I thought I'd washed it all off.'

The singing was starting up again, and the music expressed the thrill that had not yet died in him. Astrid looked very pretty, her face flushed and her eyes bright. He seized her by the hand, and pulled her into the circle.

The words were different, but the dance was the same. As they moved from light to darkness, Thorvald realised that he knew the words; on Fridarey they sung them to another tune. He roared them out along with everyone else. Astrid didn't sing, but she danced enthusiastically beside him. Her hand in his was small and cool. The ballad came to an end. 'I'll be back in a minute,' he promised, and retired into the shadows.

When he came back people were everywhere and the torches were guttering. The recorders had arrived, and the crowd pressed closer to hear the allocations. They started with the households on the island, distinguishing the whales by the marks they'd carved on their fins. Then they went on to give shares to the visiting boats that had taken part. When they came to the trading ships that had been moored in the voe, there were angry shouts from the crew.

'Two whales,' replied the recorder. 'Two whales is a fair share.'

The crew pushed to the front, hands on their knives. The islanders surged forward, and the crowd swayed. Thorvald was crushed among a group of islanders, all shoving towards the recorders. Men were yelling threats, and unsheathing their knives.

Thorvald remembered Astrid. She shouldn't be in this. He began to kick and use his elbows, making for the place he'd left her last. He saw torchlight reflected on a raised blade. A woman screamed. Other men were fighting a way through. The press of bodies hid the light. There was another scream, a man's. Where was she?

He found her, rooted to the spot where he'd left her, hands pressed to her mouth. He grabbed her, got his arm round her shoulders, and pulled her through the crowd, hitting out a passage between packed bodies and trampling feet.

Then they were safe in the sheltering dark outside the stones. He could feel her shaking. 'Best out of that,' he said reassuringly.

'I'm all right,' she said, trying to wriggle out of his hold.

He was looking back, trying to work out what was happening. There was a press of men in the middle, while the women gathered round, shouting, blocking his view.

'Let go!'

He realised he was still gripping her arm. 'Wait!' If Helgi's sons were in there, he ought to be fighting on their side.

'Don't hold on to me!'

He turned to her impatiently. She was safe now, there was no need for her to keep demanding his attention. 'You shouldn't be here. It's dangerous. You'd better go home.'

'Are you going home?' Her voice was challenging, even angry. He couldn't see her face. He'd been sure she was frightened.

'Of course I'm not!' he said. 'I'm not a coward.'

'So you think I am?'

'It's not safe for you.'

'Yet it is for you?'

'You're a woman.'

'There are women there!'

He was exasperated. It seemed as if she wanted to be in a fight. 'I tell you it's not safe. Off you go home!'

'You can't tell me where to go!'

'It's a fight, girl! Don't be stupider than you can help!' He was so annoyed that he shook her arm hard, to show that he meant what he said.

His wrist was wrenched round so he had to let go. Her fist came out of the darkness, and landed a sharp blow on his chin. Furious, he lunged at her, but she was gone.

Chapter 41

Two days later Thorvald found Helgi at the beach working on his boat. One of the boards had been pushed in during the whale hunt, and had split badly. Helgi was making a temporary repair, so that the boat could be used for the rest of the season. When Thorvald arrived, Helgi's son was sealing the crack with seal's grease, and Helgi began to tack on a patch of oiled sealskin.

Thorvald explained that he wanted to talk, and while Helgi worked he told him the whole story of the lawsuit.

'I suspected something of the sort,' was Helgi's first comment, 'I know my son Arne regards you as a friend, and friends are what he'll need, if he's to settle on a new island. For his sake, I'd like to see the whole matter resolved. Also, you're Eirik's son, so I'll help you if I can. There's nothing worse than feuds in a family.'

'I'm still not sure how it all happened. I couldn't seem to stop it.'

'Let me think,' said Helgi. 'Eirik had other friends of course, who could support you. But I don't think that's the best way.' He examined his broken fingernails, and frowned. 'You do have one powerful man who owes you a favour, don't you? Perhaps we can make something of that.'

Thorvald looked blank.

'You took Kol shipbuilder's daughter to Amundi, didn't you? What's her connection with your family? She's no kin of anyone on Fridarey?'

'No, it was a shipwreck, pure chance. She's been living at my uncle's house. When he died she asked me to bring her to Amundi.'

Helgi looked thoughtful. 'Well, whether he likes it or not, Amundi must regard that as a favour. Leave it with me.'

Amundi's hall was full. They had evidently been feasting; the tables had not yet been cleared and the smell of whale meat lingered. Helgi made his way between the tables to the high seat.

'May I speak with you, Amundi?'

A harp was being played, and the drinking continued around them, but drink never affected Amundi Palsson.

'I have a young man staying with me,' began Helgi, 'the son of an old friend. I believe he undertook an errand on your behalf.'

'Is that what the boy said?'

'He told me he had restored to you the daughter of an old friend of yours, at some inconvenience to himself.'

'And what leads you to suppose it was inconvenient for him?'

'If I were travelling here from Fridarey, I'd hardly choose to bring a young girl with me, and offer her protection on whatever boats happened to be available.'

'That seems rather unadventurous of you. Have you met the young woman?'

'No. Where is she?'

Amundi glanced across to the women's table. 'Sitting next to my daughter.'

'She looks very young. I thought she was Signy's age?'

'Fourteen.'

'She doesn't look it. So she escaped Dyflin only to be shipwrecked in Hjaltland. It seems very hard.'

'Unfortunate.'

'You met the boy, however. He is Thorvald Eiriksson of Fridarey.'

'The name sounds familiar. Why should that be?'

'Eirik Thorvaldsson of Fridarey? Does that mean anything to you?'

'Timber from Noreg?'

'You have it.'

'He stayed with you, would it be ten years ago? A shrewd man, ambitious in all that he did.'

'This is his son.'

'Is it?'

'I owe my trading connections largely to Eirik Thorvaldsson, and I would do what I could to help his sons in return.'

Amundi thought for a moment. 'Your boy Arne. He's gone to Fridarey, hasn't he, to be married? Is that correct?'

'Yes.'

'Is his betrothed any relation of this young man?'

'His cousin.' Helgi looked round the table. Nobody was listening. If Amundi chose to have a private discussion in the middle of a feast, no one would dare to overhear.

Helgi leaned forward. 'Amundi, I have a story to tell to you, for I think it may amuse you.'

Amundi smiled from time to time as he listened, and presently he laughed out loud, drowning the babble of talk around them. 'A classic story,' he roared. 'And well told. It only wants the tragic ending, and it wouldn't disgrace the court of Noreg itself.'

'But these people are real,' said Helgi quietly. 'The much-tried nephew is a lad from Fridarey, who finds himself perplexed rather than ennobled by his fate.'

'A peasant is he? I'm not sure that interests me.'

'He'll make a seaman like his father. Eirik was ambitious. Eirik's son wants a trading ship that will make him his fortune, trading from here to Island.'

'Is that what he told you?'

'He told Arne.'

'Ah yes, Arne. We mustn't forget your interest in the happy ending, Helgi, must we? Traders! They're all traders these days. Offer them a fight and they run straight to the lawcourts and sit like cabbages waiting for judges to pronounce their doom.' Amundi laughed. 'So Thorvald wishes for nothing better than a quick and peaceful settlement. And you support him, and also wish your son to have a secure future? You want to see the whole matter resolved out of court, and a fair inheritance arranged for everybody? Is that it?'

'That's precisely it.'

Amundi regarded Helgi with amusement, then grew suddenly serious. 'What is this boy to me? I have affairs of my own to think of. A boy with nothing to recommend him but a desire to go to Island? What is it to me what becomes of him?'

'I thought the matter of your friend's daughter might carry some weight.'

'Kol's daughter? What of her?'

'If it were not for the boy she might have become a thrall. Some farmer's mistress. Thorvald has restored her to her friends, and he deserves some thanks for that.'

'From me? You must be soft in the head! Kol was more of a man than most people realised, but all the wealth he had is lost. His daughter inherits nothing from him but his looks – a backhanded gift – and possibly his obstinacy. What use to me is a destitute girl who brings nothing but the clothes she stands up in? And they do little enough to recommend her. What do you propose I do with her, now that she has been so carefully delivered to me?'

'The best thing would be to provide a respectable dowry and find a husband for her. That would get her off your hands.'

'Your common sense does you credit. Though why you think I should be overcome with gratitude at the prospect I can't imagine. Don't you think I have enough women in my own household to find husbands for?'

'I know that's a problem,' said Helgi. 'But surely it wouldn't hurt you to part with a small dowry that would mean a great deal to many men? To one in danger of losing his inheritance, for example, it could solve a lot of problems.'

'I'm so obtuse, Helgi,' said Amundi softly. 'Would you mind explaining exactly what you mean?'

Never had a night seemed so long. Again and again Thorvald wished he'd never come to Papey, or heard of Helgi Sverreson. He lay on his back and listened to the wind sweeping in from the east. Draughts whistled under the door, rustling the straw. A turf had slipped from the fire, and the wind whipped the dying peats into flame. An easterly would probably last for days, so near the turn of the year. If he were to be at Svinborg before Rolf, he ought to leave within the week, but there was this business to be resolved first. Now he understood the stories about remorseless fates pursuing a man to his death.

Amundi was waiting for them the next morning. His hall was as full of people as Helgi's house, except there were no women, no babies, no boiling pots. Instead, men lounged on the benches sharpening their weapons or playing at dice. They glanced up as Thorvald and Helgi came in, then turned back to their companions. Amundi was sitting in his high seat, and he formally invited his guests to sit down. He seemed to be amused. Helgi looked anxious and kept pulling his beard. Amundi kept his eyes on Thorvald, until Thorvald felt himself redden. Amundi's lips twitched. Clearly he was intending to enjoy himself.

'What is it that you wish to ask me?'

Helgi said, 'I have come on behalf of this young man, who has no kinsman on this island. I intend to act for him as his own father would have done. Eirik was a trusted friend of mine, and I have his son's interests at heart. The proposal we wish to make is this: that Thorvald Eiriksson wishes to offer himself in marriage to Astrid Kolsdottir, whose guardian you now are.'

They could hear the howling of the gale outside. Put plainly like that, Helgi's solution sounded drastic. Thorvald was only fifteen. What had he let them do to him?

'I am prepared to consider the matter,' Amundi said. 'Since the girl has no kin and has placed herself under my protection, I have already accepted legal responsibility for her in front of witnesses. Any contract you enter into with me on her behalf will be legally binding.'

Who did this pirate think he was? And where was Astrid? Thorvald realised he was biting his nails, and clasped his hands together on his knee.

'Thorvald knows that,' said Helgi, 'and is willing to declare before witnesses that he accepts your right to enter into a binding contract on behalf of Astrid Kolsdottir of Dyflin.'

Amundi was looking Thorvald up and down. 'If we are able to agree on a contract, I am prepared to look favourably upon your offer. Would you be willing to become legally betrothed to Astrid Kolsdottir before you leave the island?'

There was a great gust of wind outside, and they felt the pressure change inside the hall. He hasn't mentioned his bit of the bargain yet, thought Thorvald: the money. She's only fourteen. Where is she? He hadn't seen her since she had hit him and run off. He cleared his throat. 'What does Astrid say?'

'Astrid?' said Amundi, as if trying to remember who she was. 'I really haven't discovered. It seemed a little premature.'

And Thorvald had left her here, at this man's mercy. They might have done anything with her. 'She does know about it?' he managed to ask.

Amundi looked vague. 'I believe my wife may have mentioned the matter.'

'And what did Astrid say?'

'I should point out,' said Amundi wearily, 'that we are here to discuss a legal contract, and as Kol's daughter is a woman in my care I am eligible to speak for her. If you wish to see her presently you shall, but it seems inappropriate to involve her in our discussion of terms.'

Helgi was trying to catch Thorvald's eye, and shut him up. But this was the only part Thorvald wasn't confused about. 'I can't discuss anything until I know she's willing,' said Thorvald firmly.

'Since she herself thrust me into the position of becoming her guardian, I cannot doubt that she is willing to trust me to make satisfactory provision for her future. But if you really need confirmation from her own lips at this stage I suppose it can be arranged.' Amundi sighed. 'Do you wish her to be fetched?'

'Yes.'

Amundi spoke to one of the men on the benches. The man jumped up, and disappeared through the inner door. There was a heavy silence, while the wind shuddered against the stone walls.

'Quite a gale blowing,' remarked Helgi.

'I had observed it,' replied Amundi.

'There are financial matters that we must consider,' said Helgi presently. 'I'm willing to stand surety for payment of a bridegift on Thorvald's behalf. There is also the matter of a dowry.'

Thorvald knew Astrid had nothing. "Nothing minus the cost of a ship that's lying at the bottom of the sea." He had just realised that he wasn't listening to a negotiation that would affect his whole future, when the door opened again. It wasn't Astrid. It was a thin harassed-looking woman with a pointed nose, who turned out to be Amundi's wife.

'I asked to see Kol's daughter.'

'I know you did,' she said anxiously. 'I'm so sorry. Astrid has gone out.'

'Gone out,' he repeated. 'Naturally you mentioned to her that this young man was expected to visit us this morning?'

'Of course I did.'

'And what did she say about it?'

'Nothing. She didn't say anything at all. A few minutes later she said she thought she'd go for a walk. And she went.'

'Very well.' Amundi turned back to Thorvald. 'Am I to gather that you feel unable to make a binding agreement until you have ascertained the opinion of the woman in question?'

'Yes.'

Amundi sighed. 'It all takes time,' he complained. His wife was still standing irresolutely. 'Don't let me keep you,' he said, and she hurried out. Amundi continued. 'Now, young man. Helgi made it quite clear what I propose to do for you? My ward will bring you a dowry of fifteen ounces of gold. That's at least as much as your disputed inheritance is worth. So you go back, and suggest to your uncle, Bjarni Thorvaldsson, that you forego your share in the land, on condition that he adopts your two brothers as his heirs, along with his new son-in-law.

'If he refuses, and I doubt if he will, tell him you'll have the support of Amundi Palsson when you bring the case before the Thing next summer. Suggest that he asks your new lawman about my reputation. I think I may say, if we're to speak honestly, that if it came to a case, with my support you'd stand a strong chance of winning. But you don't want a case. In return, you must pledge me your support, either at the Thing or in any country where you may one day have contacts. Helgi tells me that you are likely to attain more standing in the world than you have at present. Regarding your talents, I can only take his word for it. Possibly you have shown yourself to be more accomplished in his company than you have found it necessary to be in mine.

'Were it not that Helgi assures me that you are a young man of promise, I could hardly be expected to look favourably on your offer of marriage to Astrid. As it is, you'll find allies all over the islands, as the husband of Kol shipbuilder's daughter. I hope you won't forget your first benefactor, when your ambitions come to be realised.'

'I'm most grateful that you look favourably on my offer,' said Thorvald, suppressing a desire to tell Amundi what he thought of him. 'I shall be very glad to accept the terms of the contract.'

'But understand,' said Amundi in a lower tone. 'You must prove worthy of it.'

'Yes.'

'Do you still feel it necessary to find the girl before we bring in witnesses, and agree to the contract?'

'I do.'

'In that case we'll waste no more time at present. I'm sorry we've proved unable to bring her to you, but no doubt you'll overcome such a minor setback. Come to my feast this evening, and we'll announce the betrothal in the presence of witnesses.'

Where had Astrid gone?

'You are then obliged to be married within the year. Will you be returning to Papey before next year's Thing?'

'No. I'll be at sea.'

'Will you come back here after the Thing perhaps?' asked Helgi, 'if Amundi is willing to hold the wedding feast then?'

Thorvald wouldn't be beholden to Amundi any more than he could help. 'No,' he said. 'I've got a better idea. Astrid has a home on Fridarey. If she returned with me now, we could be married there, and neither of us need come back.'

Helgi looked doubtful and opened his mouth to speak, but Amundi forestalled him. 'Excellent. If there is a household there where the marriage can be held I'll make my contribution towards the feast.'

Shirva? Whatever would Bjarni think? Thorvald couldn't begin to work out the implications now.

'My uncle will act as her guardian,' he said.

'Good,' said Amundi. 'When you go back now, you can take the girl and five ounces of gold for the expenses of the marriage. Before you leave, I'll take oath before witnesses to bring the dowry to the Thing in June. Is there anyone who can collect it from me there, if you'll be at sea?'

'My uncle?' said Thorvald. He couldn't imagine how Bjarni would react, but that would have to be thought about later.

'I'll also stipulate before witnesses that you arrange a formal marriage on your own island in my absence, and your uncle will act on my behalf.'

Helgi looked pained. 'Is that quite suitable? We have the interests of the girl to consider. Now she's been restored to her father's friends should we allow her to travel in such a way?'

Amundi looked Thorvald up and down. 'If he brought her here, no doubt we can trust him to reverse the process. Also, he will be bound this time by a legal contract, so that we can have redress for any misfortune she may incur at his hands.'

'I think she'll trust me without that,' said Thorvald coldly.

'No doubt, but she is in my ward and therefore unable to make such decisions herself. However, within my own terms of reference I am satisfied. We will make our contract tonight.'

Thorvald got up to go.

'I'll follow you presently,' said Helgi. He turned to Amundi. 'I wanted to discuss the whale allocations while I'm here.'

The wind tore at Thorvald as soon as he stepped outside. He leaned back against the door for a moment and drew a deep breath of fresh air. Then he dismissed Amundi in two words, whispered in the direction of the closed door. He pulled his hood down, and set out into the wind. It was wild out here. Where would she be? He felt guilty, almost as if he'd betrayed her. He let the wind guide him, and great clouds overtook him as he strode before it towards the hill dyke.

Chapter 43

Astrid had run across the island with the wind behind her, but here on the cliffs she could hardly stand. She lay down, watching the waves. With each crash of water she could feel the ground quiver. If Amundi's great hall were flung down there, she thought, it would all be crushed to kindling in five minutes. As for Amundi himself, he was so fat he'd probably float, but then the rocks would get him. Serve him right too. She wondered what kind of friend he'd been to her father.

There were two seals in the water, twisting and diving joyously as each breaker curled over them. Thorvald . . . the last time she'd seen him his face had been smeared with blood and he'd reeked of whale. Then he'd treated her like a fool, and she'd hit him.

She watched the seals, black heads bobbing in white water, sinuous bodies rolling through surf. What Amundi's wife had told her had left Astrid too astounded to speak. She'd been too angry to trust herself to answer, so she'd left the house abruptly, and run right the way across the island. No one would think of following her here.

She wasn't sure now why she'd been so furious. What had she supposed Amundi would do with her? Help her to get to Noreg? What would her kin there do with her? Wherever she went, she would have to accept authority from someone else. She'd never fully understood that before. If Kol had lived to arrange her marriage, he'd certainly have asked her opinion. But no one else was going to care that much. Astrid began to realise for the first time how powerless her orphaned condition had left her.

She was going to have to marry somebody, and it was unlikely that she would be consulted about it. Amundi might palm her off on anybody. He just wanted to be rid of her. But why Thorvald?. Of course, thought Astrid, he wants Amundi's support against Bjarni. I even offered him Amundi's support myself, but never dreamed of him using it to attack the only people who've treated me well since my father died. I don't want to be in a plot against Bjarni. Is that why I was angry?

She realised that it wasn't. Perhaps it was Thorvald's attitude. He'd never pretended to love her, but he might, at the very least, have asked her opinion before he'd talked to Amundi.

If she had to marry him, it would mean returning to Fridarey, to all the people she had grown to know so well. It wouldn't be so bad to go back.

But there was Olaf. She hadn't given him a thought since Snorri had announced that Thorvald was about to leave for Papey Stora. She'd have to face Olaf, when she was married to his brother. I couldn't help it, she thought, suddenly frightened. I didn't do anything. It wasn't my fault Olaf liked me.

Thorvald should have spoken to her first. Those horrible old men had probably thrown their plot at him, just as they had casually sent word to her. Amundi hadn't bothered to speak to her either. Perhaps Thorvald hadn't had the chance. He might even be looking for her now.

She couldn't imagine being married to him. He'd have to make love to her, of course. The thought was so embarrassing that she squirmed. She'd seen Thorvald share his cloak with Ragna and disappear across the hillside on midsummer night. His eyes were very blue, just like Olaf's. One day it would have to be somebody. Astrid made a face at the pounding waves. The two seals had gone.

If she refused, Amundi would be furious. Perhaps he'd force her to marry. Certainly he wouldn't help her get to Noreg. They could hardly betroth her if she fought them and screamed, but where would that leave her, now Amundi had declared himself her guardian?

*

Preparing for Amundi's feast was very unlike going to the
Byrstada feast with Ingrid. The women here hardly spoke to her;
only Amundi's wife, harassed as usual, had demanded sharply
where on earth she had been. Just before the feast one of the boys
who worked in the kitchen came in from the yard with a full peat
basket. When no one was looking he came quietly over to Astrid.

'There's a man outside asking to speak to you.'

When Astrid opened the door the lamplight gleamed on wet
stones. She closed it behind her, and stood half blinded by the
sudden darkness. Someone came towards her.

'Thorvald?'

He pulled her back into the partial shelter of a peat stack. Astrid
held her arms tight round her, and wished she'd put on her cloak.
The last time they'd met she'd hit him. She wondered if he was
remembering.

His mouth was close to her ear. 'I've been looking for you all
day.'

'I was out on the hill.'

'That's where I was looking.'

A huge gust of wind swept through, and she staggered backwards.
She could only just hear him, though he was nearly shouting.

'That man, he hasn't been getting at you?'

'I've not seen him. Is that what you wanted me for?'

'No.' His hand was on her arm. 'Do you want to marry me?'

Of all the ridiculous questions. 'Isn't that what you've arranged
to do anyway?'

'I couldn't. I hadn't asked you.'

A great weight was lifted from her mind. 'Was he angry with
you?'

'Amundi? No, but he said I'd have to find you myself, because
we're to be betrothed tonight.'

She bit her lip in the darkness. 'Thorvald, is this so he can oppose
Bjarni for you at the Thing in Hjaltland?'

'No, no! This is to make it all right.'

'How?'

His mouth was close to her ear again. 'It was just as you'd said.
Helgi doesn't want a quarrel, because of Arne marrying Ingrid, and
if I don't need my share of Shirva, Bjarni can adopt my brothers as
his heirs. It's going to be tough telling my mother that, but I don't
see any other way.'

'But what about you? You won't inherit?'

It took him a while to answer her. 'I'll have wealth of my own now, you see.'

'But how?'

'A dowry.' She caught the awkwardness in his voice. 'Amundi has to pay me a dowry, for you. Fifteen ounces of gold.'

She grabbed him by the tunic. 'But that's clever! Did Amundi think of that? That'll solve everything, won't it?'

He still sounded uncertain. 'You're not angry?'

'Why should I be?'

'I thought you might be offended.'

'I had nothing,' said Astrid simply. Thorvald would never have to think, as she had had to, what was the likely fate of a girl without a dowry. 'I wasn't expecting that man to do anything generous. I'm glad he isn't lost to all his obligations. I'm sure he owes my father that much.'

'I'm glad you see it like that. Astrid?'

'Yes?'

'You don't mind marrying me?'

Another gust of wind funnelled through, bringing rain with it. 'Do you mind marrying me?' she asked him.

'I should quite like it. I've been thinking about it all day. I think we'd get on.'

The wind swept along the gutter above, showering them with water.

Astrid giggled. 'I don't mind either, then.'

In Amundi's house the women sat at a separate table, at right angles to those that stretched the length of the hearth. Thorvald, sitting among a group of men he'd not seen before, was remembering a sight that had puzzled him as he tramped the hills in search of Astrid that afternoon. He had found a small hidden voe on the north side of the island, guarded by a narrow entrance. Looking down from above, he had been startled to see two longships lying snug beneath the cliffs, safe from the storm-swept seas outside, and hidden from sight except to the closest passers by. He had dropped down below the ridge to hide, but it wasn't a raid. When he crawled forward to look again he saw islanders there, and a line of ponies at the top of the beach with baskets on their backs.

The men at Thorvald's table didn't seem inclined to talk to him, but the food was very good and so was the wine, which was white, something he had never seen before. He didn't intend to get drunk tonight, and luckily his neighbours weren't interested enough to force him to take drink for drink with them.

They were discussing some business they had just concluded, but referred to it in such veiled terms that he had no idea what it was. Presently he caught a name that he knew.

'They say it's to be his last raid, but I won't believe that until he's underground.'

'It's a bad sign though, when a man like Svein Asleifarson speaks of retiring.'

'And you don't know where they were going this autumn?'

'Magnus mentioned the Sudreyjar. It's an old haunt of Svein's.'

'Not much to be picked up there these days. I'd reckon Monige was more likely.'

'I doubt it. They were ready for him last time.'

'Englaland?'

'Rich, it's true, but too well defended. Nothing to be done so far south these days.'

'So no one knows where he's gone? If it's his last voyage he'd make for somewhere where he'd earn a share of glory.'

'You mean where the pickings are good. But where?'

'Dyflin,' said Thorvald quietly into the brief silence that followed.

They all looked at him, seemingly as surprised as if one of the dogs under the table had suddenly stood on its hind legs and spoken. A man with a hooked nose who sat opposite said, 'Can we ask where you received your information?'

'It's common knowledge,' said Thorvald.

'I see. Can we ask your source of common knowledge?'

'Several people.' How they stared. 'A friend from my island sailed with him.'

'Is that so? Naturally I should know your friend's name, but you must excuse me. Just for the moment it escapes me.'

'There's no reason at all why you should know. He's Dagfinn Erlendsson of Fridarey.'

The man nodded, and looked at Thorvald with increased interest. The others had seized upon this latest piece of gossip, and they all fell to discussing it among themselves.

'Now you've given them something to talk about for the rest of the evening.' Thorvald turned round. The man next to him looked quite friendly.

'Are you a sailor yourself?'

'I'm starting on a trading ship next year.'

To Thorvald's surprise the man seemed keen to talk to him. Naturally he expected Thorvald to take drink for drink, and the evening began to improve. When Thorvald was finally summoned to the high table, a public betrothal no longer seemed an ordeal.

Amundi called for everyone's attention, and the entire hall fell silent. Astrid was brought over to the high table, to stand opposite Thorvald. She seemed quite composed, until her eyes met his. Then he saw that they held an expression of terror.

Helgi knew the words, so all Thorvald had to do was repeat them. He didn't think too hard about what they meant, in order not to distract himself from the task in hand, which was simply to get them said.

He had to state his offer in front of them all, recite the agreement about the bride money, and name the witnesses he had brought with him. He got Helgi's sons in the wrong order, but no one seemed to mind. Amundi responded in flowing terms, announced the sum of the dowry he was prepared to settle upon Astrid, and named his witnesses. Then Helgi dictated the words of the betrothal. Thorvald recited them after him, and the contract was sealed with the handfastening between himself and Astrid. Her hand was cold, but she looked at him steadily. For a moment he felt sure he had done the right thing. He wanted to tell her so, but there were too many strangers there. It would have to wait.

The following morning he left Helgi's house early to try to find her. Before he reached Amundi's hall showers had soaked him all down one side. If Amundi Palsson insulted him again he would tell him what he thought of him. But the first thing was to look after Astrid.

There was no one in the hall. He remembered those men had said something about fetching the cargo, even if it was blowing a gale. The same boy who had taken his message to Astrid came in to attend to the fire. Thorvald asked for Astrid, and waited, studying the tapestries. He was beginning to feel quite accustomed to them.

Hearing footsteps, he turned to see one of the men who had been at the feast last night. He was tall and lanky, with a bony face and sunken eyes.

'I was hoping to find you again,' he said. He didn't sound at all friendly. 'You said last night that you were a friend of Dagfinn Erlendsson of Fridarey.'

'I am,' said Thorvald.

'Dagfinn Erlendsson killed my brother.'

'I'm very sorry. But I don't know anything about it.'

'In a tavern in Kirkjavagr two years ago. He never offered to pay compensation either.'

'I'm sure whatever he did he had reason.'

'He fled back to his ship and denied me vengeance or compensation. But I've not forgotten; I knew fate would grant me one or other in the end.'

'It has nothing to do with me,' said Thorvald.

'You deny your friends, do you?'

'No.' The man had drawn his sword. Thorvald stepped back. 'We could discuss compensation.'

Einar's sword hung on the wall at Setr, on Fridarey, waiting for Thorvald's first voyage.

'It's too late for that! Defend yourself!'

With his hands? The man raised his sword. Thorvald suddenly raced across the hall, and leapt on to a bench. He grabbed one of the swords off the wall, and faced his attacker. As long as he stayed on the bench he was taller.

The attacker's sword slashed with a sound like a whip. Thorvald ran back along the bench. The man was after him, swiping again. Thorvald grasped his hilt in two hands and parried. There was a loud clash. And again. He could do it! The idiot was trying to kill him, but he could fight him off. He kept parrying. There was no time for anything else. The man lunged at him, and Thorvald leapt free.

Thorvald had the feel of the sword now. He continued to parry while he retreated steadily backwards the length of the hall. The man was so fast, sooner or later he was bound to catch him out. Thorvald trod on a fallen sheepskin and glanced down. A flash of heat seared his arm, and his hand felt wet. Suddenly he was furious. He wasn't going to be killed by this madman. Using two hands again, he hit out. His opponent fell back, then came after him again, fiercer than ever.

There was a movement in the hall. A third sword came between the two blades, and Thorvald reeled back. People were shouting and swearing at him. Furious, he screamed back every obscenity he could think of. He was beside himself, his blood dripping on to the floor.

'Quiet!' A huge voice silenced the confusion. It was Amundi. His men cowered, but Thorvald was too outraged for respect. He pulled his torn sleeve back to expose a deep cut. Blood poured out of it and his head began to swim. He couldn't faint in front of them all. He tried to stop the room swaying in front of his eyes. Amundi was shouting at him.

Thorvald shouted back. 'Shut up! It's me that's wronged! It's your house, and your man attacked me! I want your apology!'

There was an appalled silence. Amundi's contemptuous gaze was arrested. His lips twitched with amusement. 'Magnus!' he roared. 'Apologise!'

'Never! His friend killed my brother!'

'Then leave us!'

'I demand vengeance!'

'Take him away,' ordered Amundi, and Magnus was hustled out.

Thorvald was left facing Amundi. He was quite prepared to quarrel with him now, but he wasn't offered the chance.

'One of you bandage his wound,' said Amundi. 'Give him a glass of wine. As for you, young man, take your betrothed and get out of here. If you're not off this island by midday tomorrow, there's not a man on it can protect you. Is that understood?'

'And my money?' said Thorvald coldly.

Amundi regarded him with narrowed eyes. 'My wife will give you your five ounces now. The rest I'll bring as agreed to the Thing in Hjaltland.' He turned to leave, but then paused to add, 'I never broke my word yet, remember that!'

'Now that is unfortunate,' said Helgi, while Signy prepared a comfrey poultice for Thorvald.

'You're lucky it's only a flesh wound,' said Arne's brother. 'He could easily have had your arm off.''

'That's the least of his troubles,' said Helgi irascibly. 'How can we get him off the island, with a gale blowing? Amundi knows quite well it isn't weather.'

'We can arm ourselves,' suggested his son. 'Though he might come and try to burn our house down.'

'Nonsense! We're not living in a heroic tale, and we'll start no blood feuds here! I'll go up to Amundi's myself and tell him we'll get you and Astrid off the moment it's weather.'

Chapter 45

'It's an ill wind.'
'Won't it turn?'
'No. It's an ill wind, or we're ill-wished.'
The plump girl went through to the kitchen, and came back into
the byre with hot stones from the hearth on a shovel. She threw
them into the churn, and almost at once the butter began to float
to the top. 'There's your ill wind for you!'
'It's keeping the longships here,' said the third girl. 'That's
something.'
'You might regret that yet, if you don't take care.'
'Hush, you're corrupting innocence,' said the girl with long fair
hair. They all giggled.
'If you mean me,' said Astrid, 'You needn't bother.' She was
sitting on the wooden partition that divided the dairy from the
byre. An icy draught flowed under the door. This gale seemed to
have been going on for ever.
The fair girl lifted the butter out of the churn. 'You can help me
wash the milk out if you like,' she said to Astrid. Astrid jumped
down. They washed the butter in ice-cold water until their hands
were numb.

'It's a shame you're not staying,' the girl said. 'We have a good time when the men come home in winter. Feasts almost every night.'

'The crews from all Amundi's ships are back, and sometimes there are others laid up here for the winter.'

'She likes longships,' explained the plump girl.

'Astrid wouldn't, though. She's got a man of her own. She won't miss a few feasts when she's in bed with him every night. Will you?'

'I suppose not,' said Astrid, unable to think of a clever answer.

They all burst out laughing.

'You don't sound too sure. You do want to marry him, don't you?'

'Of course she does. She came all the way from Fridarey with him.'

'He's got lovely eyes. She's done all right.'

Astrid shrugged.

'Do you want to cut the butter? Here's a knife. We'll halve it.'

Astrid had made butter on Fridarey, so she knew what to do. She began to cut this way and that, cleaning the cattle hairs off the knife as she went.

'I'll be married myself this winter,' went on the fairhaired girl. 'I'll be sorry in a way. It's been good while it lasted.'

'Just as well,' the other broke in. 'You're lucky you weren't caught out before.'

She chuckled. 'Not lucky, just careful.' She turned back to Astrid. 'You'll be all right though. It's better that he's not too handsome, it means he'll be kinder. That's the most important thing when it comes down to it.'

'Comes down to what?' giggled the other.

'Take no notice of her. How old is he?'

'He'll be sixteen at Michaelmas.'

'Well, he could still get taller. And his beard will grow, of course. You'll be all right.'

'We need some more water.'

'I'll fetch it,' said Astrid.

'Take some straw. It'll blow all over you otherwise.'

The wooden well cover ripped out of Astrid's grasp as soon as she lifted it, but she grabbed it before it blew away. She dipped the bucket, and shoved the weight back on the cover while the wind slapped her hair across her face. In spite of the straw it swept a good deal of water out of the bucket on the way back, soaking her skirt.

She found them salting the butter and cutting it into blocks. They were talking about the fight after the whale hunt.

'Knifed. Right through his shoulder and out the other side. If his lung had been touched he'd be dead.'

'They should hang that sailor.'

'That's what I said. Did you see the blood, all the way back to the hall?'

The byre door opened and a man stooped under the lintel and looked across at Astrid. 'Can we speak?' he asked.

She followed him into the yard, and shut the door, cutting off the giggles behind her.

The stranger's face showed something was wrong. Thorvald? 'What's the matter?' asked Astrid quickly.

'It's the boy – the man I should say – that you're betrothed to. There was a fight this morning.'

'What happened?'

'He wasn't badly hurt,' the stranger reassured her. 'He's gone back to Helgi's. It was Magnus. Your man's kinsman killed Magnus's brother.'

'Who is Magnus?'

'My shipmate. He'd have killed your man if he could. He attacked him in the hall. They were interrupted. Next time Magnus will take care that they aren't. I'd advise you to get your man away from the island as soon as you can.'

'There won't be any boats in this weather, surely?'

'Magnus won't forget. He was made to look foolish in front of them all.'

'By Thorvald?' she said.

'Yes. Magnus is my shipmate, but I think your man's innocent. Nothing would be gained by his death. If he asks you who gave you this warning, tell him it comes from the man who sat next to him at last night's feast, the one who told him the sailing directions for Narvey. I think he'll remember.'

Helgi's house was the most crowded Astrid had ever seen. Signy, shelling crabs by the hearth, waved to her to come in. Then Astrid noticed Thorvald on the bench, his right arm in a sling. He got up when he saw her, and met her at the door.

'Come into the barn.'

They sat down on a sea-whitened log.

'Did you see Helgi?' asked Thorvald. 'He went to look for you.'

'Are you badly hurt?'

'No.'

'This stranger just attacked you?'

'It was stupid. Dagfinn killed his brother. Who told you?'

'A man that had sailing directions for Narvey who sat next to you last night.'

'Oh, him.'

'Are you very annoyed?'

He glared down at the sling. 'Wouldn't you be?'

So this was what he was like in a bad mood. 'The man who knew how to get to Narvey thinks you should leave as soon as possible, because Magnus will try to kill you.'

'Fine. You should introduce him to Helgi. They'd agree.'

'Thorvald, I don't want you to be killed.'

'I'm not planning to be killed,' he said irritably.

'We should leave.'

'Good idea. You didn't tell me you could fly.'

'I want to get back to Fridarey,' said Astrid, surprising herself.

'People get killed there too.'

She stood up.

'Where are you going?' he asked.

'It doesn't seem to be a good moment to talk to you.'

'Come back!' She turned round at the door. 'I'm sorry. It's not your fault.'

She sat down again on the log.

'It's not going to be that easy getting home,' he told her. 'I've been thinking about it. We have to be at Svinborg before Michaelmas. As soon as the sea goes down Helgi will take us across the sound. But everyone's waiting to get the harvest in as soon as this wind stops. Even if we walk to Vagr, there probably won't be any boats leaving at present.'

She thought it over. 'Vagr's just the other side of that big hill across the sound?'

'Yes. We can walk there easily enough.'

'And Vagr is on the same island as Svinborg?'

'Yes.'

'So once we're across the sound we could walk to Svinborg?'

Clearly he'd never considered the possibility. 'We don't know the way.'

'We do. It must be east, then south.'

'But we can't just wander about the hills. We're not armed.'

'I expect we'd be a lot safer than on the sea.'

'Now you're being stupid.'

He'd been much nicer before she'd agreed to marry him. She frowned.

Suddenly Thorvald said, 'I think you might be right.'

'You do?'

'Yes. If there are no boats, we'll walk.'

Two days later the east wind died away, leaving the sound quite calm. The air was sharp and smelt of rain. When Signy arrived, out of breath, to fetch Astrid to the boat, she was ready to leave. They were still bailing when Astrid arrived. One of Helgi's sons dried a thwart for her, and they set off into the grey morning.

They rowed out between the stacks at the southern end of the voe, and Helgi glanced back to the hill behind to line up the marks, while his sons rowed on steadily. In the shadow of the red stack that guarded the passage, the water reflected greenish black. Shags stared down with yellow eyes from lime-streaked ledges. The mouth of a cave gaped at the cliff foot, while water surged on into the darkness.

When the westerly tide stream caught them, they had to row crosswise against it. The sea's surface was dark and still, rippled here and there with tiny whirlpools. Astrid didn't trust it.

'It's very calm, isn't it?' she whispered to Thorvald. There was no sound to obscure their voices, only the regular dip of oars into the water.

'I thought you preferred it that way?'

'But it blew such a gale!'

'From the east,' he explained, wondering how she could be so simple. 'Hjaltland's in the way. There's nowhere for a swell to come from.'

She watched the smooth water change colour from green to black and back again, and was silent.

They beached the boat at one end of long white sands, and walked up to the hall at Maedelboer. A guide was sent for to show Astrid and Thorvald the way to Vagr. The boy who arrived to accompany them was a silent youth, afflicted with a skin disease so that no one wanted to sit too near him.

'But he knows the way,' their host assured Helgi. 'He'll get them safely to Vagr.'

The boy grabbed Helgi's gift of whale meat, and muttered something that might have been thanks.

'I'll be there to witness the payment of your dowry money in June,' said Helgi. 'Tell your uncle I'll be glad to meet him then.'

'But you'll be back?' said one of Helgi's sons to Thorvald.

Thorvald grinned. 'Oh yes, I'll be back.'

Astrid, Thorvald and the guide walked uphill through a scattered settlement where people were already cutting the barley, and followed the line of a burn up to a pass between the hills. They took a path threading through rock and heather, and when they reached the first ridge more sodden moorland opened out ahead. Their guide spoke for the first time.

'We leave the burn here and go straight on up.'

Astrid turned round. 'Look!'

The sun had found a thin break in the watery clouds, and its subdued light was reflected in a white-flecked sea. Papey was clear of haze, a low outline rising to a rounded hill in the west. They could see a long sandy beach and turf roofed houses like grassy outcrops on the slopes above. The rigs made stripes of yellow and green right down to the shore, but the hills behind had faded to autumnal brown. It was all barely a mile away, but the sea surged through the sound between, and now the island was another world. They were almost into the hills; another hundred yards and Papey would be out of sight.

Papey Stora. A rich and fertile island with fine anchorages and great beaches suitable for boats. One face of it utterly bare, scoured rock beaten by weather; the other with lush rigs of corn, rich pasture, and grass so thick with flowers that the smell of them would guide men home from sea when the island was lost in summer mist. A very difficult place to leave, not just because of the weather.

Part Seven

The Travellers

Thorvald was uneasy. Land encircled them entirely, the sea seemed too far away, and he and Astrid were completely in the hands of the silent boy, whom Thorvald had never seen before in his life. Thorvald kept feeling for his knife. With only one good arm, he felt vulnerable. He scanned the hills again. The broken nature of the country would make it very easy for a stranger to approach without being seen.

The boy was splashing towards a loch, and Thorvald took the chance to whisper to Astrid.

'We can't see the sea.'

'Does it matter? We've got a guide.'

'We don't know who he is.'

'Helgi did.'

'I wish I'd brought my sword,' said Thorvald.

'Why didn't you?'

'It would have been heavy to carry about.'

There were otter tracks in the peat beside the loch. Thorvald remarked to the boy, 'You must get good hunting here, with so much land.'

The boy pointed to a low hill to the south surmounted by a cairn. 'That's the edge of the Vagr townland. When you reach it you'll see Vagr just below.'

Their guide clearly felt no need to exchange another word with them. He was off, back the way they had come. They watched him disappear round the edge of the hill.

Thorvald felt better without him. He looked towards the clouded sun. 'It can't be much after midday. We could be well beyond Vagr by nightfall.'

'It's all bog down there,' said Astrid. 'We should go round it.'

He followed her, taken aback by her assumption of authority. A cloud of starlings swept across the hill in front of them, their wingbeats rustling. Astrid stopped on a knoll, where white lichened stones stood among grass and tormentil. Heather lapped at the foot of the mound, but had not touched its slopes.

'Don't stop there. It's a trowie mound.'

She looked at it dubiously but said nothing, and followed him. He was quite willing to sit down a little further along. She took out a barley bannock and offered him half. He passed her his leather flask. 'Drink as much as you want. We can refill it anywhere here.'

'How quickly do we need to go,' asked Astrid with her mouth full, 'to get to Svinborg in time?'

'Helgi said we could do the journey in four days. We'd be in time if it took us a week. There's no path, but there are medes all the way to Skalavagr. If it's misty we won't see them, and we don't want to get lost. It would be worse than at sea, without a swell to tell where you are.'

'I think we should stop at Vagr tonight, and go back to the helmsman's house. I'd rather do that the first night than knock on a strange door. Do you agree?'

'Very well,' said Thorvald, smiling and reaching for his flask. 'We'll do just as you say.'

Astrid was sitting with her arms clasped round her knees. There were heather scratches all over her bare calves. Her feet were brown with sun and peat stains, but her legs were white where her skirt usually covered them. Perhaps she had brown freckles on her body, like the ones on her face and arms. Thorvald had always thought she was skinny, but he noticed now that that wasn't quite true. He could see the curve of her breast quite plainly when she sat like that. They were betrothed. On Papey he had had very little chance to think about what that would mean. He was going to have to get to know her much better.

He liked Astrid. She might look fragile, in the midst of this unknown country, but it didn't frighten her. Sometimes she was tough, and when she wasn't, he was beginning to know what scared her. Thorvald was suddenly aware of arousal, unexpected and unpremeditated. He didn't attempt to touch her, but the desire was there. He rolled over, leaned on his elbow, and watched her through half closed eyes.

'You must admit it's good,' said Astrid suddenly, 'not being dependent on anything or anybody. You can go where you want to go, just yourself. You don't have to ask for anything.'

'What?'

'Never mind. Shall we go on?'

It began to cloud over as they passed the next loch. 'See what I mean?' said Thorvald. 'If we lose sight of our medes, we're in trouble.'

Astrid glanced back. The hills between them and Papey had become grey and ominous, shrouded in a swirling mist, but ahead, the sky was bright. She quickened her pace, leaving clear footprints through the stretches of peat, and Thorvald set his own bare prints beside them.

When they reached the ridge, the wind met them, and suddenly the whole south coast of the west side of Hjaltland was before them. Vagr lay a little more than a mile away, and they could see the helmsman's house standing in its yard above the golden barley rigs. There were small lochs this side of the settlement, gleaming white, and beyond them was the sea. Thorvald looked out to a horizon lost in white squalls, and the uneasiness which had held him since they left Papey disappeared. There was a dog barking down in the settlement, and peewits calling over the moor, but he was sure he could hear the sea.

Astrid was pointing east. 'That's where we have to go, then?'

The spine of the Hjaltland hills traversed the horizon. In front of it he could count at least three lower ridges. He'd never seen so much land in his life. He looked again at the Vagr harbour, and found it reassuring. It was a proper place, green townland centred on an ideal anchorage.

'Shall we go down?'

'I just want to look at it first,' he replied.

Astrid sat down on a dyke, while Thorvald began to commit the landscape to memory: the shape of Valey, the two channels, the outline of the surrounding hills, and their relation to this hill with its outstanding mede.

Astrid took the opportunity to study him. It was hard to believe she was betrothed to him. She was beginning to grow fond of him. He'd made no attempt to touch her yet, and she wondered if, or when, he would, and what it would be like. His forearms were sprinkled with pale freckles. She hoped he wouldn't mind that, in spite of all the remedies that had been tried on her, she was covered with big brown ones. Now that Thorvald's sleeves and trousers were rolled up, she could see that his arms and legs were covered with gold hair. He probably had hair elsewhere that was also fair. Her eyes strayed over his body, trying to imagine it.

'All right,' said Thorvald at last. 'Shall we go on?'

There was a track leading down from the Vagr peat cuttings, wide enough for them to walk side by side. Thorvald took her hand, and she seemed to accept that quite tranquilly. He liked her small delicate hands. She did things very neatly. He wondered what it would be like to have her touch him. The only girl who ever had, had hands that were neither small nor delicate, but she'd been clever enough at finding out what he wanted. Ragna had never been shy. Thorvald wondered if Astrid would be. He was sure no one had been with her, and that pleased him.

'Shall we go straight to the helmsman's house?'

'Yes,' said Thorvald. He pulled her towards him and kissed her cheek. 'We'll be all right,' he told her.

Astrid blushed. Elated, he strode down the track into Vagr as if he owned all the islands, while a salt breeze blew in from the sound to welcome him.

The helmsman's family greeted them as if they were old friends. When Thorvald told them that he and Astrid were now betrothed, they brought out a jug of ale, and insisted that it be drunk at the evening meal instead of blaand. Thorvald tried to protest, being fairly sure that these people didn't have much to spare. But at least the news distracted them from their questions about his bandaged arm.

That night, as Thorvald lay in the barn, he thought about the journey ahead. Perhaps he and Astrid were taking a foolish risk.

There were a lot of small lochs and green mounds out there in the hills; there was no knowing what lurked in their depths.

But Astrid seemed unworried. She had courage. Even at sea she'd never complained, although he knew she didn't like it. After supper tonight he'd been watching her again. By lamplight her eyes were not so much green as dark. Now he'd started to notice her body, he couldn't think why he hadn't thought she was attractive before. Perhaps when he'd first seen her a year ago, she really had been skinny. Today he'd kissed her cheek, and she had blushed. Her clothes smelt of peat smoke, just like everybody's, but under that she had a faint fresh smell of her own, or perhaps it was the heather scents on the hill which had confused him. He began to imagine making love to her, and wondered how she'd respond to him. The helmsman's young sons were breathing quietly a few feet away. Thorvald slid down in the hay and undid his belt. He shut his eyes and began to conjure up an image of Astrid, bare-legged and happy, sitting in the heather below the grass-covered mound. He let his imagination drift. It wasn't difficult. The idea of making love to her now seemed pleasurable, not hard to anticipate in the very least.

Chapter 47

'I f the going gets too tough you can always come back.'

Thorvald shook the helmsman's hand. 'It won't, but I will be back. By sea, I hope, next time. I'll come and find you then.'

'You'll need to get yourself home first. You're sure of your directions?'

'Quite sure,' said Thorvald for the fourth time.

When they first looked back, the helmsman was still standing on the knowe where they had parted. He waved when they turned. The next time they looked he had gone.

'You're not worried about thieves, in spite of what he said?' asked Astrid presently.

'I don't think thieves would worry about us, unless they like dried fish and oatcake.'

'And Amundi's silver. Do you think there are trolls?'

Thorvald crossed his fingers. 'Don't be silly, Astrid.'

So he did think there might be. Astrid repeated her prayer to St Christopher, and was comforted. They followed the voe, and passed a small settlement at the head of it, where a group of children followed them curiously. People looked out when the dogs barked, and waved a greeting, but no one stopped the travellers. Chickens picked over the seaweed on the tideline, and ducks foraged among the rushes on the loch. Astrid and Thorvald crossed a bog thick with irises, and made for the hill dyke. Once over the dyke they were in deep heather. A warm breeze caressed their backs, and the sun brought out the smell of the flowers. The wind when they reached the ridge was like a plunge into cold water.

'Look,' said Thorvald, taking her by the shoulders. Astrid saw blue lines of hill fading into sky, the horizon lost in a haze of rain. Thorvald still had his hands on her shoulders. When she turned round he let go.

'You don't want to learn those hills by heart?'

He shrugged. 'I couldn't begin. But one day I'll know that coast.'

On the ridge the heather was thin and walking was easy, so it didn't take long to reach the cairn, from which they saw a patch of townland in the east. It must be somewhere in the grey distance beyond that Thorvald had stood on the ridge above Konungsborg with Arne, looking west.

'That settlement must be Thveit, from the directions,' said Thorvald.

'It's miles away!'

'Four miles is what he said. Do you think you'll manage?'

Astrid dealt Thorvald a mock blow, and he seized her wrist and held it. Laughing, she tried to wriggle free. Thorvald grabbed her in his arms and held her tight.

'Do you think I'm not strong?' demanded Astrid, pushing him away, and walking on.

It was becoming easier for Thorvald to touch her. He was aware of her every time he did so, and the current was there, faint but flowing. Thorvald glanced at the sun. It was barely mid-morning.

'I can see a loch,' called Astrid from in front. 'Two lochs.'

'Keep to the south, where there's heather.'

'But we'll have to cross the marsh sometime, to get to Thveit.'

'Later,' said Thorvald. The loch sparkled azure in the sun, amidst reeds and cotton grass. Astrid had overtaken him again. He didn't mind her walking ahead when they were alone, although it wasn't usual.

Astrid brushed through the heather, humming to herself. This reminded her of trips into the country with her father, in what seemed now to be another life. She and Kol had sometimes gone out to the foresters to select trees. Kol would walk around an oak tree, looking up into it, measuring the trunk and the length of the branches by pacing round. If he approved, he'd blaze the tree with his own mark. The cut wood wouldn't be ready for the shipyard for several years, but Kol could afford to buy ahead.

'Keep left a bit,' called Thorvald from behind her. Astrid moved downhill. The loch was curving away from them. She made for its shores, but in a few paces she was up to her ankles in water, sinking into bright green moss.

'Take care!' He was splashing after her, raising as much water as a trotting pony, and soaking her skirt.

'You said go left!'

'Not through that. Come back where it's drier.'

Astrid followed Thorvald in silence. The Thveit townland was in full view not far away, but the marshes lay between.

'There's the firth he spoke about,' said Thorvald. 'Just below Thveit, see? We're exactly where we should be.'

'Only we have to cross the marsh.'

'It's the green moss you have to watch. A man can drown in bog like that. Keep close to me. We'll try to keep to the grassy bits.'

Several times they had to retrace their steps and twice they sank in over their knees. Midges gathered in a black cloud over the unexpected feast. Astrid and Thorvald jumped across peat hags, landing in half submerged rushes. A cloud passed over the sun, and a squall of rain struck in from the west. Thorvald looked up in alarm. If they lost visibility here they'd be in trouble.

At last they crossed a wide burn by way of a stone causeway, and found that they had joined the track which led down to the noosts on the shore. Two men were coming down the track. Astrid remembered the warnings they'd had the night before, and stepped behind Thorvald, who held up his hand, and walked forward to meet the strangers. They talked with him for a minute or two, but ignored Astrid when she slowly approached them. One of the men was gesticulating towards the mass of cloud gathering on the hill ahead.

'Look here,' he said. 'I'll set you on the path.'

He led them along the shore, below the barley rigs. Presently they left the beach and met the hill dyke. There was a stile set in it, and a path leading onward.

'A couple of miles, and you'll be in Trestada. You won't get much further today.'

The path was beaten to bare earth by many passing feet. Astrid followed at Thorvald's heels. When she looked back the man was still at the stile, staring after them.

'They can't get many travellers walking through,' she remarked to Thorvald's back.

'I asked him if any boats were going to Skalavagr, but he said not now it's harvest.'

'I hope the people in the next place are friendly,' said Astrid.

'So do I.'

At least Thorvald could still see where the sun was. Sometimes the clouds seemed about to lift, then they came down and shrouded the hill heavily. He stopped as they were passing a sheep shelter.

'Let's rest. Do you want something to eat?'

They sat down in the lee of the wall, and Thorvald handed her a piece of dried fish. Mist drifted over the pass ahead, gradually obliterating it from sight.

Astrid's hair had come loose so he couldn't see her face. He touched the back of her neck, ruffling her plait. 'Are you all right?'

'Just tired, I suppose.'

Astrid wasn't tired, but she couldn't look at him. She'd wanted him to touch her like that, affectionately, and now that he had, she didn't know what to do next. She felt full of unexpected emotion that seemed about to choke her. She held her hand out, without looking up.

'Astrid,' said Thorvald. He pulled her towards him, and kissed her.

The kiss was not at all unpleasant. When he did it again, she decided that she liked it, and began to respond. His arm tightened round her. Astrid pushed him back so that she could see his face.

'Do you like me?' she asked him seriously.

Thorvald brushed his hair out of his eyes. 'I suppose that's a sensible question. Yes, I do. Did you doubt it?'

'I wondered.'

'Well, I do.' A thought seemed to strike him. 'And what about you?'

'Oh yes, I like you.'

He grinned. 'Just as well.'

By the time they reached Trestada it was raining fitfully. The path grew slippery, and grasses soaked them as they passed. They came to a dyke, and climbed over. New cut sheaves of barley drooped mournfully among stubble.

Thorvald wiped his nose on his sleeve. His tunic was turning dark at the shoulders where the rain was beginning to soak through. Astrid stopped and waited for him. Her hair felt wet and heavy, and cold drops were running down her neck and turning to a warm dampness.

'I think we should find shelter before we're wet through.'

'Good idea,' replied Thorvald. 'What are you going to do about it?'

He hadn't expected her to take him literally; he merely felt cold and irritable, but when she set off at a brisk pace across the townland, he could only follow. Squinting through the rain, he could see a scatter of turf roofs ahead. Astrid kept on uphill, and, following her, he realised she'd seen a woman leading a cow, moving its tether.

The woman was old, bent over with the rheumatics, a black shawl pulled tight over her head. He couldn't hear her answer to Astrid's question, probably because she had no teeth.

Astrid beckoned Thorvald to follow.

The woman took them into a small turf-roofed hut some way past the last house in the township. It smelt of damp and age. They heard the woman clearing some of the bruck from the platform by the hearth side. She talked as she moved about, suggesting that they sit down and take their wet clothes off. All Thorvald's clothes were wet, but he didn't respond to her invitation. He was glad when she turned back the turfs to reveal a small fire of broken peats and seaweed.

Astrid hung up her wet cloak, and warmed her feet on the hearthstones. When the woman offered them dried fish and oatmeal, Astrid said they had fish of their own that they'd be willing to share.

'No, no, you'll be needing that. I'd be shamed if I didn't feed you.'

She talked all the time: clearly she had lacked an audience for too long, but Thorvald could only make out about half of it. He was beginning to shiver, and his eyes smarted from the seaweed smoke. His wound was hurting him, and the bandage over it was quite wet. He wondered if he could remove it without anyone noticing. He moved up closer to Astrid and stretched out his feet to the fire.

When the woman left them to milk the cow, Astrid put the porridge on the side of the fire, and peered at Thorvald. As far as she could tell in the gloom, he had turned very pale.

'Is your arm hurting?'

'Yes.'

'If the bandage is wet you should take it off.'

'Then what? Let the blood drip into a bucket?'

'It can't still be bleeding. We'd better look at it.'

'I can look at it myself, thank you,' said Thorvald, rolling back his sleeve. He struggled to undo the knot with his left hand, but it was wet and stubborn. 'Can you just unfasten this?'

Before he'd unwound the bandage the door opened. A fair girl with dripping hair and a rainstreaked cloak ducked under the door, then jumped back with a cry of surprise when she saw them, hitting her head on the lintel.

'Where's Asgerd?' she demanded, rubbing her head.

'She went to milk the cow,' said Astrid.

'Who are you?'

'Just travellers. We're only sheltering the night.'

The girl looked them over. 'Why did you come here? You should have gone to Thorfinn's house. No one stays here!'

'Asgerd took us in.'

The girl had her fingers crossed as she said, 'But you should have told someone you were here!'

'We have told someone.'

'Yes, but . . .'

Asgerd appeared in the doorway. She was so bent she didn't have to duck under it. She was carrying a bucket, but when she saw her visitor she set it down by the door at once. 'It's Gudrid needing me, I suppose?'

The girl looked frightened, and started wringing her hands. 'It's not going well. Can you come at once?'

'When did it start?'

'About noon.'

'Why did no one call me then?' The old woman pushed past them and took a sheepskin bag down from the wall. 'It's always the way these days. No one calls me in until they realise they do need me after all, then they come running, usually when it's too late. She'll be lucky if it's not too late this time. I suppose you'd called in that woman from Thveit?'

The girl looked at the floor and said nothing.

'I don't know what's happening in this township. And then you come to me, expecting me to put all right, when you neglected to so much as send me word in the first place. All right, I'm coming, for the bairn's sake, but I'll have nothing to say to any of the rest of you, you understand that?'

The girl nodded dumbly.

Asgerd was putting on her cloak, and speaking to Astrid and Thorvald. 'I'll have to go, you can see that. They don't deserve that I should, but there's a bairn's life at stake, and I have to think of the innocent, whatever others do or fail to do, whatever they say when I'm not there to listen. I doubt if I'll be back tonight. It's rare for me to have guests in my house, and I'd have given you a better welcome if I had what I deserved. But there's food ready to eat, and you can sleep there on the platform. Keep the fire in, and make yourselves free of what I have. If there's not more it's not my fault, but that of those whom I won't mention. If I'm not back before you go, I'll tell you now that you were welcome and go with my blessing.'

She cut short their thanks, told them to drink the milk if they wanted it, and left them. The door shut behind her and the girl with a bang, and Astrid and Thorvald were left alone.

'Let me see your arm.'

'There's no need. It's all right.'

'Let me see it.'

Reluctantly Thorvald held it out. She took his hand and turned the arm over. A red scar was beginning to form, about four inches long. The wound had not quite closed in the middle. She touched the bruised skin gently. It looked quite clean.

'It's a pity she's gone. She'd have had some salve.'

'I don't think it's a pity. Anyway, Helgi's wife gave me some.' Thorvald rummaged in his bundle with his left hand, and drew out a greased cloth. 'In there.'

'Shall I do it?'

He watched as she rubbed it gently round the wound. She was neat and deft, and hardly hurt him at all. When she'd done, he sat back and shut his eyes again. When he opened them, she had lit a lamp, and was searching the baskets that hung on the wall.

'What are you doing?'

'Looking for something for a clean bandage.'

'You can't do that! It's not our house.'

'Only a rag, she won't mind that. I'm sure she wouldn't want you to bleed to death. Here we are.'

When she'd helped him bind his arm up, she put the fish to boil, and while she waited for it to cook, took off her wet tunic and hung it over the fire. Her unbelted dress hung loosely round her.

'Aren't your clothes wet too?'

'Yes,' he answered, without stirring. She had aroused him again, and he didn't want to move. He ate his meal absently when she passed it to him, still watching her. She seemed quite unselfconscious, and made a hearty meal. Then she put the dishes in a soapstone bowl with some other dirty pots.

'We could put more peats on the fire,' he suggested lazily.

'I don't think she has many, so perhaps we shouldn't.'

'She said we could.'

Astrid put on another bundle of seaweed. Then she sat down and began to unplait her hair, shaking it out to dry in front of the fire, and slowly combing it out. She hadn't unfastened it since they left Papey, and it was full of tangles. In the lamplight it looked black, except where red lights gleamed in it. He hadn't realised her hair was so long and thick, nor had he noticed the colours in it.

Thorvald stood up, took off his tunic and belt, and hung them over the fire. He untied his trousers at the bottom so they hung loose round his legs, and pulled his shirt loose at the waist. Then he sat down closer to her. Her face was hidden by hair, and she didn't seem to have noticed him move. He picked up a strand of hair very gently, so she wouldn't feel his touch. When he turned it in the lamplight the red lights in it shone. He began to stroke her hair. She must have noticed, but she didn't turn round.

At last she put the comb down.

'Are we going to bed?' said Thorvald. 'We'll have to move some of these things.'

They cleared the platform of dirty fleeces and spun wool, bundles of half dried plants, and some unwashed bowls. 'It smells,' said Thorvald.

'Some people wouldn't lend you their bed.'

'Why not? There's nothing wrong with me.'

The platform was narrow. Astrid lay down on the inside, with the damp stone wall inches from her nose, and heard the wind howling outside. The blanket over her was clammy, but she didn't like to curl up to get warm. She wedged herself against the wall, trying to take up as little room as possible. She'd wanted him to go on stroking her hair; she'd felt like turning round and inviting more, but she didn't know the right way. Ragna would know, Ingrid must know, but Astrid felt painfully ignorant. She'd heard women talking about men all her life; she should have listened more. The stages between Thorvald stroking her hair, and Thorvald making love to her were obscure, although her body told her they were connected. She shivered with cold. There were an unbearable number of hours to wait before the dawn.

Thorvald blew out the lamp, got into bed beside her and pulled half the blanket over him. His voice came out of the dark, close to her ear. 'Would you like an arm around you?'

She turned round. He was pleasingly warm. He put his sound arm round her, so she could rest her head on his shoulder. She tentatively did so, and as he lay still she relaxed a little, and warmed her icy feet against his legs. He didn't protest, so she wriggled closer, and closed her eyes. He was right, the bed smelt.

'I hope there aren't bedbugs.'

'So do I.'

Even if there were no bedbugs, there were certainly more fleas than usual. She could feel them biting her legs, and tried to rub the places with her feet. But fleas weren't worth making a fuss about, and at least it was warmer now. Thorvald smelt of his own home at Setr, a smell she found reassuringly familiar. Her thoughts began to lose coherence. She rolled over, and he curled himself round her. His hand was on her breast, over her dress, but she was too sleepy to do anything about it. She was glad he was there.

Thorvald lay awake for some time. The wind was rising, moaning under the door, and through the chinks between the roof and gable wall. This ramshackle hut must have withstood enough gales before this one. Cold air eddied round his back. The blanket was thin, and mostly covering Astrid. His legs itched; he'd be covered with bites tomorrow. He wondered who Thorfinn was, and whether they should have gone to his house. If they had, they wouldn't have been left alone like this, and Astrid wouldn't have unplaited her hair that way, and combed it out in the firelight. He'd never forget that. Her kisses, once she'd realised what he was at, had been cool and sweet, but they had an innocence about them which frightened him.

His left arm had gone numb under her head, and he extricated it carefully, without waking her. She muttered in her sleep, and wriggled back against him. He moved so that his hand was cupping her breast again, and felt a slight stirring of desire, but she was fast asleep now, and he was tired. Thorvald stared up at the ragged chimney hole, watching a small patch of stars appear overhead, where the wind had blown the clouds clear at last.

Chapter 48

They saw the fair girl again next morning, when she came to milk the cow. It seemed the old woman's services were still required elsewhere. The surface of the firth was wrinkled by gusts of wind, but the cloud had shifted from the hill. They followed the line of the burn upward, as it splashed its way down from the pass in a series of small pools.

As soon as they were out of sight of the township, Astrid stopped. 'I itch all over.'

'It's only fleas.'

'I'm going to wash in the burn.'

She scrambled down the gully, and Thorvald watched her stand calf deep in one of the pools, splashing water over her head and arms. Then he slid down and joined her, stripping off his tunic and shirt, and dousing himself vigorously. 'Not that it'll make much difference,' he told her.

The burn took them almost to the watershed. They picked their way delicately through patches of thistles, then were out of the marshes, walking in heather. A late oyster catcher flew across the moor piping. Just before the head of the pass they looked back. Only two small inlets of the firth still showed, and a corner of the townland. Then they were over the watershed, at the top of a steep drop into the dale, and a whole new country opened out under their eyes.

'Stop!'

Astrid halted. There was a long voe just below them, then glimpses of other voes, stretching far away towards the eastern hills. Cattle grazed between loch and sea, and by a shallow inlet they could see a cluster of dwellings which might be a hall. Beyond it Thorvald counted four ridges that still had to be traversed before they reached the hill where he had stood with Arne. The miles of land between overwhelmed him.

'Do we have to cross all those ridges?' asked Astrid, echoing his thought.

'Yes, and the voes between them. I wish we had a boat.'

He began to scramble down hill.

'Thorvald! Look up!'

Now that they were clear of the ridge, they saw the islands the helmsmen had described to Thorvald on the voyage to Vagr, like a string of jewels in a pale sea. He counted six green holms, mostly flat and fertile, one rising to a small knowe. In the open sea, the cloud was lifting fast, revealing promontories and islands. He looked south, beyond them all.

'Astrid! See that!'

She slithered down beside him. 'Where? What?'

'It's the Fitfugla Head! Look, don't you recognise it?'

The long ness was still barely an outline in the mist, but at the south of it she saw a familiar shape. She remembered her terror as they'd passed close under it, the surf breaking on the skerries barely two oars' lengths away. And she remembered Ragna, standing on the northern cliffs of the island. 'That's the Fitfugla Head, so they say. That's Hjaltland.'

Thorvald was staring out to sea, apparently absorbed. Sailing directions again. Astrid waited until he was ready.

'All right,' said Thorvald at last. 'Let's go down.'

As they descended, a shower crossed to the south, and the Fitfugla Head vanished into mist. They turned left towards the voe head, which was still lost in brooding cloud. 'They can't get much light in winter. I think this voe goes on forever.'

'We'll probably see the head of it from that knowe.'

The dale was visible from the next outcrop. There was a town-ship with rigs and houses, and they could see people in the distance cutting the barley, but it still felt uncanny, a place for trows, or worse. Astrid was bustling ahead as usual, and Thorvald followed her without a word.

They crossed the burn at the voehead by worn stepping stones. The path hugged the shore, and soon the townland gave way to marsh, and the path, once the houses were left behind, degenerated into a sheep track, hugging the dry stony ground at the top of the beach. They reached a rocky knoll where the ground was drier, and a herd of black cattle stared at them as they passed.

Astrid stopped beside Thorvald. Her cheeks were pink, and her hair, straggling as usual, was beaded with glistening raindrops. Thorvald's spirits lightened; it occurred to him that he could kiss her whenever he liked. He grinned. 'Come here.'

She responded with enthusiasm. As he tramped along behind her, Thorvald had started to worry about how to deal with her obvious innocence. But now she didn't seem coy at all.

'I'm hungry,' announced Astrid, when he gave her a chance to speak.

Thorvald looked round, with more than food in mind, but the grass was brown and sodden, and cotton grass grew among the peat hags. 'We won't stop yet. We've a long way to go.'

When they reached the boundary of the next townland, two men were at the hill dyke, mending a breach in the wall. They regarded the travellers curiously.

'Going far?'

'Skalavagr.'

'You should get there today. The cloud'll clear this afternoon. Where did you come from?'

'Papey Stora. But today we walked from Trestada.'

'Round the voe head? Why didn't you get someone to row you across?'

'We didn't see anyone.'

'Well, there are plenty of boats.' The man pointed to the noosts across the voe. 'No one walks right round Visdala. You're not from these parts? You'll be going to the hall?'

'No, we'll go on to Skalavagr.'

'You'll need to wait for the tide,' objected their new acquaintance. 'You can't cross the ford for three hours yet. Tide's running in still. You can cross at low water. You'd have avoided it if you'd been ferried across.'

Thorvald swore. He'd been reckoning on making Skalavagr by nightfall. No one had mentioned a ford.

'In a hurry, are you?'

'Yes.'

The man glanced at his companion. 'I'll row you over if you want. It won't take long.'

He set them ashore on a rocky coast on the further side of the next voe, and showed them the next mede, a big cairn silhouetted on the ridge above them. It was a rough climb, pushing through heather two or three feet high. When they got to the cairn they sat down on the stones, letting the wind cool them.

Behind them, the country which had been confusing to traverse was now clearly laid out. Thorvald turned east. There was another voe to the north-east and beyond it, the open sea, studded with distant islands. Thorvald caught his breath. 'I wish I knew. We should have asked.'

'Asked what?'

'What to look for.' He was hardly aware of her. 'That's – what? – north-east. Is that Jala? It can't be. I wish I knew what to look for. I've heard the names. It could be Valsey, I suppose, that big one, or Faetilar. But the others . . . I just don't know enough.'

'You can ask in Skalavagr.'

While Thorvald gazed at the islands Astrid studied their immediate surroundings. There were two lochans just below, set in a sweep of moorland. Beyond them she caught a glimpse of green, and drew Thorvald's attention to it.

'That must be the Thing valley, I suppose,' he said.

'Could we go that way then?'

'No, we'll follow the ridge.'

She turned south quite willingly. He didn't let her go ahead this time, but kept abreast of her.

'Fugley must be over there,' he said, indicating the western horizon.

A flock of starlings circled their hill, then flew east over the moor. An ancient dyke followed the ridge, white rocks like a broken backbone sticking through the heather. Here and there they passed green circles and broken stone enclosures. Astrid crossed herself. They seemed very far from human kind, but something inhabited this place. She was glad Thorvald was there.

Astrid stopped at the next green circle, telling herself that the saints would protect her. The wind had dropped. She could hear cattle lowing from the green ness across the voe. Someone was hammering, and the metallic sound rang out clearly across the water. The human world was only just there across the water, after all. In front of her a burn flowed between heathery banks. Its water was clear as air, falling in little pools among boulders, each fall sounding its own note in a small harmony.

'Let's stop here for a bit,' said Thorvald.

She looked at him in surprise. 'I thought you wanted to hurry on?'

'We've time.'

He'd chosen a bank above a small pool. Astrid sat beside him, dabbling her scratched feet in the water. Thorvald was staring out to sea, thinking of sailing directions, she assumed. He'd only kissed her once today, briefly, in the middle of a peat bog, and she realised she was disappointed. They were betrothed, and there was no reason why he should not make love to her. Perhaps he'd decided after yesterday that he didn't want to. She glanced at him, leaned forward, put her arm round his neck, and kissed him on the mouth. He looked so surprised that she couldn't help giggling.

He rolled over on top of her, pushing her down into the heather. 'Would you then? Would you?' His breath was warm on her face. She tried to wriggle away, but he pressed still closer. His hands seemed to be everywhere. He felt under her tunic, pulling at her dress. She pushed him away as hard as she could.

'What's the matter?'

'I don't like it!'

Thorvald's eyes were hard and unfocussed, like Einar's the night of the Byrstada feast. Suddenly she was struggling, and in panic she fought him off. She'd wanted something from him, but not this. He let go. Astrid jerked herself away, sat up, and pulled down her tunic. She didn't want him now. She felt frightened and confused.

Thorvald scowled, and pushed his hair out of his eyes. 'All right then,' he said at last. 'Shall we go on?'

'I'm sorry,' said Astrid uncertainly. She wanted to cry.

Thorvald briefly touched her cheek. He stood up. 'No doubt we'll manage.'

Subdued, she followed him along the ridge. She'd heard enough talk to know that it was wrong to lead a man on and then reject him, but she hadn't meant to. She looked at his back. She desperately wanted reassurance, but she felt she didn't deserve it, and obviously he was offended.

Thorvald didn't speak to her until they'd climbed the next hill. He stopped at the cairn and waited for Astrid. It was quiet without the heather stalks scratching against his legs. Looking down at the islands, it occurred to him that these were very gentle shores, with rounded heather hills stretching down to an unbroken coastline. A boat was rounding the green ness to the west, hardly making any headway. He couldn't hear so much as a whisper from the sea, and any smell it had was overborne by soft land smells, heather and peat and grasses.

When Astrid reached his side, she looked at him doubtfully. She was upset, he knew, and so was he, but he didn't know what to do about it. He was the one who'd been led on, then pushed away. It would have been fair if he'd forced her, but he saw no pleasure in that, even if he could do it easily. Hurt and indignant, he turned his back on her, and marched on.

The next summit marked the end of the ridge. Astrid was beginning to feel angry. He should be sorry he'd upset her. He might at least say something.

'You can see why the approaches are so complicated,' said Thorvald, looking for the seaway into Skalavagr. Then, without looking at her, he was off again.

Astrid lingered on the hill top, looking back. Their day's journey was all visible to the west of her. In a moment she would lose sight of it forever. She wanted to keep it, but time was slipping away past her. She might be angry with Thorvald now, but she had also been happy with him. This journey was too important to waste.

Three small lochs lay like descending steps down the valley. A boat was moored in the voe. Smoke rose from a dwelling under the lee of the hill. Astrid caught Thorvald up and grabbed him by the arm.

'I'm sorry. I'm just not used to it. I will be.'

He looked down at her. 'No, you're not, are you?' He wished he were alone. When Ragna was angry she shouted and hit out. If he went further than she wanted him to, she slapped him. At least he'd known where he was. Astrid didn't seem to know how easy it was to deal with him, and he resented her ignorance.

As they crossed the townland, they passed a group of women outside a house, who were boiling up a cauldron, preparing to dye fleeces. They returned the travellers' greeting, and stopped their work to stare at them until they were out of sight. Astrid was aware of their eyes still on her as she toiled after Thorvald up the opposite slope.

Just past the top they saw the voe of Skalavagr below. There was a ship moored at the end of it. Thorvald began to run. He reached the hill dyke and scrambled over. Behind green townland was a ness, where stood the largest hall he had ever seen. Along the length of the beach there were at least a dozen noosts, maybe more. They must be for the boats that came to the Thing; no single landowner could need so many. He looked up the dale to where the Hjaltland Thing met every June. At the far end he could see the sea. He felt excited; he too wanted a place in the world, to be at the centre of men's affairs, to make them happen.

Chapter 49

Astrid led the way towards the hall, while Thorvald hesitated, looking over the wall into the sheltered yard behind the building. 'Astrid! What's that?'

Astrid peered over the wall, and her face lit up. 'It's a rowan! I didn't know they could grow here.'

'Is it? I thought it must be a tree.'

Next to the rowan there were dwarf willows and some honey-suckle. Astrid hadn't seen a garden since she came to Hjaltland.

'Of course it's a tree. Thorvald, smell that. It's almost over, but you can still smell it. The lord here must be rich, to have a garden.'

He sniffed a honeysuckle flower obediently, but he was more interested in the tree. It had a grey spindly stalk and sparse leaves, but it was redeemed by clusters of red berries that hung from its stiff grey fingers.

'We had a rowan in our yard at home. They keep evil spirits from your threshold; that's why people plant them at the door.'

Thorvald crossed his fingers.

'Shall we ask if we can get a meal here?' asked Astrid.

He followed her inside. There were trestle tables set out as if for a feast. Thorvald smelt stew, and realised that he was very hungry. A woman got up from the hearth and came towards them.

Thorvald left Astrid to go forward and talk to her. Joints of meat hung from the rafters, and lines of fish were drying above the hearth. Astrid came back, and led him to a bench.

'Sit down. She'll bring it to us.'

'Is no one else coming?'

'Yes, the crew from that ship. That's why there's food cooking. Everyone else is out doing the barley. We're lucky.'

The woman dumped a dish of stew in front of them, with bread and some ale. Thorvald had never eaten a meal like this before, sitting at a table as if it were a feast, but with no one there but a girl to whom he was betrothed. He broke the bread, gave her half, and unsheathed his knife. A hen came in through the open door, and started pecking for crumbs around their feet. Then there were voices at the door, and suddenly the room was full of men. They took over the benches and tables, leaving Astrid and Thorvald squashed up at the end. The men were sunburned and uncombed, their clothes faded and seastained. The talk was all of a voyage from Katanes, and a fight that someone had had in a tavern in Hafnavagr.

Thorvald cleaned the dish with his bread. He didn't mind being an outsider here. Next year he'd be part of a crew, part of life. His present situation was extraordinary. He'd never heard any tale of a man travelling with only his betrothed for company; he and Astrid must seem an eccentric pair to anyone who bothered to notice them. With uncharacteristic insight, he realised that he wouldn't always be the person he was now. He glanced at Astrid. Next time he came abroad he wouldn't be with her, and in a way he was sorry. The thought crystallised in his mind that this journey was a rare piece of luck. Nothing like it would happen to him again. He'd leave it behind and find his proper place in the world, but perhaps there'd be something lost. One day he might look back, and regret the passing of the raw young man who sat here now.

Astrid was thinking too. Next year Thorvald would be away, and free in a way she had never been and would never know. There would be no more travelling together like this. When they met again, it would be in some ways as if they were strangers. She would have to make this one journey with him last for a lifetime. A cold fear trickled down her back, and at the same moment there was a sound from the door. Astrid looked up.

A man in a sheepskin cloak was playing a reed pipe. He carried a tray slung round his neck, laden with more pipes, and combs and needles and horn spoons.

Thorvald was staring. He had never seen a pedlar, but Astrid didn't stop to explain. The pipe had awoken a distant echo, a note that had not been struck for more than a year. Disregarding the stares of the seamen, she ducked under the table, and pushed her way through the men on the benches until she reached the door.

Thorvald made as if to follow, but by now everyone was looking, and he wasn't going to make a fool of himself crawling under the table after her. She was speaking to the man with the pipe, who had stopped his tune to talk to her. Everyone was staring. Thorvald watched, scarlet with helpless embarrassment.

Astrid was examining the pipes on the tray. She picked up one, raised it to her lips, blew two or three tentative notes, and then played a tune. Thorvald was astonished. Dagfinn had brought home whistles one year for the boys, but it had never crossed Thorvald's mind that a girl would want one, let alone play a whole tune. Astrid selected a second pipe, and played a bit more of the same tune. Then she amazed him by playing two lines of the ballad of the whales which they'd sung on Papey. How did she know how to do that? He couldn't take his eyes off her, torn between interest in her skill and fury that she should show him up like this.

Astrid tried all the pipes. Most of her audience seemed to have lost interest, but she hadn't let them disconcert her. She chose the pipe she liked best, and asked for a price. As she'd expected, the answer was ridiculous. She began to barter. The men around her were amused, and threw in encouraging remarks of their own. She smiled at them. The pedlar named a lower price, and refused to budge from it. Astrid put the pipe back. 'Oh well, never mind.'

He picked it up and held it out to her, offering her a slightly lower price.

At last a bargain was struck. Astrid had a coin which Bjarni had given her in the sheath with her knife, hanging round her neck. She tipped it out, and with the knife cut off a little less than a quarter of the soft silver. The pedlar weighed it on his finger. Others were crowding round the tray now. Astrid grabbed her pipe, and retreated.

'For Christ's sake!' hissed Thorvald. 'What do you think you're doing? What was all that about?'

She regarded him with amazement. 'I wanted the pipe.'

'Do you realise every man in the place was staring at you? You shouldn't be here, anyway. It's no place for a woman. And then you do that!'

'What of it?'

'Let's get out of here,' said Thorvald, 'before you do anything else.'

'Have you travelled far?' asked the serving-woman, as they got up to leave.

'From Fridarey,' said Astrid, with her usual willingness, thought Thorvald, to tell everyone far too much.

'Christ preserve us,' said the woman. 'I didn't know anything human lived out there. Is it true they get their winter meat from salting down shipwrecked sailors?'

'No,' said Astrid. 'Do you know of anywhere where we could stay the night?'

She looked them over. Her face was lined and rough, and Astrid noticed for the first time that she looked exhausted. 'You don't want to stay here. It'll get rough later. You could go up the dale to the monastery, but it's a fair way. No, I've a better idea. Go north towards the Thing until you reach the first loch. After that you'll see a house on your left with a big barn behind it. Ask to speak to the man of the house – the man, mind – and tell him Sigrid asks if you could stay in his barn the night. Will that do for you?'

The evening was still and gold. Astrid and Thorvald crossed a burn by stepping stones beside a ford, and followed a cart track up the dale. They walked through marsh and water meadow, in a dale so wide that on the west side the long green meadows stretched almost to the sky. They came to the foot of a loch, close under the hill, passing a green mound beside the water. Thorvald eyed it dubiously.

'Where's the Thing?' asked Astrid.

'I don't know. I think there's another loch beyond this one.'

They could hear a faint breath of wind over water, and cries of sheep from the hill. The verges of the track had not been cut for hay, so that stalks of russet sorrel and white angelica lined their path. The sea was still visible behind them, with the Fitfugla Head beyond. Even though the valley was landlocked, its horizons reminded Thorvald of the sea. It was like being in the trough of a long swell, the line of the hills being the crest of the next huge wave. A swan flew up from the loch in a series of splashes. Thorvald took Astrid's hand, his annoyance with her forgotten.

'There's the house with a barn.'

He was almost sorry. The year was turning fast, and Thorvald had a sense of time running short, a moment sliding by. He was still holding Astrid's hand. He was fond of her now. Their journey would soon be over, and then there would be nothing else like this.

Chapter 50

As Thorvald had feared, Sigrid's acquaintance invited them indoors to sleep on the benches by the fire. The wife of the house seemed thoroughly suspicious, and cross-questioned Astrid in such a manner as made it obvious she didn't believe a word of Astrid's answers. Astrid answered her with a vague innocence which she seemed to be quite unaware was infuriating.

'Does your mother know you're here?' asked the woman.

'No. She's dead.'

'I see. And do you think she'd have liked you to be travelling unescorted around the country like this?'

'I don't know,' said Astrid. 'I can't remember her.'

That was not quite accurate. Astrid could remember a journey with her mother. She'd been carried on her mother's back in a sling along a narrow street with wattle houses on either side. Her mother's hair had been tied back under a scarf, but from where Astrid was carried, she could wind and twist it round her fingers as they walked. She couldn't remember the colour of her mother's hair. She felt sleepy now, and wished this woman would stop asking irrelevant questions.

'Well, does your father know where you are?'

'No. He's dead too.'

'An orphan.' The woman was looking at her. 'But if your father had been alive, what would he have thought about you making a journey alone with a man?'

'I don't know,' said Astrid. She was exhausted, but clearly some explanation was going to be necessary. 'I'm betrothed to Thorvald,' said Astrid. 'My guardian sent us home.'

'And who is your guardian?'

'Amundi Palsson of Papey Stora is her guardian,' said Thorvald. The woman's mouth dropped open. 'He entrusted Astrid to my care. If you don't like the arrangement, you'd better complain to him.'

She didn't seem to know whether to believe him or not, but her man put an end to further discussion by demanding that they all stop blethering and get themselves to bed.

When Astrid and Thorvald passed the loch next morning, it was full of swans. A wind was blowing the water into waves, and the rich cornfields of the Thing valley were tossing like the sea.

'The Thing's further up the dale,' said Thorvald. 'I asked the farmer. All this land belongs to the monastery by the Thing.'

'Do you want to go up there?'

'There's nothing to see now but all the dismantled booths. I don't need to see those.'

In the grey distance the Fitfugla Head reared itself like a talisman, promising the end of their journey.

'If it were clear, I think we'd see Fridarey from here.'

Astrid looked at the dull haze beyond the Fitfugla Head. The day was much colder, and the wind made everything difficult. The happiness which had never quite eluded her since they left Papey seemed now to have deserted her. She longed to recapture it, but the dale which had seemed so green and lush in the evening sun was now desolate and grey. Hjaltland had turned alien, a land without comfort or shelter, offering her nothing.

Before they reached Skalavagr again they took a path round the east bank of the voe. The track soon lost itself in a swamp of withered rushes. They had to wade to their knees in brown water before they were on to higher ground, the wind strengthening as they climbed. Astrid tied her shawl round her head to stop her ears aching. As they topped the first rise, they could see the ridge in front of them, right down to Fitfugla Head.

'Due south now,' said Thorvald.

There was a single farm in a high valley, bounded to the south by a burn flowing through a deep gorge, its cliffs adorned with ferns and mosses. They followed the line of the gorge uphill, then struck for the ridge. A sharp shower met them, pushing them on and soaking them through all in a minute.

'We're running into real gales now. I wonder where Sula is.'

'I wouldn't like to be at sea today.'

'They'll be all right. But the year's turning. We don't want to be stuck at Svinborg until spring.'

The idea seemed to spur Thorvald on. He strode off so that Astrid had to half run to keep up. The hailstorm was now a grey blur to the east. To the west, the islands shone in a burst of sun, gleaming wet in a dark sea.

Astrid was pink with cold. Without stopping to think, Thorvald kissed her, and was glad to find she made no protest. Perhaps yesterday had been forgotten. He kept hold of her hand, and they began the descent into the dale. In a moment the wind was cut off behind them.

'That's better,' said Thorvald. 'Look, Fugley's coming clearer every minute.'

'Do we just head on south? It looks a bit wild to me.'

'It was you that wanted to walk.'

'But perhaps we should go where there's townland. Can't we do that?'

'There's townland to the east,' he answered. 'But the hills go in a direct line south.'

Astrid sighed. 'I wish we could find just one real place, with proper land; you know, not just peat and sea.' The wind irritated her. His kisses left her with nothing but questions she didn't want to answer, and there seemed to be nothing in this barren place but tiny settlements dwarfed by desolation, and, surrounding it all, the sea, that never ceased to force itself upon her senses. She wanted nothing more to do with it.

'How can you say that? Where in Hjaltland have you not found corn growing on the land and cattle on the hill? Where don't you get fish from the sea and birds from the cliffs? You've lived well, haven't you? What more do you want?'

Astrid shrugged.

The gale, like the country, was growing wilder. Fugley seemed to be suspended above the sea in a white haze, although its peaks were clearer than ever. Patches of sun swept over the land, turning it bright, then misty grey.

'Papey lies over there,' said Thorvald, waving his arm northwest. He looked south. 'If it were clear enough, I'm sure we'd see Fridarey.'

'Where?'

He pointed a little west of the Fitfugla Head, and watched Astrid peer into the haze just as he had done. 'I can't see anything,' she said. 'The wind makes my head ache.'

The hill began to seem endless. Astrid followed doggedly in Thorvald's footsteps across a marshy plateau. When he stopped she almost trod on his heels.

'Look,' Thorvald was saying. 'We can see the east coast now.'

She hardly cared, but that didn't stop him. 'See that island, those big cliffs over there? That's Brusey. I know it from coming up this coast with Einar. The Ness of Brusey is the main landmark once you're past Svinborg. Einar says the lord there is at least as rich as Amundi. Brusey's like Papey, you see, in having beaches suitable for boats. That's the important thing, as well as land.'

Astrid felt that something was still unresolved, but there were no words which would explain her thoughts.

Thorvald hugged her. He was looking out to sea again. 'We needn't worry about directions now either. I've sailed this coast. It's not far now.'

'Will we get to Svinborg today?'

He glanced at the bright clouds hiding the sun. 'We'll get to Konungsborg.' He was still holding her. 'Will you be glad to get home?'

'I don't know,' said Astrid. Touching him again, she felt confused. It was only yesterday she'd fought him off. 'Hadn't we better go on?'

He was glad to see her take the lead again. He realised now that she felt happier like that. He wasn't responsible for her feelings; he had enough to worry about without that, but he did like her to be cheerful. He followed, stopping frequently to survey the islands. There were so many, both east and west, that he felt a surge of excitement. These coasts were his birthright, and he was learning them well.

Astrid was running downhill into a high dale that ended in a cliff, over which a burn vanished in a shower of blown spray. They had to scramble between the rocks on hands and knees. A snipe flew out of the marsh by the burn almost under Thorvald's hand, startling them both.

The wind lashed at them when they reached the top, shoving them along across rough pitted country, where heather hid all footholds. Twice Thorvald tripped and fell to his knees. Astrid never missed her step, and remained just out of reach ahead of him, like the shadow of a cloud. They had passed the last of the inshore islands, and only open sea lay to the west between them and Fugley. Thorvald's eyes strayed to the Fitfugla Head, always tantalisingly distant to the south. There was something else behind it.

'Astrid! We can see it now! Look!'

She turned and ran back to his side. 'What is it?'

He realised she was frightened. 'No, no, look there, beyond the Fitfugla Head. It's Fridarey. We can see the island!'

There was indeed a small grey hump, half hidden by the headland. It looked insignificant, and very far away. Astrid remembered watching it vanish as they sailed north to Svinborg. She'd expected that to be her last sight of it, and now they were hurrying back towards it as fast as they could, with the autumn gales at their heels. It was the only home she had, probably the only home she would ever have. It wasn't what she had expected from life. She had a brief vision of trees in autumn, a river winding between meadows full of cattle, the towers and spires of churches inside a city wall. The world over the sea was as remote now as the stars, but still familiar in memory. All she had now was a hump of an island, bare rock and peat. Thorvald was staring at it as if it were all the treasure of Mikligard. She was going to marry him. Her heart lurched, as if he had really sighted something dangerous in the hills.

Thorvald took his eyes from his island. 'This is the hill I came up with Arne. I'll know exactly where I am when we get to the top. Come on.'

Two dales opened up before them, and Thorvald pointed out the one he'd walked up with Arne. They came to the lip of a corrie. Astrid looked down, and stopped short.

'Thorvald!'

She pointed down the hill. There were people. Campfires and skin tents. Cattle herded together. Dogs. Rising smoke.

'Astrid, get back!'

'Who are they?'

'I don't know. Let's not find out. Come on, over the ridge again, quick!'

They were too late. Dogs were barking. There was a flurry of movement below. People were running towards them, pointing them out.

'Run!'

Astrid was away like the wind, and Thorvald stumbled uphill after her. He felt a surge of panic. A girl. She mustn't be taken. He should never have brought her. If he and Astrid were caught, he couldn't protect her. He fell, and something brushed past his head. An arrow. He must still be in full view from below. Thorvald struggled to his feet, and ran, half doubled up, a shrinking between his shoulder blades as he heard barking and shouts behind him.

As soon as he was over the ridge he saw her waiting for him. 'Don't wait for me,' he yelled at her. 'Run!'

If she didn't catch the words she got his meaning, and fled, leaping over the heather clumps.

There wasn't any shelter out here. If they were pursued, they'd have to keep up their pace for miles. Maybe he could draw them off. Thorvald glanced at the horizon behind him. It was terrifyingly near, only a dozen yards uphill across the heather. At any moment figures might appear and shoot him down. Astrid was more than two hundred yards ahead now, only just visible in her dark cloak against the hill. If anyone came over the hill, they would see him first.

Thorvald took a line away from the burn across the hill. Every time he glanced back the horizon seemed to have followed, keeping right behind him like a threat of pursuit, but no figures appeared. He had quarter of a mile start on them now, and was running into the wind. An arrow wouldn't strike far into a gale. Astrid was gone. He couldn't run any more anyway. He slowed down, glancing back all the time.

He'd gone half a mile before he decided they weren't going to follow. Thorvald slowed to a walk, out of breath and shaken. Sweat trickled down his back and dripped, stinging, into his eyes. He turned south again, towards the burn. There was no sign of Astrid. Everyone had warned him the hills were dangerous. Here he was, without weapons or shelter, taking risks no man in his senses would have dreamed of. He should have realised why he'd never heard of a man travelling alone with a girl. There were very good reasons.

If anything had happened to her, he'd carry the blame forever. Where was she now? Thorvald scanned the dale, and realised how easy it was to lose someone here, and how hard it might be to find her again. Surely she'd just keep to the burn? She had that much sense, and if he did the same he'd be bound to catch up with her. There was a movement, but it was only two sandpipers bobbing beside the water. If he lost her here, he'd no idea how to search for her. The burn chattered at his feet. Thorvald brushed the sweat out of his eyes, and followed.

Chapter 51

'Please,' begged Astrid. 'You have to help me. I don't know what's happened to him. He might be hurt.'

The man stood at the door of his house, and regarded her stonily. He was chewing.

'Please,' said Astrid again.

A younger man with a piece of bread in his hand appeared in the doorway behind the first. 'What is it?' He stared at Astrid. 'Who's she? Was it her banging on the door like that?'

The first man turned his back on Astrid, and muttered something which she couldn't hear. While he was speaking, the young man went on staring at her. He bit off another mouthful of bread and ate it as he listened. When he did finally speak he addressed himself to Astrid.

'What were you doing out there on the hill anyway?'

'We were travelling from Skalavagr. Please, I have to find Thorvald. I don't know what's happened. I waited, and he never came.'

'Where did you lose him?' The man was more interested in her than in her answer, and he didn't take his eyes off her for a moment. Astrid wondered if there were a woman in the house. But the most important thing was to make them look for

Thorvald. If they wouldn't help, she'd have to go back alone, and
dusk was falling.

'At the head of the burn,' she said. 'Just below the hilltop. We
saw them camped in the next valley, so we ran away down this one.
I thought he'd follow me down the burn. But I couldn't find him.
I went back. He'd said not to, but I had to look.'

Her legs were shaking. These people frightened her. There were
no other houses near, just this one hovel just above the ford.

'It's all right,' she said. 'I'll go. I'll manage. You don't have to
help me.'

She heard them shouting as she ran away, but she didn't stop.
Thorvald might be captured, or dead. A sob broke from her as she
ran. She walked a little way, then ran again. There was no clue
anywhere, nothing to be seen but a few sheep, and a curlew crying
over the moor. The smallest outcrop might hide Thorvald. He
might be searching the hill for her just as she was searching for him.
He might be lying injured quite close by. Astrid broke into a run
again.

An hour later she was back at the ford. The light was almost
gone, and she didn't dare go further into the hills. There was danger
there, and danger on the road behind her, and nowhere to turn.
The air had turned chill, the birds had ceased to call. Her feet were
wet with icy dew.

What would Thorvald expect her to do? According to his account, Konungsborg couldn't be very far to the south. In a township
it would be safe to ask. There must be some landowner to whom she
could appeal. A man in authority would have enough men to be
able to search for Thorvald. She had to try. Astrid turned south.

Konungsborg turned out to be less than half a mile away. She
could just make out the townland in the twilight, shadowy slopes
round a darkness that must be a voe. She came upon the hall almost
by chance, a big building that loomed up on the west side of the
voe. The door stood ajar, but she knocked loudly with her fists
before going in. When she pushed it open she felt hangings in front
of her. The peat reek met her, and then she was blinking in
lamplight, and flickering firelight that cast long shadows through
the room.

There was a sudden silence. She could see figures grouped
around the hearth, and a woman got up to speak to her. Astrid
began to explain, but all the time she was examining the room

behind the woman, for someone who might be in authority. She could make out the pillars of a high seat. Its occupant was hidden in the gloom.

When the woman had heard her out, she said, 'You'd better speak about this to my father.' As Astrid followed she realised that the woman was heavily pregnant. She wasn't richly dressed, but she spoke with authority, as if she were the daughter of a man of some standing.

Astrid faced the high seat. This was no warrior who would lead a party into the hills to search for an unknown young man. He was bent almost double, and peered at her sideways as if he couldn't raise his head. His face was seamed with deep lines, and his grey hair was sparse. He questioned her closely, in a manner that showed he had known the hill very well at one time. Astrid answered all his questions, and stood waiting for his answer, swallowing with anxiety. The heat and stuffiness were making her head swim. If this man wouldn't help her, she didn't know what she'd do. Thorvald might be dead.

'Which house was it that you went to?' the man asked.

Astrid explained exactly how she had found the hut above the ford. 'They scared me. I ran away. It was obvious they wouldn't help me.'

'I see. And who sent you on this journey in the first place?'

'Amundi Palsson, from Papey Stora,' said Astrid wearily.

'Amundi Palsson! Why didn't you say so at once? Is Amundi kin of yours? What was he thinking of, to send you on such a journey?'

'He's my guardian. He betrothed me to Thorvald.'

'Njal!' A young man was instantly at her side. Astrid listened in bewilderment as orders were given, instructions passed on, and the hall became alive with a burst of activity. Men were clustering around the high seat. Astrid wasn't even conscious of her success, until the crippled man on the high seat slewed himself round to face her again. 'We can't do much tonight. There's no moon. But we know where to enquire. Don't worry. If he's still alive we'll find him. We'll find him even if he isn't. I'm quite willing to do Amundi Palsson a favour. You'll tell him, won't you, that Grim Njalsson did all he could to help you?'

'If you help me find Thorvald I'll tell him anything you like.'

There was nothing to do after that but wait. They gave her rich mutton broth and barley bread, which she ate without tasting. It seemed almost worse to be sitting still than to be alone and desperate, running fruitlessly up and down the burn. Perhaps everyone she ever loved would be torn from her. Perhaps she brought a fate with her. If Thorvald were to come back, maybe the best thing she could do for him was run away from him. She didn't want to bring a curse on his head. Astrid found herself praying fervently, as she had not done since the night of the shipwreck.

The dawn came at last, and the men left soon after. Astrid sat by the hearth, her ears strained all the time for some sound of arrival, for words which might bring news.

The old man wouldn't let her go out to search. Everyone seemed very busy. She wasn't sure how much of the bustle in the hall had to do with her. Several times men came in and spoke privately to Grim, and then left again. No one told her what was going on. When she asked the girl who'd let her in the night before, all she got was a shrug. 'Better not ask. He has ways of finding things out.'

Later on Astrid wandered about outside the hall. Yesterday's gale had blown itself out, and a thick mist was lying over the hill. She walked down to the voe, but didn't dare go far, in case any news came. Soon she hurried back towards the hall. If Thorvald never came back, one day she'd just have to walk away and leave.

'Not again,' she whispered, breaking into a run. 'Please God, not again.'

She came round the corner of the hall, and there was Thorvald, standing by the door, small and shabby beside the men who were with him, a lonely uncertain figure who looked as lost as she was.

It was a moment before she could take him in. Then, ignoring the people all round, she rushed over and hugged him, her cheek pressed against his wet cloak. 'I thought you were lost!' In spite of herself, she began to cry. She couldn't care less what any of them thought. 'I thought you were lost!'

Thorvald hugged her back, not in the least disconcerted. 'I thought you were,' he said, and held her tight. 'It's all right. I'm here now. It's all right.'

He didn't tell her to stop, but soon Astrid stepped back, wiping her face on her sleeve. They were all watching, their faces reflecting interest and amusement.

'Come in,' said Njal. 'My father wishes to speak to you.'

Grim Njalsson brushed aside their thanks, but reiterated his concern that Amundi Palsson should be given a full account of his generosity. 'It was no trouble,' he repeated. 'As soon as we knew the hill folk had driven you off, we guessed you'd have made for the shore. If you'd just stayed put at the fishermen's huts, young man, we'd have found you first thing this morning. Whatever took you back to the hill again? You gave us a much harder job, seeking you out there.'

'I was looking for Astrid.'

'I hope you've learned your lesson. That was no route to take unarmed, with a girl for company. There are more folk in these hills than you can possibly know about, and you were lucky to have got through. Surely Amundi Palsson never suggested you took that route?'

'It's harvest,' said Thorvald. 'There were no boats from Vagr. We have to reach Svinborg by Michaelmas.'

'And no one warned you against the wild country? I have authority in these parts, but I can't be expected to give you safe conduct wherever you go. What I can do is set you on the safest road to Svinborg. If you keep to the townlands on the east coast, you'll be all right. I'll give you a message to a tenant of mine who might give you shelter tonight. But keep off the hill. Don't climb up to the western ridges. Understand?'

'Yes.'

'And you'll convey my good wishes to Amundi Palsson, and tell him I was glad to offer help to any man of his?'

'Indeed I will.'

'That's the Picts' castle,' Thorvald told Astrid. 'That's where Bjorn fled with Thora when he stole her away from Noreg. They stayed in there all winter, then they went to Island.'

The castle was a high round tower, like the one that guarded the entrance to the Vagr channel, dominating the small island to the south. It seemed alien, something out of the far past.

'Is it haunted?'

'Of course,' said Thorvald, crossing his fingers. 'Even so, they weren't the only lovers to stop there. Earl Harald's mother of all people – she ended up there. There was a huge scandal. You ask Snorri.'

'What about the Picts?'

'Who?'

'Picts. You said it was a Picts' castle.'

Thorvald couldn't make her out. When he'd found her this morning, she'd wept with joy to see him again. But now he had her back, safe and well, Astrid hardly said a word. He'd expected that the moment Njal was out of the way she'd fall into his arms again, but she'd remained distant. He'd tried pointing out the place where he and Einar had moored the boat in the summer, and the spot where they had camped on the shore with Arne, and the exposed pale rock of the soapstone quarries, where a few men were still working. He showed her the place where they'd dug out the stone for Fridarey. But Astrid didn't seem interested in anything, until the Picts' castle. As if the Picts mattered, when she hadn't asked him a single thing about the unbearable hours he had spent searching for her, thinking she was lost.

'They were called Picts,' said Thorvald shortly. 'But they lived long ago, before there were any settlers here. They were gone before any stories were made. There's nothing to tell about them.'

'So what happened to them?'

'They were uncanny. Some say they lived in the trows' mounds, so maybe they weren't mortal. You can tell they were small by the passages in the tower. Einar's been in there, he says whoever built that tower was only half the height of a man. They were little and dark, people of no account really.'

Astrid sat down on a rock, her chin cupped in her hands, still looking at the tower. There were beads of dew in her hair from the damp air. She looked like someone lost in a strange country. An emotion he didn't recognise twisted inside him.

'They built tall castles for folk of no account,' said Astrid.

'It's full of holes and tunnels. Most of them are blocked up now, or fallen in.'

'Yes,' said Astrid, as if he were telling her something she knew already.

There was no getting any nearer to her. When she stood up and led the way onward, Thorvald followed with an irrational feeling of gloom. He was tired, and he hadn't slept at all the previous night. He'd lived through the worst of fears, but one thing he had not expected was this remoteness of hers. It was all too complicated.

Once they were beyond the bluff which harboured the soapstone quarries, they found themselves in extensive pastures, degenerating into swamp among the hollows. The track forked, and they took the right-hand path, keeping close to the hill dyke. Thorvald was so weary he could hardly think. He kept his eyes on Astrid's heels, and trod where she trod. She showed no signs of flagging. The day was growing hotter, a sullen sun turned the pastures yellowish, but it remained muggy. Clouds of midges followed them across the marshes.

It was a relief to meet some breeze at last. Shreds of mist were dissolving in the sun, and now a rugged coastline showed ahead.

A gleam of sunlight caught Thorvald and Astrid, and the mist and midges melted away. Thorvald was half asleep, swaying on his feet.

'Can we stop for a minute?'

'Are you all right?'

'I didn't get any sleep last night, that's all.'

'Well then, let's stop. There's no hurry, is there?'

Thorvald shook his head, and sank to his knees. The ground was damp, but among the heather there was a bit of shelter from the wind. He could hear a burn flowing nearby. He rolled his cloak round him, and shut his eyes.

The burn flowed through his dreams, and turned itself into a tune, thin and reedy, like a whisper from a departed world. Astrid was eluding him, vanishing into the marshes like a will o' the wisp. He could never catch up with her. When he reached out there was only misty air. His body felt cold and empty, lacking her touch. The tune grew less melancholy, and beckoned him on. There was sun on his eyelids, drawing him awake, but he resisted, turning his face into his cloak to catch the dissolving dream. But his arm hurt him, and the earth on which he lay was hard. Awakening, he realised the tune was separate, part of the daylight.

The sun shone with a peculiar white brightness. Astrid was sitting on her cloak a few feet away, small and dark and self-contained. He blinked at her as if he'd never seen her before, and sat up and rubbed his eyes. She lowered her pipe, and looked at him.

'Don't you like it?'

'What is it?'

'My pipe, of course. The one I bought.'

She passed it to him. He took it, held it as if he didn't quite know what to do with it, then handed it back to her.

'What tune was that?'

'Which? I played lots. You've slept for hours.'

Thorvald looked at the sun. Two hours, maybe. His eyes hurt. 'I suppose we'd better get on, then.'

'Do you feel better?'

'No.'

'I'm sorry,' said Astrid. She seemed more remote than ever.

When they came round the next hill, they found dogs circling around huddled groups of sheep, driving them slowly towards the townland. Calls and whistles echoed across the pasture. A cordon of people was spread across the hill, moving slowly towards one another in the wake of the sheep.

'We'd better wait,' said Thorvald.

He watched, wondering why this township should be so late with its autumn gathering. On Fridarey the lambs had been brought down before he and Astrid left. This must be the settlement where Grim had told him to ask for his tenant, who might be among those men down there.

Astrid touched his sleeve, and he looked where she indicated. Four sheep had broken away from the flock, running clumsily across the hill, two ewes and two well-grown lambs.

'They've not seen them. We'd better head them back.'

Thorvald moved downhill to intercept the strays, his exhaustion forgotten. He and Astrid turned the sheep, and drove them back past the herders, until they had rejoined the main flock. Astrid and Thorvald went on walking towards the hill dyke with the rest, and the sheep gathered and milled about in a dip below. The dogs circled and doubled back, until at last the sheep were driven into the pen.

'Shall we go on?' said Astrid quietly, since no one seemed inclined to take any notice of the travellers.

'No, we'll speak to them. We've done them a favour, after all.'

Thorvald went up and addressed himself to a man and woman who were standing apart from the activity around the pen.

'We're travelling south,' she heard Thorvald say. 'Just now we're needing a place to stop the night. I believe a man called Hedin Magnusson lives here. Can we stay in your township?'

The man looked at him doubtfully, and the woman glanced at Astrid. 'I'm not sure anyone here can help you,' said the man slowly.

A little girl with fair curly hair came and stood beside them. She looked the two travellers over disdainfully, and took her mother's hand.

'We've walked a long way,' said Thorvald, forgetting he'd slept most of the afternoon. 'We only need shelter in a barn.'

The woman looked at them sharply. 'We've our neighbours to think of too. They were saying you didn't look like honest travellers. We've been having quite enough trouble with strangers on the roads.'

'We're strangers, but no man ever called me dishonest.' replied Thorvald. 'You can't refuse shelter to travellers.'

Astrid realised he was too amazed to be angry, being confounded by a response so totally outside his experience. As soon as he fully realised he'd been insulted, he'd be in a rage. She went to stand beside him.

'I've no way of knowing whether you're honest or not. Who's lass is that, anyway? Did you come by her honestly? We don't want any trouble here.'

Thorvald was still puzzled, but beginning to be angry. 'We helped herd your sheep. You saw us.'

'I've nothing more to say.' The woman turned her back and walked away, and the little girl stuck out her tongue at them before following her mother.

The man lingered for a moment. 'It's nothing to do with me, you know. I'm sorry. They said at the hall that any man found harbouring outlaws will have his land forfeit, and you don't look like people of substance.' The man walked quickly away, back to the crowd among the sheep pen.

'We'll see if that's what you all say!' Thorvald was about to start after him, but Astrid blocked his way.

'Thorvald, no! You can't confront them all. We'll go on.'

'But did you hear? And we helped with their sheep! What would Einar say? Not to take in travellers! There'll be a curse on them for that!' Thorvald spat after the retreating man.

'We'll never see them again. It doesn't matter to us.'

'But I want to see them again. One day I'll raid the place, as soon as I get the chance.'

'We can walk to the next township.'

'No!' exclaimed Thorvald. 'I'm not asking anything from anybody. This is an evil country. We'll stay out on the hill.'

'But we'll freeze!'

'It's too damp for a frost tonight. Come on.'

For the next mile they tripped and splashed across bog. Another township was coming into view, lying in a fold of the hills, with a stony beach at the foot of it. Someone had been digging out soapstone there too; there was a scar of pale rock across the hill. Thorvald began to make a circuit round the place, keeping well above the hill dyke.

'Thorvald, we should go along the coast. You know what Grim said about the hills.'

Thorvald swore, and ignored her.

'Thorvald, stop!'

'Very well. Have you got a better idea?'

Just inside the hill dyke there was a small building, a shieling perhaps.

'What's that?'

He followed her gaze. 'I don't know. Maybe they use it for the lambing.' He touched her shoulder, and grinned. 'Let's have a look at it.'

The hut was half full of fresh hay. 'I'd like to set fire to it,' remarked Thorvald.

'If you do, they'll probably flay the next people who pass.'

Thorvald stood in the doorway and looked round. It was evening, and they wouldn't find anywhere much safer.

'All right,' said Thorvald, satisfied. 'What did Grim's household give us to eat?'

'Dried mutton and oatcake.'

'We must tell Amundi Palsson how generous they were with their food.'

When they had eaten, they climbed over the hay so that they were out of sight of the door. Thorvald spread his cloak out flat. 'Give me your cloak. We can put yours on top.'

She hesitated, then lay down on his cloak. There was a gap at the top of the wall, which let in a little lingering daylight. Thorvald pulled her cloak over them both, and spread more hay on top. Then he lay down. 'I suppose your feet are cold?'

'No. Why should they be?'

'Come here, just in case they are.'

When he put his arms round her she was stiff and awkward, resisting him. 'Astrid, what is it?'

He could hardly catch the muttered answer. 'I thought I'd lost you.'

'And I thought I'd lost you.' His arms tightened round her. 'I won't lose you again, I promise you.'

'You can't promise that. You don't know.'

'I know I want you.'

'But fate takes people away from each other.'

Thorvald thought of the hours spent searching the hill for her, and was silent.

'I don't want to bring an evil fate on you,' said Astrid.

'You won't. Your saints will take care of that, and I have luck of my own. You don't need to worry.'

He couldn't see her face very well, the light was growing too dim; but he felt her body relax, and hugged her tighter.

This time his touch didn't frighten her. Suddenly it was easy to let him caress her, and to touch him back. She let him undo her hair, even though she knew she'd have to plait it all again in the morning.

Thorvald rolled away from her, and began pulling off his clothes.

'What are you doing?'

'Nothing,' he said, pulling his shirt sleeve over his bandaged arm. He could have done without being wounded, but it didn't matter. He was more worried about scaring her.

But Astrid's fears had vanished. She had been brought up to know that a man would make love to her sooner or later. She touched him with curiosity rather than passion, but in a way that excited him more. When he pulled her dress over her head she made no attempt to stop him.

Naked, she could feel his skin warm and smooth against hers. She found the thorshammer hanging round his neck. Thinking it was a cross, she traced the shape of it with her fingers, and realised her mistake. His cloak was rough under her back, and the hay over them rustled and fell round her, smelling of summer. Thorvald's hair was long and thick, and brushed her face. He was heavy, but the hay was soft, and his weight was easy to bear.

Thorvald felt clumsy. He understood that she wasn't going to stop him, and he wanted her, urgently. He tried not to hurt her but he couldn't help it. She gave a small scream of pain.

'I'm sorry.'

'Go on.'

Then he was inside her and he couldn't stop. Astrid felt him shudder, and bury his face in her hair. He gave an odd gasp, and collapsed on top of her. She held him tightly. She wasn't sure what she felt, but she loved him, she'd give him anything. She felt wet and sticky; she wanted him, but she felt bereft too. There was something that still eluded her. They were together now, as they had never been before, but what confronted her in the growing dark was a loneliness she didn't want to face.

'I love you,' whispered Thorvald, for the first time in his life.

'Yes,' she said, knowing that she had to shield him from the dark into which she stared with eyes wide open, looking up over his shoulder into nothing at all.

Chapter 53

Astrid woke feeling stiff and sore. She'd bled in the night, and the hay had got through their cloaks to her skin, and she itched all over. Everything she touched felt rough and sticky. Thorvald was sleeping with his back to her, curled up like a dog by a hearth, his cheek pillowed on his shirt. Astrid found her dress, shook the hay out of it, and put it on. She took her comb from her bundle, and crept outside to find the burn. The morning was raw and cold, and the wind caught her as soon as she moved away from the hut.

The burn flowed through a small gorge about fifty yards away. There was no one in sight, so Astrid splashed herself all over. If anyone knew that she had stripped herself on an autumn morning and washed in cold water, they'd say she was out of her mind and would probably die of a chill. She felt she didn't care if she did. Her body ached, and the stickiness revolted her. She dried herself on her clothes, and dressed again. She felt better standing in the wind, with the icy touch of clean air all over her.

She shook her hair out in the wind, and began to comb it, tugging hard, almost inviting the pain which made her eyes water. In that hut, an illusion had died at last. Tough as a boy, she'd been. She should have been a boy, a shipbuilder's apprentice, allowed to know things, to run as fast as Olaf, to leap over the flames of a Johnsmass fire. She'd realised long ago that such things were impossible, and yet something in her had still resisted, until now.

The wind blew her hair free every time she managed to fasten it, so she had to go back in. She sat in the doorway where it was light, and slowly braided her plait. It hurt to walk, so she was going to have a hard time keeping up today, let alone striding ahead.

When Thorvald woke up at last, his assumption that all was now completely well between them made her feel less distant. He seemed to think they had achieved something good, and his evident happiness brushed off on to her. When they set out, it wasn't hard to keep pace with him after all.

The country here was well populated, with hardly more than a mile between one settlement and the next. By noon they had reached one of the few voes along this coast. When they had left behind the township grouped around it, they surmounted the last hill, and before them was the sea. Running down to the shore the ripe fields of grain they had seen on their first visit to Svinborg were all shorn, and studded with stooks of corn. Svinborg lay between the Svinborg Head which had been in view ever since they set out that morning, and their old friend the Fitfugla Head, now hardly more than a couple of miles away across flat townland. Between the two headlands, nearly lost in the haze, was the outline of an island, a large hump, with a smaller hump joined on to its east side: Fridarey, and the Seydurholm.

'Home,' said Thorvald.

Astrid looked across the sea, then at the mile or so of land in front of them. This last day was slipping away without being savoured, sand sliding through a glass.

'Can we stop here?'

'If you like. There's no hurry now.'

They sat down in uncut grass, damp at its roots, where skeletal flowers of cow parsley overhung them. The midday sun seemed suspended, a dark yellow circle emerging dimly through a veil of cloud. The land smelt of autumn, dying grass and heather mingling with the salt breeze off the sea.

Thorvald was lying propped on his elbow, watching her face silhouetted above him. He reached out and touched her hand. She'd been very quiet all morning. She was his now. By Yule they'd be married. She might even be pregnant now with Thorvald's son.

Or Thorvald's daughter, perhaps. He liked the idea, though he couldn't quite take it in. 'Astrid?'

'What?'

He saw her bite her lip. If she were unhappy she wouldn't give in and say so. He sat up and put his arm round her. 'It's all right, Astrid.'

She wouldn't let him see her face, and she returned his embrace fiercely. Thorvald held her to him and stroked her hair. Even three days ago this situation would have terrified him.

'Nothing's going to end,' he told her. 'I'll never go away for good.'

'But nothing happens twice.' Her voice was so muffled, he wasn't sure if he'd heard her correctly.

To reach Svinborg they had to walk around a pool where the retreating tide had left an expanse of sandflats. Astrid thought at first that the edge of the sand was strewn with gleaming boulders.

'Sealing time,' remarked Thorvald. 'There's some good hunting there for someone.'

Astrid looked again, and the boulders became a line of sleek bodies, hauled up just out of the sea's reach. 'I remember,' she said. 'You were all hunting last autumn, just after I came. We had to cure the sealskins, and they smelt.'

'They come ashore now to pup. That's when the hunting begins.'

'Olaf told me a story once, about the selkie woman who turned into a troll when her man killed her mate and her sons.'

'Olaf? It can't have been him. Olaf never told anyone a story in his life.'

'He told me this one.'

Thorvald shook his head. 'You might have heard it at any of our feasts, but not from Olaf. He's always been too shy to tell stories.'

Astrid didn't bother to contradict him. A pang of apprehension seized her, and she frowned at the island which Thorvald called 'home'. She owed Olaf nothing, but the twinge of unease refused to be quieted. She began to realise that there would be a lot to face when they got back. It wasn't just Olaf. What would Ingebjorg and Bjarni say? Would even Ingrid approve of what she'd done? A betrothal was a matter that affected everybody. Since last night she belonged irrevocably to Thorvald. There might even be a child now too. It seemed impossible that such momentous results could ensue from so small a cause. Today she should be closer to him than ever, but instead she felt quite separate, irritated by the thought of being attached to anyone or anything. Astrid suddenly broke into a run, and at once the seals slithered into the sea and swam away in a surge of white water.

Thorvald didn't try to keep up. He slowly skirted the pool, wondering where the Sula was, and if he and Astrid would have to wait long at Svinborg. He licked his finger and held it up to get the wind, which had been variable all morning. It was definitely shifting westerly. If Sula were here the weather would be right for the voyage home.

It was two days till Michaelmas. His journey with Astrid had gone extremely well. He had made love to her just in time, on their very last night. He wasn't sure why she'd been so elusive at first, any more than he knew why she should have taken it into her head to dash ahead like that and frighten off all the seals. But he'd learned now that she could be unpredictable, and that it was nothing to worry about. He was a man with a woman of his own. He would like to make love to her again as soon as possible. She was out of sight now, but the seals were still swimming at the far end of the pool, held there by curiosity. She couldn't be far away.

Astrid was waiting for him on the far side.

'We'll walk round by the voe,' he said to her as he came up. 'The Sula might be there already, you never know.'

As soon as they came over the dunes where Rolf had put them ashore, they sighted the Sula, moored on the south side of the bay beside a little promontory. Thorvald ran, slithering down the dunes and cutting across the wet sands. Astrid lingered, reluctant to face them all. The journey was over.

Thorvald hailed Sula from the beach, but before there was any response he heard a shout from behind him. Rolf was scrambling over the rocks and waving.

Rolf embraced Thorvald warmly. 'Well-timed! We only got here yesterday, and Bergfinn said he'd had no word of you. I was preparing to wait three days, but the year's turning, so it's a relief to see you.' He looked Astrid over as she came slowly up to them. 'You're back with us, I see. Didn't you find your father's friend?'

'Yes,' said Astrid, 'But then other things happened.' She looked at Thorvald, waiting for him to explain.

'We're betrothed. She's coming back to Fridarey.'

Only for a moment did Rolf betray his surprise. Then he shut his mouth again, embraced them both, and congratulated Thorvald on his choice.

'How did your suit to Helgi work out?'

Thorvald told him what had happened on Papey, while Rolf's eyes strayed to his ship, swinging slowly at her mooring as the wind changed, and to the swell beyond the mouth of the bay.

'You've done well,' said Rolf. 'If you've got your rights and avoided a lawsuit, that's the best outcome we could have hoped for.' He was still scanning the horizon. 'We'll sail with the flood tomorrow morning. There's nothing else we have to do in Hjaltland. You couldn't have timed things better.'

'How was the voyage?'

'Good,' said Rolf briskly. 'I've news for you too. We had a fair voyage from here to Biorgvin, then back to Kirkjavagr, with the timber and a passenger too – a man from Vindland who's setting up a warehouse with his partner in Biorgvin. Jens of Lubeck, they call him. We may be entering into a permanent contract with him in the spring. Also, in Kirkjavagr I was interviewed by Bishop William himself, concerning the island.'

'The Bishop!' Thorvald sounded dismayed rather than impressed. 'Why, what does he want with us?'

'I went to the monastery of St Olaf's in Kirkjavagr, as we'd agreed, and gave money for a mass to be spoken for Einar's soul. While I was there, the priest asked me, did the priest from Dynrostanes in southern Hjaltland not visit us, for such questions as mine should find their answer in a man's own parish. I told him how it was with us, and . . . well, I did say we had needs concerning spiritual matters that were not met.'

Thorvald looked alarmed. 'We don't want a priest from Hjaltland! We have our Thing! That's what we agreed to, and the Earl himself subscribed to that! We don't need the Bishop to cast his eyes on our land!'

'You don't understand. No one wants our land. This monk spoke to the Bishop, and before I left Kirkjavagr, I was summoned to the palace. The Bishop dare not go against the Earl; it certainly isn't in the Earl's interest to lose any of the revenues from Fridarey. All that's changed is that the priest from this parish will be visiting us regularly too.'

'So who is he? Where is he? And who pays for him?'

'He's here,' said Rolf simply. 'I'm taking him back to the island now. The men from Svinborg will fetch him again before winter, when it's weather. His living is the parish of Dynrostanes, and we pay our share of his keep in tithes. There's no danger to our land.'

'We should have been asked. I know Einar would have said so.'

'This isn't about our land. It's for our souls.'

'Don't we pay tax enough to the Earl, without bringing in anybody else?'

Astrid looked from one man to the other. She hadn't expected Thorvald to have such strong opinions. For her, a priest would be a relief and a blessing, but Thorvald, raised on Einar's ideas, would never see it like that.

'There's not much point in discussing it now, is there?' she said mildly. 'Shouldn't Thorvald meet this priest himself?'

Neither acknowledged her words, but Rolf said, 'Let it be, for now. I've business with Bergfinn tonight, before the feast. We've brought him grain and iron. Do you want to come, Thorvald, and present yourself to him again?'

When Astrid caught sight of her betrothed again, he was with the crew, and as much part of them as if he had sailed with them since harvest, instead of wandering across Hjaltland with a girl. At supper Thorvald was talking hard to Leif, belying the rumours that there was an irreconcilable feud between them. They ate out of the same dish, and they both drank steadily.

After the feast the priest told them the story about St Magnus refusing to fight, and singing psalms all through the battle of the Mene Strait off Bretland. The men of Svinborg countered with tales of the miracles Magnus had performed in Hjaltland since his death.

'There was a man in this very township,' one man said, 'whose head was broken when a beam fell on him. It was Bergfinn here who made his vow for him. He cast lots as to whether the man should offer a pilgrimage to Romaborg, the freeing of a thrall, or a gift of money to St Magnus's shrine in Byrgisey. The lot fell upon the gift of money, and at that very moment the man regained consciousness, and was healed.'

'That wasn't the only miracle in this township.'

Astrid had heard many such stories before, only the names of the saints had been different. The endings were always the same, blessed be the saints who made them so. Her attention strayed. They were going back to the island tomorrow. Going home.

As evening began to fall next day, the cliffs of the Nordhavn drew close, ready to enclose the Sula for her winter rest. Rolf was aft, frowning, biting his thumbnail and continually glancing back to the north-west, where the wind was setting. Astrid looked back too, to the peaks of the Fitfugla Head and Svinborg Head, but she saw nothing untoward. Ahead lay the shore of the island, the arched stack at the harbour entrance, the long lines of reddish cliff. There was the sandy shore, and the Sula's boat shed. Astrid had returned. Her own people, now, waited for her here. The island seemed to reach out to her, reassuring, but threatening too, about to enclose her, perhaps for ever. She looked back across the sea, to the distant peaks at Svinborg, faint beyond the endless swell that cut off this island and every other island, an endless barrier between her and the world outside.

Thorvald was watching for the waves crossing the swell that told him his own island was near, even though he could see the land plainly. He was coming back from the longest journey of his life, triumphant in the knowledge that it was only the first. He could smell the land now, grass and peat and heather, a particular land smell like no other. But his home would never be quite the same to him again. When he looked back the sea was a great highway that stretched across the world, always open to him now.

They slipped into the Norhavn under sail, and slid across calm water. The men began to lower the sail ready to beach Sula. Rolf took the helm as they came in, keeping the stack in line with the right-hand edge of the Sheep Rock. As they passed the cave at the harbour entrance, two seals swam alongside, watching the travellers intently, until the Sula had grounded on the sand among breaking waves.

Part Eight

The Inheritors

The tide was on the ebb, but Rolf had his mind on the next flood. It would be dark by then. He bit his nails, felt the wind, and made his decision.

'We'll offload and haul her up. Skuli!'

Skuli argued, 'How can we haul her up without the islanders? Can't we moor her by the stack till morning? It'll be dark in an hour!'

'We'll have the islanders!' Rolf's eye fell on Astrid. 'You can run, can't you?'

'Of course!'

'Good. I can't spare a man. Run to Setr and get Olaf. Tell him to rouse the townland down to Byrstada. You go to Shirva and tell Bjarni. He must get word to Leogh. Tell them we've beached in the Nordhavn. If we don't have her hauled up before the flood, she'll be pounded to driftwood before the next tide. There's a northerly blowing up, but they'll see that for themselves. Can you do that?'

'Of course I can!' Astrid was on the gunwale, ready to jump ashore.

'And don't let them argue!'

Astrid ran as fast as she could, walked just long enough to get her breath, then ran again. The sea was left behind, the burn of

Finniquoy was below the path on her left. Cattle raised their heads and stared as she passed. The hill dyke was in sight. She was vaguely aware of a red and purple sunset blazing beyond the sharp edge of the western cliffs. She was over the hill dyke and there was Setr. As she approached she caught the smell of peatsmoke. There was no time to think. She shoved the door open, and burst into the dim room.

'Olaf?'

A pot fell against stone and broke. After the bright sky the peat reek was impenetrable. Ingebjorg's voice was sharp. 'Astrid? Astrid! What's happened?'

'We're back. The Sula's in the Nordhavn. Olaf?'

'Where's Thorvald?' demanded Ingebjorg sharply. 'What's happened to Thorvald?'

'He's home. He's at the haven.'

'Astrid?' whispered Olaf.

'The Sula's in the Nordhavn. Rolf says . . .'

'You've come back!'

'Yes, yes I have. But I'm to fetch you at once. She's beached below the tideline, and she has to be hauled up tonight, because of the northerly.' Astrid was still too out of breath to explain properly. Olaf looked dazed, staring into the smoke as if he couldn't believe his ears.

'He wants us now?'

'She has to be hauled up before the flood.'

'I'll come.'

'Rolf said to tell you to rouse the townland down to Byrstada.'

'I'll do that. They've been watching for Sula for days. It's late in the season.' Olaf peered through the smoke. 'You're going to Shirva?'

He came round the hearth to the door, and focussed his gaze on her for the first time. She caught his smile of amazed delight, and before she could stop him, he'd grabbed her by the shoulder.

'You've come back!' said Olaf exultantly, and kissed her on the mouth. 'I'll see you later.' Then he was off, out of the door and away across the island.

Astrid cast Ingebjorg a look of horror, but there was no time to explain anything. 'I have to run to Shirva,' she said, and fled before Ingebjorg could answer.

She took a short cut across the stubble rigs, jumping the ditches. There was a stitch in her side, but she didn't stop running. She leapt the drain below the midden, scrambled up the wall, and was in the yard. Everything was the same. A cat blinked at her from the threshold, and the chickens scratched at the end of the yard in the last of the sunshine.

From the barn came the steady tap tap of hammer on chisel. Astrid crossed the yard. The big barn doors were wide open to catch the evening light.

Bjarni was sitting in the doorway, chipping carefully at the surface of a stone slab on the bench in front of him. Astrid moved into his light, and he looked up.

'I've come back.'

He didn't look particularly surprised, but he stopped work, and held his tools, frozen in mid-movement. She saw runes newly chipped into the stone. There were more marked out with charcoal.

'I see you have,' said Bjarni quietly, and put down his tools. 'This is quite a surprise. Is it by choice, or by necessity?'

'I wanted to come back.' Astrid felt tears prick her eyelids, but Bjarni wouldn't want her to weep over him. 'You don't mind? I can come back?'

'You're always welcome here,' he said. 'Shirva's your home, if that's what you wish.'

There wasn't a trace of emotion in his voice, but Astrid was reassured. 'I've a message from Rolf. The Sula's beached at the Nordhavn, and he has to have her hauled up before the flood.'

Bjarni stared out at the sunset, calculating. 'The flood tonight, does he mean?'

'Yes, because there's a northerly.'

Bjarni stood up. 'North-east. It won't blow a gale tonight, though.'

'He said she'd be pounded to driftwood by tomorrow.'

'You mean he's beached her now, on the ebb?'

'Yes.'

'The fool! Who does he think we are? Why didn't he moor her until morning?'

'I don't know.'

'Of course you don't. But if that's what the man's done, we don't have much choice, do we? I suppose she's high and dry by now.'

Bjarni glanced at the fading sunset. 'But we'll be doing the whole job in the dark!'

'He said I was to tell you to raise the townland down to Leogh.'

'He what?' Astrid flinched. 'It's not your fault. Call those boys, will you, and we'd better get on with it.'

'What boys?'

'Of course, you don't know. Arne and Jon. Fool!' Bjarni flung down his chisel and strode across the yard.

Astrid hung back. A few seconds later Arne raced out of the house. He spared her a quick greeting and a mystified glance as he passed, running towards Leogh. Astrid waited until Bjarni, closely followed by a lanky young man who must be Jon Helgisson, had come out again, then she made for the door.

Before she reached it Ingrid was there, flinging her arms round Astrid's neck, and hugging her tightly. 'You're back! Oh Astrid, you've come back! I can't believe it!'

'Well, it's true.'

'I'm so glad to see you! I missed you so much! Come in! Come in at once and tell me everything.'

Shirva was home now, there was no doubt about it. It was only through going away that Astrid had realised it, but here she had somewhere that was safe. The English would never invade Shirva, no war was likely to be fought over it. Even Gerda seemed pleased to see her, although she didn't go so far as to speak to Astrid directly. Ingrid bustled about, heating up the remains of the evening meal, and pressing Astrid to tell her the whole story of her journey, and exclaiming over everything. But when Astrid reached Helgi's proposal, Ingrid dropped her spoon and gaped.

'*Thorvald!*' gasped Ingrid. 'Betrothed to Thorvald! *Thorvald!*'

'Yes.'

'But do you like him? Thorvald! I can't believe it!'

'Oh, Ingrid. He's not that bad!'

'Has he tried to make love to you? *Thorvald!* I just can't imagine it!'

'Then don't try,' replied Astrid sharply.

After that, Astrid had to repeat the whole of the rest of the story again. But when Ingrid finally understood that there was to be no lawsuit, she flung her arms round Astrid's neck and hugged her.

'Don't thank me,' said Astrid. 'It was Thorvald who arranged it, and I'm quite happy with it.'

At last Ingrid started to tell her what had happened at Shirva in the last weeks. Naturally the wedding had been the main event.

'It was a good feast,' said Ingrid. 'In spite of hardly having any time. But it was the best time of year, plenty of everything. We killed two calves, and there was crowberry soup to have after the meat. Arne and Jon arrived only two days after you'd left. I was so glad to see them, but of course they had to speak to my father at once – I told you about that – the more I think about it, the more thankful I am it was Jon that came. Father couldn't believe his eyes when they arrived, he had no idea why they'd come. So Gudrun and I waited out here when they were telling him.'

'Was Bjarni angry?'

'Angry! I've never heard anything like it! Arne was as white as a cheese, and Jon didn't look much better. And I was crying, well, so would you have done. I don't know what would have happened. But Gudrun confronted him – she stood right in front of him and said, "Father, that's enough! It's a good marriage anyway. So what if there's a baby coming? It's happened before and it'll happen again. There's no harm done." He calmed down quite suddenly. I knew it would be all right, if Arne came back.'

'And then you had the feast?'

'We had the betrothal feast three days later, and the wedding feast a week after that. Father said we might as well make the timing decent, if we couldn't make it honourable. But that's the worst thing he's said, after that first scene. He's got used to it now.'

'Poor Bjarni.'

'Poor Bjarni! What about me? What about Arne? Anyway . . . where was I?'

'You'd got as far as the marriage feast.'

'That's right. We can do things splendidly at Shirva when we try. All the islanders came. It wasn't one of our biggest feasts, of course, with the Sula being away. But I wish you'd been there! And Arne only had Jon of his own kin, so we got Olaf to sit with Helgi's sons and support them, and . . . Astrid, have you thought of that?'

'Of what?'

'Olaf. Does he know you're betrothed?'

Astrid scraped the last oatmeal from her bowl. 'He will tomorrow. Thorvald will tell his family as soon as he gets home, I suppose.'

'He's going to be upset.'

Astrid shrugged, but couldn't help blushing. 'He thought I'd gone for good. He'll have stopped thinking about me by now, if he ever did.'

'That's not true,' said Ingrid. 'I've known Olaf all his life. Just because he doesn't say much, it doesn't mean he doesn't think about things.'

'I know,' snapped Astrid.

The men didn't get home from hauling up the ship until late at night. Astrid woke to see them turn back the turfs from the fire, and sit warming themselves at the hearth, talking in low voices. She was asleep again before they lay down.

The next morning the men slept until well after dawn. Astrid served them their morning meal. She liked Jon, who reminded her of his sister Signy, and Jon seemed much more interested in her stay on Papey than Arne did. They were still discussing last night's work. They'd unloaded Sula's entire cargo, and hauled her up to her shed by torchlight. Hauling up was a tricky job at the best of times, with only just enough men on the island, but in the dark it had been next to impossible. And when they'd finished, it was quite obvious that the wind was dropping. When they awoke this morning it had died away, and the sea was as calm as anyone could wish for.

'Rolf won't dare show his face for days,' said Bjarni. 'He could easily have waited until morning. He should never have beached her.'

After the meal was over, Astrid slipped outside after Bjarni, and found him going into the barn. 'I want to talk to you,' she said.

'If you wish. Come in here.'

'I want to tell you what happened to me.'

He was watching her closely. 'You went to Papey, didn't you? I hope Amundi Palsson treated you fairly?'

'You know all about it?'

He smiled bleakly. 'I guessed. Thorvald is less circumspect than he likes to think, and remember I've had an addition to my family here. Arne confirmed my suspicions.'

'Did he tell you I'd tried to make him give Amundi a message before?'

'He's told me a great deal, but to be fair to him, mostly by mistake. But you tell me your own story.'

'You may not like it very much.'

He seemed unperturbed. She told him everything that had happened, up to the moment when she and Thorvald had left Papey, but said very little about the journey back.

'I see,' said Bjarni. 'This is all very well if it suits everybody. I don't suppose they gave you much say in it. You weren't forced? You're happy about this marriage, I take it?'

'Oh yes, I'm happy about it now.'

'Fair enough,' said Bjarni, and picked up his tools. 'Go and find Ingrid, then. She's pleased to see you, though I'm glad we were spared the transports we went through when that boy turned up. I'll be in later.'

Thorvald never appeared at Shirva that day, and by the next morning after that Astrid was beginning to be anxious. Olaf had kissed her. She hadn't had the chance to explain anything either to him or to Ingebjorg. What would they be thinking of her now? Ingebjorg had seen the kiss, and knew how Olaf felt. If she'd told Thorvald that Olaf had kissed her, perhaps he'd think the worst of her too. Perhaps that was why he didn't come. There was nothing she could do but wait.

Chapter 55

Eirik and Olaf had been playing fox and geese, and the board was still set out near the hearth. The last three geese had been driven right into a corner, and Thorvald had already worked out the next move, if he had been the fox. It was easier than listening to his mother.

'I can't believe it!' said Ingebjorg again. Her spindle lay idle on her knee, and she was still staring at him as if she'd never seen him before in her life.

'Why shouldn't I be betrothed? There's nothing wrong with me!'

'But just like that! You'd never thought of such a thing!'

'No, but when I did, I began to see it wasn't such a bad idea. Look, mother, we don't want a lawsuit. Even if we won, what would we gain? I'm not going to encourage feuds in my family. I'm going to Bjarni tomorrow. I'm not stuck for money now, so I can afford to be generous. Olaf and Eirik will have a share in Shirva, and I can help them too.'

'How will you help me?' demanded Eirik.

'You'll hand them over to Bjarni, you mean,' said Ingebjorg bitterly, 'after all I've done for you.'

'It's too late for that. You won your case and brought us up yourself, and I'm glad of it. But that's all past now. I'm grown up, and I've found a way to recover what I lost when my father died. I'll go to sea, and when I'm ready, I'll have enough money to take a share in a ship of my own.'

'A share with whom?' she said sharply. 'You're not planning to leave the island?'

'I might,' said Thorvald, though he'd not meant to reveal so much. 'And I don't know who, but I have an idea. We'll be shipmates; I'll see how we get on first.'

She was still regarding him in that disconcerting way, as if he were a stranger to her. 'And your brothers? You'll leave them to work things out with Bjarni, will you?'

'I've already told you I'll talk to Bjarni tomorrow. I'll make sure they have their rights. But I've got enough money to help Olaf now if that's what he wants. I've never thought of it before, but now I've travelled a bit myself I think he could . . . But where is Olaf? I thought he'd just gone outside. He wasn't going anywhere, was he?'

'Thorvald,' she said, quite gently this time. 'You've done much more than I expected, but you haven't considered everything, have you?'

'What do you mean?'

'You really don't know why he went out?'

'No?'

'Perhaps it's as well.' She caught the question in his eyes and shook her head. 'No, if he wants you to know he'll tell you himself. So you have it all worked out. And Eirik?'

'Eirik stays here with you, of course.'

'No,' said Eirik, from the floor, 'I'm going off with the pirates, like Dagfinn.'

'Maybe. But not yet.'

Eirik resented his brother's note of authority as he had never resented blows or indifference. 'Says you! I don't have to ask you, anyway!'

Ingebjorg picked up the spindle, and slowly resumed her work. 'I suppose it could work. No one ever wanted you to have to take it to Hjaltland, certainly. But what about Astrid? Is she happy? You're sure she wasn't forced into this?'

'I'm not that cruel!'

'My dear, no one says you are. But have you talked to her? You know how she feels?'

'Of course I have! Of course I do!'

She gave him a shrewd glance, and to his fury, Thorvald found himself blushing, and slid along the bench into the shadows. 'If Olaf's not coming back, I'll give you a game,' he said gruffly to his brother.

For a second Eirik's amazement showed in his face, then he swept the pieces off the board and began lining them up again.

'I'll be the fox this time,' he announced, making the most of this rare attention.

Thorvald only caught Olaf the next morning because he heard him trip over some shoes on his way to the door. By now Thorvald realised something was badly wrong. He threw his blanket back and ran after Olaf, overtaking him by the byre. Olaf turned round, a hunk of bread in his hand.

'Olaf? What is it? What's the matter?'

'Leave me alone,' said Olaf. He tried to push past Thorvald, who grabbed him by the arm.

'What's wrong?'

'I said leave me alone!'

'Why?'

Olaf dropped his bread, and swiped Thorvald across the mouth, sending him reeling back against the wall. Olaf glared, then sprang on his brother.

They had never fought in such earnest before. Chickens scuttered out of the way as they lurched across the yard. Olaf had his hands round Thorvald's neck. Thorvald kicked out, and tried to loosen Olaf's grip with his sound hand. They knocked over the water buckets. The noise brought Eirik to the door. He stopped, aghast, then ran after them begging them to stop. He grabbed Olaf by the tunic and got trodden on. They ignored his sobs. Suddenly Olaf let go, seized Thorvald's wounded arm over the bandage and twisted it hard. Blinded by pain, Thorvald grabbed his brother and hurled him clean across the yard, where he lay sprawled out on his back.

For several seconds Olaf lay quite still. Then he sat up, and got painfully to his feet. Thorvald took one tentative step towards him, and Olaf turned and spat, savage as a cat, then shot away round the corner of the house.

A thin rain had begun to fall. Eirik was hunched by the well, weeping. Thorvald hesitated, then slouched barefoot through the rain towards Shirva, his wounded arm stuck in his shirt for a makeshift sling.

He had forgotten, until he reached the Shirva yard, that today he was supposed to deal with Bjarni. There was no one in the house but Gerda.

'They're milking,' she said, before he could speak. 'No, don't go after her. You can wait here till they're done.'

'Is my uncle here?'

'He went fishing early with Arne and Jon. You're quite safe.'

Thorvald didn't like her tone, but Gerda wasn't to know anything had changed. Arne and Jon: he had to think about them too. There'd been no time to talk when they'd all been hauling up the Sula. His arm hurt, he was shivering with cold, and his head swam in the sudden heat indoors.

'There's blood on your sleeve,' said Gerda. 'You'd better let me look.'

As he felt quite faint, he had little choice.

'You should have dressed yourself properly. It's the cold making it bleed,' she remarked. But she undid the bandage quite gently. The fire was warm on his feet. Thorvald leaned back against the wall, watching what she did through half-closed eyes.

Underneath the bandage the half-healed scar was torn apart again, and blood oozed sluggishly. Bruises made by Olaf were coming up livid the length of his forearm. Gerda washed the wound, then applied something cool, which stung a little. When she had bandaged it up again she went back to her work without a word. He watched her, too exhausted to move. When he was small he'd been frightened of her because she was so old. She had taken some sprigs from the bunches of herbs that were hung to dry, and was chopping them with a sharp little knife. She put them in a mug and poured boiling water over them. The infusion steamed gently, and she added a spoonful of honey from a stone jar and stirred it in. Some women's business, he thought idly, remembering what they'd said about Gudrun's child. He was startled when she brought the stuff to him, and told him to drink it. It was hot, and had a bitter aftertaste in spite of the honey. He sipped it slowly, warming his numb fingers on the mug.

When Astrid came in she took one look at him, and was at his side. 'What's happened? Thorvald, are you all right?'

'I had a fight with my brother,' he said sullenly.

Astrid went pale. So she did have some idea how much it mattered. 'I threw him backwards across the yard. If he'd hit the brigstones I could have killed him.'

'But he didn't hit the brigstones?'

'No.'

Her hands were clenched in her lap. He waited for her to ask why they'd fought, but instead she said, 'What did he tell you?'

'Nothing. He went away.'

'Perhaps he doesn't want you to marry me.'

'But why ever not? He once said he liked you very much.'

She didn't seem inclined to say more. 'Have you had any breakfast?' she asked presently.

'No.'

They gave him a bowl of hot porridge, which he ate hungrily, feeling much better when it was finished. He stood up.

'Where are you going?'

'To find Olaf.'

Their boat was still in its noost at the Nordhavn. Relieved, Thorvald took to the hill. If Olaf chose not to be seen, he hardly had a hope of finding him, but it was better to look than to do nothing. Rain was falling in fierce bursts, and Thorvald shook his wet hair out of his eyes as he strode along, skirting every geo.

On the west side of the Vord, he looked south into a great geo lined with precipices of copper-coloured rock. Below, the surf made thread-like patterns for about fifty yards offshore. At the mouth of the geo, gannets perched on an arch above a turquoise sea. He could see the descent into the geo, but Olaf would stick to the cliff tops, he felt sure. He turned back to the ness just below the Vord, and began to climb down the spit. The grass was slippery, but sheep had left a faint track, which he followed.

Halfway down, he caught sight of Olaf in a small hollow at the lip of the precipice. Water lifted and cascaded off brown rock far below, and kittiwakes called under the cliff. Thorvald edged forward.

Olaf heard him and sprang to his feet, fists clenched. 'Get out! Leave me alone!'

'No.' There were only a few feet between them. Behind Olaf was the cliff. A damp gust of wind came in from the sea, and rain beat down hard between them.

'Go away!'

Thorvald stepped forward. Olaf stepped back. 'Take care!'

The wind was blowing Olaf's hair across his face in wild curls. Thorvald had the rain in his eyes, and brushed his hand across his wet forehead. Olaf leapt, trying to get past.

Before Olaf could move again Thorvald was on him, and had him by the tunic. It tore, and Olaf tried to pull free, but the cloth was too strong. Thorvald forced Olaf round and held him hard against his chest. Olaf struggled violently, twisting his legs round Thorvald's, trying to bring him down. Thorvald began to slip towards the edge.

'Don't! We'll be over!'

Olaf didn't answer, but brought his knee up hard.

'I said stop! We'll be over!'

'Then let go!'

'No.'

Thorvald pinioned Olaf's arms, and Olaf fought and arched his back. His hair blew into Thorvald's face. Thorvald spat hair out of his mouth, and struggled to keep his feet.

'Olaf, stop! Do you want to kill us?'

'Then let go!'

'No.'

Thorvald knew exactly how strong Olaf was. He could hold him easily, as long as he could keep his balance.

Suddenly Olaf went limp. He knew exactly how strong Thorvald was. He couldn't get away; if he tried he'd have them over. He surrendered, an inert weight. Thorvald dared not let go. He looked over his brother's shoulder, and saw water break on rock six hundred feet down.

'Sit down!'

They stood chest to chest. Then very slowly Olaf let his legs give way, and sat down. Thorvald sat with him, gripping his arm tightly.

Olaf looked down, and saw a blur of green moving against brown. 'When are you going to let me go?'

'Soon. I want to talk to you.'

Olaf stared into the sea. His tunic was half ripped off his back.

'I can't know if you don't say.'

At last Olaf spoke. 'I said I'd go to Papey with you, if you wanted anyone.'

'I wanted to go alone. I told you.'

'But you didn't go alone.'

'But that wasn't my plan. You must know that.'

'Wasn't it?'

'I told you, I didn't want it.' Thorvald tried to make sense of it. 'I thought you liked her?'

Olaf was silent.

'You told me you did.'

'I did like her,' said Olaf, in a small, distant voice.

He'd liked her the first time he'd seen her, standing so pale and small beside Ingrid, when he and Thorvald had gone to slaughter the cattle. Long dark hair she had, a white face, and eyes like the earth, hill-coloured. She didn't talk to anyone. She was neat and quick in her movements, very slight, but when he'd looked he'd noticed her body was already a woman's. Something about the way she moved, even that first time, made him want to touch her.

When she was pleased she had a big grin, which showed the gap between her front teeth, which were still smooth and white like a child's. She made quiet remarks which most people ignored, but when he listened they were often quite funny. She was fragile and tough all at the same time. When he'd told her that story at midsummer he'd been watching her eyes change in the firelight, sometimes green, sometimes dark. He'd seen her face very clearly when she was so close. And later she'd told him about her father, while the rain sheeted down between them. At the feast she'd looked into his eyes so long, he'd almost forgotten where he was and kissed her. He'd been certain then his chance would come. Then the blow had struck. She'd gone. He'd decided almost at once, after his first despair, that he'd follow. Come the spring, he'd follow her, the first day there was a boat. And then she'd come back two days ago, pink and breathless from running, and he'd been so overwhelmed with joy that he'd kissed her without even thinking about it. She hadn't said a word. He'd run across the island, happier than he'd ever been in his life.

And then this. 'I thought you liked her.' Thorvald meant that, the fool. Not a traitor, just stupid. There was no point even being angry now. There was nothing left to feel at all.

'Then why?' Thorvald was asking him.

Olaf caught the edge of fear in Thorvald's voice. So he'd begun to understand at last, had he? Olaf should know Thorvald, if anyone did. He should have known his brother hadn't even begun to realise what he was doing. Olaf's rage evaporated, leaving only an agony of emptiness behind. But that he could keep to himself. Rain beat down on his head, misting over the white patterns far below.

'It doesn't matter,' said Olaf at last. 'Forget it. Let's go home.'

The islanders were desperately ignorant, but not nearly as poor as the priest has expected. The weather was at its early autumn best, and the temporal harvest had been plentiful, which seemed an augury that the spiritual yield might also be fruitful. Certainly the ground was fertile, already ploughed in some places, though in others he expected to find it stony and unbroken. The fields cried out for nourishment and the seed was there for the sowing.

They were willing to listen to his stories. He had learned long ago that it was the stories that mattered. If he could capture their imaginations that way, there was no need for discussion or exhortation. These folk were starved of godliness. They had no church. Once or twice he had heard the men muttering about tithes, but so far he had met with no opposition. They were aware of their own backwardness, and he knew they would find money for a church, once they saw it as a matter of prestige.

Meanwhile he celebrated Mass at the Thing place. Not a soul on the island was absent. The October sun was pale gold, the sea the colour of ice. He doubted if they had done much to prepare themselves, but they were all baptised, so he asked no questions.

When the service was done, he retired to the smithy, in the hopes that some of them might come to him.

They came, as he had expected. Nothing that they brought was new to him, though like every soul on earth, each one seemed to think his or her own case was unique. Naturally they never asked whether he had heard it all before; what he had to remember was that not one of them had ever been heard before. So he listened quietly, for the most part unperturbed. He had total faith in what he had to offer.

The first was a young man. That was unexpected. In his experience it was women who took the initiative. He hoped that a youth who came so promptly might be an ardent soul, thirsty for spiritual refreshment. For a moment he thought of St Magnus, praying on the ship's deck in the midst of the battle, while the arrows rained down round him. But it took him less than a minute to discover that this young man was not like that at all.

'My name is Olaf. I want to ask you about the shrine of St. Magnus at Byrgisey, or at Kirkjavagr. I don't mind which it is.'

'What did you wish to know about our blessed Magnus?'

'Nothing really,' said Olaf. 'Only I heard there were miracles. Cures. A man from Svinborg had his sight given back to him there.'

'And is that important to you?'

The priest didn't mind how long he waited for an answer. The boy's downbent head was a mass of thick brown curls. The priest waited while he struggled with himself.

'Yes,' said Olaf.

The next arrival was more predictable.

'I've been married nearly four years,' she told him, 'and I lost two children before this one, which is due next month. I don't know why fate willed it so. But there wasn't a priest to marry us; we were married the old way, perhaps that's why. If Rolf and I had been blessed by a priest, or even if we could be now, that would make it right. He's willing. Perhaps there was an ill fate. We couldn't prevent it then; we didn't have anything to protect us.'

It was easy enough to help her with that. But when he thought she was satisfied, and was about to leave, she said, 'Did you know that my uncle was drowned after the hay harvest?'

She seemed disappointed by his ignorance, but she was willing enough to tell him the story.

'You see,' she said when she'd finished, 'it haunts me. I think about it all the time. Not just because I loved him – I did, of course, he was my father's brother – but it worries me, even more because there's the child to think of too. Why? That's what I can't think about. Why? Einar didn't deserve to die. Whose fault was it? It was our feast; was it our evil fate that killed him? Was it Rolf?'

She brushed aside his words of comfort.

'No, no, it's not that. We did all that. Rolf paid for a mass to be sung in Kirkjavagr, and gave the monks money to pray for his soul as well. Anyway, my uncle was a good man. He deserves God's mercy. No, it's the evil fate we have here, on the island.'

He waited, while she searched for words to tell him. Gudrun looked at him, willing him to understand her. 'My husband hates his brother!' she told him at last, and burst into sobs, rocking to and fro with her head in her hands.

He only began to fear that there was more to deal with on this island than domestic sins, when his next visitor began to talk. Perhaps it was inevitable; weeds grow rank in untended ground.

'No,' Gunnhild argued. 'It was never sorcery, not the way you mean. Who is the Prince of Darkness anyway? Is that the Devil? No one ever used spells like that here. No, no,' she seemed deeply distressed. 'I never heard of any of that. I'm talking about herbs and charms, small things we need in order to protect ourselves. But no one did anything to raise that wind. I only did for Gudrun what any midwife would do. I'd do it again tomorrow. You saw for yourself at Byrstada, the child's nearly due. Its head's down now. I'm not expecting a hard birth either. It must be right. Aren't we put on this earth to help each other?'

As Jacob wrestled with the angel, so he wrought with her, and could not prevail. She argued, but she was not penitent. She was willing to pray with him, she was willing to do penance, she was willing to have him intercede for her soul. But she would not recant. He sensed a struggle scarcely begun. The incomprehension she showed at some of his questions made it clear that she had no sense of the church's great spiritual crusade against witchcraft. All she would say was that healing knowledge was a gift that could not be withheld from the needy, not even at the price of the giver's soul. Such arrogant heresy struck him with horror. She even said that not to do anything one could seemed wrong to her, for she had been taught to believe that God was merciful. She wept, certainly, and accepted her penance, but he recognised the unrepentant soul. The powers of evil had found soil here in which to take root, and already he acknowledged with foreboding the struggles that might lie ahead.

Rolf's sister came as a touch of lightness after the shadow of the dark. Having stayed two nights at Byrstada, he'd have predicted that the younger one would arrive first. He'd seen girls like Thorhalla before; no fiery spirit, but a sad, loveless soul who might easily be led to the light, and find a vocation in the spiritual life, when the temporal one appeared to offer her so little. But he hadn't expected to see Ragna this morning, and he wasn't surprised to find it was no spiritual conflict that troubled her. That didn't worry him. He saw no evil in her beyond the venial sins of the simple. Her right destiny in this world was obvious enough.

'My brother Rolf,' Ragna told him, her indignation tempered by a terror that he guessed was quite new to her, 'has arranged this marriage for me. He thinks I can leave the island in the spring, just like that, and go with him to Biorgvin, as it were no distance at all. And it isn't even an island man, he's not even Norse! He's a foreigner, a man from Lubeck. Lubeck! I've never even heard of the place, have you? He's a merchant from this city in Vindland, and now they have a warehouse in Biorgvin. And now this Jens of Lubeck is spending the winter making trading contacts in the Orkneyjar, and my brother's entered into some contract with him. Rolf says we'll have goods coming into the island that we've never seen before – wine and glass and linen cloth – stuff like that – it's going to become commonplace, he says. He says the pirates are doomed, trade's where the new wealth's going to be. "It's the best future I could have hoped for you," he said to me. "Of course if you don't get on with him when you meet him in the spring, I won't force you. But I think you'll find he's goodlooking, and certainly he's a wealthy man. To be honest, it's a brilliant marriage for such as we are." '

Ragna burst into tears, and the torrent of words continued through her sobs. ' "Such as we are!" If Dagfinn could have heard him! Rolf spoke as if we're peasants! And my other brother – the one who's gone with Svein – he knew what we're worth! We have land! We're farmers! We have a ship! I don't want a brilliant marriage,' wept Ragna, her sobs threatening to overwhelm her. 'I don't want to go to Biorgvin! I don't want to go away at all!' Her words ended in a long wail.

The priest had dealt with hysterical women before, and this wasn't a complicated matter. He knew better than to speak immediately about duty or obedience. That could come later. Instead, he described the city of Biorgvin to her, which he was luckily able to do at first hand. When her sobs began to subside, and he'd caught her interest, he dwelt a little on the virtues of courage and endeavour, using as an example the noble adventures of the great crusaders. Women too, he suggested, might take their part in daring enterprise, within their own sphere, and perhaps duty, in Ragna's case, was to be coupled with splendid adventure.

He was satisfied that he'd hit the right note. Her eyes were still red, but she was beginning to look quite eager. While she was in a malleable condition, he took the opportunity of bringing her attention to the spiritual aspects of her condition.

He had expected to see one or two of the sailors who'd brought him here. Not all of them came from islands as far removed from godliness as this one had been. None of them were in any way unpredictable, except for the last one.

Leif had grown up with the benefit of priestly instruction. He knew how to prepare himself. But the priest realised very quickly that there was confusion here. He knew when he wasn't being told everything, but he couldn't make out where the young man's tale was leading.

'In that church on Uvist,' Leif told him, 'I realised I'd been forgetting too many things. But sin isn't all black, is it? Not if there's love too. It can be more confusing than that.'

'It can be confusing, but the nature of sin is never in doubt.'

'There is a sin . . .' began Leif, and stopped. Then he started again, 'In that church, I made my own prayer. I said it in my own language. I don't have much Latin – I wanted to be a scholar once; I'd like to have studied at the Cathedral school in Nidaros, but I was apprenticed to the sea instead – So I made my own prayer in Norse. There is a sin . . . There has been a sin . . . I prayed that it might not come my way, that I'd find a way out, and not even wish to be tempted any more. Because when it's confused with what's good, it's harder to resist.'

It took some encouragement to make him go on.

'It worked,' said Leif. 'My prayer was answered. The prayer that temptation would go away. It did.' He had gone quite white, but two spots of colour burned in his cheeks. 'Not the desire. That remained. That's worse. I was praying for just myself, you see, and perhaps that's wrong. I might have killed the only person I love. I don't know. It confuses me.'

The priest was familiar with agony of mind. There was more to this, and he asked for it.

Instead of answering, Leif asked him, 'What is the sin against the Holy Ghost? Can you tell me that?'

'Why do you want to know that?'

'Because it's not clear to me, and I'm frightened.'

His voice stayed level, but the priest had seen such desperate control before.

'The sin against the Holy Ghost is the denial of God.'

'But how?'

When Leif left him at last, the priest was not satisfied. Leif was right, there was confusion, diabolical confusion perhaps. There was too much that the young man had failed to tell him. He recognised that Leif was unhappy, and mortally afraid. Anathema, he'd suggested. But no, more likely he was troubled by mortal sin which would torture him until he confessed to it. Whatever he had done, he could hardly have set himself beyond the mercy of God; it was arrogance even to think it, a deadly sin itself.

There was no such difficulty with his next visitant. He saw at once that she was a true daughter of the Church. The confessional was nothing new to her. She didn't have to be introduced to it gradually; she had prepared herself already. She had been taught what he was there for, and she didn't attempt to seek anything else.

When he realised she was from the bishopric of Dyflin, he was no longer surprised. She had been exiled for too long, poor child. In this benighted community, far from priestly guidance, she had continued to do her best, as the priest and nuns who had instructed her in Irland had taught her. Facing the long task before him, it was like finding a small lamp already burning in this outland darkness. Her presence was as much a gift to him as his blessing was to her.

Chapter 57

Within a week after Sula had arrived back with the priest, people began to fall ill.

It began with a sore throat and a headache, and that frightened them, but it resolved itself into nothing worse than a severe cold. At Byrstada the women had it, although the crew escaped infection. At Shirva they were all ill except Arne and Jon. At Setr only Thorvald and Olaf caught it. Thorvald was annoyed. He hadn't had a day's illness since he was five, and he took it as a personal affront.

'I've had enough of this,' he told Olaf, after they had kept each other awake coughing all night.

'It's the priest,' said Eirik. 'They said it was bad luck.'

A damp mist had drifted in over the island. Thorvald walked along the muddy track to Shirva, skirting the puddles, and coughing as he went. He was lucky enough to find Astrid alone for once, feeding the chickens. 'My throat's sore,' she said. 'Maybe you should keep away.'

'No,' he said, and kissed her. He wasn't feeling very well, and there was no chance of making love to her just now, but just to hold her for a moment aroused him, and he felt better.

She hugged him back. 'I miss you.'

He'd never have imagined it would be so hard to be without her, even after just a few days together. It would be different when he was at sea, of course, but in winter, when they were both on the island, this separation seemed pointless. He began to kiss her again.

'Thorvald!' called a voice behind him.

She whipped out of his arms in a flash, and he turned round. Arne was standing there, grinning. Thorvald grabbed him by the shoulders, then remembered. 'I'm ill. Better keep away,' he said, coughing.

'They're all ill here,' said Arne, embracing him. 'But Papey men never catch cold. It's good to see you.'

There was so much he and Arne had to talk about, that for a while Thorvald forgot the harder part of his errand to Shirva. He almost forgot Astrid too, until she brought ale to them while they sat on the bench outside, exchanging news of everything that had happened since they last met.

'I'm sorry I missed your wedding,' Thorvald told Arne, 'I should have guessed, when you told me at Konungsborg you'd left something on Fridarey, and you'd come back for it one day. You must have thought I was a fool not to realise what you were saying.'

'I wanted to tell you, but it's a bit hard to say to a man you might urgently need to marry his cousin. Afterwards I wished I'd said, especially when I arrived here and they told me you'd gone to Papey.' He eyed Thorvald cautiously. 'Thorvald, there's nothing between us, is there? You don't feel that what you've lost, I've gained, do you?'

'Me? I haven't lost anything now. I told you, your father saw to that.'

'I was never after your inheritance.'

'Of course not.' Thorvald saw Arne was still doubtful, and shook him gently. 'I've got what I want now, don't you realise? So have you, I hope.'

'Oh yes,' said Arne, 'And you know that you'd have my support, if ever you should need it.'

Thorvald did know. He realised that he could always trust Arne to be as he was now, to stay here at Shirva, to take his place on the farm, to be fair to Thorvald's brothers, to be a reliable kinsman to come home to. He liked Arne, but Arne, who could have sailed from Papey in the best trading ships out of Hjaltland, who had been born on an island where an ambitious man could have had anything, had chosen instead to find a quiet corner for himself on Fridarey, and secure a place in the world through an advantageous marriage. This was one kind of friend, and very necessary. Perhaps there was another kind, a man who'd share his ambitions, who would want to be partner in adventure.

'It's the same with me,' Thorvald said. 'You'll have my support as your kinsman now, if ever you should need it.'

Arne smiled. 'You must meet my brother Jon properly. Come into the house.'

'Is Bjarni there?'

'Don't you want to meet him?'

'That's what I'm here for, apart from finding you, of course. I need to speak to my uncle privately.'

'You might find him in the barn. He's been working there. Good luck,' said Arne, and sauntered off to find his brother.

There was a space in the barn where they'd been threshing barley. Sacks of grain were heaped against the wall, ready to be taken down to the mill at Finniquoy. Thorvald stepped inside, and tripped over the bench that had been set across the entrance where it was light. There was a stone slab set on the bench, the hammer and chisel still lying on it, with runes carved on the smooth surface. Thorvald leaned over, and spelled out the words with some difficulty:

Bjarni Thorvaldsson raised this runestone for Einar his brother, an excellent man who . . .

Footsteps sounded outside, and Thorvald straightened up quickly.

Bjarni had gone to the smithy early, with a couple of crabs from yesterday's fishing. He had found Gunnhild more upset than he had known her to be since Snorri was brought home wounded, and he had stayed to comfort her. Luckily Snorri was working at something which required much hammering, so as long as the noise from next door continued, Bjarni knew that they were safe.

'Nonsense,' he told Gunnhild, when he'd heard her story. 'There's no need for all this fuss. We've managed without a priest for long enough, God knows, but there was never an island since time began that managed without a midwife. The man doesn't know what he's talking about.'

'But he has power.'

'Not over me he doesn't. This isn't even his island. Don't worry about it.'

He knew he hadn't convinced her, but he succeeded in cheering her a little. Presently he even got a smile out of her.

'So you've heard all about this betrothal, have you?' he asked her.

'Of course, from Ingebjorg.'

'And what has she to say about it?'

'She's happy. So I hope you will be too.' Gunnhild turned his face towards her, and made him look at her. 'It's a way out, Bjarni. You've got to hand it to Thorvald, he's found a solution. He never wanted to take a case to the Thing any more than you did.'

'That's as may be; he's still never been near me.'

'He didn't come and tell you about his betrothal? That's bad. But he will. From what his mother tells me, he's determined to do what's right.'

'He's taking his time about it.'

'He's had a lot to deal with at home. So who told you the whole story, if Thorvald didn't?'

'Astrid, of course.'

Gunnhild laughed. 'Of course, she'd be the first to confront you. But Thorvald will come himself, you'll see.'

'I don't think she had to confront me,' he protested. 'I've had quite enough scenes from young people recently. But Astrid – I think she likes me.'

Gunnhild laughed again. 'Bjarni, you've got yourself another daughter there. I hope you're pleased.'

'The last thing I need is another daughter.'

'Nonsense. Everyone likes to be wanted. Astrid will never let Thorvald break with you. Nothing could be better.'

Bjarni gave a twisted smile. 'Better for whom?' He took his arm from round her and stood up. 'She's brave, you know. Never complained. Never made a fuss. It's been hard on her.'

'Of course it has. Don't worry, Ingrid doesn't mind. She's fond of Astrid too, and she'll never be jealous.'

Bjarni looked bewildered. 'Jealous? Why should she be jealous?'

'Never mind. Just go on treating Astrid well, whatever happens. It's worth your while.'

'I'd never do anything else,' he said indignantly. 'I'm not an ogre, am I?'

Bjarni walked slowly home, thinking about the priest. He wished Einar had been there to deal with this; in spite of the reassurance he had given to Gunnhild, there might be problems.

Einar would have known what to do. As it was, the men that were left would have to ensure that this man – for man was all he was, for all his holy office – that this man didn't gain too much influence. Rolf should have spoken to the islanders before taking such high-handed action on his own initiative.

Bjarni reached the barn, still preoccupied. He looked up and saw his brother Einar, standing by the bench which supported the half carved runestone.

Bjarni recoiled, and crossed himself. The figure moved. Not his brother. Nothing like his brother. It was his nephew Thorvald. Bjarni had never seen him as a grown man before.

Still shaken, he grasped the doorpost, and waited for Thorvald to speak. Thorvald opened his mouth, and broke into a fit of coughing.

By the time Thorvald had blown his nose, and was able to speak again, Bjarni had recovered. 'I've been hoping I'd see you. I must congratulate you on your betrothal,' he said coolly.

To his surprise Thorvald met his eyes. 'I think I've been very lucky.'

'I think you have,' said Bjarni drily.

Thorvald coughed. 'I'm sorry if I offended you, before I went away.'

'Offended me? Is that what you think you did?'

'Whatever went wrong, I'm sorry for it.' Thorvald regarded his uncle with a touch of the wariness that Bjarni had become accustomed to. 'I think I'd better tell you where I went, and what happened there.'

'You probably know that I've been told already.'

'Even if you have, it's better if I tell you myself.'

'Is it?' Bjarni unfolded his arms, and came away from the doorpost. 'Very well, young man, have it your own way. Sit down.'

Thorvald blew his nose again. His temples ached, his eyes hurt, and his head felt as though it was stuffed with moss. He hadn't expected Bjarni to kill a fatted calf for him like the man in the story, so he wasn't disconcerted by his uncle's coolness. The point was to tell the whole story as clearly as he could.

'But what's even more important,' he explained to Bjarni, 'is that I've had all this time to think about what happened here. I'm no lawman. I'm a sailor. I don't even need land, if I have enough wealth for what I want to do. What I do need is my kin.'

He found himself trying to explain to Bjarni what had gone through his mind when he stayed with Helgi's family. He didn't expect his uncle to think much of it, but it was so important that he couldn't keep silent.

'Helgi's family are so sure of themselves,' he said. 'They don't need to care about anyone else. Oh, they're hospitable, it isn't that, it's just they don't have to bother about outsiders. They've got themselves.' He sniffed, and wiped his nose on his sleeve. 'They know exactly who they are.' He glanced at his uncle's impassive face. 'It reminded me of my father. I want that back.'

'Fair enough,' said Bjarni.

Thorvald's head was throbbing. 'There's one other matter.'

'Yes?'

'I told you how Astrid and I were betrothed on Papey. Amundi says we have to be married within the year.'

'That's the law. Isn't that what you want?'

'Of course it is. But we have to have a wedding. Amundi gave me some gold. I have it here. We need to have a feast.'

'Yes,' said Bjarni, watching him. 'Can I ask you a question?'

'Of course.'

'Do you want to marry her? Apart from the contract you've made, I mean. Do you want her?'

Thorvald hadn't said a word about the journey back from Papey, nor did he intend to. But Bjarni's question reminded him of it again. No, he hadn't wanted her, not until she was thrust upon him. But they had crossed the hills of Hjaltland since then, he had made love to her since then. He remembered the warmth of Astrid's body under his, in the hay; Astrid unplaiting her hair in the old woman's house, hanging her wet tunic over the fire to dry; the way she'd looked at him in the quiet evening, before they'd walked down the hill to Svinborg.

'Yes,' he said indifferently. 'I think we'd get on well. I want to marry her.'

He hadn't realised until he looked up how intently Bjarni was watching him. To his annoyance, he blushed, just as he had done with his mother.

'Very well,' said Bjarni. 'She belongs here. Will you be married at Shirva?'

'If you don't mind.' It had been bad enough explaining; now Thorvald had to go further and ask a favour.

'No, I don't mind. When do you want this to be?'

'As soon as possible,' said Thorvald recklessly.

'Hallowmass? That seems a good time for a feast.'

Thorvald grinned. That was sooner than he'd expected. 'That would suit me very well.'

'We might as well get it over with, especially while we've got that priest on the island. We might as well make use of him. I'll recoup my losses next year, assuming no one else will want me to supply them with a wedding.'

That was a joke. Thorvald realised it was the nearest to an explicit reconciliation he would ever get. He smiled, and said, 'There is one other thing.'

'Yes?' Bjarni sounded resigned.

'Will you go to the Thing next year? If so, would you collect Astrid's dowry from Amundi?'

For a moment he was afraid Bjarni meant to refuse. There was no one else he'd trust to do it, not Arne, not Kalf of Leogh. Neither of them would be quite certain to cope with any difficulties.

'I'll do that,' said Bjarni at last. 'At least it's preferable to the other errand you had planned for me there. I wouldn't bother to go now, but there's another matter I need to attend to. You know I don't like travelling. Sick as a dog on any boat that's not my own. But I have to go to Hjaltland next year anyway, so I'll do it.'

'What's the other matter? I hope it's not a quarrel.'

'No. I thought you'd have guessed. I want to choose my own wood when the ships come in from Noreg. We need a new boat for Shirva.'

Gudrun and Ragna were sorting out wool, spreading the fulled fleeces across the brigstones to see exactly what they had. They put the coarser fleeces in the pile for the wadmal tax. The better ones they set aside on the bench for their own use.

'Is that lichen boiling yet?' asked Gudrun. 'This is the fleece we want to dye brown. We can put it in now.'

'All right.' Ragna sat back on her heels and sniffed. 'But I do want to go out soon.'

'So you said. What's all the hurry?'

'I haven't seen Astrid yet.'

Gudrun heaved herself up on to the bench, and wiped her hot forehead. 'You're not going to make trouble, are you?'

'Trouble?' Ragna's surprise was obviously genuine. 'What trouble? She's my friend. I haven't had a chance to talk to her since she got back, that's all. Is there anything wrong with that?' she added belligerently.

'No. I just thought,' said Gudrun, choosing her words carefully, 'that this betrothal mightn't be what you were expecting.'

'It doesn't bother me. Even if Rolf hadn't made his bargain with Jens, I wouldn't mind.'

'I wondered.'

Ragna shook her head. 'I never dreamed of marrying Thorvald, if that's what you mean. He's too young.'

'In the summer he didn't seem to be too young.'

Ragna shrugged. 'In the summer there wasn't much choice. I like Thorvald, but I know him too well, I don't want to marry him. Mind you, when Rolf first sprang this Lubeck man on to me, I thought of Thorvald. Then in the next breath Rolf tells us Thorvald's marrying Astrid. It felt like a fate, but as soon as I'd had time to think I knew I'd never have done it anyway. You can't marry a friend just so you feel safe, can you?'

'I don't know,' said Gudrun, without bothering to consider the question. 'So long as you're not angry with Astrid. We can put the fleeces in now. You take the pot; I'd better not lift it.'

'It was all Thorvald's idea anyway,' said Ragna, heaving the pot of dye off the fire. 'Left to herself, she'd have had his brother.'

'Olaf? Nonsense, you don't know what you're talking about.'

'You weren't at the Midsummer Feast.'

'I don't believe it,' said Gudrun firmly. 'And don't you dare spread a rumour like that around. Olaf's just a boy.'

'So was Thorvald once. I could tell you more about that, too.'

'You needn't. I'm sure Astrid never led anyone on.'

'No?' said Ragna, grinning as she built up the fire. 'But isn't it just as well I've been practising, if I've got to charm Jens of Lubeck next spring?'

Ragna wasn't free to visit Shirva until the following day. She found Astrid at the peatstack, picking out small pieces for kindling.

'Rolf told me you're betrothed to Thorvald,' she said, as soon as Astrid had greeted her. 'I came to say there's no hard feelings, not from me.'

'Thank you,' said Astrid cautiously.

'Don't thank me. I just want to get it straight. I'm glad you've come back.'

'Thank you.'

'But I won't be if you go on saying thank you. I don't know what Thorvald's told you, but anything that went on between us wasn't serious, you realise that?'

'Yes.' Thorvald had never mentioned the matter at all.

'Anyway,' Ragna was saying, 'I won't be here after the winter. I expect you've heard about that already.'

'Rolf never said anything when we sailed back. It was Gudrun that told us.'

'About the man from Lubeck?' Astrid nodded. 'What did she say?'

'She said it was very sudden. She'd no idea Rolf was thinking of such a thing.' Astrid looked at Ragna. 'How do you feel about it?'

Ragna shrugged. 'I don't know, do I, until I've seen him? Rolf can't force me to marry. I'll go to Biorgvin in the spring and look him over.'

'And if you don't like him? What will Rolf say then?'

'He'll look a fool, won't he? I'm not marrying against my will, not for anybody.'

Astrid admired her confidence. Did Ragna never experience a moment's doubt? It must be a fine way to live. 'It can be difficult though, when men start making their plans all around you.'

'I'm not scared of Rolf. Wait till Dagfinn gets back. We'll see what happens to all this authority of Rolf's then.' Ragna stopped, interrupted by a fit of sneezing.

'Have you got the cold? We shouldn't stand out here. Come in.'

'Is Ingrid in there?'

'No, she went to move the cow.'

'All right then, I'll come in.' Ragna followed Astrid into the house. 'Gudrun was fussing about this cold being around when the baby came. It was frightening at first.'

'Oh, it's only a cold. Do you think the priest brought it?'

'I don't care who brought it. And I'm not so sure about "only". Not after what happened before.'

That was what everyone had been saying. 'What happened?' asked Astrid.

'Ten years ago? There was a ship at the beginning of the season, called in for supplies. We'd had a bad winter, there hadn't been much to eat. A few days after the ship left, people began to get ill. It began with a cold, just like this time. But then there was a rash. After that, a fever.'

Astrid crossed her fingers. 'God keep us! In Dyflin people were always frightened of plague. But I thought it was safe here.'

'It wasn't plague. But I had it,' said Ragna.

Astrid listened in dismay.

'My mother took it from me,' said Ragna. 'It killed her. She wasn't strong. It killed my father too. He fought it for two weeks, but it killed him. Didn't Thorvald tell you?'

'He told me one of his brothers had died.'

'Einar Eiriksson. He was just a baby. Olaf was very ill too, and they thought he'd lost his sight. Thorvald didn't have it badly. It was mostly the babies that died, and the old people. That's why we have that extension on the graveyard. Didn't anyone tell you?'

'I don't think I wanted to hear,' said Astrid. 'I suppose there's no safe place in the world really.'

Ragna helped herself to some of the oatcakes left over from the morning meal. 'I don't know why I'm talking about it,' she complained. 'Take no notice.'

Astrid had been coaxing the fire back into life. She knew she wasn't quick about people's feelings, but something in Ragna's tone caught her attention.

'Ragna, what is it? What's upset you? It's not me and Thorvald, is it?'

Ragna shook her head. 'No, of course it's not. I told you. There's nothing wrong.'

'But there is.'

'It's different for you!' Ragna burst out. 'But I remember what you looked like when you first came here. You were just a stranger; you looked as if you weren't anybody. I don't want to be like that. I don't want to go away, where nobody knows who I am. It's what you just said, nothing's safe! You think it is, then you lose it all, just in a moment. I don't know what anything will be like now. I'm frightened!'

Even in distress, there was a toughness about Ragna to which Astrid responded. She put her arm round her, as easily as if it had been Thorvald. 'You'll be all right. It might be an adventure. He might be nice, this man from Lubeck. If he's not, you can say no. At least he won't have to go to sea all the time, and he might love you as well. If he doesn't, you can come home.'

Ragna blew her nose. 'I'm glad you've come back,' she said. 'Even if I go to Biorgvin, we might meet again. You had to manage on your own, and you've survived. I'll think of that when I get frightened. If you can do it, I can too.'

Astrid and Thorvald usually met on the far side of the hill dyke after the evening meal. Astrid had been to Setr once, at Ingebjorg's invitation, and Olaf hadn't been there. She didn't dare to ask if that were deliberate. Ingebjorg was friendly, but she didn't invite intimacy.

But today Thorvald called at Shirva, as he did every morning, and suggested that she come over to Byrstada with him. They arrived to find a lively discussion already in progress.

'That's what I heard in Kirkjavagr,' Rolf was saying. 'Apparently after he'd raided all through the Sudreyjar Svein went on to Monige, but they were ready for him there, and he couldn't make a landing. But then he overtook two English trading ships off Bretland and seized the cargo – English broadcloth, so I heard – very valuable. They left the English crew with the clothes they stood up in, and enough food to last until they reached port. I had that from a man in Kirkjavagr who'd spoken to a trader from Tyddewi who'd met some of the English crew in Abergwaun.'

'That's a typical Svein story.'

'D'you suppose Dagfinn was there?'

'It'll bring honour to the island if he was,' said Snorri.

Bjarni leaned back, warming his feet on the hearthstones. 'We may be well supplied with English broadcloth then, before the year's out.'

'Then we wouldn't have to weave the wadmal!' exclaimed Ragna.

'I wouldn't trust you with idle hands all winter.'

'You wouldn't waste broadcloth on the Earl's tax!'

'While we're speaking of Svein Asleifarson,' remarked the priest, 'perhaps I could remind you of the time the noble Earl Rognvald showed great mercy to him, in spite of the strife there'd been between them in the Earldom.'

They knew the story, of course. Everyone knew how Svein had fled in a small boat to South Rinansay, escaping the Earl's vengeance. When Svein realised Rognvald had pursued him in his own longship, he ran back to the shore with his men to launch their boat again. When the Earl's longship reached the beach it ran fast aground. As Svein's small boat rowed past, Svein stood in the prow, ready to hurl his spear at the Earl. But Rognvald had raised the shield of peace, and invited Svein to come ashore. That was how Rognvald and Svein had been reconciled, and, concluded the priest, 'That was how Rognvald succeeded in making peace between Svein and Earl Harald, and thus he brought peace and prosperity to us all.'

'Yes,' said Snorri. 'Rognvald saved his face that time. It was a neat way of getting out of another embarrassing situation. The man was no sailor. Shipwrecked twice, and lost a whole fleet through sheer carelessness!'

'Of course,' agreed Bjarni, 'he'd have killed Svein if he hadn't bungled the business. There's no doubt that's what he set out to do. He did the next best thing, when he managed to get a peace out of it.'

'What was the first embarrassing situation?' asked Astrid. They all turned to look at her. She didn't care. Now that she was beginning to piece the Orkneyjar stories together, she really did want to know.

Thorvald grinned. 'Surely we told you that story? The one where Rognvald came to conquer the islands and seize the Earldom, but he went ashore in Jala for the night, and while he was asleep Earl Paul came into the Sound, fresh from his victory at Dyrnes, and seized Rognvald's whole fleet without a blow struck?'

'Yes,' said Snorri. 'It was Svein who brought Rognvald to power. If Svein hadn't made away with Earl Paul, Rognvald would never have managed it.'

'Mind you,' put in Bjarni, 'it may have been a poor beginning, but he was one of the better rulers we've had.'

'I'm not sure,' said Rolf. 'We were Paul's men at Byrstada, and we don't forget it.'

There was an uncomfortable silence.

'Rognvald's life was exemplary,' observed the priest. 'He made his pilgrimage to Jorsalaheim, then he returned to bring prosperity to his Earldom, until his death, and now he still brings succour to the faithful at his blessed shrine in Kirkjavagr.'

'Peace, yes,' admitted Rolf, 'And there's no wealth without that. As to the shrine, it's Saint Magnus who makes that holy, surely, for all Rognvald built the Cathedral?'

'These matters may be beyond our understanding,' said the priest. 'It's not for us to judge.'

Rolf frowned, torn between the need to support his guest, and more ancient loyalties. 'Let me tell you a story,' he said to the priest. 'It's a story no man on this island likes to hear, but it will never be forgotten.

'There was a man called Dagfinn Lodvirsson, a good farmer on this island. He was my father's brother. Earl Paul appointed him to make a beacon here, after Rognvald had made his claim to the Earldom. The idea was that when Rognvald's ships came south, Dagfinn was to light the beacon on the Vord as soon as they were sighted, then the men of North Rinansay would see it and light theirs, and so the news would fly through Orkney until it reached the Earl himself.

'Rognvald got to hear of the plan. So he brought his fleet south, within sight of our shores, and went on sailing until he saw us light the beacon. As soon as we'd done it, he turned north, and went straight back to Hjaltland. Dagfinn, of course, had embarked at once for the Orkneyjar, to join the Earl's men.

'When Rognvald's fleet failed to arrive, Paul's men turned on Dagfinn in a fury, and in the fight that followed my uncle was shamefully murdered. After that they took the responsibility for the beacon from Byrstada and gave it to Shirva,' finished Rolf.

'They gave it to Eirik of Shirva,' Thorvald told the priest. 'But Rognvald was always devious. He sent spies here in a fishing boat, a man called Unn, who brought three Hjaltlanders with him. He said they were his sons, though they were nothing of the sort. He went to Shirva, and we – my family – we treated him well and gave him a place to live, for we've never turned away a guest at Shirva.'

'This Unn,' cut in Bjarni, 'was allowed to start fishing here. He won the trust of Eirik my uncle. Eirik wasn't young, and he was rheumatic. Unn offered to mind the beacon for him, and Eirik accepted.

'The second beacon was even better than the first. We used wood for it which we could hardly spare, but this time we were determined there should be no mistake.'

'But Unn soaked it with water,' said Thorvald.

'He soaked it,' repeated Bjarni. 'Then he fled, coward that he was. A spy sent to play tricks on us, but not man enough to face us afterwards!'

And who can blame him, thought Astrid. I'd have fled pretty quickly too.

'And when they tried to light the beacon . . .'

'. . . it was wet through, and they couldn't. That was the second time Rognvald's schemes had us shamed throughout the islands.'

The priest looked from Thorvald to Bjarni and back again. 'I can see that from your point of view it was all most unfortunate. But I'd like to remind you that Rognvald ruled nobly as Earl of the Orkneyjar for many years after he gained power. Moreover, he was a warrior in the service of Christ. You cannot deny that he ruled you well.

'You should know,' went on the priest, 'that many stories are being told in the islands, telling of Rognvald's noble deeds and steadfast faith, demonstrating his exemplary Christian life. Moreover, since his death he's been known to intercede for the suffering and the penitent, just as the blessed Saint Magnus has shown mercy to those who have turned to him, ever since his martyrdom.'

The islanders looked uncomfortable.

'Noble deeds, yes,' said Snorri, 'once he'd made his alliance with Svein. Christian life, I'm not so sure. Not that I'm any judge.'

'Perhaps it's about time,' remarked Gudrun, speaking for the first time. 'Magnus is the only saint we have of our own. In most places they have lots. They do in Irland, don't they, Astrid?'

Astrid nodded.

'So that's the way the wind blows,' said Snorri. 'Perhaps it's no bad thing. It's about time they noticed in Romaborg that we exist.'

'A return on our tithes, you might say,' said Bjarni, with a sardonic grin.

Everyone looked self-conscious. Tithes had been the dominant topic of conversation ever since the Sula had returned, but no one had yet mentioned them in the presence of the priest.

The priest turned to Snorri. 'How right you are to emphasise the Earl's noble deeds. I'm sure you all know Rognvald's own poem about his crusade.'

'My mother knows it all,' said Thorvald unexpectedly. 'Her brother Erling was a crusader. It's a good poem, especially the bit where they seize the trading ship from the infidels. They killed every heathen aboard, and took treasure too.'

'The Moors are much richer than any Christian king.'

'But they spared the captain,' said Thorvald. 'He was a man of honour, for a heathen. They tried to sell him in the next Saracen town they came to, but no one would buy him, so they set him free. Afterwards they found out he was a Prince of that country. He could have had them all put to the sword then, but he let them go.'

'That's right,' said Snorri. 'He said, "What saves you is that you saved my life, and treated me with respect. But I never want to see you again, so farewell." '

'If I were going east,' remarked Thorvald, 'I'd choose the sea route too. I'd go the same way they did.'

'No you wouldn't,' retorted Leif, across the hearth. 'No one does it now. They buy goods from the east from traders in Holmgardr or Konugard. A man in Birka told me that's where the silk and spice trade is. You'll get more from that than looting heathen ships, and you come home to tell the tale, what's more!'

'All right, just tell me the sailing directions to Konugard, and that's what we'll do!'

Chapter 60

The October light was thin and clear. In the Shirva oat rigs they could hear a steady hammering from the smithy, the bleating of sheep from beyond the hill dyke, and occasional voices from the yard at Leogh. There was not a whisper from wind or sea. Eirik and Kari played a game at the edge of the rig, spreading straws in patterns round them.

The shearers moved slowly down the rig, swinging their sickles, while the corn fell before them. Behind them came the bandmakers and the binders. The Shirva oat harvest was battered in places by the September gales, but the grain was heavy in the ears, and ripe before it was cut. This was the last harvest on the island. Once the oats were in, the gate in the hill dyke could be lifted, and the cattle let in over the rigs, to take what nourishment they could from the cut fields before the winter slaughter.

Bjarni led the reapers, whistling under his breath. Thorvald worked beside him. His hands were hard from rowing, but the sickle brought blisters out in different places. Thorvald bit the blisters open, spat on the raw skin, and speeded up to catch up with Bjarni, who never changed his pace.

Leif had come to help, deserting the Byrstada harvest. If Bjarni had been surprised to see him turn up with Thorvald, he didn't show it, but set Leif to work behind Thorvald, making the bands for Astrid to tie the sheaves. Leif tied the bands in a peculiar way, as they'd done it on that other island when he was a child. Last year they'd laughed at him, at Byrstada.

'What's this?' Ragna had asked, 'Cat's cradle?'

Leif had been new to the island then, and worried about what Dagfinn's sister might think of him. He'd endured her taunts for weeks, before realising that she treated everyone like that, until they had the wit to respond in kind. Astrid worked quietly beside him. Leif had hardly noticed her before, but since he'd heard she was going to marry Thorvald, he'd paid more attention to her. Sometimes she made dry remarks that most people, including Thorvald, ignored, and, listening, he realised to his surprise that she was laughing at them.

Astrid was relieved to be working with Leif. This was the first time she'd seen Olaf since she got back, and he'd given her one blank look, then gone to bind sheaves behind Bjarni. She was left with a sinking dread, not knowing how to approach him. She and Olaf might be going to live on the island together all their lives. Astrid looked across at Thorvald, but he was sharpening his sickle, and didn't notice. She wondered if he had forgotten already that he and Olaf had fought so violently.

Everyone stopped working for the morning meal and ate bread and cheese and blaand at the top of the rig. Kari fled from Eirik, who had pushed him into a ditch, and came to sit beside Ingrid, who began to plait a corn dolly for him. He watched with increasing interest.

'I'm not very good. He'll probably fall to pieces.'

'He looks all right to me,' said Astrid, looking over Ingrid's shoulder, and trying not to be aware of Olaf, who was sitting within earshot with his back to them, next to his brother.

'You should see the ones father makes,' Ingrid was saying. 'He used to make us all kinds of toys out of straw. He'll do you a better one, Kari, if you ask.'

Bjarni was sitting a little apart from Helgi's sons and his two nephews. They were arguing about the priest, but he was hardly listening. He had sown this crop with Einar, just as they had done together for twenty years. Next year it wouldn't be like that. Thirty-five years ago he and Einar had first followed the binders, their baskets round their necks, to pick up the gleanings. His father and his uncle Eirik had been the shearers then. Einar and he used to abandon their task to crawl inside the newbuilt stooks and hide. Sometimes they'd fight and the sheaves would topple over, and they'd be chased off the rig. Thorvald their father had been a hard man; his sons were adept at running away, and had supported one another from the very beginning.

Bjarni became aware of a small figure waiting patiently beside him. He looked up and saw Einar's son. Kari's face was muddy from the ditch, and he held a hank of corn stalks in his hand.

'Ingrid said you'd make me a corn dolly.'

Bjarni set down his mug, and took the corn from him. 'Watch then! Next time you can do it yourself.'

They all went back to work before their backs had had time to stiffen. Arne, on the other side of Bjarni, swung his sickle steadily. It was a fine day and a good harvest, and it was better making love every night in a bed, than snatching time with Ingrid in a sheep shelter. He'd have a child of his own in the spring. The first of many, perhaps. Arnessons. Arnesdottirs. He had no quarrel with any man, and a place in the world of his own. Yesterday he'd spoken with Bjarni.

'You'd better come with me to Hjaltland in June,' Bjarni had said. 'We have to see about a new boat, and you'll wish to see your father at the Thing.'

Ingrid and Jon followed Arne down the rig. Ingrid tied straws into bands, and Jon bound the sheaves together. Then they set up the sheaves in stooks, half a dozen together. Eirik and Kari chased each other in and out of the stooks, and Gerda, with her gleaning basket, shouted threats at the little boys as they squealed and dodged.

There was only a thin line of corn left standing, and the fieldmice were fleeing from its shelter. The shearers grasped the final handfuls, and as the last corn fell, the men straightened themselves painfully. Thorvald and Arne flung down their sickles. Bjarni wiped his carefully, and hung it from his belt. Then they turned back to help bind the remaining sheaves.

There was a tension in the field now. As soon as no corn was left standing, the women drew back, and stood at the edge of the rig with the children. Bjarni bound one sheaf and joined them. The young men worked fast. There was hardly any corn left lying. Astrid was remembering what had happened last year. The man to bind the last sheaf had been one of the crew, hired by Einar for the day to help. They'd caught him as he finished, pulled his trousers off, and beaten him with sheaves. She couldn't help hoping that this year it wouldn't be Thorvald. Or Olaf. Or Leif. She wouldn't mind if it were Arne. He'd never taken her message to Papey. She wondered if he knew what to expect. When she looked at him, he was binding his sheaf as fast as he could, his eyes roving anxiously round the field.

Possibly the men of Fridarey thought Jon would be fair game. He was binding his sheaf, apparently oblivious, humming to himself. Leif nudged Thorvald, and grinned. They drew nearer to him, but Jon threw down his sheaf and shook his head, pointing behind them, where Bjarni's row of corn lay cut.

Olaf was thinking his own thoughts, gathering together sheaf after sheaf, at the end of his row away from the rest. He knotted one more band, looked for the next row of cut corn to gather his sheaf, and found none. He looked up, blinking, and on the edges of his vision he saw them, a circle of blurred figures ready to close in.

At once he realised what they were at, and was ready. He let them come a little nearer, and at the last moment he dodged, ducking under the arms that reached to grab him. A hand brushed his back. Then he was away, running out of the corn, over green ground, over brown. He could hear them behind him as they sped across the turf and rutted track, most of them with strides much heavier than his. They were almost on him, then one by one they dropped back, panting.

But Olaf still ran, losing no speed until he was across the hill dyke, and the last shouts had died away behind him. He turned, his head cocked, listening. Not a sound. He trotted steadily on, over the hill and out of sight of the townland.

Olaf the scapegoat stood on the summit of the Vord facing north, and felt the beginnings of a wind on his face. He spread his arms wide and careered down the slope, then up to the north coast of the island. They would all have gone back to their own concerns now: harvests, weddings, churches, ships. By the time the feast was ready they'd have forgotten all about him. He would be back in time to get his share of food, not before.

Below him he could hear the first waves breaking against the rocks. He gazed out towards the hills of Hjaltland that he would never see from here, and felt a breeze like ice against his face. He sniffed it, and caught the first breath of snow.

A harsh yelping cry came down on the wind, and he turned his face towards it, straining his eyes. The geese sank lower, swooping in over the island so close above the cliff that even Olaf could see them. Their wings made a sound like a rush of air through an open door. He watched their straggling V pass over him and break, as they circled down to Gullvatn as they did every year. If the tales men told were true, they'd come down on the wind from the far north, away from the winter that already held Island in its grip.

Part Nine

Islanders

Chapter 61

Two islanders stood in the shelter of Sula's shed at the top of the Nordhavn, waiting for a shower to pass. Bjarni had come to see how the Sula had weathered the season, and discovered his nephew aboard her on the same errand.

'I was just checking the mast step,' said Olaf. 'Snorri and I put those bands round it last winter. I wanted to see how they'd held.'

'Are you working on her again this winter?'

'If Snorri wants me.'

Bjarni and Olaf were not used to talking to one another, but neither regarded the other with any ill feeling, and each wanted to make the fact plain. So they stood in the lee of the shed, exchanging such remarks as occurred to them. There were still drag marks above the high tide line from three days ago, when they had hauled up the Sula. The crew had already started work on the ship, scraping down the hull and hanging the sails and ropes up in the shed ready for cleaning.

Bjarni glanced out to the stack, and into the narrow stretch of open sea visible beyond. A shape was looming in the mist, a shadow where no shadow should be. 'Look!'

Olaf peered out to sea. Bjarni had hold of his sleeve, and was clutching his arm just as Thorvald might have done.

'What can you see?' asked Olaf, after waiting a moment. Thorvald would have told him without being asked.

'Eh?' Bjarni remembered who he was speaking to, and said, 'I'm not sure. Wait!'

The shadow drifted inward, detaching itself from the surrounding mist. It took shape: a slender prow, sweeping back to a wide belly, low in the water. Two lines of oars, rising and falling, half smothered by shreds of mist.

'A longship!'

'What?' Bjarni felt Olaf's arm tense under his hand. 'A longship? Here?'

She was close to the stack now, gliding towards the shore. Bjarni caught a gleam of colour out of the grey, a painted dragon prow.

'Should we warn the island?'

Bjarni stared into the mist, but there were no further shadows, only the one ship, no longer wraith-like, passing the stack into clear water.

'I see it!'

Bjarni let go his nephew's sleeve. 'Is your boat ready for sea?'

'Of course.' Olaf was about to run to his noost, but Bjarni held him back. 'It might be a raid,' he said. 'I doubt it. There's been none here for over sixty years. My guess is it's Dagfinn, or news of Dagfinn. It's a risk. Shall we row out?'

Olaf looked out at the ship. He could see a blurred brown shape, no detail, but a curve like a swan's neck, a line that satisfied the soul. Irrationally, he wanted to touch it. He grinned at Bjarni, and ran for his boat. The two of them launched it without a word, and rowed out into a choppy sea.

The dragon prow gleamed red and gold. Bjarni could see men aboard, some at the oars, others standing in a group aft, by the helmsmen.

'We'll keep our distance. See what they say.'

'They can't ride us down in here.'

'No, they'd have to shoot us.'

There was a shout across the water. 'Bjarni! Bjarni!'

Bjarni grinned at Olaf's back. 'What did I tell you?'

'It's Dagfinn!' Olaf raised his oar to turn, and hit Bjarni's oar with a clunk.

'Wait! Let them ship their oars first, then we can come in alongside.'

It was a good thing Thorvald wasn't there, thought Olaf; he'd resent being given orders on his own boat. Olaf smiled to himself, and waited patiently until his uncle gave the word.

The longship was much lower in the water than the Sula. Her crew must have lowered the sail just outside the haven, and now the yard projected beyond the sides of the boat, so Bjarni and Olaf had to come in behind it. As soon as the freeboard was low enough to hold on to, Bjarni gripped the gunwale. A figure detached itself from the group of men aboard, and seized his hand. Dagfinn's face was in shadow under the hood of his boat cloak. He moved stiffly.

'What is it man? You're hurt!'

'Never mind that!' Dagfinn's head was swathed in a dirty bandage, one eye hidden. He nodded to Olaf. 'It's good to see you both! I've a chest here. Can we get it ashore?'

Bjarni greeted the ship's crew with traditional words of welcome, and a marked lack of enthusiasm.

The captain replied. 'No, we'll sail while we can. We won't come ashore.'

'You don't need anything? Water?'

The man shook his head. 'We're fresh out of Gareksey. It's late in the year to be at sea, and we'll be as well to get to Hjaltland while it's weather.'

'Can you manage the chest?' asked Dagfinn.

Bjarni touched Olaf on the shoulder. 'Your boat. Can we take that?'

Olaf looked doubtfully at the sea chest that two seamen held ready. 'Not with Dagfinn as well. We'll come back for it.'

'Take the chest first,' said Dagfinn. 'Come back for me.'

'Not stupid,' muttered Bjarni, as they took the chest aboard.

As soon as they left the longship for the second time, the ranks of oars were dipped again, someone shouted farewell, and Dagfinn waved his hand.

'Where are they bound for?'

'Better not ask,' said Dagfinn. 'Einar wouldn't approve.'

Olaf bent to his oars and waited for Bjarni to speak. Bjarni said nothing. Olaf cleared his throat to tell Dagfinn Einar was dead, but the words failed to come. The moment passed.

By the time they were ashore the ship had disappeared into the mist. Were it not for the presence of Dagfinn and his chest, the whole episode might have been a dream. Dagfinn didn't help them beach the boat, but stood rigidly on the shore and waited, while they put her back in her noost.

'Shall we put your chest in Sula's shed?' Olaf had to repeat his question, as Dagfinn seemed not to have heard him.

'Oh yes,' said Dagfinn the second time, but he didn't seem interested. 'Leave it there for now.'

Dagfinn followed them to the top of the beach as they carried his chest up. Now his hood was thrown back, they could see how the bandage was padded over his eye, so that half his face was hidden. The bandage was dirty, and stained with sea water. His thick hair had been cut short in a ragged line which barely reached to his neck. His beard too had been cut back close to his face, giving him a naked look, more vulnerable than a man should be.

'Head wound, I see,' said Bjarni. 'Sword, was it?'

'I expect so. I didn't get the chance to examine the weapon very closely.'

They were walking slowly along the top of the beach. The path home stretched across the hill.

'I may have to take it slowly,' said Dagfinn. 'Don't wait if you're in a hurry.' He stopped before the upward slope.

'Olaf, catch him!'

Olaf leapt to Dagfinn's side, and the two of them caught him as he reeled and fell. His face was grey, his one eye closed. Bjarni crouched over him, holding his wrist, listening for a pulse. Then he laid Dagfinn's arm gently across his chest.

'He's not dead is he?'

'No,' said Bjarni. 'But there are more wounds on him, I think. I should have guessed. You run to Byrstada as fast as you can. Tell them what's happened. Get them out here with a litter.'

Olaf turned to go.

'Oh, and Olaf, bring a blanket. The man's soaked through. You haven't a cloak here, have you? Never mind. I'll do my best to keep him warm. Run, then!'

Dagfinn was home. He'd never expected to be here again. He lay on his back on the sleeping platform at Byrstada, listening. The wind whined round the corners of the house. He could hear the others talking on the other side of the hangings they'd set up in order to give him some peace. Ragna's voice was still penetrating.

She laughed loudly, and he winced, but he wouldn't want it different. He wouldn't want anything here different.

What a way to come home! Carried on a litter, unable even to greet his family, let alone his crew. He'd been aware of nothing but a confusion of presences, voices floating vaguely into his consciousness, hands lifting him, carrying him indoors. They must all have seen him like that, as helpless as a baby. Bjarni had been there. He had one lucid memory, after they'd come ashore, of Bjarni's face above him, framed by a misty sky, asking him if he were cold. It seemed an unlikely question for one man to ask another. There should have been a feast, and here he was, lying on his back, alone in the dark, while they did their best to keep quiet for him. Dagfinn had never lain on a sickbed in his life, until the day he had been struck down.

It wasn't as if he had good news to bring them either. He'd not brought shame to his island, he'd played his own part as well as he could, and that was something. But the campaign had ended tragically, and he would have to give them the whole tale. If he had been fit to fight until the end, he should have died a hero's death, defending the man he'd chosen for leader until all hope was gone. That hadn't happened; instead, in the final battle, Dagfinn had lain helpless among the wounded in the ships, unable even to stand. He would have chosen to die then, if the chance had been offered to him. Better dead than crippled.

At least he knew now he'd be able to stand again. But perhaps not well enough for a warrior. And his eye . . . he could remember it all, but there was no recapturing the agony, lying in a heaving ship, with a pain piercing his head like a knife blade. He'd fallen in and out of consciousness, coming round each time to the fact that he was half blind. The knowledge and the pain were inescapable. An eye lost, and not much wisdom exchanged for it either, unless it were wisdom for a man to know the limits of his own luck.

The spectre of blindness still haunted him. As he had done countless times in the last weeks, Dagfinn cautiously opened his one eye. As so many times before, there was a moment's panic before he realised it was night, the room dim in the shadow of the hangings. The hanging didn't quite reach to the rafters, being suspended by a rope that sagged in the middle, and he could see the firelight on the other side playing on the beam. He watched it, and let his eye drift along the beam. He knew every inch of the

Byrstada roof. He had lain here as a child, rebelling against sleep, straining his ears to hear the talk from the hearth side. There was the same big knot halfway along the beam, the same sagging turfs between the rafters, the same whalebone arch at the gable.

He made out Rolf's voice among the murmurs from the hall. No doubt Rolf would want to tell him how he'd managed with Sula this summer. The idea exhausted him. He didn't want to face his brother yet. It was not Rolf's presence that he craved.

The pain was coming back. It never left him alone for long. Slowly it invaded his brain like the thrust of a lance. He closed his eye, and stretched out, waiting to bear it. There were shapes growing in front of his closed eyes, both of them, green and black shapes like reflections left by the sun. Except reflections did not hurt, and this was agony. He lay quite still. There was a whine in his ears like the wind. He could still feel the heave of the sea under him. The pain grew worse. Thoughts fled before it. He wished someone would come, but he would never, so long as he had any will to resist, call out for help. Silently Dagfinn fought his demons, lying flat on his back, only the rigidity of his half hidden face betraying his struggle.

He must have drifted into a doze at last. When he woke again the hall was silent, and the firelight had ceased to flicker. He was stiff from being stretched out. It was difficult to move; there were half healed scars across his chest, and a long flesh wound down his thigh. Someone – Gunnhild, he realised now – had put salve on his wounds, and certainly they felt less hot. It still hurt to move. Dagfinn put his arm out, and half sat up.

Someone stirred. There was a slight movement across the floor, and he was aware of a human presence next to him.

'Dagfinn?'

It was only the breath of a whisper, close by his head, but he knew at once who was there. His heart leapt. He hadn't dared to think about it, let alone to ask. It wouldn't have surprised him to learn that he was never to hear that voice again.

'Is that you?'

'Hush!' whispered Leif. 'Yes, it's me.'

Dagfinn reached out his hand, and, sure enough, a hand met his. Leif's clasp was cool and dry, unlike his own. 'I came as soon as they'd gone to bed,' breathed Leif. 'Is there anything you want?'

Dagfinn was slow to answer, and then his reply came as softly as Leif had whispered to him. 'Not now.'

Presently Leif shifted uncomfortably on the floor, without letting go.

'You're cold. Why don't you lie down?'

'There's not room.'

Painfully, Dagfinn moved up closer to the wall. Leif stretched out on the platform next to him, his head propped on his elbow.

'I thought you might have gone,' whispered Dagfinn at last.

'No,' said Leif, and touched Dagfinn's cheek. 'Why should I do that?'

'I left you.'

'So? Now you're back.'

'Defeated,' whispered Dagfinn harshly. 'And not so pretty to look at now, either.'

'It's not important.' Leif's lips brushed Dagfinn's hot forehead.

Dagfinn stirred. 'I don't know what I deserve. I don't think it's this. Why don't you lie down, get some sleep?'

'I dare not,' whispered Leif. 'They'll come and look after you again as soon as it's dawn.'

Dagfinn was silent. Perhaps Leif thought he was asleep; certainly Dagfinn's sudden whisper made him start. 'Leif, go! Go back. I'm no use to you. Go back! You don't need me, not now.'

'No, I won't do that.'

'I left you.'

'Yes,' admitted Leif. 'And in my heart, perhaps I left you. But not any more.'

'The more fool you. I'll get no better.'

'Maybe not,' said Leif. 'It makes no difference.'

Chapter 62

'Don't tread on the chicks,' called Ingrid.

Gudrun stopped. 'I can't see. Where are they?'

'Everywhere. Shut the door, it's the smoke.'

'I'm just going to. Where's Ragna?'

'Here.' Ragna followed her in, and slammed the door after her. A moment later it opened again, and Thorhalla came in.

The rain was lashing down outside, and water dripped steadily into soapstone bowls where the sodden roof had started to leak. But the fire glowed, and the air was warm and heavy with peat. Einar's dog lay stretched out along the length of the hearth, twitching a little in response to the women's voices. Astrid and Ingrid had brought in piles of fleeces, and heaped them up on the benches. The women from Byrstada settled down in the free spaces between, and took out the long combs they had brought with them, ready to comb out the wool for spinning.

'Is Dagfinn any better?' Ingrid asked Ragna.

Ragna scowled. 'He's all right,' she said.

'He gets headaches,' said Gudrun. 'Gunnhild says no wonder. It was a bad head wound, besides losing an eye.'

'They were saying at Leogh it's an ill fate,' said Thorhalla. 'But if so I'm sure I don't know who brought it.'

'I'm sure you don't,' said Ragna, mimicking her tone. 'So you'd better keep quiet about it, hadn't you?'

Thorhalla pouted, and pulled off a hank of wool from the fleece beside her. 'Well, I do know something,' she said sulkily. 'The priest has been warning people against witchcraft.'

'Hush!' said Ingrid. The outer door had opened again, a cloud of smoke billowed out into the room, and under it they saw two pairs of feet.

'Don't tread on the chicks!'

'Where are they?' asked Ingebjorg and Gunnhild simultaneously.

'Everywhere.'

The others moved up, leaving them the best seats at the hearth. Ingebjorg and Gunnhild took out their combs and set to work at once, taking one handful of wool after another, combing them through each way, then twisting them between the comb backs into a roll ready for spinning. Astrid found weaving much more interesting than the endless preparation of the wool, but she sorted the combed wool carefully into different shades, blacks, greys, browns and white, ready to put in the right piles.

'We should have got someone to come in and play the harp,' remarked Ragna. 'Leif played at the combing at Byrstada last winter, remember?'

There was silence after this tactless remark. Bjarni was known to be the best harpist on the island, and this was his household. Today he had gone to the mill with the rest of the men, now that there was enough water in the burn at Finniquoy to start grinding the corn.

'We could ask Astrid to play her pipe,' suggested Ingebjorg. 'I should enjoy that.'

Astrid was twisting her wool between the combs, and caught unawares she dropped it. Thorvald must talk to his mother. She'd never imagined him doing that.

'What pipe?' asked Ragna.

'Not yet. Later, maybe,' said Astrid. Suddenly an image of the journey had come back to her, just herself and Thorvald. Now she spent her days among all these women and she hardly ever saw him. She would be married to him soon, but it would somehow make everything public in a way she didn't want. She wanted to keep something to herself.

'But what pipe?' asked Ragna again.

'The one I bought in Skalavagr,' answered Astrid reluctantly.

'Skalavagr? I thought you went to Papey?'

A flurry of rain blew in and hissed on the hearthstones. The dog whined in its sleep.

'I'm never going abroad,' announced Thorhalla. 'I'd hate to go away.'

'You may change your mind,' said Gunnhild.

Thorhalla shook her head.

Astrid was wondering what else Thorvald had said to his mother. In a few weeks she'd be living under the same roof as Ingebjorg. Thorvald would be away half the year, but Ingebjorg would always be there, every single day. Ingebjorg had always treated Astrid with an almost formal courtesy, but she could hardly do that if they had to do everything together. Astrid stopped combing her wool, and stared into the fire, ignoring the conversation that buzzed around her.

Ingebjorg's voice broke in on her thoughts. 'What do you think, Astrid?'

She started. 'What do I think about what?'

'She's not been listening,' said Ragna. 'Daydreaming about Thorvald, I suppose. Tell her again.'

'We were talking about the priest,' said Ingebjorg. 'It seems he's questioning people on the island about witchcraft, asking if we make spells, and so forth. You have more experience of churchmen than we have. What might he be seeking?'

'What sort of spells?'

'I wish we knew,' said Gunnhild, and as she spoke Astrid realised it was Gunnhild's unusually agitated voice that had been the background to her thoughts. 'He speaks of devils. I know there was gossip all over the island about the gale when . . . after the Lammas feast. But no one raised that wind, I know it. People will say anything when something happens they don't understand. They look for someone to blame. But a priest should know better than to listen to that kind of thing, surely?'

Astrid had heard this kind of talk before. She knew what the consequences could be, and she didn't want to tell them.

'Did they talk about witchcraft in Dyflin?'

'Yes,' said Astrid unhappily. 'Sometimes.'

'Astrid,' said Ingebjorg, 'if you do know anything that would shed light on this priest's attitude, I think you'd better tell us.'

Astrid looked round at them. 'I've heard this,' she said at last. 'They say witchcraft is a heresy, a crime against the church. Anathema. But I don't really know what that means. But when something bad happens, like when a well was poisoned in Dyflin, it gets talked about. Some people said the Jews had done it; others said it was witchcraft, and that some woman had made a spell. She had a grudge against a man in that part of the city, so everyone who used that well got sick, and some people died. They said then the witch should be burned.'

Ingebjorg looked sombre. 'It's a frightening thing, when the unforgivable sin has no name. Surely it only serves to put everyone in terror of their own ignorance?'

'No sin is unforgivable,' declared Gunnhild. 'I don't believe that's what the church says either.'

'You don't get forgiven if you don't repent,' said Thorhalla, without raising her eyes.

'Then you'd better start repenting now, and shut up,' said Ragna, 'Or the trows will come and get you.'

Thorhalla sat up indignantly. 'Me? I haven't done anything. At least, I never raised any gales.'

'Meaning someone else here did?' Thorhalla cowered back as Ragna leapt to her feet, and pulled her up by her plait of hair. Thorhalla screamed. 'You'd better explain yourself,' said Ragna grimly.

'Ragna, leave the child alone!' demanded Gunnhild. 'If there was an evil fate that night, we're all involved. It won't help looking for someone to blame.'

'But is the priest looking for someone to blame?' There was a crease of worry across Ingrid's brow. 'Surely not! He never knew Einar, why should he want him avenged? If he asks anyone, he'll find that no one had a grudge against him either.'

'People talk,' said Ingebjorg. 'He's visited at Leogh. You can imagine what he might have heard there.'

'But why should he regard it?' persisted Ingrid. 'He's a man of God.'

'It's his job to look for evil,' said Gunnhild. 'He may have a different idea of it than you or I.'

'She's right,' said Ingebjorg. 'It's dangerous, looking for a scapegoat. If it goes on, someone will end up suffering.'

They all crossed their fingers. 'There hasn't been a killing on this island in eighteen years,' said Ragna.

'Who's talking about a killing!' exclaimed Gunnhild. 'You'll tempt a fate, Ragna. Think what you say before you speak out loud!'

'I spoke to the priest,' said Gudrun suddenly. 'He was kind to me. He never spoke of blame. All he said was that sheep without a shepherd will stray into dangerous places, and that this island had grown far from God.'

'There's nothing wrong with our sheep!'

'He means our souls, stupid.'

Ingrid looked indignant. 'Then he should say so. What right has he to criticise, anyway? It's not his island.'

'But that's not the point,' said Gudrun impatiently. 'We need to be careful. My father says so too. We know that no one raised that wind. But everyone here did what they could to save this baby, and do you think I'm not grateful? It was Gunnhild who made sure of that. We have knowledge and skills among ourselves that we can't do without. That's not a sin, but it seems it might become one.'

'What do you think, Astrid?' asked Ingebjorg again. 'Do you think we're making too much of it?'

Astrid forgot to be shy of Ingebjorg, now that she realised how important the question was. 'No, I don't think you are. It seems to me now there are certain kinds of knowledge that have to be kept secret. People can't do without them. They needed them in Dyflin just as they do here. I think they managed by just keeping everything in its right place. Some things belong to the church, and can be talked about to the priests. Other things don't; they have to be kept quiet, but they still have to happen. People do what they can.'

'But they go to confession,' objected Gudrun. 'Aren't they supposed to confess everything?'

Astrid shrugged. 'Maybe they can't.'

'That makes sense to me,' said Gunnhild. 'Life's not so simple that you can tell the same story to everyone. Each of us has many stories, they're all true, but we have to tell the right one to the right person. There's no use pretending that there's only one tale which takes account of everything.'

Ingebjorg hadn't taken her eyes off Astrid. 'What did they do to the woman whom they thought had poisoned the well?'

Astrid had hoped no one would ask. 'They burned her.'

'Do you think that was justified?'

'I don't know. My father said there's no knowing what makes water turn bad. It can happen without anyone doing anything, but it could easily be done out of spite. There's no telling.'

'We're speaking of dangerous matters,' said Ingebjorg. 'We don't have much experience of priests here. But sometimes a priest is known to be unlucky.'

'At sea they are,' said Gudrun. 'The crew didn't want to take that priest aboard. A priest brings an evil fate on a ship, everyone knows that.'

'Dagfinn wouldn't have done it,' said Ragna.

Gudrun was about to argue, but Gunnhild forestalled her. 'Does Dagfinn know about the priest?'

'The priest visited him,' said Ragna.

'Dagfinn told Rolf a priest could be a dangerous blessing,' put in Thorhalla. 'I heard him.'

'Well, Dagfinn has nothing to be afraid of,' said Ragna. 'He has no secrets. It seems that we do. So what do we do about it?'

'We have to look after our own,' said Gunnhild.

'It's not that difficult,' said Ingebjorg. 'You can't imagine what it was like in the Orkneyjar after the Earls' wars. There were factions everywhere. I learned very young that it was dangerous to say too much. It would be a solace if one could confide in a priest the way a child confides in its mother, but life's not that simple. It's foolish to expect anyone to act out of character. The priest represents the church. He's not a midwife.' She ignored Ragna's chuckle, and carried on. 'We can't expect him to see things the way we do; we'd be foolish to think he would. There are parts of our lives that have nothing to do with him. We just have to know what face to show him. It's not dishonest. We are Christian folk and we need him. But that's not all we are. We have to remember that.'

'That's all right,' replied Ragna, 'as long as no little mischief makers with long tongues go round making trouble.'

'I'm sure we have none such here,' said Ingebjorg calmly. 'Anyone who might be tempted has only to ask herself if she'll ever need a midwife, and she'll see the answer for herself.'

Dagfinn sat in the high seat at Byrstada, surrounded by his family, his neighbours and his men. Only Einar was missing; everyone else seemed to be accustomed already to his absence. Dagfinn's legs were still uncertain and he seemed unable to shake off the heave of the sea, even after nearly a week. His head ached persistently, and the effort of taking part in an animated scene with only half his vision was exhausting, quite apart from the pain which never left him completely, even in sleep. But he had had enough of lying on his back, so he chose to ignore these things. There was much to be done, even by a man who hadn't regained his full strength.

He had been embarrassed at first to appear among them. Dagfinn knew that he was vain, but he had always had reason to be. The loss of his looks was a severe blow to him now he was beginning to feel better. Gunnhild had replaced the clumsy bandages with a band that went once round his head and covered his eye with a pad of soft cloth. The wound was still not quite healed; Gunnhild said that was because the sea water had kept it damp too long. The skin round it was badly bruised, and felt puffy under his fingers. He hadn't dared feel the eye socket itself. If the healed wound were too ugly, he would wear a patch over it. His hair and beard would grow again, but he felt ridiculous appearing in front of them all with his head so bare. One of his shipmates had cut his hair off for him with his own knife while he was still half conscious, lying in the bottom of the ship. It had been matted with blood, and there'd been no choice about it, they said. It was the only way they could get the wound clean.

They had brought his chest up from the Nordhavn, but he had refused to allow anyone to open it until now. All their eyes were on him as he took the key from its chain round his neck, and turned it in the lock. The lid creaked back, its hinges stiff with salt. Dagfinn took out a grey bundle and tossed it to his sister.

'Washing.'

Ragna threw it into a corner.

Dagfinn delved into the chest again and drew out a roll of heavy cloth. 'English broadcloth,' he said, passing it to Gudrun. Ragna and Thorhalla crowded over her to look. There was another roll of cloth wrapped in a piece of linen. Dagfinn took it out carefully, and after a moment's hesitation passed it to Ragna. 'Not for rolling in the hay,' he said. 'You can keep it for your wedding.'

So Rolf had told Dagfinn. Ragna looked at her two brothers speculatively and decided to say nothing. She unwrapped the linen and her eyes widened. There was a thin roll inside, not very long. Ragna unrolled a little of it and spread it out. 'Oh,' she said softly, bereft of words.

'Silk,' explained Dagfinn carelessly.

It was pale gold, and it shone in the firelight as if it were wet. Ragna ran her fingers over it, and it seemed to change colour as she moved it. It felt like spun water.

'Thank you,' she said at last.

Dagfinn nodded, and watched them passing the silk round and admiring it. His head hurt, and his attention was straying again. Once in a harbour tavern he had seen hair that colour, hanging straight and smooth, changing colour in the uneven light. And when at last he had put it to the touch, it had been silken under his fingers.

'Dagfinn?'

He sat up, and opened his eye. 'Perhaps you're too tired?' said Rolf.

'Of course not!'

'You didn't buy that in the Sudreyjar,' said Gudrun.

'Let's hear the story,' repeated Ragna, while her fingers still stroked the strange material.

The pain was back behind his eye socket, but he would never have told them that. After all, the first part of his story was worth the telling. His family and his crew all hung on his words. He told them how the five longships had swept down from the Sudreyjar, already loaded with stolen riches, how they had encountered the English merchant ships off Abergwaun, how the English had tried to turn close to the wind and failed, how their heavy ships had wallowed like stranded whales until Svein and his men boarded them. As for the cargo of broadcloth that had been on its way to Dyflin, they could see it for themselves. He told them about the rich monasteries on the east coast of Irland, and the fat pickings to be had from them. It had been nearly harvest, which was earlier in those parts, and in spite of what folk said about civil war in Irland, it had been no hardship for the pirates to live off the land. King Henry had asked for the Dyflin defences to be strengthened, but his authority was shaken since the killing of Thomas in Cantwaraborg, and Svein and his men had made such efforts as the English had made look foolish. The pirates had been within a mile or two of the city, and as far as treasure went, you could hardly say the English kept their wealth well defended. But Dagfinn had never sighted Dyflin; they had left the ships too far behind to advance further. They couldn't have carried more anyway, so they'd retreated, and sailed back to Ljodhus in triumph.

When they returned to the Orkneyjar for the hay harvest, they sailed into Kirkjavagr with broadcloth pinned to the sails, and with the sun shining, the fleet looked glorious enough for a king's crusade. They had left Hakon the Earl's son in Kirkjavagr, then sailed back to Gareksey, where they had feasted after the harvest.

'Gareksey!' exclaimed Rolf. 'You were as close to us as that!'

'There was a feast,' Dagfinn continued. 'The Earl came to it, and his son too. It was almost as grand as a Byrstada harvest supper. The Earl listened to the story of our summer's raiding, and then he talked to Svein about it. I overheard what he said.'

'Sitting between them, were you?' asked Bjarni suspiciously.

'This is what I was told he'd said: "Svein, it was glorious, but it can't go on. Raiding belongs to the old days, and we're neither of us as young as we were. There's something to be said for this new fashion of living in peace on one's own land. You must have treasure enough stored away. You could have peace and riches in your old age. As it is, you don't seem likely to have any old age at all." '

'Very sensible,' said Bjarni, 'For an Earl. The man should have been a farmer.'

'Svein said: "Fine words and friendly ones, my lord. You've always given good advice. I don't know that you always brought us much peace."

' "That's my business," said the Earl, "Just now I'm telling you yours."

' "Very good of you," said Svein. "Very well, I'll do it. I'm not as young as I was, and war is a demanding trade for any man. But I'm making one more trip this autumn, and it will be as glorious as my spring trip. It'll be the last one. After that I'll be a pirate no more."

'The Earl wasn't too sure about that. "I hope it will bring glory," he said, "and not death." '

'Dagfinn,' interrupted Rolf. 'Are you all right?'

Dagfinn jerked himself upright again. He could feel sweat on his forehead, and hoped they couldn't see it. For a few moments he had forgotten himself, carried away on the tide of his tale, forgetting even the ending that had to come. They had not heard the news here. Only Rolf had heard the whole story, when Dagfinn had blurted it out, half-drugged, lying on his sickbed while his brother knelt at his side. Dagfinn felt a vast weariness engulf him.

'Do you want to lie down again?' whispered Rolf.

Perhaps it would suit Rolf all too well if he did. Rolf had run the ship to suit himself all summer, and had arranged Ragna's marriage without consulting anyone. The fact that it was a good match didn't alter his presumption. He had brought that priest to the island without referring the matter to anybody. And Dagfinn suspected he'd had some hand in this Shirva lawsuit that everyone had been so anxious to describe to him. At least that seemed to have been resolved. Thorvald and Bjarni seemed quite content with one another's company today, whatever anyone said. If Rolf had been hatching quarrels there, he'd obviously failed. Dagfinn made an effort, and forced himself to sit up. 'It's nothing a measure of ale won't cure,' he announced. 'And look to our guests while you're about it!'

Leif was at his side, proffering a cup. Dagfinn permitted himself one glance. Leif's face was impassive, but his normally pale cheeks were flushed red. Dagfinn knew that look; either Leif had been drinking, or something had moved him. Dagfinn looked away, and took the cup. Leif's fingers brushed his as he gave it, and then he slipped back to his place among the crew. Dagfinn sipped his ale. The good part of the story was over, and the rest seemed worse than meaningless. What was the point of a tale, when that which lay at the heart of his life must remain forever silent, not part of any story? Leif was sitting with his head close to Skuli's, listening to some private joke. Skuli stopped speaking, and Leif laughed out loud. He seemed as remote now from his captain as the stars.

'Will you give us the rest of your tale now?' asked Bjarni. 'It can wait though, if you prefer.'

They must be craving for news. It would be cruel not to give them their answer.

'I can't make a proper tale of it,' he told them. 'But this is my news, for what it's worth. I fear you have no cause to welcome it.

'We set sail for Dyflin again this autumn. Having come so close, Svein was determined to finish the job. He took seven longships this time, and once again Hakon Haraldsson came with us. We went back to the Sudreyjar first, but we got little plunder there. After our raids in the spring they were ready for us. So we went on to Irland.

'This isn't an important part of the story, but we made landfall some distance north of Dyflin, and raided a small settlement on the coast. They must have had word of our coming. There were armed men waiting for us. A party of us had gone foraging. It's fertile country, full of trees, some of them three times as tall as a man. Among the trees it's uncanny, full of strange sounds, and you can't see any distance at all. We were cut off and ambushed by a party of warriors on horseback. The only way to get back to the ships was to fight our way through. We dropped our spoils, and tried to make a break for it, but the trees are like an enchantment. They trip you and block the way, you can't tell where you are or where you're going. A man's like a fly in a web in one of those forests. A man on a horse rode me down, and caught me a blow with his sword as he rode over me. I lost my helmet, and got myself this wound you see.

'That's the last I knew about it. I'd been fighting hand to hand before that, and lost a good deal of blood. I was lucky to be left for dead, and luckier still that later on Svein sent a party to search for us. I was surprised afterwards when they said we'd been within half a mile of the ships all the time. It's the trees that put you wrong. As it was, a couple of men managed to get through to the ships, and then the others came back and found me. The rest were lying dead where they were cut down.

'After that I was out of the campaign. I'd have been glad then to be home at Byrstada, I can tell you.' Dagfinn paused. There was no point telling them what it was like lying wounded, soaked with salt water, frozen and feverish by turns, terrified he'd lost his sight, tossing on a heaving sea, falling in and out of consciousness with no idea where they were or what was happening. His companions had treated him as well as they could. There was extra water for the wounded men, but never enough. In his fever he'd thought he was dying of thirst. But there was no need to tell them any of that.

'We sailed on,' said Dagfinn shortly, 'and this time we did get as far as Dyflin.'

Eirik's sons had the same thought at the same moment. They both looked at Astrid, sitting silent between Ingrid and Bjarni. She was looking at the fire, her face white and pinched. Olaf watched her helplessly, his hands clasped on his knees. She must still have friends in Dyflin, kin perhaps. A moment later Thorvald got up, and edged his way in beside her.

North of Dyflin, Astrid was thinking, the woods stretched down to the river. At this time of year the leaves would be red and gold, the river just visible through half naked branches. Brown leaves floating down a broad river, grey city walls beyond. She was glad of Thorvald's presence, although he was one of them. He took her hand, under cover of her skirt, and held it, regardless of the fact that Bjarni was watching.

'They took the people of the town completely by surprise,' continued Dagfinn. 'They were right inside the walls before anyone realised they were there. They took plunder, and the English never even tried to resist. The new governor surrendered without putting up a fight. He just agreed to pay Svein everything he asked for. You'd think the English would have been keeping a sharper watch out for trouble after our raid in the summer. After all, they've only held the city for a year. I wouldn't like to live in Dyflin these days.'

Did they ring the bells again, wondered Astrid, as they had rung in warning last year? St. Colum's, St. Michael's, St. John's, Christchurch, St. Olaf's by the harbour. The men of Irland will suffer a grief that will never grow old in the minds of men. I'll never see Dyflin again, she told herself, and it seems there'll never be peace for the ones left behind.

'So Svein of Orkney declared himself governor of Dyflin, and appointed men of his own to take charge there. The English swore on oath that they'd keep to the agreement. But they were English, not Norse, and perhaps that explains what I'm about to tell you.'

There was no sound in the hall.

'Svein and his men came back to the ships. They'd agreed to go back in the morning and take over the town. We camped that night further down the estuary. I was glad to get ashore at last, and feel the warmth of a fire again. I wish I could tell you more firsthand, but I was feverish still, and not as aware as I'd like to have been of what they were saying around me.'

Dagfinn glanced at his audience. His eye ached with the effort. No need to tell them how little he had cared, either, for news of the taking of Dyflin, or for anything but the terrible burning agony inside his head. A man lying wounded and mutilated longs for nothing but home, and an end to the constant pain and movement. But that would be a coward's tale.

'We'd agreed with the governors of the town that Svein should choose hostages to take home with him. None of us suspected anything, for the victory had been fully acknowledged, and binding oaths had been sworn afterwards.'

Astrid felt Thorvald's grip on her hand grow tighter.

'But that night the town governors ordered deep pits to be dug just inside the city gates, and more along the streets where they expected Svein to march in with his men. They hid armed men in the buildings round about, and covered the pits with thin planks which would collapse under the weight of a man. They disguised their traps with earth and straw.'

'What then?' demanded Bjarni. 'What then, Dagfinn?'

Dagfinn was very weary. 'Svein and his men came to the city gates next morning. The Dyfliners formed a crowd, lining the route, so that the way to the pits was clear. Svein and his men suspected nothing. They entered triumphantly, and the leaders fell right into the pits. The English rushed to bar the gates. They drew their weapons before our men had time to defend themselves. Svein and all his men were slaughtered.

'That's all,' said Dagfinn, unable to hide his exhaustion. 'Luckily we were aboard again, and ready to embark. We'd been waiting to row up the estuary into the city harbour. Instead, we were warned in time, and those of us that were left, nearly all wounded men, had just strength enough to take one ship and turn north, to save ourselves, if not the honour of our expedition.'

In Dagfinn's hall there was silence. Thorvald looked over Astrid's bent head, and met Bjarni's eyes.

'It's what Einar always said,' whispered Thorvald. 'There are no pirates left in the islands now.'

'No,' said Bjarni. 'Svein Asleifarson was the last of his kind. There's nothing to be done now but make a story of it.'

Hot metal hissed as it touched cold water. Steam rose and wreathed upward, vanishing into the darkness under the roof. There was very little light, except for the fire where the charcoal burned red, whitehot at its centre.

Olaf lifted the cooled metal from the water butt, and examined it in the firelight. He touched it cautiously, and, finding it merely warm, transferred it from the tongs to his hand. Peering closely, he couldn't even see a crack now where the blade had been broken. He laid the spade down on the stone surface beside him.

'You can file it down later,' said Snorri. 'There's a peat spade to do as well. Over there. Bring it over, will you?'

Olaf looked round. Away from the fire, the smithy was hidden behind a solid wall of darkness. He'd never worked the hot metal himself before; now he discovered it had left him isolated in a world of fire and shadow.

'Where?' asked Olaf.

'There. Can't you see it?'

Olaf knew this had to come. 'No,' he said. He was no use after all, and he couldn't hide it. Snorri was hidden in the enclosing dark. Olaf stared at nothing, a sinking fear in his stomach. He heard Snorri moving, crossing the smithy with the limping gait that Olaf knew so well. There was the scrape of metal on stone, then Snorri was coming back again. Something cold was pressed into Olaf's hand. 'Here you are then. That's the blade. See if you can work this one without me saying anything.'

Turning back to the fire, Olaf felt a wave of heat break against his face and through his shirt. Drops of sweat trickled down his back. He laid down the tongs for a moment and stripped off his shirt. The heat meeting his skin made him gasp. Snorri was working the bellows, pumping steadily just as Olaf had learned to do for him. Olaf grasped the broken tushkar blade in the tongs, and held it in the centre of the fire. He was close enough to see every detail. Slowly the metal changed colour, from grey to red, then red almost to white.

'Try it now.'

It was so hot it was all Olaf could do to reach out with the tongs.

'Hammer.' Snorri held the tool out to him. Olaf placed the hot blade across the anvil, facing the fire so he could get the light. There was the clang of metal on metal.

Snorri leaned against the wall, watching him. Olaf had ceased to be skinny, though his ribs showed plainly. He was going to be strong, broad across the shoulders as his father had been. His skin glistened pale in the firelight. He wasn't making a bad job of the metal. He hadn't wasted his time helping, these past months. He hadn't the full strength for the job yet, but that would come. Fifteen years old and a man grown. He had a man's body, and maybe a man's feelings too, if the rumours Snorri had heard were true.

'Turn it over,' said Snorri, when Olaf paused at last.

Olaf looked up, scarlet in the face. 'There's still a crack. But it's cooling.'

'Then you'll need to heat it again. Put it back.'

Olaf turned to the fire, and Snorri pumped the bellows.

'I shouldn't have needed to heat it twice.'

'Don't be hard on yourself. Give it time.'

Snorri didn't say another word until the job was finished.

'Will that do?' asked Olaf, laying down his hammer.

'Could be worse. Luckily it belongs to Magnus. He doesn't know one end of a tushkar from the other anyway.'

Olaf cooled the blade in the water butt, and laid it down. He stopped to wipe the sweat out of his eyes, leaving a trail of soot across his face.

'We'll eat,' said Snorri. 'You can file both those down later.'

Olaf looked round for his shirt.

'On the floor behind you. You can wash first, if you like.'

Olaf hadn't thought of it, but he guessed that this was a hint.

The food at the smithy was always good. Olaf ate his piltocks, and smiled dreamily at Gunnhild, who never expected him to contribute to any conversation. Afterwards she gave him a hunk of bread with honey, a rare treat, and a measure of ale. Then she excused herself, and left.

When he had finished eating, Olaf looked up, and found that Snorri was regarding him steadily.

'And whose weapons will you take down from the wall, Olaf, when you go abroad to seek your fortune?'

'I don't know,' said Olaf, startled. 'I've never thought about it.'

'You're not planning to stay here all your life, surely? Don't you want to see the world outside?'

Olaf nodded vehemently. 'Oh yes, of course I've thought of that. I'll leave as soon as I can, in the spring. It was the weapons I meant.'

'So what will you do? Will you follow your father and brother and go to sea?'

'I'd be no use at sea. Anyway, I don't want that. I told you before what I want, at the Byrstada feast. I may have been drunk, but I meant it. I like making things.'

'You could be a smith,' agreed Snorri. 'It wouldn't make you rich in a day though. Never, perhaps. But you'd have a trade of your own, and that's a kind of freedom.'

'I'd need to be apprenticed.'

'I never served my full time,' said Snorri. 'I was too old. A crippled warrior's not much use to anyone. I was just looking for a way to get back here without having to beg my neighbours for a living. I can't teach you much, you realise that?'

Olaf sat up, taut as a bowstring, and looked straight at Snorri. 'Do you know who could?'

'Alard Simkin, who taught me, is a master smith in Kirkjavagr. His smithy is right by the harbour, a stone's throw from the Cathedral. He works for the chandlers and shipmasters, but he's also done most of the metalwork in the Cathedral. It was he that made the great gates. He's an Englishman by birth. His father came up from Dunholm with the masons, when Kol Rognvald's father began work on the Cathedral. Alard's still working inside the building, I believe. He has two or three apprentices at a time; it's a big smithy. It would be a fine opportunity for a young man who hopes to become a journeyman, or even a master at his trade.'

'I'm planning to go to Kirkjavagr in the spring anyway,' said Olaf.

'Are you indeed? To work?'

'And for other reasons. If I could get an apprenticeship there, that's all I could wish for.'

'If you were a journeyman trained by Alard smith, you could go anywhere,' Snorri told him. 'A craftsman of any trade who can say he's worked on one of the Cathedrals will find work wherever he wants, if he's a member of the right guild. Skotland, Noreg, Valland, Englaland, the world's open to you.'

'What would I need to recommend myself to him?'

'Only my word,' said Snorri. 'I gave him treasure enough to last him a lifetime, out of the parting gifts Svein Asleifarson gave to me. I thought afterwards I'd been a fool to pay him so generously, but it's not every man who'll take on someone like me for apprentice. But now I'm thinking it may have been to good purpose. I'll give you a token for him, and you can take it in spring, with a message from me. We were good friends in the end. That should get you what you want, and if it doesn't at once, I have friends in Kirkjavagr whose names I'll give you, and they'll make sure anyone from my island gets his rights.'

Olaf's cheeks were red, his eyes shining. 'Thank you,' he said, stammering a little. 'I don't know how to thank you.'

'I don't want thanks. Come into the smithy.'

When they got there Snorri did not immediately remove the turfs that Olaf had banked up round the fire. He went to the end wall, reached up painfully, and took down his sword. He drew it out of its scabbard, and handed it to Olaf. Olaf took it gingerly. It was surprisingly light. He felt the razor-sharp blade with his fore-finger, holding the sword carefully as if he didn't quite know what to do with it.

'You're strong enough to wield it now,' said Snorri. 'But you'll have to learn how. I'll give you my sword and shield, but I won't have them shamed, nor left to gather dust on the wall while you grow into a peasant.'

Olaf looked doubtfully at the sword in his hands. A good knife, or a smith's hammer, would have been more use to him. He had no desire at all to wield it. A gleam of sunlight shone in at the door, through a brief parting in the clouds, and Olaf saw the blade properly. There were twisted patterns carved down the blade, and strange foreign letters inscribed below the hilt. Now that would be something, to be able to decorate metal like that. 'Of course!' said Olaf aloud. 'You always said it was Frankish. You can tell those aren't Norse patterns, can't you?'

'Yes, indeed. They don't make swords like that any more. But the hilt is Norse.'

It was a beautiful thing. Olaf weighed it in his hands. With this, he had the power to kill. If I went mad suddenly, he thought, I could sweep Snorri's head from his shoulders. He handed the weapon back to its owner, and rubbed his nose. It's a good thing I'm not mad, he decided, and giggled.

Snorri sheathed the sword and laid it down. 'You can take it with you when you go. The shield too, though there's nothing remarkable about that.'

'Thank you,' said Olaf awkwardly. 'I'm definitely going, you know, with the first boat in spring. I'd have gone anyway, but it's much better like this.'

'Are you so keen to get away?'

Olaf hesitated. 'Yes. No. I've never been anywhere else. It's going to be hard sometimes, I know that.'

'I'll tell you this,' said Snorri. 'It would be far worse to stay in a trap here. Don't end up living with an impossible situation that you have to bear all your life, just because you dare not deal with it.'

Olaf stared at him. 'What do you know about that?' he asked roughly.

'More than you think. Take my word for it. You're young. You're healthy. Get out, and make a life for yourself, while you're still able to.'

'I will.' Olaf was embarrassed, but puzzled now as well.

'Very well. Where are those blades then? You know how to use the file. I'll leave you to it.'

Rolf sat on the bench outside Byrstada in the November sunshine, biting his nails. The sea was the colour of pearl, the land a soft winter brown. Away to the south he could see the Leogh boat taking advantage of this brief break in the winter weather. She was barely moving, though her sail was stretched tight to the breeze.

His crew – Dagfinn's crew – were at Finniquoy, washing Sula's ropes in fresh water, and laying them out to dry. It was the first good drying day they'd had since they got back, and the ropes and sail had been draped over the beams in Sula's shed, still sticky with salt. This was the last major job to be done on the ship before caulking her in the spring. Skuli was an able quartermaster, so there was no need for Rolf to join them until later in the day, or at all, if he were not free. His wife was in labour, and while he hardly liked to admit to being tied to his house for such a reason as that, he didn't wish to leave. There might be good news at any time. If there were not, she might need him. Rolf chewed his fingers and scowled at the translucent sea.

There was no sound from indoors. The women were in there with Gudrun, but everyone else had cleared out. Luckily his brother had removed himself from his sickbed, commandeering one of the crew to support him, for his wounded leg was still troubling him. Leif had gone all too willingly, without asking Rolf's permission, though Rolf had given clear orders that every man was to work today. But his orders could once again be countermanded at any time, now that Dagfinn had returned. He and Dagfinn had hardly talked. Rolf had felt he must spare a sick man, but there had been changes, and he wasn't willing to go back to the way they'd run things before. He wondered if Dagfinn had any idea of his mood. Undoubtedly he did; Dagfinn had never lacked intuition. Rolf wondered if he discussed such matters with Leif. Rolf had become adept over the years at turning a blind eye to what he didn't wish to see, but he had had the measure of that situation within five minutes of Leif's coming aboard the Sula in Biorgvin, a year and a half ago. His heart had sunk; it was the last thing a captain needed, if he were to retain any order and respect among his crew. But Dagfinn had carried it off, and showed in small matters a surprising discretion. To protect the young man, Rolf supposed, but discretion in the face of such a blatant risk was laughable, if the danger had not been so great, a capital offence in fact, if anyone should choose to prove it. Pray God they never would.

But Rolf's more pressing concern was what was to happen next season. There could be no going back to sailing as his brother's right-hand man, no more taking orders from Dagfinn. Rolf had had one season to set up contacts of his own choosing, and he was a better man of business than Dagfinn would ever be. He had already considered what would happen if and when Dagfinn returned. It was unfortunate that he'd not had just one more season to establish himself. If Dagfinn were too badly injured to sail next season, the thing would be resolved. Rolf found himself hoping this might be so. He could never admit, even to himself, the significance of that wild moment when he had met them bringing his brother home unconscious on a stretcher, and he had believed for one moment, amidst all his fear and sorrow, that he might be free.

But now Dagfinn was up and about again, short of an eye, but that was unlikely to deter him. So Rolf had two choices: either to come to an agreement with Dagfinn giving the pair of them equal and joint command of the Sula, or to go ahead with the plan he had sketchily discussed with Jens of Lubeck: to take joint shares in a ship, and to run the business with Jens in Biorgvin, and himself as shipmaster travelling to and from the islands. The former course had seemed more of a possibility in Dagfinn's absence. Rolf realised that he would have to fight for his rights every step of the way, and from below too, in the old accustomed place.

The other course was full of risks: Jens was a foreigner, Rolf would have to borrow money. But Dagfinn had brought home a chest full of treasure, looted from the Sudreyjar and Irland, and Rolf could fairly demand treasure in return for his half share in the Sula. If Dagfinn objected he could take the matter to the Thing. But Dagfinn would not object. He had always been generous, even if he lacked other qualities.

The women were a greater source of uncertainty. Ragna had to agree to that marriage, whether she liked it or not. Rolf bit his nail to the quick, and squeezed out a drop of blood. Dagfinn had spoiled her. She might find Jens attractive, but Rolf could certainly expect trouble if she didn't. Rolf tried to recall the man to his mind's eye, but he could hardly remember what he looked like. At least Dagfinn had made no objection when he'd heard the news. Probably he'd been relieved to have such a tedious matter taken out of his hands. Then there was Gudrun. Would she be willing to go to Biorgvin? If she insisted on staying here, he'd hardly ever see her. There was the child to think of too. Rolf raised his head, but he could hear no sound from indoors.

The pain was familiar. Gudrun had been through it all before. It was worse this time, but quite different, because this child was alive. This child would live. It had to live. In a corner of her mind, Gudrun faced cold terror. Her body had never before come so close to its limits; she began to understand how women died, how easy it was to die. She didn't want to. It wasn't time. The pain grew stronger, like waves driven by storm, breaking further back, exposing cruel rocks beneath. She must have spoken. Gunnhild's voice came through it all:

'Of course you won't die. The baby's just where it should be. There's nothing to be afraid of now.'

Gunnhild sounded quite fierce, and somehow that was reassuring. Gudrun opened her eyes. An image of smoke-blackened beams fixed itself on her brain and was gone. She closed her eyes tightly as the next wave broke.

Everything began to change. She could feel her body, no longer her own, bearing down, opening out. Once she ceased to resist, the pain altered, transmuted itself into something else. An image of Rolf impinged itself against her closed eyes, an image of loss, far away. But then there was nothing outside any more, only her own body, and the dark inside, bearing down, changing, turning into a different being.

Then a new pain, so huge she screamed out loud. It was gone again, something wet and slippery slid against her legs. The dark cleared. Gudrun struggled to sit up properly, stretching out her arms. A small wet body, mottled pink, not herself, lay sprawled across her thigh.

'My baby. I want my baby.'

Dagfinn and Leif slowly skirted the great hole at Raiva, and began to climb towards the cliff, stopping every few yards. Dagfinn leaned heavily on Leif's shoulder. His face was white and drawn, wet with sweat.

'God, what a wreck!'

'You'll get better.'

At the top of the cliff at Raiva they could see the sun that was already hidden from the farmlands. They looked back, to where long winter shadows cast themselves across the island.

'Lundenborg is the richest city in Englaland,' said Dagfinn, once he had breath enough to go on with the conversation that had been suspended while they tackled the hill. 'The Flemish merchants have a lot of interest there now. One can't fail with the English wool trade, it seems.'

'You'd hardly want to bring wool back to the islands,' remarked Leif.

'It's the cloth. You saw that broadcloth I brought home? There's none like it. To reach Lundenborg you have to sail a long way up the estuary through a lowlying country full of farmlands and orchards. There's ripe fruit for the picking all the year round, in Cantland.'

'That's impossible.'

'Leif, you should believe everything until you've seen it for yourself.'

'I should believe nothing, you mean.'

'Very well, then. One day we'll go there, you and I, and I shall make you believe it.'

As they passed Shirva on their way back, a small knot of people broke away from the doorway and hurried to waylay them.

Ingrid reached them first. 'Dagfinn! Gudrun had her baby. It's fine. It's all right!'

Dagfinn stopped, and took his hand from Leif's shoulder. 'Is that right? So we have a son for Byrstada, do we?'

'It's a girl, but she's fine.'

Dagfinn smiled. 'Well, that's good too. I like girls. When did it happen?'

'Just after midday.'

'Maybe she'll get a boy next time,' remarked Arne, standing at Ingrid's side.

'I shouldn't mention that yet, if I were you,' said Dagfinn. 'Has she a name? Rolf should call her Thordis, for her grandmother.'

Ingrid hesitated. 'Well, they haven't. They haven't named her after our mother either. I don't know what you'll think.'

'It's not my business to think anything,' said Dagfinn.

Astrid broke in, 'Rolf named her Maria.'

Dagfinn looked blank. 'Maria?'

'I know,' said Ingrid, looking troubled, 'It's not an island name at all.'

'It's very common abroad,' said Leif consolingly.

'What was Rolf thinking of?' asked Dagfinn curiously. 'He was always the man for tradition, so I thought.'

'It wasn't Rolf's idea,' said Ingrid. 'It was Gudrun's wish. Something about a blessing. Rolf said he saw no reason why he should gainsay her.'

'I don't know that I'd be pleased,' said Arne.

'Well, it's new,' said Dagfinn, 'but none the worse for that. Maria Rolfsdottir.'

'We'll get used to it,' said Ingrid practically.

Dagfinn crossed his fingers. 'In any case, may the gods preserve her.'

Skuli waited by the burn in the shadow of the smithy. Two figures came round the house and slipped across the yard. He heard scraping noises against the stone wall, then a pebble slid off the roof and bounced on the brigstones. Somebody swore. Skuli recognised the voice, and grinned. Then he left his hiding place and strolled quietly in at the smithy door.

'All right?' whispered Ragna to Thorhalla.

'I'm safe, but I don't think we ought.'

They were balanced on the ridge of the smithy roof. The mouth of the chimney hole was black below them.

'You're not going to back out now?'

'I just don't think we ought.'

'Don't be silly. Nothing will happen anyway.'

'Then why do it?'

'Oh shut up. You go first.'

'No!'

'Hush, don't squeak. Someone will hear. I will, then.'

'Wait!' Thorhalla sounded terrified. 'You shouldn't be asking anyway. You know who you're supposed to marry!'

'Don't be a fool. Nothing will happen, I promise. I've done it before. Nothing ever does.'

Ragna took a skein of wool from under her belt and held it over the opening. Thorhalla peered into the dark, her eyes round with fright. Ragna let go the skein, holding the end so that it unwound and bounced down into the smithy as it unravelled. Thorhalla's heart was thumping, but Ragna's voice sounded clear and firm. 'Who holds my wool end?' she called, and prepared to wind the skein in.

There was a tug from below and the thread fell from her fingers. 'I, Skuli Hedinsson!'

The words echoed in the empty smithy. Thorhalla screamed, and Ragna jumped, lost her footing, and fell heavily on to the roof, where she clung to the ridge.

'Ragna! Ragna, where are you?'

'Here, of course.' Ragna sounded furious. 'I'll get him!'

'What was it? Did you hear? Ragna, come back!'

'I'll catch him!' Ragna leapt to the ground with a thud, and vanished. Thorhalla was left too petrified to move. The smithy door slammed below her. Footsteps ran across the yard, there was a stifled squeal, and silence. She gasped in terror, then descended carefully, still trembling. As soon as she was down, she fled towards Byrstada, away from the unknown spirits that haunted the smithy on Hallowmass Eve.

Skuli caught up with Ragna on the far side of the Byrstada barn. Half scared, half laughing, she tried to push him off.

'Come on,' said Skuli. 'All's fair. The one who catches your wool end is your own true love, isn't that right?'

'No! My own true love is a merchant from Lubeck, and don't you forget it! I'm sure he never hangs around in other people's smithies where he has no business to be.'

Skuli kissed her.

'I told you never to do that again!'

'It's cold out here. Come into the barn.'

'No! I tell you, I have to look after myself now, or what will Jens of Lubeck say?'

The dark had gathered so thickly he could no longer see her face. 'Nothing will happen to you that this Jens need know about, I'll see to that,' said Skuli. 'I promise.'

'But can I trust you?'

'Oh yes,' said Skuli, and kissed her again.

'Promise?' demanded Ragna, when he had done.

'I swear by my honour.'

'Ha!' said Ragna. 'I'll come in for a bit. After all, I'm not married yet, am I?'

'I wish I could marry you myself,' said Skuli regretfully, putting his arm round her, and leading her into the barn.

Ragna was not back by bedtime. Thorhalla couldn't sleep, but she didn't dare tell anyone what they'd done. Nor did she dare investigate outside, for who knew what ghosts might be walking? At last someone crept to the sleeping platform where she lay. 'Ragna?'

'Ssh! Are you still awake? It must be gone midnight.'

'Where have you been? What happened to you?'

'Out. Nothing.' Ragna stripped off her tunic and got into bed. Thorhalla moved up. For one who had been out in a chilly November night, Ragna was not at all cold. 'Ragna, what was it? That voice, what was it?'

'Voice? Oh, that. What did you think it was, you goose?'

'Was it human?'

'What do you think?'

Thorhalla was silent for a while. 'If you don't tell me, I'm going to tell Rolf. I'm scared.'

'Do what the hell you like. I'm tired.' Ragna turned her back, taking up more than half the bed, and refused to speak another word.

Thorvald and Astrid were married the following afternoon. It was the first time there'd been a priest to celebrate an island marriage with a mass, but the old ceremonies of good luck were not omitted, and the feast afterwards was a good one. It was the second wedding feast to be held at Shirva in one year.

When the feasting was over and the tables cleared away, the islanders seized hold of Astrid and Thorvald and carried them shoulder-high round the hall. They dropped Thorvald with a bump, grabbed him by the arms and legs, and swung him high in the air a few times for luck. Astrid was let down more gently, and when Thorvald was allowed to get up again he came back to her side, looking hot and dishevelled.

'A story,' people were shouting. 'We should have a story!'

'A love story!'

While Bjarni was telling the first story, about Rut the Islander and Queen Gunnhild of Noreg, Thorvald took the opportunity to whisper to Astrid. 'We'll get away as soon as we can. I'm not being put to bed by this lot.'

'Is that what'll happen?'

'Yes, but they'll do a lot more drinking first. I'd rather take my clothes off for myself. Watch out, I'll tell you when it's time.'

Thorvald leaned back, and let Rolf pass him the drinking horn filled to the brim. He didn't drain it. When no one was looking he poured most of it over his shoulder on to the floor.

Bjarni's story came to an end.

'Serve him right,' said Ragna. 'Hard on Unn though, don't you think?'

'She found consolation elsewhere,' said Dagfinn. 'I don't think we need be too sorry for her. Skuli, how about a story? I'm sure you know more love stories than anyone else here.'

Skuli acknowledged the compliment with a sinister grin. 'I can give you a new one I heard in Biorgvin this summer. It comes from Nerbon.'

'Is it sad?'

'Of course. It's the story of a lover who sought in every way to win the favour of his lady. She was his lord's wife, but he was willing to pay the penalty and die, for the reward of one night in her bed.'

'Latin,' remarked Rolf.

'But when it came to it, he knew he could not dishonour her, and so they slept with a naked sword between them.'

He looked straight at Thorvald and grinned. Thorvald looked back blankly.

'Didn't it get in the way a bit?' asked Olaf.

'You're not impressed?' asked Skuli.

Thorvald shrugged. 'Let's have it, anyway.'

Skuli stood up, and began his tale, and Thorvald whispered in Astrid's ear. 'Go on out now. If anyone asks, say you'll be back in a minute. Get your cloak if you can. Then make for Setr, fast. I'll catch you up. Wait! Don't look as though I'd told you. Go in a minute.'

Astrid nodded, and caught Ragna's eyes on them, so she looked attentively at Skuli. When she glanced at Ragna again, she was watching him too.

Astrid got up and slipped past the row of people on the platform. No one challenged her.

Outside the moon was almost full, bright as a lantern. A sharp wind caught her, cold from the sea. Astrid hadn't been able to get near her cloak, but she had her shawl. She pulled it over her head, and turned towards Setr.

The land was white under the moon, the hills outlined against a charcoal-coloured sky. There were shadows across the track, and she lost the path for a moment. Wet grass soaked through her boots. Once she was past the knowe the way shone clear. On her left she could hear the waves breaking in Hjukni geo.

Someone was following fast. 'Thorvald?' she called.

He caught up with her and grabbed her arm. 'Come on! There isn't much time!'

Seconds later there were shouts behind them, and a light appeared, dotting over the moonlit fields like a will o' the wisp.

'Come on!'

They ran until they reached the Setr yard. 'Here!' He thrust her inside the house, and pushed past. She could hear him scrabbling in the dark. Then a turf was lifted off the fire, and his face was caught in a red glow. His hair fell over his forehead, shadowing his face, and his hands seemed to be in the fire itself.

Thorvald lifted out a half burned peat, and lit the lamp.

'I'll bar the door. Hold the lamp, quick!'

She held it up while he found the heavy bar, and lifted it into its sockets. The bar was thick with grease and dust. Thorvald wiped his hands on his tunic, and stuck a wooden pin through the latch as well.

'There we are. Safe.' There was a smudge of soot across his cheek. He grinned, and gave the door a satisfied kick. 'Come to bed. We'll blow out the lamp before they come. That'll fool them.'

'What about your mother? You've locked her out.'

'She'll stay at the smithy. And my brothers won't expect to come home tonight. Come on.'

She watched him, uncertain and bewildered. He tore off his tunic and trousers, and sat down to pull his socks off. There were shouts outside, coming closer. Thorvald stopped, his shirt half over his head. 'Come on! We have to blow the lamp out! What are you waiting for?'

She took off her shawl and tunic. The air was freezing on her skin. The hem of her dress was damp, but she scrambled into bed without taking it off. She didn't feel safe. She'd never slept in this house before. She felt as though she shouldn't be here. This was where Ingebjorg lived, and Olaf and Eirik. Thorvald's bed was chilly. She shivered, and clutched her dress close around her.

Thorvald was standing over the fire, quite naked in spite of the cold. He seemed a stranger; she couldn't make herself recall what it had been like between them before. He blew the light out, and the dark closed in. There was light outside; moonlight coming through the chimney hole, then a warmer light. Footsteps echoed on the stones. Shouts and jeers came from all round them.

His hand reached out in the dark and touched her face, and he was climbing into his bed beside her. 'Just in time.' He sounded gleeful. 'They'll never get us now.'

There was a tremendous banging on the door. She clutched him, genuinely scared. It was hard to remember it was all a game. His skin was warm under her hands.

'You're frozen,' said Thorvald. 'Come here.'

She hadn't been close to him like this since they got home. The only times they'd been alone were out on the hill, where it was far too cold to undress. She'd forgotten him. Astrid laid her cold hands against his chest. But there was too much happening at once. The thumping on the door grew louder. The flickering glow of many torches gleamed against the chimney hole.

'Open up! Open the door!'

'Thorvald! We know you're in there!'

'Not yet he isn't. Give him time!'

'Come on boy. You're not dead!'

The banging ceased. There were thuds, and crashes on the roof above them. The rafters creaked. Astrid pulled the blankets over her head, and pressed her face against his chest.

'Whatever's that?'

'It's someone sitting on the ridge pole banging his feet. Several people, in fact.'

'The roof will fall in!'

'No it won't. My father built this house. He'll have made it strong.'

'Thorvald! Thorvald!' They were turning his name into a chant.

'Answer us, or we'll have the roof off!'

He shouted suddenly, making Astrid jump. 'Go home! You're not coming in here!'

'No, it's you that's supposed to be doing that!'

'Get lost!' roared Thorvald from his bed.

'No, don't do that. Shall I tell you where to look?'

Astrid raised her head. The roof was still intact. She could feel Thorvald laughing. 'Take no notice,' he said cheerfully. 'They'll go away when they've had enough.'

'Are you sure?'

'It's a cold night, and they can't get in. There's more drink at Shirva than there is in our yard.'

There was more thumping, and the roof shook. Thuds and bumps were interspersed with shouted taunts and encouragement. Then a splash of water came down the chimney hole, and the fire hissed furiously.

They heard Rolf's voice in the yard. 'That's enough. He'll not let us in. Leave him in peace now!'

His advice was drowned in catcalls, but presently they heard slitherings and scrapes as the invaders descended.

'Don't think much of your hospitality, Thorvald!'

'We'll know where not to call again!'

'Cheated! What's a wedding without a bedding?'

'Leave him!' shouted Rolf again. 'I'm sure he's managing the bedding without any help from you.'

Their voices died away, and only the moon shone across the hearth.

'Astrid?' He had stopped laughing, and wriggled down close beside her. It was getting warm at last. The bedding smelt of Thorvald, and of Olaf too. Perhaps they had the same smell.

Astrid began tentatively to touch him again. His skin was very smooth. It had been a long time since she had known him like this. Outside was the sea, holding her on his island, perhaps for ever. But he had locked it out; she realised that when he was with her, he would always have the power to do that. She found his thorshammer hanging on its chain round his neck, and closed her fist over it.

She found herself holding him tightly, frightened of something, a shadow out of the future.

'There's nothing to worry about,' said Thorvald. 'No one's going to try to get in now.'

'I wish you never had to go away.'

It was the last thing he'd been thinking about. He didn't say anything for a little while. 'You know I shall have to go. But not yet.'

So he couldn't see the shadow. The night was quite still now. There were no sounds of any human presence, only the soft whine of the wind, and the faint wash of the sea breaking on the rocks. It was her turn to shield him from the things he could not see, and would never see. Astrid leaned over him compassionately, and kissed him. A current of stronger feeling tugged at her. He slid beneath her, and held her. The current caught at them both, then swept them slowly out into the depths of their own particular sea.

The feast at Shirva lasted until dawn. Most of the guests fell asleep on their benches. Outside, the sun rose red and huge, casting a path across the sea, and over the little winter lochans at the south end of the island. Near the shores of the pools a thin film of ice had formed. As the breeze shook the reeds there were small cracking sounds as the ice snapped round the bent stems. The grass was flecked with white. Olaf stood still, shivering, watching the sun rise against the endless blur that always surrounded his island. The bands of pink were fading into grey. Olaf left the loch and turned towards the smithy, his feet crushing the frozen grass.

Chapter 67

'Eirik, you're not looking,' said Thorvald. 'Try again.'

'But that's just like the one you did!' protested Eirik.

'It isn't.' Thorvald bent down, and rubbed out the figure Eirik had drawn in the ash. 'Look, I'll draw it again.' He wrote four runes in the ashes with his forefinger. 'There you are.'

Astrid stopped by the hearth. She had been walking up and down the room to keep warm, drawing thread from her spindle as she went. She absentmindedly went on spinning as she watched, until the distaff wheel bumped on the floor. She wound the thread up slowly, and started the next length.

'Can you write my name too?'

Thorvald looked up. 'Do you want to try as well?'

No one had ever suggested that she should interest herself in writing. 'Can I?'

'Why not? Except I don't know how to do "Astrid". Let me think.'

He took a handful of cold ash from the edge of the hearth, and spread it over the earth floor, smoothing it with his fingers. Then he stopped to think. Astrid waited, willing him to know the right signs. She'd never thought of it before, but suddenly it felt import-ant. She wanted to see her name.

' ⅄ ', wrote Thorvald.

He bent over the ashes, his tongue sticking out as he concen-trated. Four more signs followed the first one. 'I think that's right.' He looked at his work critically. 'I'll ask Bjarni when I see him, just to make sure.'

She was crouching beside him, her spindle abandoned on the bench, looking at his handiwork with awe. 'Is that me?'

'Does that say "Astrid"?' asked Eirik, leaving his writing, and leaning on Thorvald's shoulder to see.

The door opened, bringing in a blast of wind. The three by the hearth peered into the gloom beyond the lamplight.

'Who's that?' called Thorvald.

The door banged shut, and Leif marched over to the hearth. The cold seemed to hang about him, and there was frost on his boots. He stood over Thorvald, and without a glance at the others, said, 'I've come to announce a killing.'

Eirik gaped at him from the hearth. Astrid stood stock still. Thorvald got up slowly. 'Tell me,' he said.

There was blood across Leif's cheek, and his mouth was a thin line.

'There's blood on your hands,' said Eirik hoarsely.

'Tell me!'

Leif shook his head, and held up his hands as if to push some-thing away. His hands were shaking, and they were covered with blood.

'Sit down,' ordered Thorvald.

Leif sank on to the bench, but kept his face turned away. When his cloak fell back, they could see more blood on his tunic, a thick black stain in the lamplight.

'You're not hurt?'

Leif shook his head, and clenched his fists on his knees, keeping his face hidden.

'I've killed a man.'

'Who?'

'I've killed a man.' Blood had soaked into the cuffs of his tunic. Leif looked up, and met Thorvald's eyes.

'Start at the beginning,' said Thorvald.

'I shouldn't have gone!'

'Gone where?'

'He asked me to go out with him. To talk, he said.'

'Who? Leif, tell me who!'

'Svein from Danmark.'

Svein with his straggly hair. Svein, who had told the story of the king's nephew at the ill-fated Byrstada feast. Svein, who had lowered the flit boat that took Astrid and Thorvald ashore at Svinborg.

'Asked you to go with him where?'

'Nowhere. It was an excuse. I should have guessed.'

'What did he want?'

Leif shook his head, and made a despairing gesture.

'Tell me,' said Thorvald. 'You must, if you want me to stand witness.'

Silence. Eirik and Astrid looked at each other. In response to the question in the child's eyes Astrid gave a tiny shrug. Thorvald never took his gaze from Leif's face.

'Did he threaten to betray you?'

Leif jumped as if he'd been struck. 'What do you know about that?'

'Nothing,' said Thorvald. 'Am I right?'

There was a long pause. Leif unclenched his hands. Where the blood had dried, cracks had appeared over his knuckles. Leif spread his fingers, examining them. 'He said he could bring evidence.'

Thorvald seemed to understand. Eirik looked at Astrid again, but she was as puzzled as he was. She shook her head.

'He was probably lying,' said Thorvald.

'He said he could bring evidence against me. He said I had no reason to be proud, for I couldn't deny what I was. He said he could prove it, that he had evidence.'

'So you killed him?'

Leif shook his head. His white cheeks had taken on a sudden rush of colour. 'I said I was not ashamed of what I was, for he had shown himself a baser man than I, with his bribery and threats. I said I would never sell myself to anyone. Whatever I have done,' he turned and looked Thorvald in the eyes, 'I have never had to do that.'

'What did he say then?'

Leif's face was hidden again. 'He said I was not a man at all.' It was said so quietly that Thorvald had to lean forward to catch the words. Astrid wasn't sure she'd heard him right; it made no sense.

'I would have killed him, if it had been me,' said Thorvald.

'I drew my knife on him. He would have drawn his. He moved back, and I slipped. I caught him below the ribs.'

'And killed him?'

'It went straight through his clothes. It just slid into him.' Leif shuddered. 'I've been in a fight before, it's not that. It's the way it happened. There wasn't a fight. It just slid in. He was screaming. He went on screaming. He wouldn't stop.'

'And then?'

'I didn't know what to do. I did it again.'

'Knifed him?'

'I couldn't make him stop.'

Thorvald had never known a killing on the island. Not in your lifetime, Einar had said. Einar had been proud of that. It couldn't be said of any other island, so far as he knew. But now Thorvald had been called as witness, and he knew his law.

'You've notified the killing at once, that's the main thing,' said Thorvald, with a coolness he did not feel. 'That makes it man-slaughter, not murder.'

'I didn't know what to do. It was too dark. I couldn't even see him. I stabbed him again. He was screaming. Then he stopped.'

'You've seen men killed before,' remarked Thorvald. 'He deserved it. He'd never have let you alone.'

'I'd never quarrelled with him before.'

'You couldn't help the way it happened.'

Leif was still shaking. 'I couldn't have let it go. He'd have done what he threatened.'

'Given evidence against you?'

'Not just me.'

'You'd no choice then. You had to be loyal.'

Leif's eyes were desperate. 'You know what this means?' he whispered.

Thorvald knew the law. If Svein had been right, if there had been a crime committed, if there were evidence to support Svein's charge, and if there were witnesses; if such a crime were proved before the Thing, the penalty would be death. The Fridarey Thing had never condemned a man to death since Einar had set it up. Thorvald had realised why Leif was here the first winter he came, but he had never admitted it, even to himself, until now. Irrelevantly, he found himself wondering if Einar had known too, and if Einar had fully realised the risk that Dagfinn had taken.

Leif's head was down on his clenched fists. 'What have I done? I never meant it! I never meant to disgrace him!'

'Hush, take care!' Thorvald was aware of Eirik's frightened uncomprehending gaze. 'You haven't disgraced anyone. You've only committed manslaughter. That can be dealt with quite easily. There was a quarrel between you and Svein. I'll bear witness to that. No one else has to be mentioned.'

Leif sat up. 'Thank you, Thorvald,' he said with an effort.

'It's a good thing you came here at once. You've notified me of the killing; I'll bear witness to that. You'll have to go before the Thing. Just say there was a quarrel. The Thing can deal with that. It's quite straightforward.'

Leif pushed his hair out of his eyes. 'I know. They'll charge me with manslaughter.'

'You'll have to prepare your defence,' said Thorvald, 'and summon what support you can before the Thing meets.'

'Support?' said Leif. 'This isn't my island. I don't even know if the crew would support me. Svein wasn't unpopular.'

'Dagfinn and Rolf must support you.'

'No!'

'They must, both of them. Dagfinn's your captain. He'd have to show support for his own man, and so would Rolf.'

'I can't ask him that! Not on his own island!'

'All the more reason why he must. It would be a disgrace if he didn't come to your defence. He's your captain. You don't have to say he had anything to do with it.'

'He didn't!'

'Even easier. Give an account of the quarrel, and call me as witness. I'll say I know you for an honourable man, and Dagfinn and Rolf will support me. The islanders will accept it. It's not as if Svein had any kin here, or anyone to avenge him. All the islanders will want is to have their own peace kept.'

'Svein's captain should be the one to avenge him,' said Leif.

'Svein is dead. No one wants Dagfinn disgraced. I can't think of anything that would do worse harm to the island.'

Leif was silent.

'You have my support,' said Thorvald.

He waited patiently for a response. Leif had reacted fast enough eight months ago, he remembered, on the day of the launching.

'I stand in your debt,' said Leif. 'Are you sure you want to be involved?'

'Don't be stupid. Anyway, I'm getting quite good at solving lawsuits.'

Leif stopped trembling, and brushed his hand across his eyes.

'What did you do with the body?'

'Nothing.'

'You mean he's still lying where you killed him?'

'I couldn't shift him.'

'Did you cover him?'

Leif shrugged. 'What with?'

Thorvald stood up. 'You're laying yourself open to a serious charge. You'll have to cover him and lay him somewhere decent, or you'll find yourself in real trouble!'

'It's pitch dark out there.' Leif sounded dazed.

'Then we've the chance to do something about it before dawn. You should get washed too, before anyone sees you. Astrid! Have some hot water for him when we come back. Leif?'

'I'm coming.'

'We'll go to the smithy first, and I'll fetch Olaf. With three of us, we can get the body as far as the graveyard, and cover it. Then I'll summon the Thing as soon as it's morning.'

'I don't understand,' said Eirik fretfully, while Astrid ladled jugfuls of water into the big cauldron over the fire. 'What was all that about? Why did Leif have to kill that man?'

'I don't know,' said Astrid. 'But Thorvald will sort it out.'

'Huh.' Eirik was unimpressed. 'And he didn't finish writing your name either.'

Chapter 68

Astrid tramped through the snow to Byrstada. Olaf's old boots hardly kept the cold out, in spite of being stuffed with wool, and her toes soon went numb. She didn't care; the sky was clear and pale, and the island was showing a new face. It would be dark again in a couple of hours, back to firelight and lamplight, but just now it was as bright as summer.

Gudrun's baby was three weeks old today. The first time Astrid had seen Maria, she'd thought her quite un-human, red and fragile, an alien thing that might or might not survive. It was better to stay detached, until the child obviously began to thrive. Astrid had seen the way Gudrun looked at Maria, and she'd been afraid of such intensity. I never want to feel like that, she thought, crossing her fingers inside a double layer of mitten, it isn't safe. Thorvald had never talked about a child. She didn't want one. She had already taken enough risks in loving.

Today was the first day it had been properly light for a week. Suddenly elated, Astrid began to run, going round in circles, making patterns in the untouched snow, then jumping as far as she could and going backwards, to confuse any passer by who might try to work out where she'd gone.

By the time she reached Byrstada the snow had soaked right through her boots and socks, and her cheeks were tingling with cold, but even so she hesitated. The light was so rare it seemed a shame to leave it. Astrid dived under the lintel into the encircling gloom.

It took her eyes a moment to adjust. All the women were inside, huddled round a bright fire.

'Come on in,' said Ragna. 'We've just finished the milking, and we're thawing out.'

They moved up to make room, so that she could warm her wet feet on the hearthstones. Astrid sat down, and struggled with her sodden leather bootlaces.

'She smiled today,' Thorhalla informed her.

Thorhalla had never addressed a single sentence to Astrid before. Taken aback, Astrid asked, 'Who?' and they all laughed.

'You'd better not have a baby,' said Ragna. 'You'd probably forget you'd got it and leave it lying around somewhere. Have a look at this one.'

Obediently Astrid looked. Maria was propped in the curve of Thorhalla's arm. Her cheeks were fat now, and she had turned a proper colour. There were red blotches on her forehead, and she had vague blue eyes that didn't seem to be looking at anything. While Astrid watched her the baby gave a little cough and brought up a mess of milk.

'I don't think I want one,' said Astrid. 'Not yet, anyway, but she's very nice,' she added quickly.

Gudrun laughed. No ghosts seemed to haunt her. She was spinning wool as she watched her baby, standing under the light from the chimney.

'Are the men still at the Thing?' she asked Astrid.

'I suppose they must be. I didn't see anyone when I came over.'

'They'll be frozen,' said Ragna. 'At least that means they'll want to get the whole business over as fast as possible.'

Gudrun frowned. 'As long as that old man from Leogh doesn't decide he wants to make an issue of it. He needs to do something to establish himself as lawman.'

'He won't stand against both my brothers,' said Ragna decidedly, 'not when Dagfinn's brought back glory to everyone on the island. And after all, what did Svein have to do with anyone here?'

Gudrun glanced at her, but said nothing.

'Can I take the baby?' Ingrid asked Thorhalla.

Thorhalla handed over the child reluctantly. Neither she nor Ingrid seemed to have any attention for anyone else.

'Thorvald's speaking for Leif, isn't he?' said Gudrun. 'He thinks it'll all be straightforward, does he?'

So Gudrun knew. Astrid found it hard to gauge how much anyone else understood. When Thorvald had told Ingebjorg what had happened, Ingebjorg had made no comment at all, nor had she mentioned the matter to Astrid since. It was Thorvald who had eventually explained to Astrid what kind of crime it was that carried the death penalty in this case. He had made her swear never to speak of it to a single soul. 'After all,' he'd said, 'Svein only assumed they'd done that. He might have had proof, possibly, but as for witnesses, it seems unlikely.'

'Why is it so terrible?'

'It's against nature,' said Thorvald. 'But Dagfinn has always been a friend to me, and now Leif is my friend too. I'm bound to give them my support, and in this case that means avoiding the law. There's no other way. It's better if we just forget the whole thing, even between ourselves. I shouldn't have told you.'

'Thorvald says it's a straightforward case of manslaughter,' said Astrid to Gudrun now, 'and should be dealt with easily.'

'Thorvald!' said Ragna, laughing. 'Perhaps he should be our lawman now, after his last success.'

'It's a good thing someone from the island was willing to speak for Leif,' said Gudrun.

'Look!' interrupted Ingrid. 'She's smiling again! Look, Astrid.'

'Yes,' said Astrid, looking. 'So she is.'

'You ought to show some interest,' said Ragna. 'You'll probably have a child yourself before the year's out.'

Gudrun crossed her fingers. 'Don't tempt an evil fate, Ragna. You shouldn't say so out loud.'

'Well it's true. Thorvald will get a bairn on her soon enough. Hasn't he been trying, Astrid?'

'What do you think?' said Astrid absently, and wriggled her bare toes in front of the fire. They were thawing out, and her chilblains itched.

'There's time yet,' said Gudrun. 'Ingrid, what did father say about this meeting today?'

'Not much. He was telling Arne and Jon how there hasn't been a killing here for eighteen years, and it was bad to have the peace broken. They started talking about the killings they've had on Papey. They don't realise that father doesn't see it as something to be proud of.'

'But father didn't say anything else about Leif's case?'

'No. Did Rolf say anything?'

'Not much.'

'Yes he did,' said Thorhalla. 'He was arguing with Dagfinn behind the hangings. He said Dagfinn should never have brought Leif home, and if Rolf couldn't get his own ship one way, then he'd get it another.'

Ragna leapt to her feet, and before Thorhalla could duck, she fetched her a swinging blow across the ear. Thorhalla screamed, and Ingrid clutched the baby to her bosom.

'Don't you dare!' shouted Ragna. 'You should know better than to repeat what your own family say to each other in their own home! Telling tales on your own brothers!'

'If Dagfinn and Rolf quarrelled,' said Ingrid mildly, 'that's hardly news to us. I wouldn't worry.'

Gudrun addressed herself to Astrid. 'Have you started on the weaving at Setr?'

Astrid sighed. 'Yes. Ingebjorg's very good at it, isn't she?'

'Good?' said Ingrid. 'She's said to be the best weaver we've ever had on the island. You're lucky to have the chance to work with her. I wish I could.'

Gudrun winked at Astrid, as she scooped up her now restless infant from Ingrid's lap. 'Tough, is it?' she asked her, over Ingrid's head.

Astrid found herself admitting what she'd hardly allowed herself to recognise. 'Yes, it is, sometimes.'

Ingebjorg had treated her very well from the beginning, but she was never warm, as Ingrid had been. Astrid had grown too used to Shirva, and Setr did not feel like home now. She even missed Bjarni. There was no man at Setr, except for Thorvald, of course, but he'd be gone in the spring. Olaf hadn't spent a night in his own home since Thorvald and Astrid had been married. His blankets remained neatly folded on the sleeping platform. Ingebjorg never mentioned Olaf's absence, just as she had never mentioned what had happened the night Astrid had come back to Fridarey. Olaf was sleeping at the smithy, and Astrid hadn't seen him to speak to since the wedding.

The other problem was the weaving. Ingebjorg never criticised her work. She seldom offered advice or made suggestions, but her own immaculate cloth, along with her lack of comment on Astrid's efforts, had unsettled Astrid. Last winter at Shirva they'd admired Astrid's skill, but admiration did not seem to be one of Ingebjorg's gifts. She only unbent when Gunnhild called. This happened almost every day in winter, and Astrid was always relieved to see Gunnhild make Ingebjorg talk and laugh like an ordinary person.

When Astrid got home from Byrstada, Ingebjorg had gone out. There was a pot of beef simmering over the fire, and the loom stood half threaded in its place against the far wall. Reluctantly, Astrid turned to the task of threading it up for the next weaving. She had to stand on the stool to tie the warps to the beam, and then fasten a stone weight to each one at the bottom. It would have been easier with two people, the way she and Ingrid used to do it, one to thread the warp, and the other to tie the weight.

The daylight was almost gone, and she was about to light the lamp, when the door opened.

'Thorvald?'

Whoever it was had stopped just inside the door. Astrid stood on the stool, waiting.

'No.'

'Olaf!' She hurried into speech to hide her embarrassment. 'Is the Thing over?'

'An hour ago. Isn't Thorvald here?'

'No, but wait for him. He'll be upset if you don't.'

Olaf hesitated. He'd expected to find his mother here. It hadn't occurred to him there'd be no one in but Astrid.

'Stay here till he gets back.'

He couldn't see her. The snow outside had made the falling twilight glow. In here it was all shadows. There was a note of pleading in her voice that he didn't like.

'All right. I'll stay.'

He felt his way across the familiar room to the hearth, and sat down. Astrid watched him pull off his wet boots.

'What happened at the Thing?'

'Nothing, if you mean about Leif. They reported the killing. Thorvald spoke for Leif. Leif has to pay a fine in compensation for Svein's death, and pay the islanders for burying him. Svein has no kin to receive compensation here, so it goes to the island as a recompense for breaking our peace. That was what they spent most time discussing. No one seemed that bothered about the cause of the quarrel.'

'So Leif's free?'

'Yes. There's no one here to avenge Svein.'

Astrid lit the lamp. Married she might be, but she had her dark hair loose down her back. Not when she went out, presumably. She looked pale. Perhaps she wasn't happy. She hadn't changed. He didn't know why he'd expected to find her different.

'Thorvald should be here soon,' said Astrid, when the silence seemed to have grown too long. 'I was setting up the loom. I'll go on, if you don't mind.'

'Of course I don't mind.' Olaf spread his socks on the hearthstones. His bare toes were raw and red. He began rubbing them gently. 'I'm not a guest,' he couldn't help adding. 'I live here.'

She didn't answer, but he sensed he'd hurt her. He watched her, his eyes slowly adjusting to the lamplight. She tied a single warp to the beam, then climbed off her stool to tie a weight on it at the bottom.

'Wouldn't it be easier to tie all the threads first?' he asked.

'No, they get tangled. It was easier when Ingrid and I did it together.'

He got up. The floor was damp and cold. She looked down at him from the stool.

'Where are the weights?' said Olaf. 'You tie the thread at the top, and I'll fasten them at the bottom.'

Olaf caught the dangling thread and knotted a weight to it. He still found her beautiful. There was nothing about her to show that she was married at all. He'd thought her beautiful the first time he'd seen her. When he'd admitted as much to Thorvald, Thorvald had laughed at him. Olaf took another weight. She was just above him, stretching up to reach the beam. Her skirt brushed his hair as she moved.

'You've been working on this with my mother?'

'Yes.' She didn't sound very happy.

'She likes you,' said Olaf suddenly, breaking a confidence for the first time in his life. 'I heard her tell Gunnhild. My mother said you were a pleasure to have about the place, and she thought she could learn to love you very well.'

Astrid was astonished. Olaf would never tell her that if it were not true. But for him to say it at all . . .

'Thank you,' she said at last. 'I'm glad you told me. It helps.'

'I shouldn't have,' grunted Olaf, and tied another weight. It was growing easier to be in her company every minute. He stopped listening anxiously for his brother, and allowed himself to thaw out in her presence, as he let the heat of the room gradually begin to warm his hands and feet.

Chapter 69

A few shags were sheltering on a stony slope, but when the young dog that had been Einar's slithered towards them, they shambled off into the sea below. Thorvald called the dog to heel, and she reappeared, trotting along the cliff edge waving her tail. From below came the crooning of eiders, like distant gossip. Thorvald and Astrid had just crossed a dyke when some sheep sprang from the shelter of it, their fleeces tawdry yellow against the crisp white ground.

'There you are,' said Thorvald. 'Four ewes. That's it.'

'How did you know to look here?'

'You learn to guess. We can go home now.'

Out of the shadow of the hill the sun glowed golden. Brown patches of grass were beginning to reappear through the frost.

'Do you think I'll learn to guess too?'

'Sure to, if you come with me a few more times.'

'It's knowing where to look when they're missing.'

Thorvald pulled off his woollen hat, and stuffed it into his belt. The sun was so low in their eyes they could hardly see the farms below.

'You'll know.' He turned her face towards him and kissed her. 'We've got four months still, doing it like this. You'll manage.'

'Of course I'll manage.'

He kissed her again.

There was a feast at Shirva that night.

'You'd think Bjarni would have had enough feasts for one year,' remarked Ingebjorg.

'There's always been a feast at Shirva the first night of Yule.'

Ingebjorg stopped combing Eirik's hair, and looked at her eldest son, who was crouched on the floor, washing his hair in a bucket. 'Yes, but he's given two wedding feasts this year, besides his own seven day feast.'

'It's still Yule,' said Thorvald, emerging from the bucket.

'I remember the last Yule feast at Shirva,' said Astrid, handing him the cloth to dry his hair. It was becoming much easier to talk to Thorvald in front of his family. She was deliberately making a habit of it; after all, she couldn't be shy in her own home for ever. She'd found Ingebjorg much gentler to be with since Olaf had repeated his mother's words about her. 'I went and hid in the barn halfway through. I didn't want any feasts, this time last year.'

'Things have changed a bit.' Thorvald was rubbing his head vigorously. 'Have you finished with that comb?'

Ingebjorg brushed Eirik's fringe once more, and handed the comb to Astrid, who began to tease out the knots in Thorvald's hair. He sat still, watching Eirik struggle into his best tunic, the one embroidered with red and green braid. It had once been Thorvald's. Thorvald could remember Olaf wearing it at Gudrun's wedding.

As if in answer to the thought, the door opened, and when he looked out from under his wet hair, there Olaf stood, in his best clothes and new boots.

'Olaf! Aren't you on your way to the feast?'

'I thought I'd go over there with you.' Olaf squatted at the hearth next to his brother. 'There mightn't be another chance for a while.'

Astrid went on struggling with the tangles in Thorvald's hair. She was quite aware of the surge of happiness that went through him, almost as if she could feel it herself. She knew how much he had been missing Olaf, although he'd never said so. She guessed he'd only recently realised that when he came home next winter, Olaf would be gone, for who knew how many seasons?

'Olaf,' said Ingebjorg presently, as if he'd never been away, 'can you bring in more peats, if you're ready?'

Olaf went out with the empty basket.

'There you are,' said Ingebjorg to Eirik, fastening the clasp on his shoulder. 'Now sit still and try to keep clean. You don't want to disgrace Bjarni's feast.'

'Kari will be there,' remarked Eirik. 'I asked him.'

'That's fine.'

'Kari's grandfather says that fate will now treat Shirva well, because Bjarni is an honourable man.'

'Is that so?' said Ingebjorg, taking a jet brooch from a small wooden box in the recess behind her bed, and carefully fastening her own tunic.

They were ready to set out. Olaf set fresh damp turfs over the fire. 'You won't need a light out there tonight,' he told his mother. 'There's a fine moon.'

Astrid, in the far corner by their sleeping platform, helped Thorvald fasten his tunic. 'You look beautiful,' she whispered.

He was startled. 'So do you,' he managed to say. 'At least we won't disgrace my uncle tonight.'

'He should be proud of us.'

The first night of Yule. Three hours after noon the sun vanishes into the sea. With it warmth drains from the land, and in the sharpened air the lochs and puddles freeze. The island is still, the air so cold it hurts to breathe it. The surrounding sea is dark, and the faint sound of its swell drifts across the island. The wind has blown the stars clear, brilliant in the empty night, faint only where the moon rises over the Seydurholm. In their configuration rests the only certain fact, telling that it is midwinter of this one year, on this one island. Below the stars the island lies silent, telling nothing.

Yet there are people down there, moving slowly over the frozen fields, from Byrstada, from Leogh, from Setr, all converging, the islanders making their way to Shirva through the night.

A wind creeps in from the sea; thick clouds roll over the land. In the north the stars are gone. Mist drifts along the cliff tops. No one is out there now. The islanders are feasting by the light of their own fire.

Midwinter. It seems the darkness will never lift again, but tomorrow the sun will reappear, as the islanders have known it will since the first stone huts were raised upon the island. Nothing ends. Nothing happens twice. There are no voices now, no language to be heard, only the waves that break forever on those shores.

And there this story ends.